Sherlock Holmes's
School for Detection

Other Mammoth titles

Sherlock Holmes's School for Detection

Simon Clark

ROBINSON

ROBINSON

First published in Great Britain in 2017 by Robinson

Copyright © Simon Clark, 2017

1 3 5 7 9 8 6 4 2

The moral right of the author has been asserted.

A CIP catalogue record for this book
is available from the British Library.

ISBN: 978-1-47213-687-9

Typeset in Whitman by Hewer Text UK Ltd, Edinburgh
Printed and bound in Great Britain by CPI Group (UK) Ltd, Croydon CR0 4YY

Papers used by Robinson are from well-managed forests and other responsible sources.

Robinson
An imprint of
Little, Brown Book Group
Carmelite House
50 Victoria Embankment
London EC4Y 0DZ

An Hachette UK Company
www.hachette.co.uk

www.littlebrown.co.uk

Contents

Acknowledgements

Once again, it's only right that the acknowledgements section contained in an anthology of Sherlock Holmes stories should begin by recognizing Sir Arthur Conan Doyle, the medical doctor, turned writer, who created one of the most enduring, and loved, fictional characters of all time.

My thanks go to Duncan Proudfoot and Emily Byron at Robinson for making this anthology possible in the first place.

And much gratitude to you, the reader, for your undiminished appetite for new Holmes and Watson adventures. Happily, I share that appetite, too. I also whole-heartedly thank my wife, Janet, for her advice and feedback as I once more recruited such a fine team of writers for this volume that you now hold in your hands.

All of the stories in this anthology are in copyright. The following acknowledgements are granted to the authors for permission to use their work herein:

THE ADVENTURE OF THE ORKNEY SHARK © 2016 by Simon Bestwick

INTRODUCTION © 2016 by Simon Clark, PROLOGUE © 2016 by Simon Clark and THE CASE OF THE WRONG-WISE BOOTS © 2016 by Simon Clark

THE MONSTER OF THE AGE © 2016 by Paul Finch

THE GARGOYLES OF KILLFELLEN HOUSE © 2016 by Cate Gardner

THE BELL ROCK LIGHT © 2016 by Guy Haley

THE CASE OF THE CANNIBAL CLUB © 2016 Carole Johnstone

THE ADVENTURE OF THE AVID PUPIL © 2016 by Alison Littlewood

A GENTLEMANLY WAGER © 2016 by William Meikle

THE SPY AND THE TOWERS © 2016 by Nick Oldham

THE PRESSED CARNATION (or A SCANDAL IN LONDON) © 2016 by Saviour Pirotta

SHERLOCK HOLMES AND THE FOUR KINGS OF SWEDEN © 2016 by Steven Savile

Introduction

There is film of Sir Arthur Conan Doyle talking in a most revealing way about how he created Sherlock Holmes.

This monologue, recorded in Doyle's garden in the summer of 1927 by the Fox Film Corporation, is one of the earliest sound films, and can readily and freely be found on the internet today. The vignette of Doyle, in the company of his dog, Doley, lasts about ten minutes. Five minutes are devoted to Doyle chatting about Holmes and five minutes focus on his unshakable belief in Spiritualism.

For me, the first five minutes shine a brilliant light on to how Doyle effectively created what we now understand a modern detective to be: an intelligent seeker of truth. Doyle, in his charming, avuncular way, talks about how he used to enjoy reading detective stories in his youth. However, he became increasingly annoyed by innumerable detective heroes who appeared to identify the villain by sheer chance, or by tales in which the author didn't explain the detection process at all. As a fledgling author, Doyle decided to write crime stories that would employ scientific methods. His detective would carefully build a case scientifically, methodically accumulating clues and facts, until he could intelligently unravel the mystery and so solve the crime.

Doyle's professional background mentally equipped him for such a task. He had studied medicine at the University of Edinburgh Medical School from 1876 to 1881. This would have demanded long periods of concentrated study, attention to detail, the ability to remember extensive lists of tongue-twisting terminology relating to drugs, treatments, and parts of the human body from the crown of the head to the tip of the toe. What's more, he was fortunate that one of his lecturers was none other than the remarkable Dr Joseph Bell. In the film, Doyle speaks admiringly of Bell, who could not only make accurate diagnoses of his patients' illnesses, but could also deduce their nationality and occupation, and so on, by using 'his power of observation'.

If anything, it seems to me that it's Doyle's scientific education under the guidance of teachers like Dr Bell that prepares a fertile ground for Sherlock Holmes's creation. Just to read a few pages of Bell's manual for surgeons, written in the late nineteenth century, reveals a machine-like mind, setting out precise step-by-step instructions to guide a surgeon through the most delicate and complex of operations. For those with a strong stomach, *A Manual of the Operations of Surgery* makes for fascinating reading. Bell's manual also clearly indicates his determination to pass on his expertise to the next generation of physicians.

Doyle brought this forensic attention to detail to his fiction. He admits in the film to developing a 'hundred little dodges' for the detective he would write about. These 'dodges' are the techniques of observation that Holmes would employ, such as noticing that an individual has spatulate fingers, for example, indicating that they regularly play the piano or operate a typewriter. Doyle's hero wouldn't make guesses about the criminal's identity or haphazardly stumble into a house full of thieves. No, his detective would be the equal of a scientist. He'd search for clues, perhaps scrutinizing a document written on a train to determine which route the document writer had taken by comparing the varying quality of the handwriting – jerky scribble indicating where the carriages had bounced over level crossings, or smoothly formed words penned while the train was at rest in a station. All these clues would have meaning for Doyle's investigator. Although often deeply cryptic to policemen and the investigator's friend, they would form a message of exquisite clarity for Mr Sherlock Holmes – a message that would ultimately solve the mystery.

All of which brings me to this anthology, *The Mammoth Book of Sherlock Holmes's School for Detection*. Just as the education of medical doctors evolved over the centuries, from physicians who were little more than happy-go-lucky amateurs, to the rigorously trained, well-qualified professionals of the nineteenth century, so it must have been that the government would demand that their police should also be adequately instructed in the science of detection. If we imagine that a private detective of the genius of Sherlock Holmes really existed, then the nation's leaders would ensure that he pass on his expertise to a new generation of investigators. After all, just one unfortunate slip at (let's say) the Reichenbach Falls could rob society of the world's leading solver of crimes. Therefore, it would be only logical that strenuous attempts would be made to persuade Holmes to take students under his wing in order to teach them his own remarkable methods. So, surely, a School for Detection would be born. Of course, it would be a most remarkable school, boasting one of the most remarkable men of all time. Its students would be presented with baffling mysteries, shocking crimes, and all kinds of danger.

And yet, always in the background, would be the wisest of mentors.

In this book you will find a host of 'new cases', imagining what might have happened if the great Sherlock Holmes had decided the time had come to educate a new breed of investigators – a breed wedded to using the power of observation and the latest scientific techniques in order to become consummate warriors in the fight against crime.

Simon Clark
April 2016

Prologue:
Holmes Receives a Most Intriguing Proposal

My good friend, Mr Sherlock Holmes, vigorously brushed his hands together in much the same way a master craftsman might, dispelling the dust after a hard day's work had been done, and done well.

It was a crisp, sunlit morning in the autumn of 1890, and Holmes wore a distinct air of triumph as he approached Baker Street. "Hah! Watson! It's as if the fellow wanted to be caught! As if with all his heart he longed to spend many a year in jail."

I humphed by way of disagreement. "The blood on your chin suggests otherwise."

"A scratch, Watson, nothing more."

"The thief fought like a demon!"

"A mere tussle."

"Good Lord, it was the most violent boxing match I've ever seen."

Holmes's eyes flashed with excitement. "There's nothing like fisti-cuffs to make one feel so fiercely alive."

"Those grazes on your face—"

"Pah! I do not feel them."

"You will, when the heat of battle's left your veins."

"What I feel is elation! Triumph!"

"And rightly so, Holmes. You captured a mean-spirited burglar."

"Such a glorious morning, Watson. Look at the sunlight illuminating the road. It could be made from gold – pure, shining, imperishable gold."

"Ah, yes . . . most picturesque."

"My appetite's up. I'll ask Mrs Hudson to prepare a feast. Bacon, sausage, eggs, buttery mushrooms, an entire raft of toast." He paused before crossing the road to allow a hansom cab to speed by, the horse's hooves making a rapid-fire clatter. "A wash and brush-up would be in order, too."

"And I'll attend to those cuts on your face."

"As you wish, old friend, as you wish!"

A figure approached the door of my friend's home at precisely the same moment we did, and I began to suspect that breakfast might be delayed somewhat. The man, clad in a brown overcoat that reached his ankles, wore his bowler hat pulled down to his ears.

Sherlock Holmes's sharp eyes swept over the figure. "Inspector Lestrade, good morning!"

The Scotland Yard detective's own small eyes narrowed as he noticed Holmes's bloody face, yet he made no comment in that respect. "Good morning, Mr Holmes." He nodded to me. "Dr Watson."

"Inspector, you have had quite a night of it, too," Holmes exclaimed. "Enjoying a tussle with both the living and the dead."

Lestrade endeavoured to conceal his surprise, yet astonishment flickered across his face. "I daresay, Mr Holmes," said he, "you've read an account of the arrest I made yesterday evening in the newspapers."

"On the contrary, Inspector, I have seen no newspapers whatsoever in recent days. I do, however, read the clues here before me with absolute clarity, as if reading the sharpest of newsprint."

"Then how do you fathom there's been a crime involving cadavers and a living person?"

"Your right boot: a nail is stuck in the leather – a small nail with a domed head of the type so often used by coffin-makers. You experienced a violent struggle that involved kicking as well as punches. That's how you picked up the coffin nail in your boot. The pungent aroma of embalming fluid emanates from your clothes. You've recently manhandled a corpse, a gruesome and decidedly unhealthy business, prompting you to scrub your hands with a brush until they're bright red." Holmes's large nostrils twitched. "Yes, a scent of carbolic soap, too: efficacious in killing bacteria generated by dead flesh."

"Yes," Lestrade exclaimed with astonishment. "You are correct."

"Naturally."

"An undertaker's assistant crept back into the premises to steal items of jewellery that were to be buried with the deceased." Lestrade gave a queasy swallow as if his breakfast might make a vivid reappearance. "There was an altercation with the scoundrel. Coffins fell to the floor. Those grim boxes weren't devoid of tenants, if you apprehend my meaning?"

"Most clearly, sir. Now . . . before I noticed the coffin nail, odour of embalming fluid and whatnot, I observed that you wore the expression of a man with a burning question on his lips."

Lestrade spoke humbly: "Yes, sir. I am here to make a request of great importance."

"Then we should continue this conversation indoors. After you, good sir."

Twenty minutes later, the three of us sat in Holmes's sitting room, which was cluttered with laboratory equipment that he'd been using for a series of the-Good-Lord-knows-what experiments – a large scorch mark on the ceiling suggested that those experiments were as dangerous as they were volatile. My nostrils also detected the distinct acrid smell of singed human hair. As for Holmes himself, he'd exchanged his overcoat for a purple dressing gown. When I attempted to clean the wounds on his face with cotton wool soaked in alcohol, he'd impatiently shooed my hands away.

Inspector Lestrade sat in an armchair. The man didn't lounge back in a relaxed manner. Instead he sat bolt upright, hands clasped tightly together on his knees. He opened his mouth to speak.

Holmes leaned forward, interested to learn what had brought the policeman here.

Before Lestrade could utter a word, I issued a stern command: "Inspector. Kindly withhold all information about why you are here until Holmes consents to my treating his wounds."

Lestrade clamped his lips together.

Holmes frowned. "Tsk, Watson. I will recover without dabs, daubs, ointments."

"Holmes," I said firmly, "you are my friend. I am also a doctor. I would fail as both a friend and a physician if I did not care about your well-being."

Holmes acknowledged my concern with a smile. "Of course. Regrettably I allowed professional impatience to get the better of me. Dab away."

I used the cotton wool to wipe blood from the sharp features, which would be instantly recognizable to millions of people around the world.

A moment later I pronounced, "Nothing serious, though there will be bruising."

"Thank you, Watson." Holmes's smile was a warm one. "I appreciate your care."

Lestrade cleared his throat. "Uhm. Dr Watson, with your permission?"

"By all means, Lestrade."

Holmes energetically used a poker to jab smouldering pieces of coal in the fireplace – flames soon blazed, filling the room with the most sublime warmth. After that, he sat down on the sofa, one long arm thrown out along its back.

Closing his eyes, he uttered a single word: "Proceed."

"Mr Holmes," began Lestrade, "I am here today to beg you to accept a vital role in an educational establishment."

Holmes opened his eyes in surprise. "Extraordinary. I anticipated you sought assistance in a criminal case."

"Your help in our mission to educate would be most useful." Lestrade spoke with utmost respect, if a trifle ponderously.

"What, pray, would I teach?"

"Why . . . what you are so brilliant at, sir. Solving crimes."

"At which university?"

"This is a new establishment. Its headquarters are at 1 Russell Square, here in London. The Imperial Academy of Detective Inquiry and Forensic Science will train students from not just Great Britain but the four corners of the world."

Holmes's expression registered equal measures of surprise and amusement. "You wish me to don a professor's cap and gown, and lecture students in some dull classroom?"

Lestrade appeared eager to dispel such a notion. "Naturally, you would lecture students from time to time. However, you would also act as their mentor as they undertook their own investigations assigned to them by either your good self or Scotland Yard. This would grant students practical experience in the field, as it were."

"How remarkable."

"On certain occasions students would, in effect, be apprenticed to you. They would accompany you on your own investigations."

"Dr Watson is the sole individual customarily by my side."

Inspector Lestrade's voice rose in order to convey the importance of his mission here today. "Mr Holmes, you are the most famous detective in the world."

Holmes acknowledged the declaration of his exalted status with a slight, although hardly modest, nod.

Lestrade continued, "You solve every case that comes your way."

"Not every case, sir."

"Nobody ever gets the better of you."

"Some have, Inspector. Several individuals have defeated me." He grimaced with displeasure. "*C'est la vie.*"

"Sir, modern society requires a first-class police force in order to defeat the cruel, destructive forces of crime. Anarchy will triumph if people, such as your good self, do not see to it that the police forces of the world are modernized." He turned to me in the hope I would help plead his case. "Dr Watson, you will agree that nobody should diagnose illness, prescribe drugs, or saw the bones of living men until they have studied for many years."

"Of course," I said. "All medical practitioners must undergo rigorous training and pass exams before they are permitted to treat patients."

"Thank you, Doctor." Lestrade threw out his arms towards Holmes to implore him. "Sir, please help us. We are fighting the most titanic war against crime. You are the only man who can elevate the humble police officer to where he, and she, will become an effective detective.

These investigators you create will become the intelligent, logic-driven weapons that will destroy criminality."

"That's quite an inspiring speech."

"Verily, one from the heart, sir."

"No, sir. The brain. The heart solely exists to pump blood. Isn't that correct, Watson?"

I laughed softly. Holmes was clearly jesting. Yet, equally, I saw that Lestrade's proposal interested him.

Lestrade pressed on. "Not only will you educate police officers. There are so many who will benefit from learning your astonishing methods, such as those engaged in espionage on behalf of our government, or men who will become bodyguards."

"Who will draw up the students' curriculum? Slavishly adhering to an educational framework formulated by some dry-as-dust committee will be deeply tedious." Holmes rose to his feet before pacing the room.

"You will have a free hand, Mr Holmes. Devise whatever lessons you think fit."

"Lestrade, Dr Watson has developed something of a career alongside that of medical practitioner. He writes up my investigations for publication. Yes, he has an inclination to render such accounts in a very colourful fashion, when he should really concentrate on my scientific approach as I build up deductions that ultimately solve the case. Nevertheless, I would not wish that he cease producing those articles."

Lestrade nodded. "Dr Watson would be wholeheartedly encouraged to continue with his writings."

Holmes went to the window, where he gazed out at pedestrians and hansom cabs in the street below: the teeming multitudes of this great city were going about their daily business as usual.

Holmes murmured, "Transmuting the dull base metal of men and women into the shining gold of proficient detectives?"

Lestrade rubbed those pink, well-scrubbed hands of his together with great enthusiasm. "Dr Watson's reports about you are a joy to read. Is there anyone in this world who has not heard of the great detective,

Mr Sherlock Holmes? Have not millions been thrilled by your ingenious unravelling of the most complicated of crimes? What's more, rumours reach us at Scotland Yard that you've helped the royal families of Europe, not to mention a sheik and maharajah or two. What a benefit to society it would be if you trained students to apply your scientific methods in order to fight crime. Just picture—"

"Lestrade, enough." Holmes raised his hand. "Such praise heaped upon me is quite as stimulating as cocaine – just as addictive, too."

"I only repeat what others say. You are the master detective. The best."

Holmes smiled. "I will not disagree, although I risk irritating Dr Watson here with a shameless display of egotism."

"I ask again, Mr Holmes, will you offer your services as tutor and mentor?"

Holmes stood with his hands clasped behind his back as he once more gazed thoughtfully into Baker Street. "The Imperial Academy of Detective Inquiry and Forensic Science?"

"Yes, sir."

"Despite the institution's cumbersome title, I am intrigued. Instructing your raw recruits will be a most stimulating challenge to my intellect."

Lestrade leapt to his feet. "Then your answer is 'yes'?"

"It is, Inspector. An emphatic 'yes'. Now, if you'll excuse us, Inspector; Dr Watson will have patients to attend to, and I have a rather interesting puzzle to solve, involving . . . ah, but to say more would betray a confidence."

And so it was that my friend, Sherlock Holmes, became teacher to a fascinating array of students. Moreover, in the course of those duties, he brought that razor-sharp mind of his to bear on a wide range of mysteries that were at times either baffling, thrilling or downright dangerous.

As Holmes so rightly pointed out, The Imperial Academy of Detective Inquiry and Forensic Science is a woefully ungainly name

– so much so, that the establishment became more commonly known by the much more succinct title, 'The School for Detection'.

In closing, I will add that this is but a small selection of those extraordinary cases which I am now, at last, permitted to lay before you, the discerning reader.

John H. Watson, M.D.,
London

The Adventure of the Avid Pupil
Alison Littlewood

I have long found it greatly to the credit of my friend Sherlock Holmes that he has always clung to what he sees as right, regardless of any desire for personal glory. Indeed, he often insisted that I forbear from making my little accounts of his cases, particularly as his fame grew; he even came to disdain the approbation of the public. He was ever a law unto himself. Unlike other men, he did not require the approval of the world, but trod his own path within it. Thus, it chafed upon my senses all the more painfully when it appeared that another might turn Holmes's talents to the purpose of furthering his own reputation.

I brought the matter to Holmes's attention as we sat one evening perusing the papers. Only a brief time had elapsed since he had agreed to pass on his skills in observation and deduction in a new School for Detection, and to mentor some of its students; and such was the subject upon which I opened.

"That fellow, Simon Smedley," I said. "Is he not one of your apprentices?"

"He is," Holmes replied. "A young police officer under Inspector Lestrade's tutelage, and very keen to find improvement, though I do believe his mind to be fixed upon still greater things."

"Indeed! For I find I must warn you, Holmes, of what I heard from his own lips this very afternoon."

Holmes did not react to my tone. He merely raised his rather expressive eyebrows and tilted his head for me to continue, and I did so with alacrity. "I heard him boasting at my club – indeed, to all who would listen! He said that he was not only learning all that the master knew, but that as any pupil should, he would soon surpass him; at which time he would begin his own academy, one which would not only improve upon your own, but usurp its ripest fees."

I felt my cheeks suffuse with blood in my indignation, and yet Holmes sat quite undisturbed. He drew on his pipe and let out a cloud of blue smoke so that, for a moment, I saw him through a fog.

"Well, Holmes – what do you think?"

He set down his pipe, leaned back and closed his eyes. "I think," he said, "I may have a little nap, Watson, if you have no objection. I find the demands of the academy, along with my own cases, have left me somewhat enervated this evening."

"But Holmes, something must surely be done! For I carried out a little detection of my own, and it took little time to discover that the fellow has been repeating his boasts all over the city. He is claiming to all who will hear him that he shall soon be a detective the like of which London has never seen. You should write to Lestrade – tell him, indeed, that you will no longer assist the man in his endeavours to take your place."

To this, he made a low sort of grunt.

"Holmes? Is the man's boast so empty, then, that you intend to do nothing?"

His eyebrow rose once more, though his eyes remained closed. "Not at all, Watson. No, he is a rather intelligent fellow, and keener than mustard, as you have so ably and forcibly recounted."

"Why, then—"

He quelled my indignation. "I apologise, Watson. I am in somewhat low spirits, I shall admit. But there can be no harm in the increase of knowledge and the improvement of skill, can there? I should think there cannot, at any rate. And if we were to dismiss every man of whose manner we did not approve, we would become lonely individuals indeed." He sighed. "Perhaps the pupil *should* one day outflank the master."

"But he is nought but a swaggerer, Holmes – a buck, a swell!"

Another tilt of the head informed me that Holmes concurred with my judgement, and yet he could not be prevailed upon to denounce the effrontery of the man. Instead it was I who was forced to subside, trying to focus once again upon the newspaper; though I soon found myself staring into the fire, listening to its hiss and spit, occasionally interjecting with my own impatient sigh. It was but a short time later that I deduced, from my own observations, that the reigning master detective, Sherlock Holmes, was fast asleep.

2

The next morning I professed to Holmes that I should very much like to observe a little at the school of detection, in order to broaden the scope of my memoirs and to witness any new side to his character that the endeavour might have brought to the fore. I did not imagine him a natural tutor. He was too impatient of others' slowness for that, and a little too inclined to enjoy baffling those around him with his own peculiar genius; but in reality I wished to discover a little more about our friend Simon Smedley. In due course, I found myself in a seat in an almost circular, steeply banked lecture theatre, watching Holmes standing in the pit below, next to an object which, despite its covering sheet, I could have little doubt was a human cadaver.

Naturally this was no new sight to me, although its presence in this room, surrounded by eager students leaning over the heads of their fellows to better absorb the sight, made it somewhat difficult to tear my gaze away. However, I wished – before Holmes began – to make a study of Simon Smedley's appearance. He was seated in the middle seat of the middle row, his eyes shining palely. The day was gloomy and I could hear the constant assault of rain against glass somewhere behind and above me, but even allowing for the shifting light, I must say that I found him wanting. His black hair lay flat and lank and lifeless; his forehead was a little too smooth; his snub nose was too like a child's; his wide-set blue eyes stared rather unpleasantly and, to finish the impression, he possessed a receding chin and a flattish skull that nobody could covet.

I could not fault his rapt attention on Holmes, however, as the master began to speak.

"To discover the story of what happened to a body," he said in stentorian tones, "one must see its wounds. We must know who he was; what tool was employed to stop his breath; we must see the place in which the deed occurred. We must understand his life, in order to understand his death. Only by making close examination – by the most minute observation – can we hope to succeed. It would be a remarkable man indeed who expects to solve a crime without leaving his rooms."

He swept the sheet from the table and a stir went about the galleried seats, for what lay beneath was indeed a corpse, but what a corpse! It was that of a man of middle years, and it was torn and mutilated and stabbed with myriad injuries.

"I shall ask each of you to step down," he said, "and demonstrate your aptitude in making out the cause of a wound. Tranmer!" He pointed to a callow youth in the first row, who glanced around him before leaving his seat. A moment later he was at Holmes's side, who, despite the lad's gangling build, stood a head taller.

Holmes pointed. "Left leg. Double puncture marks, small and close-set. What do you suppose to be the origin? And pray, do not tell me a vampire did it."

A titter went about the room, gradually subsiding into the shifting of feet as Tranmer first bent to the body and then started back, his hand pressed to his suddenly bloodless face.

"Come now, no squeamishness!" Holmes said. "For many of your fellows are officers, and they will mock you. We must not be deterred by the small matter of odorous unpleasantness, for it is in examining the first effects of the crime that our best clues may be found. The cause, if you please."

Tranmer cleared his throat. "He – he has tripped, perhaps—"

"Nonsense!" Holmes waved a hand about the room. "Can anybody enlighten our young friend?"

I heard the shuffling as someone got to their feet. I knew before I turned that it was Simon Smedley. "It is snakebite," he said, "as encountered in your own case of 'The Speckled Band'."

"Exactly," Holmes said. "Of course, I possessed certain advantages. Enquiring into the life of Dr Roylott informed me that he was accustomed to travelling throughout the tropics and that he possessed several Indian animals. An examination of the room revealed a dummy bell rope and ventilator to allow his swamp adder to pass into his intended victim's room. A deduction as to the cause of death provided the key to preventing the lethal bite."

"And yet there *was* a bite," said Smedley. "You frightened the creature into turning on its master; it took his life in seconds."

Holmes bowed. "You have made a study of me."

I stirred uncomfortably. I had written an account of the case myself. Had I done my part, then, in fuelling this upstart's pretentions to my friend's position in the world? And yet there was something in the assiduousness of Smedley's pursuit of knowledge that made me see why Holmes would hesitate to curtail his progress.

For now, however, Smedley remained silent.

"You see the importance," Holmes declaimed, "of knowing who a man is: his habits; his enemies; where he came from; of seeing the circumstances in which he was struck down. Only then may a complete picture emerge. This very week, a finely dressed man – a gentleman, by his attire – has been found at the Thames Embankment, his body cast into a sewer as if it were something worse than worthless. It is thoroughly perplexing the police, and I dare say it shall continue to do so, unless they can discover who he is and where he came from. And yet no one even appears to be searching for him."

"The victim of a cut-purse." Smedley had not yet retaken his seat.

Holmes bowed. "The lack of injury to his person would suggest otherwise."

"But you will solve it, will you not?" a voice called from the back of the room.

Holmes's lips twitched. "Contrary to expectations," he said drily, "I cannot take upon my shoulders every case in London."

The lecture theatre was reduced to silence. Holmes paused for a moment, leaning against the table on which the much-maligned cadaver lay. The pattering of rain seemed suddenly very loud; the light shifted and flowed across my friend's face. He appeared exhausted, his complexion almost grey. I shifted my gaze to his student. Smedley was seated once more, leaning forward, his too-pale eyes agleam amid the shadows. In that instant, he reminded me of nothing so much as a predatory cat, poised and watching and awaiting the moment to strike.

The rest of the lecture brought a repeat of the same performance, though with different actors and examples of the detective's art. Holmes revealed his knowledge of examining stab wounds – their width, angle and positioning, whether made by sword, ice pick or stiletto; the numerous effects of strangulation, and some insight into how a bullet may be matched to a weapon. None of his listeners proved so well informed as Smedley, however, and he asked several pertinent questions, pressing Holmes until the hour grew quite late. I found myself drifting as Holmes went on, speaking of the importance of bringing all the senses to bear upon a case, and concluding with his ability to identify the type of tobacco from its scent and the need to follow one's nose.

Not content even at that juncture, Smedley once more rose to his feet.

Holmes did not speak. Indeed, he looked by this time quite spent; he squinted along his aquiline nose and made an impatient gesture.

The young man gathered himself. "Are we to apply these theorems on the actual streets of London at any juncture?" he asked. The question could have been impertinent, and perhaps it was, and yet it was asked purely in a tone of enquiry. Something about it set me prickling, however. It reminded me of the way that Holmes would question a suspect, wearing the face of innocence, without giving them any intimation that was what they were.

Holmes inclined his head. "When you are ready," he said simply, and he turned his back, preparatory to leaving the hall.

Smedley's face darkened at once. I was reminded that he was, in fact, a practising police officer prior to taking up his place in the school; he must have encountered several real cases before now.

"However." Holmes stopped without turning. "A little sojourn on to the streets of London would not harm any of you, I am sure. Tomorrow!" And with that, he swept from the room.

A short while later, I met my friend with a view to taking a hansom cab together back to our rooms at 221b Baker Street. He was little inclined to speak, and I was scarcely less so; it was an effort to raise our voices to be heard above the sound of the rain, constantly lashing the cab roof and the driver's oilskins, and hissing about the streets. I could not prevent myself, however, from making some little outburst when he asked how I had found his lecture.

"It was informative, Holmes – too informative, perhaps! Why, the fellow asked all he could – he is intent upon learning what he can about you, and you tell him everything!

"Of course, my dear fellow. Is that not the purpose of a teacher?"

"But it has ever been your way to hold a little in reserve, has it not? Why should you now—"

"I am mortally tired, Watson." Holmes settled back into his seat, lowering his hat over his eyes. "Pray, let us discuss it another time."

I blustered, I admit, but I subsided, valuing the peace of my friend above my own indignation. I really did not like his appearance; his cheeks had remained quite bloodless. And I supposed there was little to be done, if Holmes was truly intent upon giving away every last one of his secrets.

3

I had not intended to spend a further day away from my consulting rooms, but Holmes's proclamation about an outing into the streets had piqued my interest. And so the next morning I found myself once more at the School for Detection, surrounded by the eagerness of youth, and watching Holmes as he unpacked a series of boxes. The rags he removed soon spilled from the table, and still there was more; I could smell old fustian, see the rusted black of a clerk's jacket along with indifferently clean aprons and pinafores. From another box he removed pairs of spectacles and hats; next, he produced face pastes, paints and powders, and several unpleasantly real-looking wigs. Finally, he took out several mirrors.

"This," he said, quite unnecessarily, "is a lesson in disguise." He smiled and gestured about him.

I knew Holmes to be a master of such subterfuge. During the course of his investigations he had donned the appearance of everybody from a clergyman to a groom to an opium addict. I had in the past looked him squarely in the eye and entirely failed to recognise him. He could not only mimic to an uncanny degree the way of standing or walking of other men; he could control the musculature of his face so closely that the shape of his visage almost appeared to change with his character.

"We shall each adopt the dress, expression, posture and habits of another, proceeding in that guise into the heart of London," he continued. "But it shall not be so simple! For sometimes, you may find it necessary to throw off pursuit. How useful it would be, then, if a disguise could be adapted or exchanged – the moustached clerk turning in an instant into a bearded fellow with a stoop? Such is your challenge. You will enter the street in pairs: one to flee, one to follow. When one is caught, the game is up and your positions are reversed. Half an hour, I think, will suffice to affect your transformations." He gave a rare smile.

An excited shuffling ran about the lecture theatre and I realised that, once more, Simon Smedley had risen to his feet.

"Yes, Smedley?" There was no trace of irritation in Holmes's voice, though I bristled at the imposition.

"Thank you. I merely wish to point out that there is an irregular number of students in the room."

"Is there? Then I thank *you*." Holmes paused, never taking his eyes from Smedley. "Very well. I shall myself adopt a disguise, and I shall be your pursuer, at least until such time as you give me the slip."

Smedley did not smile, but he could barely conceal his eagerness as he nodded, and all made their way down the steps to discover what personage they could possibly become. They had seized what clothing they wanted. Some stepped into voluminous skirts where they were, whilst others concealed their finds and retired to try them in privacy before revealing themselves. There came many muted guffaws and excited murmurs as they blackened their teeth and held up various wigs, while Holmes turned his back on it all and left by a side door.

A short time afterwards, the students began to return, wearing the most outlandish array of costumes: a beggar, his beard too well trimmed and his cheeks too well fed to ever have it to perfection; a costermonger and a hawker of penny bloods, a little bundle of pamphlets ready in his hand. A passable clerk stood to one side, and a clergyman who gave me pause. His round eyeglasses sparkled in the light, and some mild arrogance in the tilt of his head, under his low-crowned hat, was so fitting that I almost thought he was real. I started when I realised that it was Smedley.

"Good day, sir." I looked around at the tremulous voice and saw a woman in the mourning weeds of a widow making her way towards me. I did not stand; I knew it was not necessary, though the be-ringed hands with their prominent knuckles, clutching a walking stick, were quite convincing.

"Holmes," I said, "good heavens! I had expected better of you."

For of course, it was he. And he looked enough like a woman – the higher pitch of his voice even made him sound like one – but it was a remarkably simple disguise in comparison to many I had seen. He had had to do little, after all, with his visage, save to conceal it beneath a thick black veil. And yet such a thing would be an easy matter to cast off, would it not, if anybody pursued him? But the skirts would scarcely be so simple.

"Did you, Watson?" he asked mildly. He surveyed his students at the bottom of the amphitheatre. "Perhaps you are right. This dye is nasty stuff – pah! There is little wonder that widows complain of their eyes. It is not merely tears that irritate them so, I'll warrant."

"It is a pity not to lead more by example, Holmes. I know you to be a master in disguising your features, even when they are in plain view. Why, nobody would recognise you, if you really did not wish them to do so."

He stared into space for a moment. I could just make out his fine nose, his wan cheeks. A casual observer could certainly imagine him a woman, her face hollowed by the privation of loss. He even wore a rather intricate jet brooch at his neck.

He drew a deep sigh. "And yet there is a gentleman cast into the sewer whom no one knows. How he would wish, if he could cry out from the ground, that somebody would recognise him!"

"Ah. And you really have no interest in the case?"

"A little interest perhaps, though very little time. And yet I find my absorption is growing, Watson. It seems that half of London is taking some measure of concern in the matter. It is perhaps in the nature of man, is it not? For I fear it is the very horror of it which has them all pondering the solution. Why, it has become quite a matter of importance, in notoriety if not in difficulty."

"Difficulty? Why, I thought you stated there to be quite insurmountable problems."

"Not if examination had been made, I am certain. Though it is too late for that." He roused himself. "Now, where is Smedley?"

A low cough made me start, for it came not from some distance, but almost at our backs. I turned and saw that Smedley had crept around the row of seats, not next to our own but directly behind us; and I wondered at once how much he had overheard. I was instantly ashamed of my comments on Holmes's guise, and yet my friend was not in the least perturbed.

"Capital! You apprehend me already," he said, forgetting even to speak in the higher register. "It is my turn! Come, let us proceed at once." He called out more loudly, "Do not forget: be artful! Evade, dodge, melt into the very walls!" He glanced at his watch. "We reconvene at two, to consider what we have learned. For now: London!"

"London!" came the echoing cry, as the motley gathering of every class and occupation tried to spill all at once from the door.

Soon I was alone in the room. I glanced around at the shadowy ranks of seats, imagining the eager faces that had filled them, there and then vanished. Perhaps, in later years, it would seem that each group of hopefuls had passed through this place in a trice; it could not signify, after all, what one trifling individual might boast.

I smiled to think of Smedley's endeavours at shaking off Sherlock Holmes amid the streets he knew so well, and I decided I would step out for a time and enjoy luncheon at my club. Today, at least, I should not have to listen to the young buck's boasting.

Outside, the sky was lowering, the clouds swollen and heavy with as yet unfallen rain. It was not so dank as yesterday, however, and for now there was no downpour; only an ever-present dampness that hung in the air, the humidity turning all things grey with mist. I wondered how that would help Holmes's students to make their various escapes, then banished them all from my mind.

I decided I would trust in the weather's abeyance and walk. As I did, I began to realise the air was not merely redolent of rain, but of the river; I could smell the heavy brown scent of the Thames. I wrinkled my nose. For the first time in an age, I could detect the taint of human ordure; the sewers must be overflowing into its channel. I comforted myself at the thought that at least the system was much improved since the time of the Great Stink. I could not recall it, but I had been told of its awfulness; men were even forced to hang blankets soaked in chloride of lime at the windows of the Houses of Parliament, to keep out the noxious stench. Still, with these conditions, and with such a quantity of rainwater, it was little wonder that even the marvel of engineering that was London's sewer system was struggling to cope.

Thankfully, after a pleasant repast of cutlets and kidneys, I returned to find that the day, as well as my mood, was brighter. The latter was not to be sustained for long, however. It was well short of two o'clock, and yet I had not quite re-entered the lecture theatre when I heard the exulting tones of a familiar voice in the passage.

"That's right!" Smedley crowed, for it was he. "Under twenty minutes! I would swear to it upon my life. I slipped into an emporium, circling aimlessly – he was hindered by his skirts, ha! – and from thence it was a simple matter to make my escape by the doors into the opposite street."

There came to my ear the scornful laughter of one of his fellows.

"I employed no great trickery, nor was it needful to change my guise to outwit him. He is losing his sharpness, I tell you – he is worn down! Unless the accounts of his skills are all the invention of his buffoon of a friend, and never even existed."

His contemptuous tone became too much, and I strode around the corner to see that his eyes were alight with triumph and mirth. He lowered them at once at the sight of me, then glanced over his shoulder, gave a shallow bow and stole away. His friend looked around and followed likewise.

I was glad to have routed them, though I would have welcomed the opportunity to give vent to my anger. How dared he! And yet I do not think that it would have rankled so deeply if it were not for the memory of Holmes in the simplicity of his disguise. He could do better – I had seen better! If anything, in the course of making my reports of his many capabilities, I had rather taken the side of subtlety and muted praise. Anything else would have been anathema to Holmes's proud sensibilities.

I still stood there, breathing heavily and glaring at the space where Smedley had been, when some small sound behind me made me turn. There, framed in the doorway, was Sherlock Holmes himself. He was stooping, and although it made his semblance of a worn-down widow the more convincing, I could not help but feel there was something of reality in his deportment. For a moment he leaned against the jamb, before throwing back his veil to reveal a waxen countenance.

"There you are, Watson," he said gruffly, as if it were I who had been off chasing wild geese about the alleys and byways of London.

"I am indeed! Though I did not expect to see you for a while yet, Holmes."

"Ah – no. That is true."

"What on earth happened, my dear fellow? Are you well? You look quite spent."

"I am well, to answer one of your questions, Watson. To reply to the other: hmm – well, perhaps I am a little tired, after all."

"And yet the churlish fellow has been here crowing that he was lost to your sight within minutes! How could that be so?"

"The luck of youth, Watson, or perhaps the legs. Curse this veil!" He rubbed at his eyes, which were quite red.

"You are ill."

"No, it is simple. He gave me the slip. I could not even find him again to reverse our roles."

"He has been making much of it, Holmes. And he will do so again when the others return, I have no doubt of it."

"Then pray accompany me to my office. It would not do to be mocked whilst wearing a dress, I suppose, even if it is one of such a sombre colour."

He went past, his skirts rustling against the wall, and I followed him down seemingly endless corridors until we entered a spacious room with a decently solid mahogany desk. He did not immediately remove his outer vestments, however, but slumped into the chair, picked up a pipe and slipped it into his mouth, staring contemplatively into space. He had not even taken the trouble to light it. I opened my mouth to remonstrate further, but a sudden sharp rap upon the door gave me pause.

A moment later it opened to reveal a police officer. He did not notice me at my place in the corner, seeing only Holmes; he murmured an apology and turned to leave, but Holmes bid him enter. He started in surprise, staring at Holmes's attire, then shuffled forward as if he were not quite certain how to proceed. Holmes merely waited, though I could hardly bear to stand by and see the twitch of the impertinent fellow's lip; and yet the comicality of the scene kept returning to me, and I was forced to swallow back my own unwelcome amusement.

The constable's next words made it entirely evaporate. "Sir, I wonder if you are able to accompany me to the Embankment?" he said. "For there has been a body found – a woman this time – and we should very much appreciate your eyes at the scene."

Sherlock Holmes stood in a dignified manner, despite the rustling of the crepe. "I shall join you forthwith," he said. "Just allow me a moment."

The constable raised one sly eyebrow. "To remove your dress, sir?" he asked.

"Quite so," was Holmes's colourless reply.

4

It was a dismal sight which met our eyes when we stepped from the hansom near the bank of the Thames. It was almost a pity that the skies had begun to lighten, clearly delineating the scene that lay before us. The constable led us towards the brown water until we saw, just over the banking, a narrow platform just above the level of the swollen river. There lay an elderly woman, foully begrimed and soiled. Her dress must once have been white, though now it was greyed with water and discoloured with more abhorrent matter still. Her face was the same grey as her dress and her hair was tangled and matted, flowing loosely like waterweed about her shoulders. She had not the dignity of a cap; perhaps it had been lost.

Holmes did not hesitate. He jumped down to join another officer who was at the woman's side, and he leaned over the corpse. He viewed her without repugnance or compassion. Then he peered around and I thought he looked for me: then I realised he was staring at the wall.

I went towards him, thinking to offer my opinion as a man of medicine, and yet I was distracted by rapid steps behind me. I turned and my spirits fell as I made out, hurrying from a hansom cab which must have followed closely upon our own, none other than Simon Smedley.

He nodded and touched his hand to his hat, and opened his mouth to speak to me as if his being there were the most natural thing in the world. And yet he said nothing, but merely let out a long "Ah," and I realised that he too was gazing down at the body, not in pity, but with the same rapt eagerness he had demonstrated in the lecture theatre.

The similarity of the scene struck me. And yet here were no banks of seats or plinth or respectfully covering cloth: there were only the lighters out on the river, the blank rushing water, the glare of the sun spearing through the broken clouds.

"Smedley?" It was Holmes who spoke and I was pleased to hear that his tone was peremptory. Smedley felt it too; he gave a start, and in a moment he had overwritten his fervent expression with a more apologetic look.

"I thought it was you, Mr Holmes!" he said. "I caught a glimpse of you at Russell Street, you know, and felt I had better take my turn at once. I am quite sure you had caught up with me at the emporium, after all."

At this most blatant of excuses, I stared. It was as if the man had not known me to have overheard his words in the passage; and he had, after all, taken the time to remove his own disguise. But Holmes spoke before I could.

"This is a most pressing case. You must return to the school at once."

Smedley's eyes flashed. "Ah – of course, if you wish it. I am ready to be your most humble servant. But I am here, am I not? Perhaps I would not be entirely in the way if I could observe the master at his work?"

Holmes stared at him for a long moment. I could have burst. I waited for him to dismiss the fellow, but Holmes only turned back to his task and gestured over his shoulder for Smedley to follow.

Smedley shot me a look; his lip curled. Then he strode, ahead of me, to the narrow and slippery steps. I had no choice but to follow at his heels, until four of us were crowded on the little platform with the body. At once, I noticed what Holmes had been looking at. I could hardly fail to do so, so noisome was the stench that emerged from it. Behind us was a large, brick-lined opening, which dripped with foetid matter, clots of loathsome origin still clinging to the stained walls of the outflow.

"The sewer." The constable's explanation was scarcely necessary. I took out my handkerchief and pressed it to my nose. "The body came from in there. We only found her in this place because of the rain; the system is overflowing into the river, as you may see."

I looked again at the pitiable remains. She was coated in filth; she must have been submerged in it. It struck me then that perhaps she had even drowned in it, and I pressed my kerchief more tightly across my face. And yet, when I peered at her more closely, I could not help but think she must have been dead before her subterranean journey began.

Holmes knocked into my side.

"Steady, Holmes!" I said, alarmed at my precarious position, and he spoke at the same time.

"Apologies, dear fellow . . ." he broke off.

There was no more, and after a moment, the constable continued his account. "She was seen by a trawler-man, out on the water. He saw her white dress and came in a skiff to examine it further. Lucky she didn't wash into the river, or she might not have been found for a week."

"And then," said Holmes, half under his breath, "we might never have discovered where she came from, or what her life was."

"What her . . .?" the constable sounded puzzled, and I could well understand why. It was hard to imagine this pitiful creature ever having a life; it was a sad reflection on reality that any life might have ended in this. I reflected on what Holmes had said about the horror of the case resulting in glory for the victor, and I cast a glowering eye upon Smedley, who stood close by, missing nothing.

"Her dress is somewhat expensive," Holmes said. "The stitching is very neat. And it is plain in colour, but see this lace, and this quilling! Sadly bedraggled now, of course, but it is fine work. Have the police received any enquiries after a missing woman, Constable?"

He gave it that they had not.

"Like the other." Holmes spoke under his breath, though not so low that Smedley could not drink in his words. "And her clothes are stained with ordure but there appears to be no blood, no visible injury, no damage to her attire other than could be expected from her being consigned to the filth of London." He gave a sympathetic sigh, then turned to the outflow. He stared into its dark emptiness; I saw his nostrils twitch.

"Well," he said, "it is a pity."

"A pity?" Smedley inched forward; it was as far as he could go without positively stepping on Holmes's shoes. I did not know how he could go closer to that dreadful hole. The foul miasma came from it in damp waves, stronger and more putrid than any quantity of fresh air could possibly efface.

Holmes suddenly sagged. "Constable," he said, "do you possess such a thing as a lantern?"

"Holmes, you cannot mean it!" I expostulated. I looked again at that black tunnel mouth. It was unthinkable. A man could not even stand straight within it; he would have to stoop, balancing himself by running his hand along those filthy bricks, breathing in . . .

No. He could not do it. And yet the constable nodded, calling to his colleague to bring the light, and the relief in his voice was such that I knew this was what he had intended all along; that Holmes, not he, would make his staggering way along that dreadful conduit, until he found – what?

"It leads north, I take it," Holmes said.

"It does. The tunnel lets on to the main passage, which is both taller and wider than this opening. By following it against the flow, one might find the source."

"Indeed." The lantern was put into Holmes's hand and he held it high, revealing more clearly the parlously stained brick. The light wavered and I realised his hand was shaking.

"Holmes?" I stepped towards him. There was something wrong, I knew that now. I remembered all his speech about enduring a little odorous unpleasantness, but this was no mere disgust; he looked truly ill. His eyes were damp and I realised they were streaming. "Holmes, please."

"If I may, Mr Holmes." It was Simon Smedley who spoke. "Perhaps I might be of assistance."

I turned. "Perhaps he could," I said. It was infuriating, but my friend's health must come before my annoyance.

"You do not look well, Mr Holmes."

"Nonsense. I have some little irritation of the eye, that is all. The veil, you know—"

"And now the stench." Smedley spoke eagerly. "Pray, allow me to help. I have listened to your lectures most assiduously, Mr Holmes; I have studied your ways. I am quite sure, if I can discover where this woman came from, I can solve it all."

Holmes looked into his face with new respect. "You know, I almost believe you could, at that."

"I could! And after all, Mr Holmes, you cannot take *every* case in London."

"I cannot."

"I can . . . follow my nose. I shall make my report with all haste."

Holmes only looked the more intensely weary. He turned to the constable. "I take it that you have spoken to a representative of the sewer company?" he asked. "It is safe to pass – it will not flood again today?"

"We have, sir, and it will not. Levels have been falling through-out the forenoon. It shall be unpleasant, to be sure, but it will be safe."

Holmes turned and stared out at the murky river. After a moment, and without looking at Smedley, he held out the lantern. Smedley reached out; his fingers closed around the handle.

"There is just one thing I should like to ask before I embark on my adventure," the man said, his voice low and insinuating.

"You do not need to name it." Holmes raised his head and met his eye at last. "Should you solve it, I assure you, the discovery shall be yours alone."

5

We made a taciturn party during the ride back to Baker Street, accompanied only by the constant rumble of the wheels of the hansom cab. I kept opening my mouth to speak, but really, I had nothing to say. I could not approve of what had just passed; nor could I wish my friend to be in the dark and malodorous tunnels beneath London. And yet I could not but reflect upon the rough pursuits that Sherlock Holmes had not hesitated to undertake before, during the course of his investigations. Was this to be the future, then? Would others take his place, one after the next, whilst he retreated further into his lectures?

It made me somewhat melancholy as we stepped out into the early evening. I looked up into the clearing sky before we entered at the door, only to find that Holmes had reached it before me and was striding up the stairs two at a time.

"Hold, Holmes!" I called out, and followed after him. I found him already ensconced in his chair, lighting his pipe. A blue-grey haze – the spiced scent was an unspeakable relief after the awful vapours emerging from the tunnel – rose before him, obscuring his features.

"Really, Holmes," I said, mildly, and then all my indignation returned. "He is a cad – he is taking advantage of your position! He will steal all your cases away, beginning with this. Why, he will solve it before you!"

Even through the pall of smoke, I saw the white flash of his teeth. "I very much doubt it, Watson. For I solved it myself this morning."

I started and he laughed at my astonishment.

"Just so. Inspector Lestrade will be calling upon us shortly to discuss my conclusions. I think he shall find all to be satisfactory."

"But who . . . what . . .?"

He settled back into his seat, though all his tiredness seemed to have evaporated. "It was actually quite elementary," he said. "Did you not wonder why nobody should be looking for the unfortunates discovered by the tunnels?"

"Of, course, but—"

"And why both of them should be found in such a place, and yet with no marks of unnatural death upon them?"

I sighed with exasperation. "Pray, explain it to me. For I find I am once more at a disadvantage, and much out of sorts at that."

"I thank you for it, Watson. You have ever been a dear friend to me, and I am indebted to you for guarding my interests so zealously."

"You are teasing me, Holmes."

"I am; and yet I am sincere."

I bowed.

"Did you happen to notice a small piece in the newspaper about St Michael's Chapel? It has long been used as a place of worship, and yet its congregation is much depressed in these godless times."

"I did not," I replied. "Are they dissenters?"

"They are not. But there have been some strange occurrences at the chapel. Children going into fits, women fainting, men vomiting and so forth."

"And the cause?" I spoke impatiently, for I could not possibly see how the two things could be connected.

"Foul air," he said. "Emerging through the boards from the burial pit below. It was closed some years ago, naturally; the Burial Laws have seen to that. And yet people complain of a dreadful stench, and not only that, but of biting insects – 'body-bugs', they are calling them – rising from beneath their feet. The vault was never sealed, you see. It is packed to the rafters with coffins and festering bodies, and yet there is no lath or plaster; only the floorboards, which have naturally shrunk over time to emit the scent of the dead."

I frowned.

"It has happened before, Watson. Enon Chapel – you have heard of it? It was constructed before we were born, in 1823, but it remains quite notorious. Over twelve thousand bodies were interred in the burial pit beneath, until anyone attending there became terribly ill. Ironically, it was Enon Chapel that became a great impetus for the Burial Laws, and led to the development of new cemeteries just outside the city."

"I never heard of it."

"Have you not? It was turned into a dancing salon – before the bodies were even removed. In fact, they turned it into something of a morbid attraction. Wait!" Holmes sprung to his feet and returned with an ageing handbill, curling and yellowed. I read:

ENON CHAPEL – DANCING ON THE DEAD – ADMISSION THREEPENCE. NO LADY OR GENTLEMAN ADMITTED UNLESS WEARING SHOES AND STOCKINGS.

"Shoes and stockings!" I exclaimed. "But Holmes, what does this have to do with – it does not make sense! Old bodies would not emit the sort of stench you describe. And there would be no insects, not so long after interment."

"Ah." Holmes was suddenly grave and I realised that he was waiting.

"Oh," I said.

"You see, you hit upon it. There would only be such a fetor if the vault had been reopened and was being used again for burials."

"But that – that would be illegal!"

He smiled. "So it would. And yet such is the case. The vault is full, of course. The only way it could accommodate further occupants is by finding some additional room. In this instance, it was an easy matter, since the church is situated above an open sewer."

I grimaced. "You have investigated the tunnels already, then?"

"Not so. Do you think me a fool? I sent for a map of the system; I am already well equipped with a map of the city. It was simplicity itself to compare the two."

"So our victims—"

"Are not victims at all, in the sense you mean. They were buried, in the full knowledge of their families, in a grave the like of which can scarcely today be found in London: within the sanctified walls of the church. That is why no one looked for them. Their relatives were not to know that their loved ones had ended in the sewer, and from thence been borne to the Thames – almost onward to the sea estuary itself. If it were not for the recent rains, they might never have known it."

"A terrible thing. But, Holmes – how on earth could you be sure of it?"

"Why, did you not wonder about my choice of a widow's guise this morning? I had all the facts before me, and yet I thought I would pay a little visit to the chapel for my own satisfaction. I made there certain enquiries about the cost of such a burial. I found the curate a rather grasping fellow, and somewhat down on his luck. He was most sympathetic to my plight, particularly when he saw what a fine brooch I wore. Did you notice that little touch? I was rather proud of it. I needed to look as if I had a not inconsiderable sum set by."

I stared at him. "But Holmes – Smedley! He was to accompany you, was he not?" And then I understood how neatly he had worked it, and a smile spread across my features.

"You see it all, Watson," he said warmly. "Smedley has been like my shadow; waiting, I am sure, for just such an opportunity as he found today. And yet I seem to have hit upon the very means to shake him off, have I not?"

"By making him believe *he* had been the one to shake *you* off. Why, Holmes, you are a genius."

"Not at all. I simply know that there is little use in observation, if you do not trouble to read the papers."

I thought of Smedley, his pale eyes penetrating the shadows of the lecture theatre, so intent upon Holmes's words; and it suddenly returned to me where he had gone. "And now – your rival?" I exclaimed.

"He is, this very moment, exploring the foulest underbelly of London, armed only with a lantern and a small quantity of oil. There, he may discover for himself the source of the body. I have no doubt he is equal to the task."

My smile faded as I thought of it. He would be stumbling through the dark, filled with its thick, damp, mephitic vapours, with only a little light for company. I imagined the shadows that would shift and dance about him; the choking pestilence; the uncertainty of the ground beneath his feet. Who knows what he would be forced to wade through before the tunnel's end? And what an end! To discover the vault with its rotting corpses and skeletons in their cerements, the coffins each piled one atop the next until they burst; the stink of it; the horrors. What dread thoughts must pass through his mind at the sight? What dreams would proceed upon it? I almost pitied him.

It was in a softer voice that I spoke. "You might have simply dismissed him, Holmes."

He gave a grin that was almost wolfish. "Ah," he said, "but where would be the enjoyment in that? Though I must admit, my plan was almost undone by the weather. Did you notice I ascertained that the tunnels would not be subject to another flood? I wished to bring him lower. I did not actually mean to kill the fellow."

I inclined my head.

"At any rate, Watson, I have broken with my usual reticence. You shall be able to read about it later this very day, in the evening edition. Smedley will no doubt see it too, when he emerges. A burial pit discovered beneath London – it will have created quite the stir by then, I imagine."

"It shall." I let out my breath. "Why, Holmes! I do believe you have solved it all, without even heeding your own lesson. What of your advice – your talk of observing the body and the place it came from, of understanding the life to perceive the death? Were you not, after all, incorrect?"

He turned and met my eye, for the moment holding aside his pipe. "Not at all," he said. "For did I not say that it would be a remarkable man indeed who could expect to solve a crime without leaving his rooms?"

I stared at him. After a long moment, he drew on his pipe and breathed out, slowly and with evident satisfaction, and I could not help it, I began to laugh. Upon the instant, Holmes was laughing with me; and for once we entirely lost ourselves in a veritable contagion of mirth.

The Pressed Carnation (or A Scandal in London)
Saviour Pirotta

London, 1893

It was coming up to Christmas and I'd just been to see the Gaiety Girls at the Palace Theatre when, on a whim, I decided to drop in on Holmes in his rooms in Baker Street. I found him laying the table with china and a ruby-coloured plum cake.

"Good evening, Holmes."

The great detective looked up from the teacups. "You have come just in time, Watson. I am expecting company."

"Anyone I know?" I asked, hanging up my hat. It was freezing outside and Holmes had turned the gas up full. He'd made a half-hearted attempt to decorate the room for the coming festivities. There was a bunch of flowering holly in a vase on the windowsill and a few greeting cards from friends ranged along the mantelpiece.

"A student from the School for Detection," he answered, putting out freshly pressed napkins. "Some colleagues from his class have invited him up to Scotland for Christmas. They are very keen for a foreigner to witness the joys and excesses of Hogmanay. He has asked to see me before he takes the 10.15 from King's Cross."

"I take it he is one of your favourite pupils," I said, eyeing up the cake, which he'd placed on one of Mrs Hudson's best cake stands.

Holmes went to the window and looked out. There were carollers across the street, which added to the cheerful aspect of the evening. "He is a young gentleman from the Continent. A very gifted student who, in time and with proper guidance, could be the young Holmes of Central Europe! There's a clue to his identity, Watson. I wonder if you can guess anything as to his parentage before he reveals it. Here he is now."

Even as he spoke there was the sound of a hansom rattling to a halt outside the building. We heard Mrs Hudson answering the bell, then the quick rat-a-tat of agile footsteps hurrying up the stairs. Holmes came away from the window and opened the door before the visitor had time to knock.

"My dear sir, how are you?"

The man who came in was young, no more than twenty-two or -three. He was slim and well dressed, with a well-tailored modern lounge coat and a matching waistcoat. An elaborately tied bow adorned his neck, while a large amethyst flashed on the middle finger of his left hand. He had a short, mouse-coloured beard, which was combed forward into a neat point. His face looked vaguely familiar but I couldn't for the life of me recall where I might have seen or bumped into him.

"Watson, this is Vaclav," said Holmes, taking the young gentleman's hat and top coat.

"Good evening, Doctor," said the young man. "I have heard a lot about you. You are Mr Holmes's chronicler."

"He is indeed," added Holmes. "Sometimes a sensationalist one, I fear. Please, take a seat. Will you have tea and cake?"

"Thank you," replied the visitor, shaking my hand before sitting down rather stiffly in Holmes's basket chair. "The English make very wholesome cakes. No milk in my tea, please, Mr Holmes. And I wouldn't mind a drop of something stronger in it, seeing as we're not at a lecture now. I am terribly worried." He spoke perfect English with a light foreign accent, which I recognised right away as coming from somewhere east of the Rhine.

"I can indeed detect you are exceedingly anxious," said Holmes. He took the stopper off a decanter and poured a generous tot of brandy into the young visitor's tea.

"How so?" said our guest, his mouth falling open. "I thought I was hiding my anxiety rather well."

Holmes chuckled. "You forgot to take off your gloves when I took your hat and you also neglected to wipe your shoes on the doormat. Both signs that there is something troubling you."

"I apologise for my lack of manners," cried our well-bred visitor.

"No offence taken," smiled Holmes, handing him the tea. "As to what weighs so heavily on your mind, I have deduced that too."

The young man nearly dropped his cup in astonishment.

"Your bowtie is somewhat lopsided," said Holmes, "and your shoes seem to have been very unprofessionally shined, for there is still shoe polish adhering to the heels. That leads me to think that you had to polish your shoes and dress yourself without the aid of your trusted valet this evening. I can also see that one side of your face is not shaved properly and the length of the bristles suggests this has been going on for a few days. Your valet has gone missing. Is that not true?"

"The rogue has absconded," cried our guest. "He's been with me for four years and he has never had any cause for complaint. Indeed, I treat him more like family than paid staff. I can't possibly travel up to Scotland without finding him first. Mr Holmes, I've been forced to cancel my little sojourn."

"It's nearly Christmas and the season to drink and make merry," I ventured from across the room. "Are you sure the fellow is not lying drunk somewhere?"

"He has been missing for three days," replied our visitor. "Besides, Banks does not drink. Nor does he eat red meat or take refined sugar. He is decidedly Spartan in nature. He is very keen on sports and keeps himself in impeccable shape with boxing and running."

"Perhaps he had an accident on one of his runs," said Holmes. "Watson is right. He might be lying injured in a ditch."

"No, I am certain the fool has run away," insisted the young man, gulping down his tea. "I have checked his room and he has taken all his stuff with him. His clothes, his shoes, his boxing gloves and the few knick-knacks that he inherited from his Russian grandmother!"

"Did he take anything of yours?" asked Holmes.

"No, only his own things as far as I can tell," answered our guest without hesitation.

Holmes poured more tea and brandy. "And do you have any idea why he might run away?"

"None whatsoever," came back the reply. "As I said, sir, Banks and I are like brothers. He seemed in an ebullient mood the morning he disappeared. He had received a Christmas card with a Russian stamp on the envelope that made him very happy. I assumed it was from his mother. Piter – his first name is Piter – has a Russian mother and an English father, which accounts for his English surname. They live in Moscow. I remember him humming some Russian country song as he cleared the breakfast dishes. We were expecting delivery of a live Christmas tree from Harrods on the Brompton Road. I believe the custom is popular in London, too. Banks was very keen to start dressing the tree. He had already purchased ribbons and baubles for it at a market in Pimlico."

"How old is Banks?" enquired Holmes.

"He'll be twenty-six next March," answered the student.

Holmes cut into the plum cake. "You said he is very lean and in excellent shape. Describe him some more to me."

"Green eyes. Full mouth. Typical Slavic nose! Keeps his fair hair very short, almost shaved to the skull. Most of the time one can't even tell it is blond. The chap must be at least six foot four but very light on his feet. And very strong!"

He stopped and looked at the famous detective almost pleadingly. "You must help me find him, Mr Holmes. It is terribly important that he returns to my employ."

"I take it you have not informed your country's diplomatic corps about the business," said Holmes. "Nor been to our police here in London?"

"No, sir. I would rather solve the problem without help from either party."

Holmes reached for his cherry-wood pipe and lit up. "You say Banks has been gone three days. When did it occur to you that he had run away?"

"The same morning he left," answered the young man. "I'm using the upper rooms of a family property on Vicarage Lane in Mayfair. Banks had made me breakfast and laid out my clothes for the day. My friends from the school were going ice-skating. I was keen to join them. When I returned home, he was not there. I thought he might be reading or napping in his bedroom so I ran up the stairs to check. That's when I found out that all his things were gone."

"Had the Christmas tree been delivered?" asked Holmes.

"Yes! I found it propped against the back door when I came home."

Holmes poured the student another cup of tea. "How did Banks come to be in your employ?"

"He was recommended to my father by a family friend back home," said our guest. "Banks might only be in his twenties but is an accomplished valet. He has very impressive references. I believe he has also served with high-ranking military officials in the Ukraine."

"And I presume your father pays his wages."

The young man nodded. "Yes! Since it is not yet decided whether I will go into my country's secret service after I graduate, I cannot use funds from the public purse. My father's accountants transfer Banks's wages into his bank account on the last day of every month. I give him a weekly allowance for our living expenses from my own funds. He keeps detailed house accounts, even though I don't ask him to do so."

"I see," said Holmes. He got up to refill the kettle and put it back on the stove. "Well, you have only been at my school for one term but here you are about to tackle your first case already. I was telling Watson before you arrived that you are one of our most promising students. I am sure you will find your missing valet."

Vaclav sat up in his chair. "But will you help me, Mr Holmes? I will not be able to do it without you, and I cannot stress how important it is for me to find him. For reasons I can't tell you, my life depends on it. I have confided certain secrets in him that might reflect very badly on me with the family if they are divulged. Indeed, they would make me an outcast. They would cause a scandal."

Scandal!

That one word made me sit up in my chair. Now I knew why the young student seemed familiar. He had the same facial features, the same colour hair as Wilhelm Gottsreich Sigismond von Ormstein, Grand Duke of Cassel-Felstein and hereditary king of Bohemia. He was a member of the Bohemian royal family.

Five years ago Holmes had helped the king of Bohemia avoid a scandal that would have wrecked an alliance through marriage of two of the most powerful houses in Europe. Now a younger relative of the king's was begging us to avoid a second catastrophe.

"I will help you," said Holmes to the prince. "Have you been inside the valet's room since you first discovered his disappearance?"

"Only for that instant in which I realised he had run away," replied His Highness promptly. "I opened his wardrobe to see if his clothes were there. I found only empty clothes hangers. I thought it wise not to disturb the crime scene, so to speak, although no crime has been committed, as far as I know. There is a little bathroom off his room. I checked in there too. His toiletries and shaving equipment are missing too."

"Go home, and make sure the room remains undisturbed until we meet again tomorrow morning," said Holmes. "And get a good night's rest. We need clear heads to solve this mystery. We'll see you at your house at ten precisely."

The prince departed and Holmes turned to the plum cake for a second helping. A good mystery to solve always gave him an appetite, even though it was not always for wholesome food or tea.

"I believe he's a member of the Bohemian royal family," I said, as Holmes cut himself more cake.

"The king's oldest nephew," confirmed Holmes. "Son of his younger brother. Prince Vaclav Alfons Antonin von Ormstein. Tenth in line to the Bohemian throne."

"I hope he finds his valet," I said. "He seems very attached to him and relies on him a good deal."

"I hope so too," said Holmes. "Not that His Highness need fear the poor fellow will reveal any dark secrets."

I gasped. "How so?"

But Holmes would say no more about the matter. After we had polished off the excellent plum cake, and I fortified myself against the cold with a shot of brandy, I made my way home.

Holmes and I reconvened in Mayfair the next morning, outside one of those grand yet somewhat shabby houses owned by foreign nobility. They always seem to be neglected, despite their owners' wealth and power.

The prince answered the bell the moment we rang. He ushered us across a vast hallway, its furniture and marble statuary shrouded in dustsheets, and up grand stairs to his humbler quarters. Here the prospect was brighter. There was a somewhat gaudy wallpaper on the wall, with a blue and white willow pattern, and lilies in tall Chinese vases at the windows.

The prince offered us tea, which Holmes declined. He wanted to proceed with the investigation right away.

"I still have not heard from Banks," said the prince as he led the way down a corridor, turning on the gaslights. "Here is his room."

We all three stood in the open doorway and looked in. It was simply furnished, with outdated wallpaper on the walls and a gaslight with a glass shade between two windows. There was a small veneered wardrobe against one wall, a chest of drawers with a small mirror on top of it and a rather grand-looking bedside cabinet next to a single bed. A Lloyd Loom chair, piled with overstuffed cushions, stood in one of the windows. A second door led into what I took to be the small en suite the prince had mentioned the night before.

"I expect you have followed my instructions and not disturbed the scene since our meeting yesterday," said Holmes.

The prince replied in the affirmative.

"Well," Holmes said, putting on white theatre gloves, "look around the room carefully, as I taught you. What can you see?"

The prince cast a slow glance around him. "As I said yesterday, Banks has removed all his possessions. His clothes and shoes, his beloved boxing gloves that he always kept by his bed and blackened frequently, and a Russian icon of the Madonna he inherited from his grandmother. It used to sit on his bedside cabinet. He has taken his pictures off the wall too."

"And what else?" urged Holmes. "Do you see anything amiss?"

His student looked slightly bemused. "Amiss?"

"Is there anything in the room that strikes you as unusual? Perhaps some things are not in the spot where they should be? They have been moved, or taken out of the room completely."

The prince cast his glance around once more. "A stool has been brought in and left by the wardrobe. It usually serves as a lampstand on the landing. But surely that's too trivial a matter to be considered a clue of any sort. Banks could have brought it in for any number of reasons."

"Nothing is trivial when conducting an investigation," admonished Holmes. "What else can you tell me?"

The prince surveyed the room again slowly. "Nothing!"

"Now, please join Watson in the doorway," said Holmes. "Watch carefully how I examine the room. Do not speak until I tell you." He adjusted the white gloves on his hands and stepped forward. For a long moment he stood immobile between the bed and the wardrobe, his heavy-lidded eyes almost closed. Then he knelt on the carpet and very slowly ran his gloved fingertips along the valance hanging off the bed. These he held up to the gaslight and inspected carefully before brushing them clean. The same process was repeated with the cushions on the Lloyd Loom chair. Then he stood up, sniffed the air, and tried the catches on the windows to make sure they were locked.

After another lengthy pause, he turned to the prince and pointed to the wall above the chest of drawers where now I could see a nail protruding from the wallpaper.

"I assume one of the missing pictures was hanging there."

"A framed cutting from a Russian newspaper," agreed the prince. "I believe it was about Banks's mother. She belonged to an archery club and had won some sort of trophy in a competition."

"I see." Holmes cleared his throat. "Well, it is obvious to me that a second person has been in this room besides Your Highness since your valet disappeared. Someone who got here before you."

The prince looked startled. "How could that be? Both doors are kept securely locked at all times and we never open the windows on account of the smog."

"My guess is that he picked the lock on the front door. It's the old-fashioned kind that any thief worth his salt would be able to pick."

"You mean the intruder was a common burglar?"

"He definitely was not common," said Holmes. "The man is quite wealthy. He is also short, unhealthily overweight and short-sighted."

The prince looked lost for words.

Holmes indicated the stool near the wardrobe. "You said this would normally be on the landing. I believe it was brought in here so that someone could reach for the suitcase on top of the wardrobe. Am I right in presuming your valet kept his suitcase up there? Being over six feet tall, he would have been able to retrieve it without having to stand on a footstool."

"That explains how you deduced that he is short, Holmes. But what about his girth, and his short-sightedness?" I said.

"Yes," added the prince. "And how can you tell he is wealthy?"

Holmes sniffed the air again. "I detect a slight whiff of geranium, oakmoss and coumarin, all ingredients in a newly launched and very expensive men's cologne called Fougère Royal. Available from Harrods too, like your Christmas tree."

He held up his gloved right hand. "Our intruder was also wearing a very expensive woollen overcoat. He left traces of the wool along the valance on the bed and on the edges of the cushions on the chair as he brushed against them. Which proves to me that he is quite a stout fellow."

He pointed to the bed, which was at a slight angle to the wall. "See, he pushed the bed away with his hips without noticing when he knelt to look in the bedside cabinet. As for his short-sightedness, notice that the looking glass on the chest of drawers has been pushed right back from its usual place. Its legs have left a double trail in the dust. Our secret visitor had to lean forward to discern the writing in the framed cutting."

"But for what reason did the visitor come into the room?" asked the prince. "Nothing seems to be missing apart from the things that Banks himself took."

Without answering, Holmes stepped up to the bedside cabinet and drew it carefully away from the wall. "I have come across a few of these in wealthy London homes. Genuine antiques, and very handsome pieces. Imported from France. Probably Louis the Fifteenth or Sixteenth."

He turned the cabinet round slowly until its back was facing us. Right away I noticed a small brass button in the top corner. Holmes pressed it and a section of the wood sprang open, revealing a secret compartment. There was an old toffee tin inside, and a sheaf of letters tied up with a ribbon. Holmes opened the tin. It was stuffed full of banknotes.

"Your valet's life savings, I believe," said Holmes to the prince. "Do you not agree that, if the fellow had absconded, he would have taken his money with him? And his personal correspondence?"

The prince undid the ribbon and sifted quickly through the letters. He handed them back to Holmes. "Are you saying that he was taken against his will?"

"I am saying that your valet was murdered," answered Holmes, "and that someone removed his belongings to make it seem as if he had run away."

The prince took the news with a look of horror in his eyes. "But why would anyone want to kill my valet? We have only been in London a few months. He knew no one here. He could not have had any enemies."

"His killer is the same person who removed his belongings," said

Holmes. "A wealthy and portly man who is also short-sighted. It should not be difficult to find him. As to the motive for the crime, I am yet to make my mind up, but I am sure we will find proof of it soon enough." He held up the batch of letters. "May I borrow these, Your Highness? I assure you that whatever sensitive information lies within them will remain a secret between us.'

The prince hesitated only for a second. "Please, take them. I know they are in safe hands."

We left the house and the prince locked the front door. Shaken by Holmes's announcement, he had decided to spend the night at a club where his father had bought him temporary membership. I myself was returning to my old room in Baker Street. Mary, my wife, had gone to visit family in Norfolk that very same morning, so I would not be missed.

"We shall meet again tomorrow at two in the afternoon," said Holmes to the prince as we dropped him off outside his club. "By then I should know the identity of your valet's killer. Please try to get some rest; we have a long day ahead of us."

While the hansom clattered through Marylebone, Holmes turned his attention to the letters.

"Anything interesting in there?" I asked.

"Hmmm," said Holmes, more to himself than to me. He had drawn a greeting card out of an envelope and was looking at it intently. Pasted to it was a pressed flower, a carnation. It was very faded, and a few desiccated petals cascaded on to Holmes's lap as he sniffed it.

"Ha, here is proof enough," Holmes said mysteriously. He held out the card. "Can you detect any lingering perfume on this carnation, Watson?"

"No," I said after taking a deep sniff. "It smells oddly of some chemical or other. Perhaps it's the paste holding it to the card."

"Perhaps!" Holmes went quickly through the letters again, then tied them up with the ribbon and tucked them inside his coat. "When we get to Baker Street, Watson, I want you to distract Mrs Hudson long enough for me to slip upstairs and then out of the house again without being seen," he said. "And I might be very late back. Do not wait up for me."

"I shall do as you say. But what on earth do you plan to do?"

However, there was no time to explain. Our cab drew up outside our lodgings and Holmes addressed the driver. "Please wait for me here."

We let ourselves in to find Mrs Hudson laying the table in the dining room.

"Good evening," Holmes muttered as he slipped upstairs.

I smiled at the spread on the table. "Mrs Hudson! What a repast you lay before us."

"It's just cold mutton and tomatoes," she replied.

"But how artistically laid out," I continued, "and I smell the most delectable aroma coming from the kitchen."

Mrs Hudson beamed. "Spotted dick pudding, Dr Watson. You shall get an extra helping for your generous compliments." She opened a cupboard to fetch beer and glasses. "Take a seat! Where's Mr Holmes gone?"

"He has an urgent appointment."

"What a shame! His dinner will get spoilt."

"But it's cold mutton, Mrs Hudson."

"Silly me, so it is." The landlady opened the beer. I could hear the floorboards creaking in the rooms above us as Holmes moved about. Whatever was the fellow up to? The door to the bathroom closed with a bang and I heard water splashing. A good fifteen minutes later it opened again and Holmes cleared his throat loudly.

"Mrs Hudson," I cried.

She looked up from her beer. "You made me jump. Whatever is the matter?"

"I smell burning. The spotted dick!"

Mrs Hudson ran to the kitchen. At the same time I glimpsed Holmes coming down the stairs. He had a grimy overcoat on, with a dark hood concealing his head. I couldn't see his face but I guessed he had put on one of his elaborate disguises. He left without greeting me and a moment later the hansom clattered away.

Mrs Hudson returned to the dining room looking flushed but cheery. "False alarm, Doctor! The pudding is doing beautifully."

Despite Holmes's warning, I was determined to wait up for him. After pudding, which was exceedingly good, I excused myself and left Mrs Hudson to partake of port on her own. Holmes's rooms looked cheery enough with the decorations and the glowing lights of Baker Street outside, and I raked up the fire to make it cheerier still.

For a while I busied myself making notes in my medical journal. That done, I tried reading a book. But my mind was not focusing on the story. I kept thinking about the case in hand, and wondering what the great detective was up to or where he had gone. Sleep soon overcame me and it was well past dawn by the time Holmes shook me awake.

"Have you just come in?" I asked.

"I have been here a while," replied the detective, who had removed his disguise. "You were sound asleep. I did not have the heart to wake you."

I sat up on the chaise longue. "Did you find the killer, Holmes?"

"I did indeed, Watson. I had to visit no less than five different locations around London, but I found him. I followed him home, too, so I know who he is and where he lives."

"And what do we do now?" I asked.

"Now we need to link him to the crime. Prince Vaclav will be here soon. I shall see if he has any ideas on how to proceed. We have covered this kind of investigation at the school so I expect him to come up to expectations."

I had urgent patients to attend to that day, my reason for not joining Mary in Norfolk, so I had breakfast with Mrs Hudson and left. By the time I returned for a quick cup of tea between rounds, the prince had been and gone. Holmes was at his desk, writing out late Christmas cards and smoking a pipe.

"Watson, when is the deadline for the Christmas post this year?"

"The day after tomorrow." I noticed he was puffing on his cherry-wood pipe and not the clay contraption that he reserved for long bouts of deep thinking.

"You do not seem to be giving much thought to this case," I added.

"There is not much to think about, Watson," he replied. "The prince and I have the matter in hand already."

I very much wanted to stay and find out what Holmes and his illustrious protégé were going to do next. Indeed, I have to admit that the mere mention of the prince brought on a surprising pang of jealousy. Up till now I had always been Holmes's most trusted assistant and confidant. Now I seemed to have a talented usurper to contend with.

I drained my teacup and was checking my bag for medicine when there was a knock at the door and a young bandy-legged chimney sweep sauntered into the room. It took me a few moments to realise it was the prince in disguise.

"I shadowed our suspect all afternoon, sir," he said to Holmes, nodding at me by way of greeting. "He is having a late-night supper with a friend tonight at Williams's Boiled-Beef House in the Old Bailey. At eleven o'clock. He has reserved a table for two at the back of the establishment."

"The room reserved for the rich," said Holmes. "Beef at ninepence a plate. Bravo! You have done well, Your Highness. Send round a message and book a table for us, too. I have never had the pleasure of dining at Williams's Boiled-Beef House but I hear its beef platters are very good. Interesting that our quarry is dining at the Old Bailey."

The prince nodded, flushed by his mentor's praise. "I conclude from its location that the killer must be meeting with a lawyer or someone linked to the legal profession."

Holmes rose from the desk. "We must put the rest of our plan into action at once." He opened the door for me. "Instruct Mrs Hudson not to prepare an early supper on your way out," he said. "Unless you want a meal yourself."

I tried not to look too disappointed. "Shall I be joining you and His Highness at the Boiled-Beef House?"

"I am afraid not," answered Holmes. "I am arranging for Lestrade to be lying in wait in a carriage outside the restaurant. You must wait for us with him. Bring a gun, and keep out of sight inside the carriage. There's a chance you might be recognised by the suspect if he lays eyes on you."

"Recognise me?" I said. "Am I acquainted with the rogue—?"

"If everything goes according to plan, he might be very flustered," cut in the prince, not giving Holmes the chance to answer my question.

"Or he might be exceedingly calm, Your Highness," said Holmes. "Remember what I explained during my lecture 'On Criminals' Reactive Tendencies and Their Uses for the Detective'."

I looked from Holmes to the prince. "What are you planning to do?"

Tutor and pupil both smiled at me, Holmes taking a dramatic puff on his cherry-wood pipe. I had rarely seen him in so mischievous a mood. Having an audience for his superb powers seemed to be doing him a world of good. "All will be revealed in due course, Watson," he said. "Now, if you wait a second, His Royal Highness and I shall accompany you downstairs. We must pay a visit to the Royal Institute of Architects and then we shall need to talk to Inspector Lestrade of New Scotland Yard."

Eleven o'clock that evening saw me sitting inside a carriage across the road from the splendidly named Williams's Boiled-Beef House. Lestrade was there with me, along with another member of the London constabulary whom I did not know. It was bitterly cold with a promise of snow in the air. Despite the weather and the late hour, the street seemed to be unusually busy. People loitered outside pubs, chatting in loud voices. Hawkers called out their wares. I recognised a knife-sharpener oiling his lathe. He had been plying his trade outside the house of the American opera singer Irene Adler when Holmes and I had been working on the case that subsequently became known as 'A Scandal in Bohemia'.

The man was in Holmes's employ. He had been planted there by Holmes himself. It slowly dawned on me that most of the other hawkers were part of the elaborate charade, too. A young posy-seller with auburn hair looked familiar, as did a chestnut-seller with a shiny bald pate.

The clock in the nearby church of the Holy Sepulchre struck the hour.

"It's gone eleven but there's no sign of Holmes," grumbled Lestrade, taking my place to peep through a chink in the carriage windows. I found another peephole in the torn curtain. Two sailors, arms linked, were making their way into the restaurant. They both had dark hair and droopy French moustaches but I recognised them right away.

"I think you'll find Holmes is dead on time, as is his wont," I said as the glass door swung to behind the sailors.

A long half-hour gave way to three-quarters. It was getting close to midnight. The local pubs and coffee houses spilled out their last drunken customers, who stumbled past our carriage without giving it a second glance.

The glass window at the Williams's establishment was steamed up with heat and, try as I might, I could not see in. I was starting to doze – it had, after all, been a long and hectic day – when the eating-house door opened and a middle-aged gentleman in a black dinner jacket stepped out. My mind cleared in an instant. The gentleman was short, ruddy-faced and wore round, horn-rimmed spectacles. I was looking at a murderer.

But it was not the first sight of a cold-blooded killer that made me gasp. I knew the man. He was an eminent doctor with a wide following in the medical community and professional links to the royal family itself.

He calmly hailed a cab and was about to climb in when the girl selling posies darted across the street. There was a loud cry and her flowers scattered all over the ground.

"Oh, sir. My poor posies, sir!"

I could not clearly see what was happening, for the hired carriage was in the way, but I heard the girl continue to protest most dramatically.

"But, sir, you knocked my posies to the ground. They'll not be fit for selling now. How about some compensation? It's almost Christmas, sir."

"This is a trick," shouted back the doctor. "*You* ran into *me*. I do not owe you a farthing." A moment later the carriage was in motion, its wheels now trampling the girl's posies in earnest. The flowers were ruined but the ruse had worked. The short pantomime had given Holmes and the prince the opportunity to leave the eating-house unobserved by the doctor. They ran across the road and tumbled into the carriage.

"That was a dramatic piece of misdirection, Watson," Holmes grinned as our own cab took off after the doctor's vehicle.

"And a very successful one too," added the prince with pride. "I must say you are scintillating in the classroom, Mr Holmes, but you are *mesmerising* on the job."

"How very nice for the both of you," sniffed Lestrade, echoing my feelings perfectly. He spoke to the driver. "Don't get too close to the quarry. We don't want him to see us."

The cab slowed down at once.

"But not so slow," snapped Lestrade. "We don't want to lose the man."

"I am acquainted with the fellow, Holmes," I gasped. "He is Dr —"

"I recognised him, too," replied the detective. "A respected fellow in the medical community. Specialises in treating diseases of the Tropics and Subtropics. Has also published papers on the effects of malnutrition on children in workhouses and penal settlements. Close friend of royalty and member of a grand order. A confirmed bachelor!"

"Darned if I know how a fine gentleman like him ends up committing murder," I said.

Our carriage trundled past Saint Paul's Cathedral to the end of Fleet Street and nudged its way on to Waterloo Bridge.

"I know where he is heading," I said to Holmes. "The doctor also teaches student nurses at St Thomas's Hospital. He is heading towards Lambeth."

A large crowd had gathered on the bridge to see a costumed dare-devil attempt a dive into the Thames, impeding our carriage. "Don't lose sight of him," Holmes urged our driver as Dr —'s hansom cab came off the bridge.

At last we were on terra firma, too, and the carriage picked up considerable pace along the Belvedere Road, the doctor's cab still visible in the gloom ahead of us. It stopped outside a side entrance to St Thomas's, which overlooked the river. Lestrade ordered our driver to slow down and we saw the doctor let himself into the hospital grounds.

St Thomas's seemed almost deserted. A few lights shone through the screens at the ward windows. Occasionally the shadow of a nurse or patient moved in silhouette across the cloth.

We watched in silence as Dr —'s empty hansom cab set off into the night. A thick mist was coming off the river now, spreading around the various pavilions.

Holmes shifted in his seat. "We'll give the good doctor a little while," he said. "Then we'll go in."

A few minutes passed, with the fog getting thicker. At last Holmes opened the carriage door and stepped out. "Watson, bring your revolver," he said. "Your Highness, please come with me. And Lestrade, you wait outside as we discussed. I take it you have other men to assist you."

Lestrade nodded. "They are waiting at their posts as planned."

Quickly, we approached the side door. Holmes fumbled in his pocket for his tools and a few moments later the door clicked open. He had picked the lock. We entered a windowless corridor with tiles on both walls and linoleum on the floor. There was a terrible smell of disinfectant in the air, masking a deeper, more repugnant stench. The smell of blood!

"I borrowed a lantern from a constable, Holmes," I whispered, trying to take my mind off the stench. As a doctor I was used to the smell of blood, but this foetid odour was something else. It was the smell of death!

"Light it now but keep your wits about you – douse it immediately if you as much as hear a footfall," replied the detective. "Follow me."

The prince and I padded along behind him and down a short flight of steps until we came to a second door, this one made of metal. Again Holmes picked the lock. It swung open to reveal a dreadful chamber that every hospital has but tries to hide from the gaze of the visiting public.

My lantern illuminated two rows of tables on which lay a dozen or so hapless cadavers, covered in grey shrouds.

"Is Banks in here?" whispered the prince, his voice muffled by the horror that always overwhelms the young when faced with proof of man's mortality.

Holmes put a finger to his lips. "He is not here, no. But listen!"

We could hear a faint scraping sound, like the scratching of mice in the walls. Holmes asked me to shine my lantern around while he stood in the middle of the room, getting his bearings. At last he moved towards a wall.

"Watson, the light."

I shone the lantern in Holmes's direction.

"Closer, man, closer."

He was standing in front of a tall glass display cabinet filled with odd jars and boxes. I could not tell what he was doing in the faint light, but a moment later the cabinet swung open like a door. Instantly, a musty and familiar smell assailed our noses. It was the muddy stench of the Thames.

Holmes beckoned us forward and I followed him and the prince down another flight of steps. These were worn and slimy with damp and algae. At the end of yet another corridor we came to a doorway. There was no door in place and the smell of the river became stronger.

The sound of scratching had been replaced by another noise in the room ahead.

I snuffed out the lantern. Without its light we found ourselves in pitch darkness, but I had been on enough adventures with Holmes to recognise that dreadful noise. It was the sound of someone dragging a heavy object along the floor.

We waited in the dark, all three crouching low, as the unholy noise continued. Then, at last, a door opened across the room and we saw, silhouetted against a faint light, the shape of a man dragging a heavy bundle out into the open. He was a short man, rotund, with glasses that caught the outdoor light.

The ghastly vision lasted only a brief moment. Then the door was kicked to and once more the dark swallowed us.

"We have him, Holmes," I whispered.

"Yes, let us pounce now," urged the prince.

"Patience, the both of you," answered Holmes. "The mouse is yet to venture fully into the trap."

We waited for what felt like hours but could have only been ten or twelve minutes. Presently we heard shouting outside.

'Police! Stop! You are surrounded."

Holmes, the prince and I charged across the room and burst through the door. We stumbled out on to the foreshore of the Thames, the great pavilions of St Thomas's rising behind us. The fog was still a pea-souper, but we could see Lestrade standing on the edge of the river. He was pointing a gun at a boat which Dr — was frantically pushing away from the bank with an oar. The shrouded corpse lay on the planking behind him.

"I said stop or I will shoot," warned Lestrade as Dr — fitted the oars in the rowlocks. He glared at Holmes. "I'm afraid my men and I were waiting at the wrong spot. It's this blasted fog. The man surprised us. But we'll have him yet." He turned once more to the boat. "Stop, sir, I beg you."

Dr — ignored the plea and proceeded to row.

"Do you not understand?" said Holmes to Lestrade. "The man wants you to shoot him. He knows there is no other way out of his predicament."

The boat was almost out of sight in the fog by now. Suddenly a loud shot rang out from somewhere to our right and Dr — slumped forward over the oars. Two of Lestrade's men dived into the river, striking out towards the boat, while a third joined us on the bank. He was replacing a pistol under his belt.

"The fugitive was getting clean away, sir."

"Well done, Patterson," said Lestrade. Behind us, lights were coming on all over the hospital. Several doors opened and people came running out. "Keep everyone indoors," Lestrade ordered his men. "No one is to venture on to the foreshore till we clear up. But ask for some orderlies to help us carry the bodies. And get someone to prepare hot tea for our lads in the water."

The men who had dived into the river returned, dragging the boat in their wake. Dr —'s body was bundled ashore, and two orderlies with a stretcher came and took it away to the morgue.

Lestrade's men placed the shrouded corpse on the wet ground. "Well done, gentlemen," said Holmes. "You go and warm yourselves up with a nice cup of tea. The prince would like a few quiet moments with his valet."

The police retreated towards the hospital, leaving Holmes and me with the prince. The detective knelt on the ground and, taking a knife from his pocket, slit open the shroud.

"Is he indeed your valet?"

The prince's teeth were chattering with the cold. He nodded miserably. "That is Piter."

Holmes peeled the shroud further till he had exposed the corpse's torso. The poor wretch was wearing a dark jacket, still buttoned. Holmes opened it and, using his knife again, slit away the lining. A small blue envelope came to light. The prince swooped on it, uttering something in a German-sounding language.

Holmes put away the knife. "Is this the missing letter you did not want discovered?"

The prince smoothed the envelope with his hands. "It is. I shall be forever grateful to you for retrieving it, Mr Holmes. You are my saviour."

Footsteps crunched on the shingle behind us. Lestrade and the orderlies had returned for the valet's body.

Holmes stood up. "Put the letter away, Your Highness. I trust that now it is back in your possession you will want to keep it."

"A memento," whispered the prince, slipping the little envelope into his pocket.

Holmes and I accompanied the prince back to his club where he started to pack for his journey to Scotland. His friends would arrange for a temporary valet to look after him until a suitable replacement was found.

Back in Baker Street, Holmes turned up the gas.

"I take it there will be no court case," I said while he put the kettle on the stove.

"There will be no need of one," said Holmes. "Both victim and perpetrator are deceased."

"Good," I sighed, settling into the basket chair. "Then there will be no adverse publicity for the prince and his family. Another scandal for the House of Bohemia has been averted."

Holmes served up some brandy.

"I am so glad we saved His Highness's reputation," I said. "But I still cannot understand why Dr — killed the prince's valet. Or why that letter would undo His Highness if it fell into the wrong hands."

"It is perhaps one of the easiest cases we have tackled," responded Holmes. "A simple case of blackmail gone horribly wrong."

"Blackmail?"

"Take notes for your stories, Watson: a prince's valet goes missing but the prince is reluctant to contact the police for help. He is afraid there might be a scandal that would ruin him and his family, so he comes to us for assistance. He has, it seems to me, something to hide.

At first glance it does indeed appear as if the valet has run away. Perhaps he has taken some valuables to sell. But no, the prince is adamant that the valet took only his own possessions. He is sure of this without even checking. When we search the room, we quickly establish that a second person, apart from the prince, has entered the room. And we soon discover that the valet has left his life savings and his personal correspondence behind him. That proves that he did not run away. Someone else removed his possessions to make it look as much."

"By this time you were convinced that the valet had been murdered," I said.

"I had a hunch," Holmes corrected me. "A very strong one. I thought if the valet had been taken against his will and was still alive, he might have succeeded in making contact with his employer. There were other clues that pointed to another complication in the mystery: the chintzy décor in the house, the valet's fondness for Christmas baubles, his strict physical regime designed to make him look like a Greek god. I chose to ignore those until the main part of the mystery had been solved. I focused on the doctor's motives but drew a blank. Why would a wealthy, well-connected doctor kill a penniless foreign valet? And then I looked through the letters we found in the secret compartment at the back of the bedside cabinet."

"The card with the faded carnation?"

"And I knew right away that my hunch was right. There was more to the handsome valet than meets the eye. Remember, the carnation had no perfume. I thought that curious. Carnations are well known for holding their fragrance long after they have been pressed and withered. Moreover, this one smelt slightly of chemicals, as you yourself pointed out."

"Yes, I thought perhaps it smelt of the glue holding it to the card."

"It smelt of the dye it had been left to stand in. To alter its colour."

"Change its colour?"

"From white to green."

"I don't follow you," I said.

Holmes got up to check the kettle. "Green carnations are a symbol, Watson. They are used as badges by certain men to identify themselves to others of their ilk. Men whose honest passions are reviled by the puritan classes. They are often worn as boutonnieres in molly houses. Now I was sure beyond doubt that the valet's tastes ran to the Greek side of things. He'd pressed and kept the green carnation as a memento of his first visit to a London molly house. But there was another letter in the bundle. It was from the valet's English father who had moved to London. The man is a gambler and a drunk. He was heavily in debt and he was looking for his son to bail him out. That's when I realised that the valet had been murdered by a man he was blackmailing."

"Dr —," I gasped.

The kettle boiled and Holmes filled the teapot. "The valet must have met him in a molly house, perhaps even before he received the letter from his father. We can never be sure. All we know is that at some point the valet started blackmailing Dr —. He would expose him if he did not pay up, ruining his career and landing him in jail."

"But would that not have exposed the valet's unlawful activities, too?"

"Such men often agree a deal with the police," said Holmes, handing me a cup of tea. "They testify against prominent victims on the understanding that they themselves are allowed to walk free. Their identity is held secret by the police, so there would have been no danger of scandal for the valet and the prince."

"Dr — met the first few demands. I know this because I checked with his creditors yesterday morning. He had unpaid bills all over town. The man was running out of money. So he murdered the valet."

"But how did you know Dr — was the killer?"

"We knew from our investigations that the murderer was short, plump and short-sighted, and that he frequented molly houses. I dressed up in suitable attire and went out looking for him in one molly house after another till I found him."

"You went out resplendent in Mrs Hudson's Sunday best," I cried.

"Holmes, that's why you told me to keep her occupied. You raided her wardrobe and cosmetics chest while she prepared dinner."

"And very proficient you were at misdirection," chuckled the detective. "Once I'd established who the murderer was, I knew all I had to do was connect him with the crime. I had to find some proof, and I also had to retrieve a missing letter that the prince was terrified might fall into the wrong hands. His Highness and I thought up a plan that might help us achieve both aims. It is my theory, Watson, that when a criminal thinks his vile act has been discovered he is lured back to the scene of the crime. He must check that there is nothing there that might incriminate him, or to get rid of any remaining evidence."

"So you and the prince let Dr — know that his crime had been discovered."

"The *mise en scène* was the prince's idea. He really is an impressive pupil. He found out where Dr — was to dine yesterday. Then we decked ourselves out as Breton sailors and had a very loud conversation across the table at Williams's Boiled-Beef House, making sure he overheard. We spoke about the body of a half-Russian valet that had been discovered by the police and how they were homing in on the murderer. The trap worked, Watson. The rest you know."

I watched Holmes light his pipe. "I wonder how he killed the poor valet."

"I'm sure the autopsy will reveal the method used, but I would bet my best pipe that he poisoned him."

"You are probably right," I said. "We doctors have access to much stuff that could be lethal if administered wrongly."

"Dr — hid the body in one of the basements under the morgue. The hospital is built on the ruins of medieval cottages and their cellars remained under the foundations when it was built. I discovered as much when I checked the plans at the Royal Institute of Architects. He was no doubt waiting for the right moment to dispose of the body in the river."

There was a long silence in the room. The sun had come up and a trader across the road was setting up a stall to sell mistletoe. It was almost Christmas.

"There is one last thing, Holmes," I said. "What was in the letter that the prince should be so desperate to retrieve?"

Holmes undid the bundle of letters and, taking out the memento with the pressed carnation, placed it carefully on the mantelpiece alongside the Christmas cards. "Piter Banks must have been a very charismatic young man," he said. "Despite his lowly position in life, he cast a spell not only on Dr —, but on His Royal Highness the Prince Vaclav, too."

The Case of the Wrong-Wise Boots
Simon Clark

One

Mr Sherlock Holmes stood in front of his sitting-room window. The bright November sun shone through the glass, transforming him into a silhouette figure – one that was tall, very thin, with a precisely delineated profile that I daresay every human being in the entire world who has access to a newspaper would recognize in an instant. Such is my friend's fame.

Earlier, the door had opened to admit six students who had enrolled in what is now commonly known as Sherlock Holmes's School for Detection. Four were men, two were women. All were aged between twenty and thirty years of age. One of the men wore a turban. The two women were from very different backgrounds: one, the daughter of a bishop, the other, the wife of a railway engineer. Despite differences in class, nationality and education, they all had a single ambition. They wished to learn the science of detection.

I sat at the table with a list of the students' names in front of me. Beneath each name a paragraph had been included, forming a brief biography. After graduating from the school, the majority would join a variety of police forces. However, I noted that one was destined to become a sultan's bodyguard. Another fellow would enter the Admiralty's intelligence office. Holmes's former students have included not only police officers, military men and bodyguards, but archaeologists, for they find that an understanding of forensic science will help unlock the secrets of the ancients when they, for example, excavate a castle or enter an Egyptian tomb.

Holmes said, "Welcome to my home, ladies and gentlemen. Let us begin."

They produced notebooks and sat up straight, pencils at the ready.

Their faces shone – they were eager to learn from the undisputed master of rational deduction.

Holmes continued: "For six weeks you've studied the foundations of detection in the classroom. You will also have read articles by my friend Dr Watson here, where he has recorded my investigations in all manner of cases." Holmes slowly paced back and forth. "After being confined to the classroom, the time has now come for you to work in the field. To each of you I will assign an unsolved case, which has been passed to me by Scotland Yard. Initially, you will work on the case alone with no help from me. Five days from now, bring me your findings and I will . . ." He made a languid gesture with his hand. "I will explain where you have gone astray in your investigations, as you surely will."

"Sir." This was the bishop's daughter, a petite woman with blonde ringlets. "Sir. I protest. You presume us to be incompetent."

"You are not incompetent, Miss Charlton, nor are any of you here, otherwise you wouldn't be sitting on my chairs. You are, however, lacking practical experience. Until, for example, you have examined the corpse of a murder victim, smelt its clothing, its hair, its hands, you can't possibly begin to gather the vital evidence you need." Holmes turned to a young gentleman with gold spectacles. "Mr Garret, why would you bring such a sensitive organ as your nose to within an inch of a cadaver?"

Mr Garret blinked nervously. "Ahm . . . well . . . uhm. Decay . . . odours of decay."

Miss Charlton gave a defiant toss of her head to show she was not intimidated by Holmes. "A scent of decay will indicate how long the individual has been deceased."

"Interesting," said Holmes, clearly not impressed by her statement. "However, it's important – vital! – to employ one's sense of smell at every crime scene. Might we not catch the telling scent of the murderer's cologne on the victim, or the assassin's favourite tobacco, which will assist in his, or her, identification? If the murderer is a printer we might catch the aroma of ink on the deceased. If the killer is a chef, then maybe the sharp tang of garlic, and so on. Moreover, bear in mind that those scents, which might be so revealing, are likely to dissipate rapidly. So – " he ran his finger down the side of his distinctive hawk's beak of a nose – "use this vital instrument the moment you arrive at the scene of a crime."

All six bowed their heads as they inscribed pearls of my friend's wisdom into their notebooks.

"I will now assign cases," Holmes told them. Immediately those six heads lifted in order to give him their undivided attention. "Miss Charlton. A man in Dover has woken each morning to be greeted by a mysterious sight." Her eyes widened in anticipation at what Holmes would reveal. "The flowerpots on his garden wall have been repeatedly shifted sideways by twelve inches. You will find out why this has happened as well as identifying the individual responsible for moving them."

Miss Charlton's expression of eager anticipation switched to one of outrage. Her hitherto milk-white face flamed red with anger. "Mr Holmes. Why . . . this is so hurtful. You are mocking me."

"Mocking you? How so?"

"You are asking me to investigate what is clearly a trivial matter. A practical joke, no doubt. Is it because I'm a woman that you wish to make fun of me?"

"In this matter I am blind to your sex, Miss Charlton. I assigned you the case because I believe you have a highly developed ability to notice what others don't."

"Now you patronize me, Mr Holmes."

"I shall prove it." He turned to the others. "Can anyone tell me what is missing from my clothing? It was there when you arrived just minutes ago."

Five baffled students gazed at Holmes, from his feet to the top of his head. Only Miss Charlton kept her steady gaze on his face.

"Does anyone notice anything different about me?" Holmes allowed himself a smile of amusement. "Miss Charlton. Please enlighten your fellow acolytes."

Miss Charlton sat up straight with a telling flash of triumph in her eye. "I noted that on the sleeve of Mr Holmes's jacket there was a single red hair. The hair came from a man of forty years of age or above. The hair is no longer there. Mr Holmes must have removed it when he went to look out of the window."

"Excellent, Miss Charlton." Holmes nodded with pleasure. "I added the hair from my collection of items that have proved to be valuable clues in the past. Now, perhaps you will explain why you decided that the hair came from a man?"

"The hair was no longer than an inch in length, and it is still customary in England for men to wear their hair short."

"You are correct. What made you conclude that the hair belonged to a man of above forty years of age?"

"The colour."

"Oh? What would hair colour reveal about age?"

"It was clearly dyed red, for I noticed that the hair near the root was silver, proving he was of mature years."

"And your deduction, therefore, proves that you are the perfect individual to assign to the most mysterious case in my portfolio."

The young woman smiled. I could tell that her respect for Sherlock Holmes had been renewed. He hadn't been making fun of her after all.

Holmes picked up an envelope from the table. Handing it to her, he said, "This contains the address of the gentleman troubled by errant flowerpots." Holmes gave another envelope to the man in the turban. "Mr Paswan, a fifteen-year-old boy, who cleans boots for decidedly meagre wages, has recently provided his destitute mother with a large house. You will discover how a poor slum urchin became rich."

"Thank you, Mr Holmes. I am grateful that you place your faith in my abilities."

"To the devil with faith, Mr Paswan. I am testing you, sir. As I am testing all the students here. If any of you fails to unravel these mysteries then you must leave the school. Whether you will become a detective now hangs in the balance. Succeed in these tasks or suffer the shame of expulsion."

The students exchanged worried glances. No doubt each one feared that all too quickly their dreams of becoming a professional investigator would be over and done with.

Holmes spoke to the remaining students in turn while handing over more envelopes. He pointed out that behind even the most apparently trivial of mysteries there might be secrets of an altogether more serious nature. Many will recall the shocking crime of the Falmouth Poisoner, where Holmes discovered why blackberries gathered in the vicinity of a certain farm had suddenly acquired an unusually bitter taste.

Holmes had no sooner finished allocating the cases when a knock sounded on the door downstairs.

"Ah, Watson," Holmes said. "Mrs Hudson is out this morning. Would you be so good as to admit our visitor? He has an interesting story to tell. I would like my students to hear it, for what he has to say will be most instructive."

Two

I ushered the stranger into the sitting room where the six students sat in a row. Holmes stood with his back to the fireplace, his keen eyes studying the man and, no doubt, making penetratingly accurate deductions as easily as most people would read a newspaper headline.

The stranger clearly recognized Holmes from illustrations in the press. "Mr Holmes, good morning. Thank you for agreeing to this consultation at such short notice."

"Good morning, sir. This is my associate, Dr Watson. These young people are students – they are learning the science of detection."

The stranger wore clothes of excellent quality – everything crisply brand new from the black hat he nervously turned round and around in his fingers to his highly polished shoes. He was perhaps forty years of age, clean-shaven, with a receding hairline that gifted him a high fore-head of gleaming skin. All in all, my impression was of an honest, softly spoken fellow who would be pleasant company. Only the anxious darting of his blue eyes revealed that his was a troubled soul in need of my friend's professional help.

"Mr Holmes," he began in gentle tones that bore a distinct Scottish accent. "My name is Charles Keppel. I am the son of the late Sir Benjamin Keppel, who invented the prism-reflector gun-sight. Consequently, I inherited a considerable fortune upon my father's death ten years ago." Keppel suddenly appeared unsure of himself, perhaps doubting he should continue. "Mr Holmes, do you wish to hear what befell me? It is an extraordinary story. In fact, so extraordinary that many refuse to believe me."

"Please, Mr Keppel, take a seat." Holmes indicated a comfortable chair. "Your story promises to be of great interest. I did request in my letter that you would consent to my students being in attendance so they could hear it, too. Is that still acceptable?"

"Yes, sir, it is." He took his seat.

Holmes nodded his thanks. "Now, I know nothing of your misadventure, so you have a fresh pair of ears for your story. Indeed eight pairs of ears, if you include my friend, Dr Watson here." He smiled to put the man at ease. "How may I help you?"

"Sir, I am here to beg you to find someone."

"Who?"

"Me."

It's not often that I see my friend react with such surprise.

He stared at the man in astonishment. "You ask me to find you? You, yourself?"

"Yes, sir."

"Mr Keppel. Consider the mystery solved. You are here in front of me."

"I apologize," he said in a flustered way. "What happened to me is so bizarre that it has left my nerves badly shaken. I've not expressed myself clearly."

"Pray, continue."

"When I begged you to find me, I should have asked you to find the other me. My other self. Do you understand?"

"Not entirely."

"Ten days ago, I walked along one of those streets of fine Georgian homes one finds south of the river, when I suddenly paused outside a particular house and I thought to myself: 'I live there'."

The students' pencils flew across the paper as they wrote down Keppel's words.

I said, "Sir, recognizing where one lives is hardly remarkable, is it?"

Keppel's eyes blazed with horror. "It's not remarkable at all, Dr Watson, but until I drew level with the house, I didn't know I lived there. It was only when I saw the brass knocker in the shape of a lion's face that I remembered. I looked down at my clothes. I wore a yellow suit made of tweed and I'm not afraid to say that I shouted out in fright."

Holmes shot a sideways glance at me, hinting that he suspected we were in the presence of a lunatic.

Mr Keppel recognized the meaning in that glance, too. "I am not mad, sir. I am the victim of some abominable crime or curse."

"Can you explain why you suspect that to be so?"

"Tweed cloth is something I have detested since childhood. I never wear tweed. I have never owned a pair of brown boots. However, when I looked at my feet I saw them shod in brown leather." His hands shook with fear. "I tell you, Mr Holmes, it was as if I'd been sleepwalking, then I had suddenly woken to discover that I wore strange, detestable clothes. In my hand was a Gladstone bag that I've never seen before in my life. I knew my name was Charles Keppel. Yet when I opened my jacket to retrieve my wallet, I noticed a name tag sewn to the lining. Printed there were the letters 'RFW'. My heart pounded so fiercely I thought it would erupt from my chest."

"You wore a stranger's clothes?" asked Holmes.

"No, I declare they were mine because they were a perfect fit."

"What did you do then?"

"I opened the wallet, which also bore the initials RFW. Inside, there were banknotes. Also, there was a photograph of myself standing beside a lady."

"What is the name of the lady?"

"I don't know, sir."

"You had your photograph taken with a lady whom you do not know?"

"I must know her . . . at least, I presume I do." He shook his head in despair. "The truth is, I don't know her name. She is a stranger to me, yet I posed with her for a photograph. It is all most strange."

"Disconcerting, too," Holmes added. "Anything else?"

"There were calling cards in the wallet. Each bore the same name: Major Robin Fox-Warren. There was no address."

"Ah," I raised a finger. "The initials RFW. We can link that name to the letters on the clothing tag and wallet."

"Yes." Keppel clenched his fists in distress. "For some reason I had assumed another identity."

Miss Charlton added an observation. "Or had a false name forced on you."

Keppel shuddered. "Major Robin Fox-Warren? I've never served in the army, so it's perplexing that my nom de guerre includes the rank of major."

Holmes rested his fingertips together. "Extraordinary."

"And my tale becomes yet more extraordinary. Of course, I rang the doorbell. The butler opened the door. I recognized him as Joplin; he'd served the household when my father was alive. When Joplin saw me, his face turned white. He exclaimed, 'Good heavens! It can't be.' I rushed past him into the hallway. An elderly woman appeared. I knew the lady to be my mother, although she looked much older. Bowed down with grief, too, almost as if life had cruelly beaten her until she could no longer stand upright. When she saw me she cried out before fainting to the floor. I shouted to the butler, 'Don't just stand there, man. Fetch the brandy!' Yet he did not move. His eyes bulged in horror as he stared at me. Then he managed to utter, 'You're dead.' I shouted that he could see me there in front of him: flesh and blood. That's when Joplin said these words that I'll never forget: 'Mr Keppel, sir. You vanished from this house two years ago. No one's clapped eyes on you since. A body was pulled out of the river. It wore your clothes and had your watch. Everyone – your friends, your family – everyone knows you to be dead.' My mother began to wake. Of course, I rushed to her, and, picking her up, carried her to a sofa where I gently set her down. On opening her eyes she flung her arms around my neck and sobbed. Meanwhile, the household staff came to find out the cause of the commotion. When they saw me they began screeching. Such a hullaballoo!"

"You say," began Holmes, "that the butler claimed you'd not been seen for two whole years?"

"Yes. However, at that moment it seemed to me that I'd only stepped out of the house for an hour or so. Yet I'd been absent for two years."

Miss Charlton said, "Moreover, you left as Mr Keppel, but you returned as Major Robin Fox-Warren."

"Yes." Keppel still appeared dazed by his experience. "This entire situation preys on my mind. I cannot sleep for thinking of the woman who stands beside me in the photograph. I wonder what I have done in this lost period of my life. How did my other self, Major Fox-Warren, spend his days? Was he a good man? Or did he . . ." Keppel trembled. This softly spoken gentleman must have conjured distressing possibilities in his mind. "What if, when I was this other fellow . . . what if I did terrible things? Or sought gratification in vile behaviour?"

"You remember nothing of the last two years?" asked Holmes.

"No. I cannot even remember what errand had taken me to Juniper Terrace last week, unless some unconscious impulse guided me there. That's why I implore you to find out all you can about Fox-Warren. Where he . . . I . . . lived. I want to know about his activities."

"Have you consulted a physician?"

"Yes. He gives me powders that should make me sleep. Alas . . ." He gave a miserable shrug.

"Don't worry, Mr Keppel. I will visit you tomorrow to examine the tweed suit, your brown boots, wallet and Gladstone bag. I presume you still have them?"

"Yes."

"Don't have the clothing washed. Nor should anyone else touch the items you carried when you – shall we say – awoke to your real self? Would two o'clock be convenient?

"It would, sir. And let me say how relieved I am, Mr Holmes, that you are coming to my aid. I don't think I could bear this distress for much longer."

"Then I shall see you tomorrow. Dr Watson will be present, along with two of my students."

Three

The next day found Holmes and I in a hansom cab, riding towards Keppel's home in Juniper Terrace.

London has become an artificial realm. Marshes drained, streams built over, ditches culverted. Roads and buildings eradicate meadows: virtually every square foot of soil lies beneath brick and stone. We denizens of London move through this manmade world, seemingly immune to nature, untroubled by changes in the season. However, November rains had arrived with a vengeance. Horses that pulled carts and hansom cabs splashed through puddles. Pedestrians struggled with umbrellas. The long skirts of ladies flapped like flags in the breeze. The pungent smell of rain filled our nostrils. Holmes and I were forced to shuffle to the furthest extremity of the cab's bench seat to avoid a steady trickle of rainwater that leaked through its roof.

Sherlock Holmes and I sat with our sodden hats in our hands. A bead of rainwater trickled down Holmes's high forehead – although it would take much more than a wintry downpour to dampen the blazing fires of thought within that astonishing brain.

Holmes said, "Watson, yesterday I sent telegrams to various government departments with requests for information."

"Ah, questions about Keppel?"

"Yes. I've discovered that Mr Charles Keppel is what he claims to be, the only son of a famous inventor. Keppel inherited considerable wealth upon his father's death. He is also a widower with a daughter of sixteen. Currently she's attending a finishing school in Switzerland. Scotland Yard confirms that Keppel vanished two years ago. A body pulled from the river was considered to be his."

"Then clearly a mistake regarding identification?"

"Understandably so in this case. The head was missing. Flesh had decomposed considerably. The cadaver was identified as being Keppel's from his watch found in a pocket."

"Keppel might have procured a corpse and dressed it in his clothes in order to vanish."

"Or did he discard the clothes, forgetting to remove the watch? Were they worn by another individual who then fell into the Thames?"

"Have you discovered any information about Keppel's other identity? The major?"

"Ha! The splendidly named Major Robin Fox-Warren. Absolutely nothing. Careful, Watson, the roof has sprung another leak."

I shifted sideways to avoid a renewed soaking. "This vehicle leaks like a sieve."

"Indeed so. Ah, but to return to our topic: there is no record of a Major Fox-Warren serving in a British Regiment. The identity appears to be a complete invention."

"Surely your instincts are suggesting a particular state of affairs regarding Keppel?"

"Watson, you know my methods." He gave a wry smile. "I prefer the cement of at least a small number of facts before beginning to construct a case. I must confess, however, this is an exceedingly interesting example of human behaviour. After all, not many gentlemen succeed in completely vanishing from society and creating a new identity before reappearing again. Ah, we've reached our destination. Make lively, Watson, it's still raining cats and dogs out there!"

Four

We stepped through the front door of number 9 Juniper Terrace, entering a sumptuous entrance hall, which boasted a curved stairway that gracefully swept up to the next floor. Our overcoats dripped rainwater while the framed portraits of men and women from an earlier age peered sternly down at two decidedly damp visitors. A maid took our coats while the butler guided us to the morning room, where Charles Keppel stood before a blazing fire.

"Gentlemen, welcome." The relief on Keppel's face was plain to see. This was a worried man who needed answers before he could resume a normal life. "Would you care for a sherry?"

Holmes spoke politely. "Thank you, Mr Keppel. However, I shall decline."

I thanked the man for his courtesy, adding: "I believe my friend, Mr Holmes, wishes to get to the matter in hand."

"Of course, of course."

Holmes said, "Two of my students are due shortly. I would like them to observe how I conduct my investigation."

"Naturally, they will be most welcome." With both fear and eagerness he asked, "Sir, have you discovered anything of my other self yet?"

"I'm afraid not, the hunt has only just begun."

"Then I am at your disposal. Let me show you the clothes belonging to Fox-Warren. They are . . . oh . . ." Keppel paused, flustered. "That's peculiar, isn't it, gentlemen? I am already referring to my other self as if he is a living human being who is entirely separate to me." He shuddered with distaste. "Yet he and I are one and the same."

Holmes nodded. "You will find this perplexing. Nevertheless, I am certain that the more you learn about your alter ego, and his – *your* – life over recent months, the more your anxieties will ease."

"Yes . . . thank you. I'm sure they will."

"Before I examine the possessions you arrived with last week, may I interview your mother?"

"My mother?" He seemed doubtful.

"The lady does live here, doesn't she?"

"Yes."

"I wish to ask her a few questions."

"She's very frail."

"It will take but moments."

"She has a weak heart. Distress could be harmful."

"Dr Watson will be present. If my questions unduly trouble her, he will terminate the interview. Isn't that so, Doctor?"

"Of course. I will keep an eagle eye on her, Mr Keppel."

Consenting with a nod, the man led us to a sitting room that over-looked a lawn. A cheery fire burned in the grate. Sitting close by in a wingback chair was an elderly lady. Despite her frailty she'd dressed for the day. Strings of gleaming pearls adorned her neck. She sat upright in the chair, clearly mustering reserves of energy to appear composed and ready to receive visitors. Her only concession to advancing years was the tartan blanket arranged across her legs to keep draughts at bay.

Keppel introduced us before asking his mother if she would answer a number of questions. Holmes added that he would prefer it if Keppel wasn't present during the interview.

"I will do what I can to help, Mr Holmes," she said in a clear voice. "I have read much about this great detective. Moreover, if he can dispel your worries, Charles, then the result will be a happy one."

The tartan rug slipped from her lap. Her son immediately hurried to pick it up.

"Och," he exclaimed.

The lady's eyes narrowed, as if she didn't care for her son using the Scottish word which corresponds with the English "Oh".

He arranged the rug over his mother's lap. "It just won't do if you catch a chill."

"Thank you, Charles. Now leave me to speak with these gentlemen."

He withdrew from the room.

The moment the door closed, Mrs Keppel leaned forward to whisper, "Did you hear that, gentlemen? Charles said, 'och'."

"Yes," Holmes said. "He has quite a Scottish brogue."

"Goodness knows why." She raised her hands in bafflement. "He has never had a Scottish accent."

Holmes nodded. "Then the mystery concerning your son is deeper than I first thought."

"Please sit, gentlemen. Ask your questions."

Her blue eyes, which so resembled her son's, were bright. Age hadn't clouded her senses.

When we sat down Holmes asked, "Would you please describe the circumstances of your son's disappearance."

"Certainly, Mr Holmes. When I woke up on the morning of the first of October, 1893, my maid informed me that Charles had left the house on the stroke of six o'clock."

"He took luggage?"

"No, merely the clothes he stood up in."

"After your son left on that morning two years ago, nothing more was heard of him?"

"Nothing whatsoever. His money at the bank wasn't touched. He appeared to vanish into the very earth. Later . . ." She shuddered. ". . . the police found a body. They identified it as my son. Of course, his return last week proved that to be incorrect. Thank heaven."

"Your son is a widower?"

"Sadly, his wife, Daphne, succumbed to pneumonia three years ago. Charles was utterly distraught."

"Was he able to continue with life as normal?"

"Yes, he conducted his duties with absolute diligence."

"Where was his place of work?"

"Here – one of the rooms serves as an office. Charles is – was – kept busy with his investment portfolio." She nodded firmly. "When he is fully recovered he will take up the reins of business again."

"I'm sure he will be restored to his former self, Mrs Keppel."

"And I do hope he sheds that Scottish affectation. So unsettling."

"You must have been overjoyed to see him again."

"Oh, yes, Mr Holmes. No matter how old a mother becomes, she will always love her children."

I noticed her eyelids grow heavy. Her voice became weaker, too.

Holmes, meanwhile, continued briskly, "After your son returned, did he have different preferences for food?"

"Hmm? I didn't quite catch the question."

"Holmes." I rested my hand on his forearm. "Mrs Keppel is tired."

"I have just a few more questions."

"No, Holmes. No more questions."

"Yes, of course, Watson. I understand." Holmes stood up. "Mrs Keppel," he said gently, "thank you for your time. I will do my utmost to help your son."

"I believe that you will." She sounded drowsy. "After all, you are the world's greatest detective."

"Thank you, madam."

We bade the lady farewell. As we walked towards the door, she suddenly called out. "There is something else. Two nights ago I happened to pass Charles's bedroom door. He shouted in such a strange voice that I decided he cried out in his sleep. What he said frightened me."

"Can you recall his exact words?"

"Yes. He shouted, 'Gwyneth. Hide the baby.'"

"Does your son know a lady called Gwyneth?"

"No. He has never mentioned anyone by that name."

Holmes thanked her and we returned to the morning room to find Keppel in pleasant conversation with two of Holmes's students from the academy: the feisty Miss Charlton, and Mrs Jacob, who was robust, round-faced, with a no-nonsense manner. I was certain that Mrs Jacob could efficiently deal with troublemakers if they required "dealing with".

I explained to Keppel that we'd left his mother to rest. Holmes then asked Keppel to show us the clothes he'd worn and the bag he'd carried when he had arrived home last week.

"Of course," he replied before turning to me and asking, "Dr Watson. Firstly, however, may I ask you a question?"

"By all means."

"Might it be that the reason I disappeared so abruptly and cannot remember what happened thereafter is due to a bout of amnesia?"

"I would not make such a diagnosis lightly and without a lengthy examination; nevertheless, amnesia isn't beyond the bounds of possibility."

Keppel nodded slowly, no doubt deeply worried about his condition.

"Dr Watson, I've heard that amnesia can occur after a blow to the head."

"A head injury might be responsible. There are other causes, too, such as physical illnesses, narcotic drugs, too much alcohol—"

"Madness?"

"You exhibit no signs of mental instability."

He took a deep breath. "Thank you, Doctor. The notion that I might be mentally unbalanced terrified me."

Mrs Jacob spoke bluntly. "The mad don't know they're mad, do they, Doctor? If Mr Keppel fears he's insane, then it proves he's sane, doesn't it?"

I suspected that in a rather artless way Mrs Jacob had good intentions, endeavouring to allay Keppel's fears.

"It's true, madam. The insane often lack insight into their malady. Uhm, perhaps Mr Holmes is keen to continue his investigation?"

Keppel did appear somewhat relieved, because he asked us to follow, before briskly leading the way down a passageway.

Holmes said, "I wish to make this an exercise for my two students. Mr Keppel, would you kindly show the ladies the items of clothing and so on in question? Dr Watson and I will remain here while the ladies conduct their examination without me breathing down their necks, as it were."

The two students entered a room, followed by Keppel. Holmes beckoned me back along the corridor.

He whispered: "Watson, as well as giving the ladies an opportunity to test their observational skills, it was something of a ploy so that we might speak alone for a moment."

"You already have an opinion about this case?"

"Far from it. In fact, I need your own opinion on a certain matter." Holmes glanced in the direction of the door through which the trio had passed. He clearly wished that we would not be overheard. "Watson, does Keppel suffer from amnesia?"

I smiled. "You know my methods, Holmes. I couldn't possible make a diagnosis based on so little information."

Holmes chuckled. "Very droll. Yes, I've used the 'you know my methods' line many times before. Nevertheless, I would welcome a modicum of guesswork."

"It's possible that Keppel did lose all memory of his past life and took himself away to create a new identity."

"This would be spontaneous, without him realizing he was adopting a new name?"

"Yes. Moreover, it might also lead to him acquiring a Scottish accent, or preferring to eat different kinds of food."

"What triggers amnesia?"

"As I've mentioned, there can be many causes: a head injury, drugs, alcohol. Or the patient might develop an abnormal mental state, such as dementia praecox – which might even lead them to believe, for example, that they are Napoleon Bonaparte, or God."

"Might Keppel be suffering from dementia praecox?"

"Those afflicted often become paranoid and believe they hear voices telling them to act bizarrely. Keppel has given me no indication so far that he suffers from those symptoms."

"What do your instincts tell you about the man?"

"As a doctor, I'm reluctant to rely solely on instinct."

Holmes smiled. "Please indulge me."

"Keppel's wife died three years ago. To suffer terrible grief in such circumstances is only natural."

"Of course."

"It is possible that grief overwhelmed his nervous system, resulting in a breakdown that banished all memory of who he was, and he simply left home and wandered away."

"Therefore we can picture him living as a tramp, perhaps. Either having his clothes stolen or giving them away, such was his mental confusion. Those clothes were then worn by a man who drowned, and came to be identified as Keppel."

I nodded. "Gradually, a new identity grew. He genuinely believed himself to be Major Fox-Warren."

"And his wanderings took him to Scotland, where he acquired a new accent."

"It is a distinct possibility."

"Thank you for your thoughts, Watson, most illuminating. Now, it's time we joined our two novice investigators and heard their findings."

We entered the room. A suit of yellowish tweed hung from the wall. A pair of brown boots had been placed beneath the clothes. The Gladstone bag, which Keppel had been carrying when he came to his senses, stood on a table. Beside the bag, a wallet and a postcard-sized photograph. Keppel stood by the window. I was greeted by the novel sight of Miss Charlton standing with her nostrils just an inch from the sleeve of the tweed jacket. Meanwhile, Mrs Jacob dipped her entire face into the leather bag and was loudly inhaling.

This unusual activity surprised me so much that I exclaimed, "Upon my soul."

Miss Charlton glanced back at us. "We remembered your instruction, Mr Holmes. Always use one's sense of smell."

Holmes gave a brisk nod. "Excellent. What does your sense of smell reveal?"

"Merely the scent of wool."

Mrs Jacob lifted her face from the bag. "Leather." She inhaled again. "Lavender, too."

"A potpourri," Holmes pointed out. "Herbs left in the bag when not in use would freshen the interior. Anything else?"

"There is something . . . though it's a something I can't quite catch."

Holmes bent over the bag, his large nostrils flaring, that sensitive organ detecting the weakest of odours. "Faint, yet unmistakable. It's brandy." He removed clean shirts from the bag. After that, he pulled out sheets of newspaper that had been used to line the bottom. "Ah-ha." He removed a tiny object that glinted between his finger and thumb.

Anxiously, Keppel asked, "Mr Holmes, what have you found?"

"That which I expected to find after smelling brandy. A splinter of glass." He held the bag so the light fell inside. "There's staining from spilt liquor."

Mrs Jacob said, "A broken bottle of brandy is hardly relevant, surely?"

Holmes examined the newspaper. "It is extremely unwise to dismiss any facts when attempting to unravel a mystery. From the evidence of nostril and eye, I would deduce that the Gladstone bag contained a bottle of brandy, which was broken on, or shortly after the fifteenth of October. The accident occurred when you, Mr Keppel, embarked on a journey in a hurry."

Keppel's eyebrows rose in surprise. "How the dickens do you know that?"

"Moreover, I suggest the bag was thrown from an upper floor of a house or over a wall. After all, brandy bottles are formed from thick glass – hard to break at the best of times. Bearing in mind the bottle shattered in the bag, hence the odour and fragment of glass, it reinforces my conclusion that the bag fell a great distance before striking the ground. The newspaper is dated the fifteenth of October. Someone, probably you, sir, emptied out the broken glass from the bag. After that, you lined its interior with newspaper in order to absorb the spirit. If you were not travelling in a hurry, you could, of course, have simply left the bag open for a while, allowing the spirit to evaporate."

"Goodness gracious."

"You have no recollection of, for example, fleeing a building after throwing the bag from a window?"

"No."

"Nor realizing the bottle had been broken? Nor taking steps to soak up the spirit with a newspaper? Because you will have intended buying these shirts after your rapid departure, and common sense dictates that you wouldn't place new clothes in a bag sodden with alcohol."

"Mr Holmes, I have no memory of those events whatsoever."

"Then, for now, these objects will speak on your behalf." Holmes studied the bag's exterior. "You also regularly carried this on a bicycle near the coast."

"Did I?" The man stared at Holmes as if he were a warlock with the power to see all and know all.

Holmes pointed at the leatherwork. "Chafing here and here suggests marks left by straps of the kind used on a bicycle to hold items in place. The bag is regularly wiped clean of soil thrown up from the tyres, yet sand in the soil makes it gritty enough to abrade the surface of the leather, forming these lighter patches."

"Good lord."

Holmes lifted the suit from the peg, raising it to his face, so his nose almost brushed the fabric near the collar. "A scent of perfume on the shoulder. A lady was fond of resting her head there. Very faint. Therefore, you've not been in this suit in the presence of the lady for several weeks."

"Remarkable." Keppel's mouth dropped open with astonishment.

Miss Charlton bent her head towards the garment. "Yet I smell nothing but wool."

"It does take time to train all of one's senses. After all, the wine connoisseur cannot differentiate between grape varieties immediately. It takes much practice and dedication. Now for the other items. Ladies, please give me an account of your findings."

Miss Charlton pushed back the blonde ringlets from her face. She spoke in a refined, almost queenly way. "We examined the picture of Mr Keppel and the lady. I judge her to be near the same age as the gentleman. The pair stand arm in arm, gazing directly at the camera. The plants and window in the background are painted on a sheet, which is quite usual for a posed tableau in a photographic studio."

Mrs Jacob picked up the photograph. "The name and address of the photographer is stamped on the back. A Mr Jeremiah Poole, Station Street, Manchester."

Holmes glanced at his other student. "Miss Charlton. You are particularly adept at noticing the tiniest of details. What do you read from the photograph?"

"The couple are dressed in high-quality clothes. A dark suit for Mr Keppel, trousers neatly pressed. The lady wears white muslin from neck to foot. Mr Keppel's face is darkly tanned, hinting the portrait was taken in the summer. And . . ." Her voice tailed away, as if afraid to reveal a fact that might alarm Keppel.

"And?" Holmes prompted.

"The lady wears a wedding ring. The couple appear to be husband and wife."

"Good lord!" Keppel reacted with shock. "I am not married. I swear I'm not. I'm a widower."

Holmes sprang at the man as if intending to hit him. And hit him he did, yet he did so with a name: "Gwyneth!"

"I – I beg your pardon."

"Gwyneth, sir. What does the name mean to you?"

"It means nothing. How – how did you come by this name?"

"Your mother heard you crying out in your sleep. Specifically: 'Gwyneth, hide the baby.'"

"Sir, I know of neither a Gwyneth nor a baby."

Holmes acknowledged the man's words with a nod. "Very well, I shall now examine the contents of the bag." Holmes moved briskly, keen as a dog following the scent of a rabbit. "Ah . . . shirts of the kind that can be bought in any high street. One cotton handkerchief. Toothbrush. Comb and hairbrush. Nothing remarkable. We shall return to these items later in order to scrutinize them in forensic detail. I daresay there were other garments here, weren't there, Mr Keppel?"

"No."

"Really?"

"Well, it's not proper to say."

"You mean, not in front of ladies?"

"Of course." For the first time I noted anger in Keppel's expression. "To say any more would be ungentlemanly."

"Sir, these ladies will eventually become detectives. They will bloody their hands when examining murder victims. They will investigate the most depraved crimes. Therefore, they will encounter far worse than a man using the word 'underwear.'"

"Very well." Keppel's face turned red. "There were undershirts and – and the like as well."

"Where are they now?"

"Burnt. I got rid of them in the kitchen fire."

"Then there is nothing to be learned from them. It is a pity that you are selective when preserving evidence for my students, and me, to examine."

"My apologies."

"At least the boots are still here. Let us see what they can tell us."

Holmes had no sooner uttered these words when a commotion broke out. Angry shouts followed by the high, piercing scream of a terrified woman.

A man's voice bellowed, "Murder! Murder!"

Holmes immediately dashed along the corridor. I followed, with Keppel hot on my heels. We rushed into the hallway to discover a wild-eyed man standing at the bottom of the staircase. Rainwater sprayed from his waterproof coat as he waved his arms. Each hand gripped a gun. One was an old flintlock pistol of the type our forefathers would have armed themselves with to fight duels. The other weapon was a modern revolver. A pair of housemaids cowered on the stairs, screaming. The butler lay on the floor while pointing up at the armed stranger. I realized it was the butler who'd bellowed "murder" when he did so again.

"Murder!"

The wild-eyed man was perhaps thirty years of age. He had black, curly hair. His eyebrows formed thick, black arches above blazing eyes.

The gunman yelled, "Where is the devil? I'll blast him to Hades! I swear I will!" He spun around, sending droplets of rainwater flying from his coat. "Ah! There's the wretch!" His eyes fixed on Keppel. "Fox-Warren! For what you did to my sister, you will pay with your life!"

He pointed the ancient gun at Keppel, who stared at the man in horror. The furious stranger pulled the trigger. I saw the hammer fall. I expected to hear the tremendous bang of the pistol, and for Keppel to fall down dead.

The hammer made a loud *click*. Yet the gun did not discharge. The weapon glistened with rainwater. Clearly the gunpowder had become damp, rendering the pistol useless.

However, the stranger raised the revolver. "I do this for the memory of Gwyneth."

A dark shape moved with a blur. This was Mrs Jacob – she used the curved handle of an umbrella that she seized from a stand to hook the stranger's wrist. She tugged hard.

The pistol fired with a painfully loud bang. The bullet smashed into the wall, sending out a jet of dust. The maids screamed again.

Both Holmes and I pounced. We brought the stranger down. He cursed, struggled, kicked, and swore he'd kill the pair of us. Swiftly, he scrambled to his feet. That's when Holmes delivered a well-aimed jab that would have brought a whistle of appreciation from a champion boxer. The stranger fell to the floor.

And, upon my soul, that's where he lay. Dead to the world.

Five

The stranger opened his eyes as I tied the last knot in the rope that bound his hands together behind his back. As he half lay in the armchair he blinked, dazzled by the light streaming through the windows. The sun had just begun to break through clouds that had delivered such torrential rain. The man appeared dazed. Holmes's expert punch had certainly done the trick. The butler appeared at the doorway. He'd quite recovered after being pushed to the floor when the stranger had burst into the house, brandishing the pistols. The butler announced in appropriately sombre tones that the police had been summoned to deal with the would-be murderer.

Keppel stared at the intruder, no doubt aware that he'd narrowly avoided being shot.

Keppel spoke gratefully. "Thank you, Mr Holmes. I should be dead if it wasn't for your presence."

Holmes examined the old pistol. "Mr Keppel, you must thank Mrs Jacob here. Her quick thinking and swordplay with the umbrella saved your life. That and the downpour of rain, which soaked the gunpowder in this antique." He placed the pistol on the table.

"Thank you, Mrs Jacob." Keppel gravely shook her hand. "It was most brave of you."

"My pleasure, sir," she said in that direct way of hers. "Disarming criminals is part of a detective's duty – isn't that so, Mr Holmes?"

"Indeed it is, madam. Would you please take a seat? You too, Miss Charlton. Both of you will find the next few moments quite educational."

The two ladies sat side by side on the sofa. Admirably, they remained calm, despite the recent life-and-death tussle.

The stranger roused himself, managing to sit upright, even though I'd bound his ankles and wrists. Naturally, we'd taken the precaution of checking his pockets for hidden weapons. Fortunately, there were none. His pockets yielded nothing more than coins and a one-way railway ticket from Manchester.

The man's expression became fierce again as he thundered at Keppel, "You scoundrel. You are not a man, you are vermin!"

Holmes said, "Please calm yourself."

"I will not be calm. Nor will I be civil to you or your gang of kidnappers!"

Holmes pointed at the pistol. "If it were not for the rain spoiling the gunpowder, you might be facing a charge of murder."

"Ha! I don't fear the hangman!"

"No, I see that you do not," Holmes said. "You purchased a one-way ticket from Manchester, which indicates you did not believe you'd return home."

"Being hanged for killing that monster would be a fair price to pay."

"I daresay this choice of antique pistol, with such a wide bore, reveals that you aren't an accomplished marksman. I presume it's loaded with pieces of lead shot, meaning that you'd probably hit your target even if your aim was poor."

"Indeed. I realized I'd have a better chance of killing the wretch with one shot from that blunderbuss of a weapon rather than the revolver."

"You know the gentleman?" Holmes indicated Keppel with a nod.

"He's no gentleman. And neither are you, if you are his friend."

I decided to speak up. Clearly facts needed airing before the conversation could proceed much further. I addressed the stranger. "Do you not recognize the gentleman standing before you?"

"No."

"He is Mr Sherlock Holmes."

The stranger's jaw dropped open in astonishment. "Mr Holmes, the detective?"

"I am that particular Holmes," my friend conceded.

"I heard you were a good man. Why do you rub shoulders with this villain?"

Holmes regarded the stranger with interest. "Soon the police will arrest you. I cannot prevent that. Nor would I wish to. After all, you intended to commit murder today. However, I do believe you can help me."

"Help? How?"

"Tell me all you know about this individual." He pointed at Keppel.

The stranger glared at Keppel. "That swindler, thief, charlatan . . . he's Major Robin Fox-Warren."

"Therefore, you do recognize him?"

"It's to my eternal regret I know him at all."

"Mr Holmes," began Keppel, "must you really engage this madman in conversation? He assaulted my staff and tried to kill me."

"This fellow did intend to cause harm. Yet he recognizes your other self, as it were. I must question him before the police arrive."

"Sir, I protest. I—"

Holmes raised his hand. "Hush. The man might have vital information."

Keppel nodded, albeit reluctantly, and remained silent.

Holmes turned to the stranger. "The man you tried to kill is Mr Charles Keppel."

"No, sir, he is Fox-Warren."

"May I have your name?"

"I'm Thomas Rawcliff, and you're correct. I come from Manchester."

"The accent and the railway ticket indicated so," Holmes said. "Mr Rawcliff, the ropes are still necessary I'm afraid. You have a violent nature."

"That's not my usual manner. I am a land surveyor."

"Then what prompted you to attempt murder?"

"You, too, would wish with all your heart to kill a monster like Fox-Warren!"

"Oh? Why would I do such a thing?"

"If he kidnapped your sister and forced her to marry him!"

"Gwyneth?"

"Yes, Gwyneth. The kindest, most gentle lady you're ever likely to meet."

"And this man, whom you recognize as Fox-Warren, married her against her will?"

"I absolutely declare it so. Oh, she seemed to go along with it, but only because he had some hold over her. He met her in Manchester at a tea dance. As soon as he found out she had money of her own, he lied his way into her heart and proposed marriage."

"The man you believe is Fox-Warren is actually a Mr Charles Keppel."

"Ah, so he confesses that he's a confidence trickster?"

"On the contrary. Two years ago he lost his memory. After walking away from this very house, he adopted another identity."

"He is lying to you, Mr Holmes. Why, when I first met him in Manchester, he spoke with a London accent. When I saw him again a few weeks ago, he'd adopted a Scottish brogue, no doubt to fool his neighbours that he was a fellow countryman."

"I doubt that he is deliberately deceitful. After all, upon recovering his memory last week, he approached me for help. He desperately wishes to learn what happened to him."

"Ask him about my sister and their young child, sir. Demand the truth."

Keppel burst out: "I have no recollection of the lady or child."

"You must! After all, it was you who murdered them!"

The silence that followed this outburst was long and absolute. Nobody moved. Even Holmes appeared shocked by the terrible accusation.

At last, the doorbell rang.

"Ah," Holmes murmured. "No doubt that will be the police." He took a deep breath. "The case has just become more complicated, and infinitely more serious." He fixed his sharp gaze on Rawcliff. "We only have a moment. Please quickly answer the questions I will now ask."

"Why should I help you?"

"Because if the man you know as Fox-Warren is a murderer, he must face justice."

"Very well, Mr Holmes."

I heard deep voices as the arriving constables spoke to the butler in the entrance hall. Holmes would have mere seconds to interview Rawcliff.

"Mr Rawcliff, you claim that your sister and her baby have been murdered. Has this been reported to the police?"

"They say the murder cannot be investigated because my sister and niece are missing."

"Where were they living when they vanished?"

"Scotland. The address is Harbour View, Bothy Road, North Reiff."

"Where was Fox-Warren employed?"

"A shipping company. It's located beside a jetty where coal is loaded on to ships. Ha, I can see him now, riding his bicycle through sand dunes to the office."

I recalled Holmes's deduction that the Gladstone bag had become marked due to the abrasive action of sand. My friend was right again!

"Did Fox-Warren discuss his life previous to meeting your sister?"

"No. My father once joked about him being 'a regular man of mystery'. The joke has turned very sour."

"You say you recall seeing that man – " he indicated Keppel – "cycle to work. Yet you, yourself, reside in Manchester?"

"I went to stay with him and my sister in Scotland for a few days. You see, Gwyneth became frightened. She was anxious about Fox-Warren's behaviour. She witnessed him talking to strangers in the garden at night. Then she woke up one morning to find that his boots had been moved by an intruder."

"Moved? How?"

"My sister didn't elaborate."

That's where the interview ended. A pair of constables entered the room. They recognized Mr Holmes, of course. After politely discussing the incident with him, they untied Rawcliff and escorted him from the house to a carriage with bars across its windows. Their captive was locked inside and the horses drew the vehicle away.

Holmes gathered us together. "This case," he said, "has become an altogether different beast." He turned to Keppel. "As a matter of considerable urgency, we must search for your wife and infant child."

"I have neither wife nor child. At least, none that I remember."

"Nonetheless, Mr Rawcliff stated otherwise. I have lines of enquiry here in London regarding the case. Therefore, I will send my students on ahead of me to Scotland. Watson and I will follow later." He gazed out of the window. "Storm clouds are gathering again. We should make all haste." Even as he spoke, thunder rumbled threateningly. The room grew darker by the moment.

"Mr Holmes," began Miss Charlton, "has the case taken a tragic twist?"

"Very possibly. You best steel your nerves when you arrive at the house in Scotland – there's a distinct probability that you will be greeted by the most terrible of sights."

Six

The telegram arrived just as we finished breakfast. Sherlock Holmes read what was printed on the slip of paper.

"Excellent," he said. "Our two students have already made their initial examination of the house in Scotland." He paused, frowning, before reading the next part of the telegram aloud: "Have examined footwear belonging to Keppel. All filled with chrysanthemum petals."

"Chrysanthemum petals?" I echoed. "A strange kind of joke to play on a fellow."

Holmes regarded me with his deep-set eyes. "That is no practical joke, Watson. Someone has just issued a death threat."

"Against whom?"

"I suspect it is aimed at either Keppel or his wife. Perhaps both."

"What now?"

"To Scotland! As quickly as we can, and pray we're not too late!"

Seven

Sherlock Holmes and I boarded the express train for Scotland. Holmes had written two letters before we left. One letter to Inspector Lestrade requested that Mr Thomas Rawcliff be released if he agreed to swear on his honour that he would immediately travel north to join us at Harbour View, North Reiff. The second letter to Charles Keppel begged him to make all haste to that address, too.

I have known Holmes for a very long time. He would not make such requests unless the matter was of the gravest urgency.

Holmes and I were fortunate to have a carriage to ourselves. Presently, busy streets, smoky chimneys and houses gave way to open pasture where cows grazed. The locomotive sent out warning blasts with its whistle as it thundered over level crossings.

I said, "The telegram sent by the two students was a surprising one. They considered the fact that the footwear contained flower petals was of importance."

"I believe the clue is highly significant."

"I must say, all this sounds very mystifying."

"When I explain my findings to you, they will seem childishly simple." He gave a dry smile as he lit a cigarette. "Yet no further elaboration will be forthcoming until I have examined the footwear myself."

"Rawcliff claimed that Charles Keppel murdered his own wife and child. Do you think this is the case?"

"There is no evidence of death yet. All we know is that Mrs Keppel and their daughter are missing."

"It's quite extraordinary that you've asked both Keppel and Rawcliff to join us in Scotland. Isn't Rawcliff likely to attack Keppel again? After all, Rawcliff despises the man."

"Ha. When you mix two highly volatile chemicals together, that's when the fun begins."

"Fun? Hardly fun, Holmes, this is a serious matter."

"Agreed, friend Watson. And yet bringing two volatile chemicals together in the same vessel can produce dramatic results of great interest." Holmes settled down, his long legs stretched in front of him. "There is a chance, is there not, that Keppel might recover memories of the time he was Major Fox-Warren when he sees his old home?"

"Familiar surroundings might produce such an effect. But why ask Rawcliff to join us there?"

"The man stayed with the family for a while. He may have vital information." Holmes closed his eyes. "Speaking of information, I believe you have some for me."

"Oh yes . . . about Gwyneth Fox-Warren?"

Holmes kept his eyes closed. "Proceed."

"I spoke to Rawcliff's father by telephone. He told me that Gwyneth is thirty-eight years of age. She was a spinster when she met a Major Fox-Warren. After a brief courtship, they married at a register office. Then they moved to Scotland, where Fox-Warren found employment at a shipping office."

Holmes's eyelids snapped open. "Ah, Watson. We'll refer to Fox-Warren as Keppel to avoid confusion. After all, we know that Fox-Warren is an alias, even if Keppel did not consciously set out to deceive anyone."

"As you wish."

"Thomas Rawcliff believes that his sister was forced into marriage."

"The brother is possibly being overly protective. Gwyneth's father makes no such claim. Moreover, he's adamant that his daughter truly loves Keppel."

"Rawcliff also spoke about Keppel marrying the lady for her money."

"Well, Holmes, does it seem likely, considering that Keppel is a wealthy man?"

"Although when he married Gwyneth, he had no knowledge of his real identity. Might we suppose he genuinely believed himself as poor as the proverbial church rodent?"

"Possibly." We were briefly plunged into darkness as the train passed through a tunnel. "Her father explained that she and Thomas inherited shares in a quarry from their maternal grandfather. The father suggested that cash yielded by the shares is comparable to the salary earned by a bank manager."

"Meaning that although she is not rich, she will have sufficient money to live in modest comfort."

"Yes, absolutely."

"Now I suggest we make our way to the restaurant car. We still have a long journey ahead of us, and a leisurely meal in your agreeable company, Watson, will be a very pleasant way to spend the time."

Eight

The journey from London to Scotland was a long one. Indeed, after the locomotive pulled into Edinburgh Station, we were required to board another train, which carried us with much puffing and blasts of steam through the hills to North Reiff. Fortunately, the station that served this small town was within walking distance of Harbour View, a detached house built from dark granite and set alone on a hillside, granting it, as the name suggests, clear views of the harbour. By this time, it was dark. Holmes and I carried our bags, containing essentials for a visit of some days, to the house. A light burned from a downstairs window.

We approached the front door. Oddly, at that moment, the light in the window went out.

"Most peculiar," I uttered.

Precisely at that instant the door flew open. A creature that seemed all teeth and blazing eyes leapt out with a fierce snarl.

"Put your hands in the air. Stand absolutely still, or I will blast you to hell!"

A light flared as a lantern was uncovered, and standing before us, aiming a shotgun at my head, was a petite woman with blonde ringlets. A second woman behind her held the lantern.

"Good evening, ladies," Holmes said calmly. "I gather you were expecting someone else."

Miss Charlton lowered the shotgun. "Oh! Gentlemen, please forgive me. I didn't see who it was. We feared that the intruders were back."

Holmes nodded. "Ah, you've had unexpected visitors?"

The holder of the lamp stepped forward. Shielding my eyes against its glare, I recognized Mrs Jacob.

Mrs Jacob spoke with anger. "Yes, some rogues have been prowling at the dead of night."

"We heard footsteps on the garden paths," added Miss Charlton.

Holmes's eyes glittered with amusement. "So tonight you threw a welcome party! Excellent, ladies. I admire your courage."

"Please do come indoors, gentlemen. The east wind is biting."

Holmes and I entered a hallway panelled in dark wood. The Keppel abode possessed a solidity and honesty that was in keeping with the nature of the Scottish people who'd built it. This was a good home in which to raise a family, bathed as it was with healthy sea breezes and set on open hillside far from the unwholesome smog found in our cities. I inhaled deeply. Was that the appetizing aroma of beef stew? My stomach concurred, almost purring at the prospect of a hearty meal.

Holmes asked, "Did you have difficulty gaining access to the property?"

Mrs Jacob replied, "We made enquiries with the local constable. He was most obliging and took us to the landlord, who lives nearby. When I explained that we were assisting you, Mr Holmes, the landlord immediately gave me the keys. He invited us to stay here, as the town's only hotel is not suitable for ladies."

Holmes set down his bag, and, declining offers of tea, immediately asked the ladies to tell him all that had occurred since their arrival here two days ago.

Mrs Jacob explained that they'd interviewed the owner of Harbour View, who revealed that his tenants, the Keppels, had vanished. Apparently, a friend of Mrs Keppel's had discovered the house abandoned and raised the alarm. Naturally, the landlord checked the house. However, he found nothing unusual. His tenants' clothes were still here. Letters had recently arrived, addressed to Major Robin Fox-Warren, and lay on the mat behind the door.

Mrs Jacob indicated envelopes on a hallway table. "We took the liberty of opening them. They're from local traders, merely monthly bills for supplying groceries, and the like."

Holmes nodded. "The landlord found nothing that concerned him?"

"Nothing. In fact, he seemed quite satisfied with the house."

Holmes allowed himself a dry smile. "One imagines that the landlord's examination of his house centred on the state of its paintwork and to check that the bathtub hadn't been left to overflow. It's highly unlikely that he would search for clues indicating kidnap or homicide."

"Do you suspect murder, Mr Holmes?" asked Miss Charlton, her blue eyes wide with apprehension.

"That, for the moment, I cannot say."

He flexed his fingertips, as a pianist might before playing a piano. For Holmes, the house was his instrument. His highly trained mind could play the fabric of the world around him. As a pianist could produce sweet notes by touching the piano keys, Mr Sherlock Holmes could extract telltale information from a human hair, a footprint, a scratch on a clock face.

Indeed, those sharp eyes swept over the hallway. His two students, eager to learn from the master, watched his every move. When his eyes darted to a scuff mark, which inscribed a line from the middle of the stone floor to the front door, their own eyes darted in imitation of his.

Miss Charlton said, "Mr Holmes, what do—"

I coughed while holding my finger to my lips. She nodded, understanding, thereafter remaining silent. Holmes did not care to be questioned while he perused a crime scene.

During his examination, he murmured, "Always look for detail. The smallest, most apparently insignificant detail can contain the biggest of truths." His eyes began to gleam with an undeniable intensity, excited by some aspect of the window. He suddenly pointed at the floor. "See the elongated scuff mark? Someone, probably Keppel, ran along the passageway from the back of the house. He ran like a man who feared for his life. Indeed, he moved so quickly that when he tried to stop in the middle of the hallway, such was his speed that momentum caused him to slide across the stone slabs, leaving that mark."

Mrs Jacob asked, "He fled from an attacker?"

"No. The individual he feared had reached the unlocked door. Keppel ran here in order to lock it, thus denying his enemy entry to the house."

"You found something of interest on the window," said Miss Charlton.

"Indeed so. Flakes of putty have fallen from where it sets glass panes into the wooden surround. Keppel's enemy tried to break down the door. Or so it appears to me."

"We noticed no damage," Mrs Jacob pointed out.

"No, the door's strongly made from oak. It held. Yet vibration from an attempt to kick it open loosened a little of the putty."

Mrs Jacob lightly tapped the glass. "The window is vulnerable."

"Easily broken," added Miss Charlton.

"Absolutely. Which makes me recall, most vividly, that when we arrived here we were greeted by Miss Charlton armed with a shotgun."

"We found the gun in a cupboard," Miss Charlton revealed. "Shortly after we arrived here, we heard stealthy footsteps at night, suggesting that a trespasser lurked in the garden."

Holmes nodded. "There you have the bones of the explanation. Picture Mr Keppel hearing such sounds as he and his family are in the kitchen. Keppel races to this point, sliding to a stop, the leather sole of his shoe producing that mark upon the floor. His enemy is approaching the house, perhaps snarling threats. Keppel slams the bolts across. His enemy hurls himself at the door. At that moment, Mrs Keppel appears with the shotgun that you armed yourself with. The intruder, fearing for his or her life, promptly fled."

Holmes clearly found his investigation stimulating because he showed no sign of weariness after the long journey.

Mrs Jacob frowned. "We found nothing amiss in the house. Although now I fear there were clues that we simply did not see, such as the flakes of putty."

"You are students, ladies. There is no shame in not knowing. That is why you have enrolled in the academy. To learn. To equip yourselves with knowledge."

They were visibly reassured by this and exchanged smiles of relief.

"I take it," said Holmes, "that you found no trace of violent struggle?"

"No, sir."

"Then all we do know is that Mrs Gwyneth Keppel and her child disappeared approximately two weeks ago."

I added my own thoughts: "And the only person who might be responsible for that disappearance or have some knowledge of it is Mr Keppel."

"Who, unfortunately, has lost all memory that his family even exist. Quite a conundrum." He paused. "Nevertheless, there is an intriguing clue. Mrs Jacob, you sent me a telegram stating that certain footwear contains flower petals."

"Yes, I'd best show you."

Mrs Jacob led us upstairs to the master bedroom where the Keppels once slept. Neatly lined against one wall was the family's footwear.

Holmes asked, "Ladies, the boots haven't been touched since your arrival?"

Miss Charlton shook her head. "They are as we found them."

Holmes crouched down in order to study the footwear. First in line: a man's boots and shoes. Next to those: a lady's slippers and dainty leather shoes – these belonged to Mrs Keppel. Then, at the end, rather touchingly, indeed poignantly, were tiny shoes belonging to an infant. These were made from soft fabrics and had silk ribbons rather than laces.

Holmes murmured, "Mrs Keppel's shoes and those of the child are placed so the toes are pointing to the wall. Mr Keppel's footwear has been placed with the heel to the wall – the toes point outwards."

I said, "Mrs Keppel reported to her brother that an intruder had rearranged the footwear in some way."

Holmes picked up a man's boot. "We can presume that this is how she found them. Mr Keppel's boots being reversed. And filled with – " he tipped the boot: dried flowers poured into his open hand – "chrysanthemum petals."

"A child's joke?"

"Keppel's daughter is a mere babe in arms. We can rule out tomfoolery from her." Holmes tipped the petals back into the boot and replaced it on the floor. "A bedroom is sacred. A veritable sanctuary. Knowing that an intruder had walked past their bed as they slept would be thoroughly terrifying."

I said, "The position of Keppel's footwear and the petals, what do they tell you?"

"My dear Watson, it would be foolish to jump to conclusions." He walked towards the bedroom door. "It might be informative to study the building's exterior, even though it's dark. If a storm should blow in, it could obliterate any remaining evidence."

Mrs Jacob hurried away to collect the lantern. We then followed Holmes outdoors where the ocean winds blew in such a chilling way. The moonlight granted a clear view of the harbour. Sailing ships lay at anchor, their masts swaying as waves rolled through the harbour mouth.

Holmes examined the exterior of the house, its garden and outbuildings, his sharp eyes glinting. At the rear of the house was a paved yard. Holmes asked Mrs Jacob to shine the light on to the wall that boasted wooden trelliswork. A sturdy climbing plant snaked its way up through the woven slats. Holmes gave the trellis his particular attention. He is a tall man and, standing on tiptoe, he was able to extend his hand until it reached perhaps eight feet from the ground. His fingers worked at something attached to the trellis.

"Ha!" Holmes held out strands of fabric. "Threads from clothing, caught by a nail. See? A distinct yellow – the same colour as the tweed suit that Mr Keppel was wearing when he returned to London."

"Mr Holmes," began Miss Charlton, her eyes wide with astonishment. "Do you suppose that the gentleman scaled the trellis?"

"I believe he climbed down from the upstairs window. He may have been imprisoned there." Holmes glanced down at the stone slabs. "Alas, there is no soft earth to capture any footprints."

Mrs Jacob said, "When you examined the Gladstone bag, you stated that a bottle of brandy had been broken inside it."

"Yes, it seems that Keppel packed what he could into the bag, including the brandy. For some reason he was prevented from using the stairs. Therefore, he threw the bag from the upper window, shattering the bottle within. He then climbed down the trellis, snagging his suit on the way."

Miss Charlton frowned. "Why would he take brandy when escaping?"

Mrs Jacob answered eagerly: "He must have known he'd be spending the night outside. He believed that the brandy would keep out the cold."

"Precisely." Holmes smiled. "Now, the time approaches eight o'clock. I need to go into town and speak with the police constable. Ladies, please remain here with Dr Watson."

Miss Charlton protested. "How will we learn, if we cannot observe you?"

"Believe me, you are learning. Therefore, please examine window latches for signs of forced entry. Also, examine each window ledge for signs of a ladder being placed against it."

I realized that both women were afraid of being left on the fringes of the investigation. However, Holmes had taken pains to involve them at the heart of this mystery, inviting them to search for valuable clues. Both women nodded.

Holmes struck off along the path, carrying the lamp to light his way. He'd only covered a dozen paces when a face appeared out of the gloom with the suddenness of an apparition.

"Mr Holmes," panted the newcomer. "I came as soon as I received your note."

"Mr Keppel, thank you for being so prompt."

The man's stark face, set with large, frightened eyes, stared up at the house as if it were some phantom. "Och! Is this my home?"

"Indeed it is."

"I have no memory of it," he cried. "Yet I'm told I lived here for nigh on two years – and with a wife and child." He pressed a trembling hand to his mouth.

Holmes called to me from across the yard, "Watson, please take Mr Keppel inside. Brandy is what this gentleman needs right now."

"This is like witchcraft," Keppel exclaimed. "I have no recollection of the town or its station. I had to ask directions to Harbour View in a tavern. The men there knew me. Yet I didn't recognize a single face. They thought I'd gone mad." His eyes shone with horror. "The men were frightened of me. Strong sailors they were – they shrank back, trembling. They believe I killed my wife and child, and now they feared I'd returned to slaughter their own families."

"Please come indoors," I said gently. "You've had a long journey."

Holmes nodded his approval as I helped the man towards the door. Then, without another word, Holmes walked swiftly in the direction of town.

I confess: this was a remarkable situation. Here I was in the company of two aspiring investigators, who at once began checking the window latches. Meanwhile, I guided Keppel into the kitchen. A large pot bubbled enticingly on the stove. Immediately, I searched through cupboards for a little something to fortify the man. I could find no brandy. However, a bottle of rum occupied a shelf. That potent spirit should restore his nerves.

And as for the man himself? Mr Keppel, the baffled amnesiac, sat at the table, shaking his head, while repeating, "I remember nothing. I do not recognize this place. Witchcraft, Dr Watson. It has to be – it's sheer witchcraft."

Nine

Fortified by tea laced with rum, Charles Keppel relaxed in an armchair by the kitchen fire. The two ladies and I sat at the table, enjoying a handsome supper of beef stew prepared by Mrs Jacob earlier in the day. Sea winds flowed through the trees, conjuring up loud sighs that made me shiver. Those sounds resembled human sighs of regret, even despair, as if the natural world knew that a tragedy had occurred here.

The ladies wrote about the day's events in their notebooks. The investigation would be valuable experience for them when they, one day, set out on their own careers as detectives. The British police force had long been the domain of the male. Now, however, the world was changing. Women would soon be solving crimes alongside their male colleagues.

The stew had been so delicious that I yielded to temptation. Helping myself to another bowlful, I contentedly ate the extra portion. The room was silent, apart from the sighing of the breeze and crackle of blazing logs in the hearth.

Such peace is conducive to quiet reflection. I recalled the morning when Mr Keppel had arrived at Holmes's rooms with a strange tale to tell. That he appeared to have lost his memory two years ago, met a lady in Manchester, married, and come to live here on the Scottish coast.

Yes, I appreciated that Keppel might have suffered from amnesia. After all, I'm a medical man. I've treated similar cases before. So it's entirely possible that Keppel had experienced a condition that erased his memory. Moreover, he'd unwittingly developed a new identity under the name of Fox-Warren. Of course, there were a number of mysteries that clouded the picture. The man called Rawcliff insisted that Keppel had murdered a mother and child. The ladies, upon their arrival here, had discovered Keppel's boots filled with flower petals. Curious, very curious. As I spooned deliciously rich gravy into my mouth, I realized I was utterly bamboozled by the case.

The ladies continued writing. Their eyes fixed on the points of their pencils. Then I noticed something remarkable. The words they wrote were all connected together with no breaks. What's more, their writing grew larger. Their expressions were strangely fixed into ones of absolute concentration. I glanced across at Keppel. He stared into the leaping flames in the fireplace. As I watched, he extended his hand, the fingers splayed out. The flames almost licked his hand.

"Hmmm . . . I . . . I say . . ." I intended to warn the man to draw his hand back from the fire, because I saw smoke rising from his jacket sleeve. "Sir . . . ah . . . you should. Hmmm."

I shook my head, puzzled. Why on earth wouldn't the words leave my lips in a lucid way?

Suddenly, the gentleman's fate became unimportant to me. I returned to eating the stew. Before I could dip the spoon into the gravy, a small head popped up. A mouse, or rodent of some sort. Its eyes were bright, like shining black glass. A drop of gravy rolled along one of its whiskers.

Plop. Its head submerged beneath the surface of the stew.

"Nasty," I muttered.

I stirred the bowl, trying to oust the rodent trespasser. Gravy splashed out across the white tablecloth. Spots of brown even fell on to the ladies' notebooks, but the two students didn't even notice. They continued writing, the pencil points sliding through blobs of gravy.

When I glanced around the room, dozens of holes were appearing in the walls. From each one peeped a hairy face. Glittering eyes! A host of pink rodent noses!

Lurching from the chair, I launched my attack. The spoon became my Excalibur. I slashed at rodent heads. The room spun. When I paused to catch my breath, I saw that Mrs Jacob and Miss Charlton continued writing. They no longer restricted their notes to the paper: their pencils scratched across the tablecloth through puddles of gravy. Their mouths hung slackly open. Their eyes were dead.

Keppel leaned close enough to the fire for his sleeve to turn black.

Miss Charlton jumped to her feet crying, "Air! I need air!" She flung open the back door before vanishing into the night.

And there in the armchair. A man on fire! Keppel's jacket had caught alight. He chuckled with pleasure, his eyes bulging.

A figure entered the room to snatch the tablecloth from the table – both the bowl of stew and Mrs Jacob went flying. The figure dragged the burning man away from the fireplace then wrapped the tablecloth around him, putting out the flames.

It seemed to me at that point that I quickly rose to a great height above the Earth, where I gazed down at the kitchen far below. The newcomer pulled the smouldering jacket from Keppel before hurling it outside into the yard. He then recovered Miss Charlton; the lady had thrown herself into a bush. After that, he helped Mrs Jacob from the floor and sat her on a chair.

I watched all this feeling extraordinarily calm. Even when the newcomer put a cushion beneath the head of a seemingly dead body on the kitchen floor, I experienced no distress. Especially when I realized that the corpse was none other than myself, Dr John Watson.

I recall nothing else until opening my eyes to sunlight falling through a window. I lay on a sofa covered by a blanket. Holmes sat in an armchair nearby.

Immediately, he smiled in a kindly way. "My dear Watson, are you yourself again?"

My throat was dry. "I am. Thank you. What of Keppel? He burned . . . covered with fire. The ladies?"

Holmes held out a glass of water. "Here. Drink. No, friend Watson, don't try to talk. I'll tell you what happened. The police agreed to my request. They released Thomas Rawcliff on the understanding that he would immediately board a train for Scotland so that I might interview him here at the scene of the crime – and make no mistake, this is the scene of a crime, and possibly the most brutal crime of all. He arrived last night while I was speaking to the police constable in town. Rawcliff tells me that he found an extraordinary scene here. Miss Charlton had concealed herself amongst bushes. Mrs Jacob was quite unconscious. You, Watson, lay on the kitchen floor in a seemingly inebriated state, while Mr Keppel had slumped by the fire, his clothes burning. Rawcliff quickly smothered the flames. Fortunately Rawcliff's timely arrival meant that Keppel didn't suffer any injury."

"Drug," I managed to say. "Narcotic placed in the stew . . . we all ate."

"Indeed so."

"It induced hallucinations. Mice . . . lots of mice . . . I believed myself to be flying."

Holmes affectionately patted my arm. "You slept for more than twelve hours. Mrs Jacob and Miss Charlton are still resting upstairs."

"Speaking as a doctor, sleep is often the most efficacious of remedies." I licked my dry lips. "Someone entered the house . . . added a drug to the stew."

"Undoubtedly the same intruder that crept in here when it was occupied by the Keppel family and who rearranged Mr Keppel's footwear and filled it with flower petals."

"What were they hoping to achieve?"

"My belief is that the intruder came here tonight with the intention of abducting Keppel. They doped your supper, intending to render everyone unconscious. Thereafter, the kidnap victim could be removed without the crime being resisted or witnessed."

"Keppel is still here?"

"Yes, he's in the kitchen."

"Then Rawcliff arrived just in time to prevent the abduction."

"I believe so. However, the criminal will surely attempt to take Mr Keppel again."

"This is a most perplexing case."

"It is also much deeper than I first believed. For certain individuals it is dangerous, too."

"Rawcliff did attempt to shoot Keppel."

"Keppel is no longer in danger from Rawcliff. No. Whoever has been creeping unnoticed into this house poses the greatest threat."

"How so?"

"If you feel up to it, I'd like you to see Keppel's footwear once more, for what they have been filled with is most revealing."

"Flower petals? It has to be an absurd practical joke."

"Come, Watson. Tread lightly, the ladies are still sleeping."

We entered the master bedroom. The boots and shoes were just as we'd left them. The footwear belonging to Gwyneth Keppel and her child were placed with the toes pointing to the wall. Charles Keppel's stout boots faced outwards, the heels touching the skirting board.

Holmes' shrewd eyes fixed on me. "Watson, surely you have attended a military funeral, especially that of a cavalryman?"

"Ah . . . of course, the dead man's horse is led behind the coffin. And the deceased's empty boots are fixed into the stirrups. But they are placed the wrong way round. The heels face forward, the toes of the boot point in the direction of the horse's tail."

"In that case, the thief employs a well-known funeral ritual. One especially familiar to a military man. And the chrysanthemum petals?"

"Yes, I think I have it." My voice rose and he quickly shushed me, lest I disturb the ladies sleeping in the next room. "Chrysanthemums," I whispered. "Chrysanthemums are flowers that the French bring to funerals."

"Then the reversed boots and chrysanthemums suggest the intruder warns the footwear's owner that they are in danger of being killed."

"And the intruder is French?"

"Very possibly. I daresay he, or she, arrived from France comparatively recently, otherwise they would know that the English don't decorate the coffins of their dear departed with chrysanthemums."

"Then what is our Gallic wrongdoer endeavouring to achieve?"

"The thread of this case has become strangely tangled, due to one of its key players being unable to recollect what happened. Until Charles Keppel can remember events that took place here, I shall have to rely on scant clues and conjecture, which is unsatisfactory, but needs must."

"You are able to form an idea of what happened?"

"Yes, I believe so." Holmes stood at the window, gazing at ships in the harbour. "Picture this, Watson. Keppel lives here with his wife and infant child. Everyone hereabouts, including his wife, knows him as Major Robin Fox-Warren, a former military man. I've spoken to local shopkeepers and they all insist that you wouldn't find a happier family in the town. The couple loved to stroll down to the harbour with the child in its perambulator. Now into this scene of domestic joy creeps a villain. They frighten Mrs Keppel by coming into the garden at night. We know this because she confided in her brother. It seems to me that the intruder demanded something of either Mr Keppel or Mrs Keppel, although I favour it was specifically Mrs Keppel."

"Then she might know the intruder?"

"Indeed so. What happened when events reached their point of crisis, I cannot say for sure. Nevertheless, it seems that the intruder did make demands of some sort from Mrs Keppel. She refused. So, in order to frighten her into submission, the intruder entered this very bedroom when she and her husband were asleep. The intruder rearranged Mr Keppel's footwear so as to inspire thoughts of the reversed boots of a dead cavalryman."

"That is a rather subtle threat."

"Which suggests the intruder then filled Keppel's footwear with what the French would recognize as funeral flowers."

"Therefore, the intruder is sending a coded message to Mrs Keppel, warning her that her husband will be murdered if she doesn't yield to certain demands."

"Precisely."

"Why didn't the intruder approach Mrs Keppel and openly state they would kill her husband if the demands weren't met?"

"Perhaps they did. However, Mrs Keppel might have rebuffed them and poured scorn on such death threats. Now imagine Mr and Mrs Keppel's reaction when they awoke one morning to discover that someone had entered their bedroom to play that sinister game with the boots? Surely they would be terrified. They would know that the individual making the demands was not only deadly serious, but had made it their business to breach the sanctity of their bedroom while they slept."

"Yet the couple did not yield?"

"I suggest that they simply could not meet this wicked person's demands, and for some reason were too afraid to go to the police. Then matters came to a dramatic climax. You saw the scuff mark on the floor in the hallway where it can be presumed that Keppel skidded to a halt by the front door in order to lock it. There are signs that an attempt was made to break the door down. We can imagine the panic. Keppel would be desperate to make sure that his wife and daughter were safe."

"Ah," I said, remembering. "Keppel's mother heard her son crying out in his sleep."

"Correct. Even though he cannot remember what happened when he is awake, when he is asleep he recalls a moment of deep terror when he cried out, 'Gwyneth, hide the baby.' At some point, possibly just minutes after he begged his wife to conceal the baby, the intruder entered the house and made Keppel a prisoner in an upstairs room. Keppel put certain belongings into his Gladstone bag, including a bottle of brandy. He opened the window. Threw the bag out. After that, he climbed down to the ground using the wall trellis. He then fled."

"No doubt to search for his wife who escaped with the child."

"No, you are wrong."

"That's what any other man would do."

"Yes, any other man would do exactly that. He'd search for his wife and daughter. He'd also alert the police."

"Then why didn't he run into town, shouting that his family were in danger? I would have been hollering at the top of my voice."

"Yes, you would. However, Keppel seems especially vulnerable to mental stress. We've speculated that the death of his first wife caused him to suffer so much grief that he experienced an attack of amnesia. When the intruder tried to break into this house, Keppel must have experienced such a monumental degree of anxiety that once again he suffered a mental breakdown. When he at last came to his senses again a few days ago, he found himself standing outside his London home. Some unconscious urge guided him there."

My blood ran cold. "Holmes, you speak of the shock of witnessing someone attacking the front door that brought on a fresh bout of amnesia. What if, in fact, it was seeing the murder of his wife and child that caused the breakdown?"

"I have considered that possibility, Watson. On this occasion it pleases me to say that you are wrong. Keppel did not witness murder."

"How can you be sure?"

"The events of last night." He paced the room. "You were drugged in order to allow an unknown individual to attempt the abduction of Keppel. They were unsuccessful, thank heaven. However, it begs the question: *what is the motive for kidnapping the man?*"

"Ah . . . I think I see."

"Go on, Watson. Let's see if our thoughts flow along the same channel."

"The scoundrel believes that Mrs Keppel and the child are alive. They hope that if they abduct Keppel, they can hold him to ransom to force Mrs Keppel to agree to whatever is demanded."

Holmes's face glowed with pleasure at my answer. "Therefore, the would-be kidnapper believes that Mrs Keppel has hidden herself away. Moreover, they believe that Mrs Keppel will meet the villain's demands as soon as she knows that her beloved husband is in danger." Holmes gave a sharp nod. "I shall inform Rawcliff and Keppel of my conclusions." Excitement blazed in his eyes. "Then it's high time that I set a trap for the rogue who has inflicted so much anguish on this poor couple."

Ten

Upon my word! What an extraordinary turnaround. That thought flashed through my head on entering the kitchen to find Keppel and Rawcliff conversing as if they were old friends. Just days ago, Rawcliff had burst into Keppel's house, hell-bent on shooting him in cold blood. As the pair chatted, Rawcliff guarded the door, shotgun in hand.

Keppel turned to me and spoke in that pleasant Scottish brogue, "Och, Dr Watson. I fancy that you're now fully recovered. That is good to see."

Rawcliff nodded a greeting. "It's a devilish thing to do, stirring opium – or whatever it was – into the stew."

Holmes leaned over the pot on the stove, his sensitive nostrils flaring as he inhaled. "I daresay the drug was an exotic one. Not only did it induce a soporific state, it generated quite striking hallucinations."

Rawcliff slapped the shotgun. "If the devil comes back, I'll pepper him. He'll never dope anyone else."

Holmes said, "I rather think that whoever doctored the stew won't try that particular trick again."

"Then we're safe?" asked Keppel.

"On the contrary, we face a determined foe. They won't give up so easily. We must be on our guard."

As he digested Holmes's cautionary words, Keppel rubbed the reddened side of his face where the fire had scorched him. Apart from that mark, he didn't seem to have suffered any harm.

Holmes asked, "Mr Keppel, you still have no recollection of the time you spent here as Major Fox-Warren?"

"Absolutely none. Nor of being married to this gentleman's sister."

"I shall not pretend that your amnesia has made this case a straightforward one. You are my main witness, yet you don't even remember living here."

"I am very sorry, Mr Holmes."

"Don't concern yourself, Mr Keppel. Now . . . if I can turn to Mr Rawcliff?"

"I shall do what I can to help, sir." Rawcliff seemed embarrassed. "I have not yet apologized to everyone concerned, especially Mr Keppel, for my shameful behaviour when I ran into his London home brandishing pistols. I had, as they say, got the wrong end of the stick. I was mistaken. Mr Keppel is a good man."

"Thank you, sir," Keppel extended his hand towards Rawcliff. "I am glad we can renew our acquaintanceship as friends and allies." They shook hands.

Holmes said, "Mr Rawcliff. I should very much like to know something of your family and your sister's inheritance."

"Of course. We are an old and respected Manchester family. My sister and I inherited shares in a stone quarry from our maternal grandfather. The dividend yields a modest sum to us each year."

Excusing myself on the grounds of checking on the health of the ladies, I quietly withdrew from the kitchen as Holmes conducted his interview. I climbed the stairs to the bedroom occupied by the two students.

Having knocked on the door, I heard Mrs Jacob say somewhat sleepily, "Please wait a moment."

When she opened the door I saw that although her eyes were bloodshot, the woman appeared quite well.

"Dr Watson." She pushed stray hairs back from her face. "Good morning."

"Good morning, Mrs Jacob. I'm here in my professional capacity as a doctor to make sure that you and Miss Charlton have suffered no ill-effects from the drug."

She gave a faint smile. "It was rather intoxicating, wasn't it? I fell asleep with my head in the gravy. Miss Charlton is dressed. Will you step in?"

Mrs Jacob opened the door to reveal Miss Charlton. I satisfied myself of their good health simply by asking some questions about their well-being. They both declared themselves to be feeling in the pink, and that they would come downstairs for a light meal. I said that would be an excellent idea.

On returning to the kitchen, I found that Holmes had already left the house.

Rawcliff explained: "Mr Holmes said that he would take himself off for a walk while he considers the case."

I nodded. "From time to time he prefers to be alone with his thoughts." I turned to Keppel, who stood at the window. "Mr Keppel, I'd recommend that you eat something . . . Mr Keppel?"

He didn't reply – his eyes were wide and staring.

"Mr Keppel? Do you feel unwell?"

Keppel suddenly jabbed a finger at the window. "There," he hissed. "A man is watching us from the hillside."

His statement had all the dramatic effect of a pistol shot signalling the start of a race. Both men raced out across the yard. Rawcliff pulled back the hammers of the shotgun as he did so. The hunt was on!

The figure vanished as fast as a rabbit into its burrow. That didn't stop the two men. Their blood was up. They were determined to catch their prey.

I followed, urging caution. "Careful, gentlemen. He might be armed."

They didn't listen to me, such was their excitement. Both scrambled up the grassy slope. I realized that I must follow the two men and be there when they caught the fellow who spied upon the house.

I glanced back down at the harbour, filled with ships. There, upon one of the piers, stood a solitary figure dressed in black. A man as straight as a mooring post. That was Holmes – hands clasped behind his back, gazing out over the water, as his sharp mind weighed clues, calculated probabilities, and refined theories with the aim of ultimately reaching the most lucid of conclusions.

Rawcliff shouted, "Quickly, Watson! We'll soon have the scoundrel in our hands!"

Eleven

My face burns with shame as I write down the next part of my story. Many an individual, upon initiating a tragedy, must wring their hands in anguish and yearn to turn back the clock. To make different choices. To avoid the mistake that plunged them into utter catastrophe. The error I made led to bloodshed. My failure caused so much suffering that I will feel the searing hand of remorse for ever more.

But I must return to the events of that day. The two men were like greyhounds in pursuit of their prey, bounding up the hill after the stranger who'd been watching the house. Both Charles Keppel and Thomas Rawcliff believed they chased the mendacious individual who had crept into the house on at least two occasions: once to rearrange the footwear and fill Keppel's boots with flower petals – a coded death threat. On the second occasion, the trespasser had added a potent drug to the beef stew.

On that sunlit morning, I'd been overcome by the fever of the hunt, too. The men were younger than me. Nevertheless, huffing and puffing, I followed. Rawcliff had the shotgun. He bellowed that he'd shoot the man if he did not stop.

By this time, I had to pause in order to catch my breath. My two companions soon vanished over the hill. I plodded after them, grunting with exertion, yet determined to be there when the villain was captured. At last I caught up with them as they searched a tract of gloomy woodland.

After twenty minutes, we all agreed on a single point of fact. We had lost the man we had been chasing. Nevertheless, the pair insisted on continuing their search.

I said, "Very well. I ask you not to kill the fellow. Holmes will need to question him about the missing lady and child."

"Don't you fret," said Rawcliff. "We'll deliver him in one piece."

"Although we're likely to give him a good hiding first," added Keppel.

Rawcliff vigorously nodded his approval, and both men sprinted away before I could caution them against any action that could be construed as torture.

Eventually, I made my way back to Harbour View.

This is where I must confess that I'd been recklessly negligent in leaving the ladies alone, because Holmes's students from the School for Detection were gone. A teacup lay shattered beneath the table, while on the door there was a telltale smear of glistening crimson.

Twelve

Holmes spun towards me as I approached the harbour, shouting at the top of my voice. Breathlessly, I explained what had happened. That the two men and I had pursued a stranger, and upon my return to the house I had discovered that Mrs Jacob and Miss Charlton had vanished.

We hurried back to Harbour View. No sooner had we entered the kitchen than Keppel and Rawcliff arrived. Their search had been fruitless. I confess that the fear impressing itself so powerfully upon me at that moment was that we'd been tricked into pursuing the stranger, who had the express intention of luring us away. I revealed my concern to Holmes.

"I suspect you're correct, Watson," he said before hurrying away to search the rooms for any sign of the ladies. He returned a moment later. "They must have left of their own free will. Their coats are gone."

Rawcliff was clearly worried. "But the smashed cup? Blood on the door?"

"Indicating that they departed in an extreme hurry. The question is why?" Holmes turned to me. "Watson, was the back door open or closed when you arrived?"

"Closed."

"Has it been shut since your return?"

"No."

Holmes examined the bloody fingerprints on the outward-facing side of the door. "There isn't a great deal of blood." He pushed the door. "Ha! Progress!"

A piece of paper had been fixed to the woodwork on an inward-facing panel.

"A note?" I felt incredibly foolish. "Forgive me. It never occurred to me that I should look there."

"Don't worry, Watson, for we are relentlessly approaching the heart of the mystery." He leaned forward to study the paper. "One of the ladies must have pricked her finger on the tack when she pinned the note here. She was in such haste she didn't concern herself shedding a little blood, nor did she waste time sweeping up the shattered cup. Mrs Jacob and Miss Charlton believed they were faced with a matter of life and death."

"Then it appears neither of the ladies has been seriously hurt," I said, relieved.

Holmes read the note: "'You do not know me. Take heed, I know the whereabouts of Mrs Fox-Warren. She lives. As does the child. They are held prisoner in Chapel Cottage. To save their lives come at once.'" His eyes narrowed as he examined the piece of paper. "There is a roughly drawn map showing this house, and Chapel Cottage just along the road from here. There is also a postscript added by either, presumably, Mrs Jacob or Miss Charlton: 'Mr Holmes. We hasten to Chapel Cottage.'"

Rawcliff gripped the shotgun. "We must go to the cottage. Come on!"

Holmes held up his hand. "No!"

"You read the note, sir. It reveals that my sister and niece are held captive!"

"Please, Mr Rawcliff. There has been too much fruitless rushing to and fro. The time has to come to exploit brain, not muscle."

Keppel threw out his arms. "Mr Holmes, I agree with Rawcliff. We should hasten to Chapel Cottage. It's barely a hundred yards from here."

"Then you remember Chapel Cottage?" Holmes's shrewd eyes fixed on the man. "Your memory is returning?"

Keppel froze in astonishment. "By heaven. The old chapel! I remember standing before iron railings, seeing the place at twilight when bats flew around the eaves. Oh, Mr Holmes. I recall holding a bonny wee baby girl in my arms – soft, blonde hair . . . a pink bonnet. There's a lady, too. Resting her hand upon my arm. She's laughing."

Rawcliff's eager eyes searched Keppel's face. "You remember my sister?"

Keppel sighed. "A ruined chapel, a baby, the woman laughing. But I remember nothing else of consequence."

"Try harder. Tell me what happened to my sister. You must!"

"Sir," I began, "trying to force Mr Keppel to remember will make matters worse."

"Then I will go to the cottage."

Holmes blocked Rawcliff's path as he rushed towards the back door.

"Mr Holmes, out of my way!"

"No."

"I will push you aside."

Holmes spoke with great authority: "Watson and I will visit the cottage, although I am certain we will not find your sister, the baby, or my two students."

"They will be there. The note!"

"It's my belief that a boy has been paid to deliver this note when its writer was confident that the three of you had left the house and the two women were alone."

"For what purpose?"

"The plea to rescue mother and child was a ruse to draw the women from here in order to capture them."

"Why?"

"That I have still to determine. However, it proves that our enemy is keeping a close watch on this house. That's right, gentlemen, we are being spied upon. I confess that our enemy has been getting the better of me. Something which is painful to admit, and which demonstrates that our foe is much more intelligent than I gave them credit for."

Rawcliff went to the doorway in order to gaze at the hillside. "Then the devil is out there, watching us at this very moment?"

"Yes, that is why you must step back inside. Nothing must be done that tells our enemy that we know we are being watched."

Keppel groaned with despair. "What now, Mr Holmes? Your students will be in danger."

"I'm sure their lives are safe for the moment. Our enemy has a plan and it is still in its early stages."

Rawcliff snarled with frustration. "Dash it all, man. We must search for this devil. He may have kidnapped my sister and niece."

"No. He does not have them." Holmes spoke with confidence. "If he had, he would be long gone."

"Then let us find the villain!" Rawcliff brandished the shotgun. "I'll force the truth out of him."

"How can the four of us search this entire landscape? He will see us rushing up the hill towards him and vanish again."

"Then what the devil do you propose?"

"I will bring our enemy to the house."

"Sir, you are not capable of that!" Rawcliff's eyes blazed with anger. "You have proved yourself to be incompetent. You are not the great detective after all. You are a man who blunders into people's lives, pretending to make wonderful deductions. But you deceive us. You are a confidence trickster!"

"I say," I began in my friend's defence, "I will not allow you to insult Mr Holmes."

Sherlock Holmes placed his finger to his lips. "Hush. Let Mr Rawcliff have his say."

"But he's making vile accusations."

Holmes murmured, "There is truth in them. My work has been slipshod. I have allowed my students to be kidnapped. I have been found wanting."

Rawcliff's eyes flashed with triumph at being proved right. "This false genius conducts haphazard investigations. Yes, oh yes! Sometimes he is successful and catches the villain. Only by chance! Only by some happy coincidence!" Rawcliff suddenly leant back against the kitchen wall, his shoulders heaving. "And . . . and I do not know whether my sister is still alive. When she was a child she nearly succumbed to a fever. I was ten years old and the prospect of her dying tore my heart in two. I saw her lying in bed struggling for breath and fearing each minute would be her last. She was my little sister. I loved her. Just the day before she became ill, I watched her play with my boat in a puddle – a nasty, slimy, filthy puddle. I should have stopped her but I did nothing. I'd been negligent. Vile germs had entered her blood because of my failings." He wiped his eyes. "I'm sorry, gentlemen. You should not see such weak emotion in a man."

"You care about your sister," I said. "That is to be admired."

Rawcliff's eyes were so wounded-looking. "I fear for my sister's life, just as I feared she'd die because of my neglect when I was a boy. I apologize for insulting you, Mr Holmes."

"It's I who should be apologetic. I've grown complacent. Now, however, the time has come for me to put matters right."

"Tell me how I can help." Rawcliff had regained a grip on his emotions. "I will take any risk to find Gwyneth and her baby."

"I, too," said Keppel with utter determination.

"Very well." Holmes's confidence grew as he spoke. "What I will ask of you, Mr Rawcliff, will seem strange. Yet please follow my instructions to the letter."

"That I will, sir."

"I want you to hurry into town. Make a show of rushing, as if you are in a desperate panic. Go to the nearest undertaker and have him bring a coffin to the house."

Rawcliff's eyes widened in surprise. Nevertheless, he nodded. "I will do that."

"Inform the undertaker that your sister's body has been discovered here in the attic."

"My God!"

"Of course, no such discovery has been made. However, that is what you will tell the undertaker. After that, go to the post office, send a telegram to this address saying that Mrs Fox-Warren is deceased and her funeral is to be arranged."

"This is most disturbing, Mr Holmes."

"I agree. My intention is to create a disturbance in the minds of certain individuals." Holmes lightly pressed his fingers together. "When you have sent the telegram, go to a tavern. Order whisky as if to calm your nerves. Reveal to the bartender that your sister's corpse has been discovered. Make your performance a believable one. Shed a tear. Tremble. Drink more whisky. Do you understand?"

"Yes, but—"

"Please do as I ask. Time is of the essence."

"Yes, Mr Holmes."

"Oh, please leave the shotgun with Mr Keppel. He will guard the house when we leave. Watson and I won't be long but we must examine Chapel Cottage. Also, it will benefit my plan if our enemy sees us searching the address contained in that little note."

Rawcliff paused at the door. "What do we do then, Mr Holmes?"

Holmes's thin, austere face was serious. "Then comes the most difficult part of all. We must wait."

Thirteen

The pace of events quickened. Early that afternoon, Rawcliff hurried into town on his morbid errand. Meanwhile, Keppel guarded the house, while Holmes and I visited the nearby chapel and its associated cottage. Holmes gazed over the railings at broken panes and sagging roofs. Both buildings were in a state of dereliction.

"Hmm . . . we'll discover nothing of importance here." Holmes eyed the overgrown lawn. "The grass hasn't been disturbed whatsoever."

"So the note begging the ladies to come here was a ruse?"

"Absolutely, Watson. Our two students were clearly abducted as they made their way here."

"We could explore further along the road."

"I admire your determination, yet we would be wasting our time attempting to search this wilderness alone. No, it's high time to progress to the next stage of my plan."

"Involving an undertaker, a coffin, and Thomas Rawcliff playing the part of a grieving brother? Extraordinary!"

"Indeed so."

"May I ask you to elaborate on your strategy?"

"Ah, Watson, you know me better than that. Suffice to say that what I have planned will surprise everyone."

"I can't help but worry about the telegram that you asked Rawcliff to send, and its effect on its recipient. After all, news of a death will be shocking."

Holmes gave a dry smile. "I handed Rawcliff a receiving address and alias that I use for deceptions such as this. That little message will trouble no one, yet it might well bait the trap I have set."

"Goodness, I can't even begin to guess at what shenanigans you have concocted."

"Ha, shenanigans. A word that suggest tumultuous mischief. How perfectly apt. Now it's time to make a show of hurrying, as if we're thoroughly alarmed. After all, our enemy will be keeping an eye on us."

Holmes moved quickly. I did likewise, trying to adopt a worried expression. When we reached the house, Holmes rushed indoors. Keppel stood in the kitchen, aiming the shotgun, ready to fire. When he saw it was Holmes and me he sighed with relief.

"I'm sorry, gentlemen. Truth of the matter is, I feel as if every movement I make is watched."

"It surely is," Holmes declared with feeling. "We are being spied upon."

I huffed with annoyance. "Then our enemy will always be one step ahead of us. We cannot act without being observed."

Sherlock Holmes told Keppel that his visit to the chapel had revealed that neither Mrs Keppel and her child, nor the students, were there. Holmes added that he needed to check the interior of the house again. Why, I cannot say, and he did not offer any explanation. Moments later, he briskly entered the kitchen, every inch the man who has embarked on a mission of huge importance.

He announced, "I am going into town. Watson, please accompany me. Mr Keppel, you will kindly remain here. Soon a steamer trunk will arrive. Please accept its delivery and leave the trunk downstairs. Also, Mr Rawcliff will return with the undertaker and a coffin. After he deposits the coffin in the sitting room, leave the shotgun in the pantry, and lock the doors. Thereafter, accompany Mr Rawcliff and the undertaker back into town. On no account leave by yourself or with any other individual, whatever they might tell you. Are my instructions clear?"

"They are, Mr Holmes."

Holmes and I immediately set out for the nearby town. Bright sunshine sparkled on the sea and I could smell brine on the fresh breeze. Yet my thoughts centred on Mrs Jacob and Miss Charlton. Goodness knows what cruelty they endured. Holmes clearly shared my concern because his pace was unrelenting. And whereas I became breathless, his vigour grew with every step, his eyes sharper, his concentration more intense.

When we reached the town he marched towards its small police station.

He broke his silence. "Watson. What I will request of you will appear extremely bizarre. Nevertheless, humour me. It is vital we are successful today, otherwise I fear our two students will die."

"Of course. I know that you never make frivolous requests."

"Excellent." He paused at the police-station door. "After you, Watson. I do hope you will forgive me for what I'm about to do to you."

Fourteen

Compression. Pressure on every square inch of my body. Absolute discomfort. There are scarcely powerful enough words to describe the torture I endured after entering the police station.

Suffice to say that Holmes asked the constable to supply a large trunk of the kind used to carry prodigious amounts of belongings. The constable, realizing he would be assisting Sherlock Holmes, the most famous of detectives, eagerly procured the required item. The trunk, when stood on end, was four feet tall and covered with labels: evidence of its travels.

I had expressed surprise when Holmes asked me to step inside. I complied, however. Lives depended on my cooperation. Fortunately, Holmes had already employed a hammer and a nail to knock air holes into the lid.

Then the torture. I, Doctor John Watson, a fellow of generous girth, crammed into that confined space. I was bundled, still within the trunk, on to a handcart. From what I could hear within my tin box, I gathered that a station porter had been hired to push the handcart, which bore the trunk that contained me. Of course, due to the secrecy of Holmes's plan, the porter was oblivious to the trunk's living contents. Every bump in the road made me flinch with pain. It was impossible to arrange my limbs in a comfortable way. My head repeatedly clunked against the hard interior. Despite the ventilation holes, the interior was stuffy and smelt of mould. I lay there compressed into a living ball of arms and legs.

At last! The porter reached his destination, Harbour View. I heard Mr Keppel take delivery of the trunk. Both men were panting as they dragged it, and me, across the floor. There they left me to my suffering.

My plan had been to free myself from the trunk because, such was the simplicity of the lock mechanism, I could release the catch from within. I would then make my presence known to Keppel – no doubt to his immense surprise, as Holmes hadn't told the man that I'd be concealed in an item of luggage. The atmosphere thickened to the point that my chest ached. Yes, I had intended to climb out. Even so, I became very drowsy. Whether I fell asleep or even passed out due to the scarcity of oxygen, I cannot say. In any event, I became unconscious for a considerable amount of time.

At last, I awoke in that infernal prison of a box – nay, torture chamber! Absolute silence. A sense of stillness. The need to escape burned inside me. Even though using my hands was difficult, due to the confined space, I managed to move the steel catch that secured the lid in place.

Moments later, I emerged. Rather than springing to my feet, I unfurled my limbs before slithering out, no doubt resembling a snake sliding from a box. When the feeling returned to my numb feet, it was with nothing less than an agony of pins and needles. Eventually I managed to stand. I knew better than to move around the dining room where I might be glimpsed through a window. Instead, I retreated to the passageway. There I waved my arms and danced a peculiar jig to restore circulation.

Thereafter, I checked the kitchen without leaving the corridor. Empty. No sign of Keppel. He must have obeyed Holmes's instructions, leaving with Rawcliff and the undertaker.

I went to the sitting room, where I saw a grim object that chilled me to the bone. A wooden coffin stood on trestles in the middle of the room. Fortunately, the curtains were closed. Nobody could peer in to see what happened next.

I quickly released the catches and opened the lid. A pale figure lay within the casket. Long fingers extended from white hands that were crossed upon the chest.

The figure opened its eyes and a familiar voice said, "Why, thank you, Watson. I wondered if you'd nodded off in your own container."

"Nodded off? I damn well near suffocated."

Holmes sat up in the coffin. He patted the wooden sides in such an affectionate manner that I shuddered.

He remarked, "If I ever ordered clothes made from wood, I can't imagine that they would ever be as snug as this. Or as comfortable."

"Holmes," I cried in anguish. "Do get out of the dreadful thing. This is the stuff of nightmares."

Holmes put his finger to his lips. "Please . . . whispers only. I should hate it if our enemy guessed that the house wasn't deserted."

With that, he allowed me to help him out of the coffin.

As he used those long, pale hands of his to smooth out the creases from his black jacket he said, "You now understand why I organized such unusual modes of transport for the pair of us?"

"The house is being watched by the villain. You have contrived to make it appear that Keppel, Rawcliff, your good self and I have left the house."

"Correct. Our enemy has watched us all leave. What he has witnessed entering this building is the trunk and the coffin. The trunk he will dismiss as the late arrival of luggage. The coffin is another matter entirely. He will be immensely interested in its presence here. After all, what does its delivery by an undertaker signify?"

"That someone is deceased."

"Moreover, our vile watcher will know that the deceased isn't one of the four men, because he saw them leave here alive."

"Ah. That is why you asked Rawcliff to send the telegram, believing that he may have been overheard in the post office."

"To make doubly sure, I then had Rawcliff visit a tavern, which in all towns is the perfect source of gossip, rumour and tittle-tattle galore. An apparently grief-stricken man downing whiskies while babbling about his dead sister will become the talk of a small town within moments. The entire borough will be fizzing with speculation and exaggeration."

"You believe the villain will hear that Gwyneth is dead?"

"I find it hard to believe that he will not. No doubt, he'll now want to confirm who will occupy this little ship on its voyage into the afterlife." He tapped the coffin with his knuckles.

"Why would the watcher be so interested in who will be put into the coffin?"

Holmes looked directly at me. "Because he is desperate to find Rawcliff's sister. He wants Gwyneth Keppel."

"Why?"

"Ah . . ." Holmes held up his finger. "I do believe we will discover 'why' and 'who' very shortly. If I'm not mistaken, I've just heard the click of a window catch being forced." His voice dropped to a hiss. "I shall replace the casket lid, like so. Now we should conceal ourselves behind that sofa before our visitor arrives."

Fifteen

Holmes and I waited. A macabre tableau indeed – a gloomy room, curtains closed, the dreadful coffin. I heard faint sounds from another part of the house – a click, a scrape, a creak of a door. Stealthy footsteps . . . slowly becoming louder. The trespasser approached the very room where Holmes and I remained crouched behind the sofa. My heart pounded. Its drumbeat quickened, growing louder, until I could believe that the intruder would hear my heart and run from the house before we could discover their identity.

Hinges gave a squeak. The sound of respiration. More footsteps. Closer and closer. Then the soft clunk of the coffin lid being raised.

A gruff voice exclaimed, "My God. What devilry is this?"

Holmes's sharp elbow found my side. "Now," he hissed.

We leapt to our feet.

From the gloom, a pair of bright, angry eyes flashed at us.

There, standing beside the empty coffin, was a familiar figure, for I recognized Thomas Rawcliff. Yet it was a Thomas Rawcliff shockingly transformed. The face now bore a scar running from his upper lip to his right eye. The man's eyebrows were grey, not black as before. His forehead was wrinkled. His hair was long, reaching down over the collar of his black coat.

Holmes spoke loudly: "Sir, whom did you expect to find in the coffin?"

"Blast you!" The man's rough voice blazed with such violence I flinched. He slammed the coffin lid back down with a bang. "Gwyneth? Where is she?"

"Ha!" Holmes stepped forward. "That proves to me she is still alive."

Rawcliff had undergone a fearsome transformation. Indeed, almost monstrous. His eyes were set beneath heavy lids. He'd aged thirty years within hours. Then I realized that the gloom had deceived me. This was not the Thomas Rawcliff I knew, but another man. One who resembled him to a remarkable degree.

The brute raised his hand to reveal an axe. "Tell me where the girl is, blast ye. Tell me, or I'll put the pair of you in a box like this." He swung the axe down, splintering the coffin lid.

The moment I saw that the axe had bitten into the wood so deeply that it had become stuck, I leapt on the man. Holmes, too. The stranger was ferociously strong. He threw me on to the sofa.

As he tried to free the axe from the coffin wood, Holmes struck out. His expertly delivered blows cut the man's cruel face. Immediately, the man abandoned the axe and punched Holmes so hard that he fell back against the coffin, whereupon both he and that long box went crashing to the floor. I hurled myself on to the monster, forcing the man off balance.

I fought for my life. The brute, roaring with fury, gripped my throat. The pressure became agonizing. My head began to spin with the lack of oxygen.

My attacker's screams of rage turned to a yell of pain as his hands abruptly left my throat. Holmes stood there, panting. The way he held an ornamental figurine, cast from bronze, suggested he'd used it to knock the fight out of the man.

I dragged open the curtains, admitting the light from the setting sun. The intruder lay there clutching his arm, his face twisted in pain.

Holmes took a deep breath. "Sometimes it's more effective to deliver a sharp blow to the elbow rather than the head. The humerus is a most effective communicator of pain."

The stranger managed to sit upright.

"Careful, Holmes, he's still dangerous."

"Wise advice, Watson." Holmes raised the figurine as if it were a club. "Sir, you will accept my advice and remain seated."

"Uh . . ." grunted the man. "Damn you. I'll get even, I swear I will."

"Ah, a man with a highly developed instinct for revenge. I thought as much. Now you will tell me where you have hidden the two ladies who were in this house."

"Damn you, I won't. You've signed their death warrants. My friends will cut their throats."

"I expect that's the order you've given your gang if you don't return to your lair by a specific time. Six o'clock this evening, perhaps? And it's now a quarter past five."

"Keep guessing, you dog. You won't find out where those two lambs are kept." He chuckled. "The lambs are going to kick and bleat when they feel the blade's kiss."

I seized a heavy candlestick from the sideboard. "You will tell us where they are. If you don't . . ." I raised the candlestick.

"Go ahead. Spill my brains."

Holmes gripped my arm to prevent me doing as I threatened.

"Watson. I suggest you do not break your Hippocratic Oath."

The man glanced up at me in surprise. "You're a doctor? Dr Watson? I've heard of you. You work for that detective."

"You haven't realized who we are?" asked Holmes. "Then you presumed we were friends of Charles Keppel?"

"Is that what he calls himself now? He went by the name Fox-Warren."

"You have been keeping this house under surveillance."

"I've watched it. Aye, sir. I make no secret of that."

"Gwyneth saw you creeping through the garden. You managed to enter the house at night to turn her husband's boots around."

"That's what they do with a dead soldier, don't they? Stick his boots wrong-wise in his nag's stirrups."

"And you filled them with chrysanthemum petals, flowers of mourning in France. You were sending a coded message to Gwyneth. One that threatened the death of her husband if she didn't yield to your demands."

"Sharp as a razor, aren't you?"

He made as if to climb to his feet. Holmes pushed him back down.

"Stay there, sir."

"Then the ladies will die for sure." The man's face acquired an expression of cunning. "Of course, we can trade like men of business, can't we? Let me go. I'll set your pretty lambs free."

"You'd do nothing of the sort. The ladies would testify against you. You'd kill them in order to prevent that."

"Ah, I remember you now. You're the detective with the big beak of a nose. Holmes. . . Sherringham Holmes."

"Sherlock Holmes," I corrected. "You are now in his custody."

"Nah, I'm not. Because I'll tell you why you're going to give me a head start from the coppers. Why don't I take you to the ladies, just the three of us?"

"The moment we're close enough," said Holmes, "you'll shout a warning to your compatriots. They'll pick us off with their guns."

"All right, gents. Have it your own way. Meanwhile, listen to that clock. It's ticking away like I don't know what. And you're right, you know? At six sharp my lads start carving."

Holmes nodded. "In that case, I will find a clue upon your person that tells me where your gang are holding the ladies captive."

The man laughed. "If you're expecting to find a map in my pockets with X marking the bloody spot, you'll be sadly disappointed." He laughed even louder. "At least you have one coffin. Save some money. Pop both lasses into the same box."

I studied the man's face. "You resemble Thomas Rawcliff. You must be related."

"Oh, Doctor, that took you a piece of time to work out. With a mind as dull as yours, I won't be coming to you with a cough, otherwise I'll be needing one of these." He tapped the coffin with his boot.

I glanced at Holmes. "Clearly, this fellow and Rawcliff are of the same blood. That means he will be related to Gwyneth as well. What's your opinion?"

Holmes said, "Time is running out. Questions concerning family relationships must wait." His sharp eyes fixed on the ruffian. "You will give me your name, sir?"

"Can't hurt my prospects, can it? I'm John Lavelle."

"A French surname, yet you have the distinctive strains of a Manchester accent."

"Ha, a brilliant detective? The village idiot could have figured out that titbit. Dear me, you are a poor muddle of a thing."

"Well, this poor muddle of a thing has just discovered where you're keeping the women."

"You're bluffing."

"On the contrary. You are holding them in a building once used to smoke herring, but which hasn't done so for a long while. The route there is through sand dunes."

Lavelle couldn't have looked any more shocked if I'd kicked him. "How the devil did you know that?"

"As I tell my students, always use your nose. There's a faint, yet distinct odour of fish and wood smoke on your coat. It's faint because the building hasn't been used for smoking fish for some time. There are traces of ash on your boots from where oak chips were once left to smoulder beneath the racks of herring. There are also particles of sand on your boots. These are fine, windblown particles found in sand dunes, not the coarse, grittier particles of the type found on the beach here at North Reiff."

"Damn you," the man growled. "Knowing about the blasted hut won't help you. The women are as good as dead."

"Then I shall launch my intelligence against the brutal nature of present circumstances – and we shall discover who comes out on top."

The man uttered a torrent of foul curses.

Holmes turned to me. "The cellar has a strong door. I propose we make good use of it."

Lavelle jumped to his feet. This time I had the satisfaction of slamming my fist into his belly. Before he could recover his breath, Holmes and I dragged him into the passageway. Holmes opened the cellar door while I shouldered the man through – there he slithered down the steps into that windowless crypt of a place. Holmes shut the door, locked it, then pocketed the key.

He slapped me on the shoulder. "You're a good man to have in a crisis. Now . . . my estimation is that we have thirty minutes to free my students. I trust you're up for a sprint?"

I assured him I was before collecting the shotgun from the pantry and checking that both barrels were loaded.

As we left the house, the setting sun cast its blood-red light on the sea. Holmes pointed to a dirt track that led down towards the shore.

"This way, Watson!"

We ran along the track towards dunes, which formed little hillocks of pale sand topped with grass. The windblown sand here was indeed different to that of the beach, just as Holmes had pointed out earlier; very powdery and soft.

Holmes was hardly out of breath, while I gasped like a steam locomotive of a particularly ancient vintage.

My friend scanned the acres of dunes. "We're looking for a shack where fishermen brought the herring they caught to be smoked."

"But, Holmes, there are dozens of shacks here. How do we identify the one where the ladies are being held?"

"We can ignore buildings still used by fishermen." His long finger indicated a cluster of huts from which grey fumes rose. "Those are in occupation. We need to find a solitary building that appears dilapidated."

I checked my pocket watch. "Fifteen minutes to six, Holmes. If Lavelle gave orders to kill the women at six, we're running out of time."

"Then the time has come to muster every atom of strength. We must elevate our powers to the extraordinary." He dashed up one of the sandy hillocks. From that high vantage point, his keen gaze raked the dunes, searching for what he knew with all his heart must be there.

At last! He pointed in triumph.

"Over there, Watson," he cried. "Two hundred yards away – a shack standing in isolation."

Holmes leapt from the dune, almost as if his sheer force of will could carry him through the air to his destination. Even though such a thing as a flying man is impossible, he dropped in an extended arc, landing in the soft sand, and instantly began running in the direction he'd pointed. I followed, panting hard, tightly gripping the shotgun.

Soon I could see the shack more clearly – a structure consisting of boards, standing amid dunes. A man of surly appearance mooched around it, smoking a cigarette.

"We have our destination," Holmes murmured as we took cover behind a dune.

"Any sign of the ladies?"

"None. Although I pray that they're inside."

"It's five minutes to six."

"Then we must act without delay."

"I'm ready."

"Good man."

I cocked the shotgun. The weapon had been loaded with, I surmised, birdshot. This would still prove lethal to a man if fired at close range.

Holmes patted me on the shoulder. "I favour a direct approach, given that we literally approach the deadline."

"I agree."

"Conceal the gun beneath your coat. Can you put your hand in your pocket and hold the barrel through the fabric? Yes . . . exactly like that. Perfect. We'll walk purposefully towards the shack while trying to give the impression we're simply there to ask some trivial question."

I nodded.

"Very well, Watson. Good luck, old man."

Holmes strolled calmly towards the shack. I kept at his side, holding the gun inside my coat so it remained out of sight. When we were thirty yards or so away, the man with the slouching walk noticed us.

Holmes's plan instantly fell apart, because the stranger clearly had a finely developed instinct for danger: he dashed back into the hut. Immediately, I heard male voices shouting in French followed by the shrill cry of a woman.

"Come, Watson! Be ready for battle!"

Holmes had no other weapon than his fists. I swung the shotgun from under my coat. Suddenly figures spilt out of the shack. One man gripped a rifle. Two other men held a woman each in their arms: Miss Charlton and Mrs Jacob. The students were frightened, yet both fought like tigresses. The men holding them produced knives from their belts, which they held to the women's throats.

The thugs unleashed a torrent of French at us that was so barbaric I couldn't understand what was being said, other than the word *morte*, meaning 'dead'. Holmes and I nevertheless grasped what they attempted to communicate. They were using the women as hostages to guarantee their escape. If we tried to stop them, the women would be slaughtered.

The man with the rifle, a gaunt figure wearing a red neckerchief, aimed the weapon at us.

Holmes said, "A standoff, I'm afraid. We have reached stalemate."

"Forgive me, Holmes," I replied. "I have been known to gamble. And I think this is the time to chance our luck."

I fired the shotgun into the air.

Already in this narrative, I have confessed that my face burns with shame as I write. I did gamble with the lives of the two women, and with our own lives. I am mortified to admit that I made a terrible mistake that had tragic consequences. I should have waited a little longer. Patience might have averted tragedy.

The terrific explosion made by the shotgun made everyone freeze. For a moment we became statues, not moving, not saying a word. The two women were the first to recover from the startling effect of the gunshot. They struggled to break free. The men's bravado appeared to desert them. The one who had held Mrs Jacob fled into the dunes. He was followed by the man with the rifle, who tossed the weapon aside as he ran.

Mrs Jacob scooped up a handful of sand before throwing it into the face of the bully who gripped Miss Charlton. He was a towering figure with a black beard and dangerous, blazing eyes. He clawed at those eyes with his free hand to remove the grit that blinded him. That was the moment when Miss Charlton wriggled from his grasp and raced towards us. Mrs Jacob paused, selflessly placing herself between the knifeman and the younger lady. When she was satisfied her fellow student was safe, she followed.

Mrs Jacob hurried towards us. I went to meet her. The man whom she'd temporarily blinded cursed in French while stumbling away in the direction of the shack.

Then that dreadful moment. The bearded man suddenly seemed to become possessed by an impulse of absolute evil. Having started to run away, he abruptly changed his mind. He dashed towards Mrs Jacob. Catching hold of her, he held her in a fierce grip.

The knife blade caught the red light of the sun. A moment later he cut Mrs Jacob's throat.

Blood cascaded down the front of her dress. She took another step towards me, her desperate, beseeching eyes fixed on mine. Then she fell.

The man's laugh thundered in my ears. Clearly, he'd taken vicious pleasure in cutting her flesh. He lifted his hand high above his head, brandishing the knife in triumph. I fired the gun again. This time the shot struck the knife, sending it spinning away through the air. The man, clutching his hand, dropped to his knees. It was then I noticed that scattered around the knife on the sand were the bloody remnants of several of his fingers.

Sixteen

Holmes stood in a room at the police station. Dressed severely in black, tall, very thin, with a white face that was almost skull-like in the gloom, he wore an expression of sadness. Earlier, we had been at the railway station to say farewell to Mrs Jacob as she was carried on to the train. Yes, I'd managed to save her life after the vile creature had wielded his dagger. Her lower jaw had absorbed most of the blade's force. She'd suffered a deep laceration there, as well as a shallower cut to her throat. Fortunately, her windpipe and major arteries hadn't been damaged. Nevertheless, Mrs Jacob would require a long convalescence to regain her strength (in parenthesis, I must add that forever thereafter the unfortunate woman could only speak in whispers: the knifeman had cruelly robbed her of her voice).

I blame myself. Firing the shotgun into the air in the hope of frightening the women's abductors into surrender had been a gamble – a gamble which I lost, and for which Mrs Jacob had to pay the price.

I had also found myself saving the life of the man who'd tried to slay Mrs Jacob. My shot had removed three of his fingers and he, too, almost bled to death.

The townsfolk were so enraged by the brutal attack on Mrs Jacob that they hunted the remaining two kidnappers down. It must be said that the pair suffered a good hiding before being handed over to the police: some rough justice before the full magisterial justice of the criminal courts.

Miss Charlton later confirmed that they had been abducted by the men as they walked to Chapel Cottage after receiving the note. She added that, apart from being locked in a small storeroom in the shack, they'd suffered no other ill-treatment.

I sat there at the police station with a heavy heart, wishing I could turn back time so as to avoid firing the ill-considered warning shot.

Holmes placed his hand on my shoulder. "I know you are blaming yourself, old chap. But what else could have been done which would have resulted in a happier conclusion? Both women might be dead if it hadn't been for your quick thinking."

"Nevertheless, I was responsible for the students' safety. It was my duty to . . ." I couldn't finish the sentence. Memories of a heavily band-aged Mrs Jacob wouldn't leave me.

Before I could find more words of self-blame, the door opened. Miss Charlton entered. She was followed by Thomas Rawcliff and Charles Keppel. After them came two powerful policemen, who didn't shilly-shally when it came to dragging Lavelle into the room. He was in chains, and they clinked loudly as the constables hauled him to a straight-backed chair where they forced him to sit.

Holmes began speaking in that commanding way he always adopted when revealing his deductions: "Mr Lavelle had two motives," he declared. "The lesser motive shielded the greater one, obscuring it from my view."

Lavelle growled, "You might have used your tricks to find out where your two little lambs were caged. You won't trick a confession out of me, by God."

"Whether or not you confess is immaterial, because I'm now able to piece together your intentions. It's all rather childishly simple. Largely, because your motive sprang from your quite childish nature."

The man glared at Holmes. *If looks could kill . . .*

"Your physical resemblance to Mr Thomas Rawcliff here is quite remarkable."

Lavelle snarled, "He's no blood of mine – at least, none that I'd admit to."

"Nor, I daresay, does he welcome having you as an uncle. The facts are quite mundane. A similar story could be told about many a family." Holmes continued briskly, "Thomas Rawcliff has told me that his mother's maiden name was Lavelle. Her father had left his native France in order to build up an honest business, quarrying limestone in England. Monsieur Lavelle had a son and a daughter, the daughter, as honest as her father, married a gentleman from Manchester; she would become the mother of Thomas Rawcliff and his sister, Gwyneth. The second son, the individual you now see in chains, was a rogue."

Thomas Rawcliff nodded. "My uncle turned to crime when he was a young man. His father told him that he would never inherit one penny of the business and struck him out of the will. Later, in order to escape arrest after a robbery, my uncle fled to France. All this happened more than thirty years ago. Our family never saw him again."

"You did not," Holmes pointed out. "Your sister, however, did. You told me, Mr Rawcliff, that you and your sister each inherited shares in a quarry from your grandfather upon his death."

"That's correct, sir."

Lavelle grunted. "Money that was rightfully mine."

"Ah," breathed Holmes, "which brings me to explaining this individual's despicable behaviour. Mr Rawcliff, you've told me that your sister, Gwyneth, and yourself received dividends from your shares in the quarry. Not a large sum, yet a welcome addition to your income. I haven't discovered how yet, but Lavelle learned that his father had died some years after the event. He then decided to get his odious hands on what he believed was his."

"And is mine." The chains rattled as Lavelle gave a self-righteous shrug of indignation.

Holmes said, "Members of Lavelle's gang have been eager to answer my questions. They hope, no doubt, for leniency from the court if they cooperate, so I've been able to piece together what happened over recent weeks. Lavelle found out where his niece lived, whereupon he and his gang came here to Scotland. He promised his associates money if they helped him. So it was that Lavelle secretly approached his niece, threatening to harm her husband if she didn't hand over considerable sums of cash. Of course, the amount she receives from the quarry isn't large, so the lady could not pay what was demanded. Lavelle believed she was lying, so continued to intimidate her by breaking into the house and filling her husband's boots with chrysanthemum petals – chrysanthemums being the flowers that the French use at funerals. He intended this as a coded warning. Eventually, his patience gave out. One night he tried to smash his way into the house. Mr Keppel here, alas, has no recollection of what happened. Yet we know he urged his wife to hide the child, which she did successfully."

Keppel sighed in despair. "If only I could remember what happened, then I could help you, Mr Holmes."

"Worry not, sir. I see clearly enough what happened just weeks ago. We can imagine that as Lavelle finally entered the house, so Gwyneth fled with her baby into the night. Lavelle seemingly has a taste for kidnap. We can picture him imprisoning Mr Keppel in an upper room with the intention of extorting money from his own niece. Yet Mr Keppel escaped. Shortly thereafter he suffered another bout of amnesia, erasing all memory of what happened, and he returned to his old home in London. Am I correct in my deduction about your own part in this, Lavelle?"

"Go to blazes."

"Very well, I will draw my own conclusions. Mr Keppel asked me to discover what he'd done with his life for the past two years, as he has no recollection of it. Accordingly, we arrived here to investigate. Two of my students had already made their way to Harbour View. Lavelle mistakenly believed we were relatives or friends of Gwyneth and Charles Keppel. He kidnapped Miss Charlton and Mrs Jacob in the hope that when Gwyneth returned from hiding, he could pressure her into surrendering her inheritance to him."

Keppel shook his head. "The villain did all that in order to extort money from his own niece? The risk must have been phenomenal."

"Ah, I daresay by that time the other gang members were thoroughly disillusioned with Lavelle. Imagine those Frenchmen living in a shack on the Scottish coast. They will have grown fearful for their safety. No doubt muttering to each other that the police would come asking questions before long. Lavelle, here, will have been promising them lavish shares from the inheritance that would come to him. Perhaps by then he even feared his own gang might turn against him, so he became increasingly desperate. And yet . . ."

Everyone turned to look at Holmes as he paused. Even Lavelle gazed up at him from beneath his shaggy eyebrows.

"And yet, this wasn't really about the money – not in Lavelle's eyes."

"What was it about?" I asked, mystified.

"I can sum it up in one word." Holmes paused again. "Revenge."

"Hah!" Lavelle's heartfelt reaction to the word "revenge" was more eloquent than a lengthy confession.

"Yes, revenge," Holmes said. "Lavelle experienced utter rage when he learned that his own father had cut him out of the will. Indeed, Lavelle here did lust after wealth. But what he really wanted was to ruin his niece's life. In the twisted monstrosity that is his mind, he somehow believed he could make his own dead father suffer if he inflicted mental torture on Gwyneth. Coded death threats against his niece's husband would produce nothing less than agonizing worry in her heart. And after he'd finished with Gwyneth, he would have turned his sadistic attention to Mr Rawcliff, his own nephew."

Thomas Rawcliff clenched his fists, no doubt longing to rain blows down on his vile uncle. At last he mastered his emotions and turned to Holmes. "Thank you, sir, for bringing this monster to justice. I only wish that you could find my sister."

Holmes rested his fingertips together. "I'm sorry that I have failed you in that respect. However, I am certain she is safe. The child, too."

Keppel reached out to clasp Rawcliff's hand. "Although I am an empty vessel when it comes to memory, I swear that I will help you . . ."

He took a deep breath. "After all, your sister is my wife, and the mother of my child."

Later, when the men left the room, and Lavelle was back in his cell, I stood in the office with Sherlock Holmes and Miss Charlton.

Holmes spoke apologetically: "Miss Charlton, I regret that I plunged you into such a nightmare."

"Not a nightmare, Mr Holmes." She smiled. "A most exciting adventure."

"Your resilience continues to astonish me."

"I have learned the science of detection from books and from lectures – now, however, I have finally discovered what it is truly like to battle evil. The last few days have taught me what it means to be a detective."

"Then I am grateful for another worthwhile outcome."

She turned to me. "Will you write an account of this case for your readers, Dr Watson?"

"Eventually, Miss."

Holmes smiled. "Knowing my friend as I do, he will reorder reality into episodes of breathtaking excitement. What's more, his readers will finish the last page satisfied that all wrongs have been righted, every mystery solved, and no question remains unanswered."

Ah, if only that could be so. I end this account knowing that Mrs Jacob has been scarred for life. Moreover, this story has a conclusion that is fragmented, because I promised myself I would record events accurately, without resorting to a fictitious happy ending. Yes, I can add that Lavelle and his gang were sent to jail with a ten-year sentence apiece. And, indeed, Miss Charlton travelled to Dover where she did find a satisfactory solution to the mystery of the flowerpots that appeared to be moving of their own volition atop a garden wall; and just as the incident of the wrong-wise boots appeared trivial at first, the matter of the shifting flowerpots turned out to be a grave one. Miss Charlton thwarted an assassin, who had moved the pots in order to improve sightlines when the time came to slay a visitor to the house with a sniper's rifle. As Holmes himself would declare: the most insignificant of occurrences might shine a revealing light on a mystery that has the power to change lives. Or end them.

Happiest of all, Mrs Gwyneth Keppel returned before Holmes and I left for London. By Jove, was there a happier reunion? The moment Charles Keppel saw her, the log-jam cleared inside his head. Memory returned. He wept with joy when he recognized his wife and baby daughter as they passed through the garden gate. Needless to say, there were detailed explanations on all sides. He had to confess he wasn't the man she thought he was. Indeed, he had a different name entirely. There were anxious moments when she hardly dared ask if he had been free to marry her. When he reassured her that he had been, they passionately embraced, kissing each other, and the baby in her arms.

I swear I even saw Holmes blush at such a storm-burst of emotion and pure love.

Gwyneth explained that when her uncle had attempted to break into the house, she had fled to the harbour with her baby. Being aware of her uncle's violent ways, she boarded a ship that was captained by a certain gentleman she knew from the town. He always sailed in the company of his wife, so it was soon agreed that Gwyneth and the baby would travel with them to safety. It wasn't the best of solutions, as Gwyneth had no way of letting her husband know about her sudden ocean voyage. She could only hope that wicked Uncle Lavelle would have vanished by the time she returned.

At this point, I am tempted to write: *all's well that ended well, and the family lived happily ever after.* Alas, are there always such pleasant outcomes in life? I heard that six months after Gwyneth was reunited with her husband, a worrying incident occurred. Mr Charles Keppel tried to board a train in North Reiff without a ticket. He declared that his name was Major Fox-Warren and he must join his regiment. The stationmaster, upon realizing that the man wasn't himself, persuaded him to wait in the ticket office. Mr Keppel soon came to his senses and was astonished to hear that he'd claimed to be someone he wasn't.

Of course, he returned home to his wife and child. Mostly, there are happy times. He remembers that he is Charles Keppel of Harbour View. Yet his lapses of memory gradually become more frequent. What follows is a melancholy observation, for I suspect that one day he will face his greatest personal mystery of all, when he gazes at his reflection in the mirror and asks, "Who is that man?" and forever afterwards is unable to answer that simple question.

A Gentlemanly Wager
William Meikle

I was having a smoke by the fire that day in May of 1898 when it all began, and I had thought that Holmes was asleep, but then he spoke, breaking a silence of several hours.

"I have been considering the value of a partnership in crime solving," he said. "In particular, the roles of primary investigator and companion, and how the dynamic between the two might be approached during the training of the Russell Square recruits."

I smiled rather wryly at that, for Holmes had almost always, throughout the length of our acquaintance, insisted that he was quite capable of handling most of our investigations on his own. Indeed I have, more than once, looked back to consider that my own involvement was more happenstance than foresight and planning. I did not, of course, bring that to Holmes's attention—it would have seemed like a slight on his very persona. Besides, he was already continuing, so clearly did not expect conversation—rather he was, as he has done on many previous occasions, merely using me as a lens through which he might focus his thought processes.

"You know young Wilkinson—Mycroft's lad? I consider him a leader: a future primary. And Green, Lestrade's plodder; he is most definitely destined to be a follower, a companion, an information-gatherer—rather than one to be entrusted with reaching any conclusions off the back of their own intellect. What say you, Watson?"

I was so surprised to be asked that it took me quite a few seconds to gather my thoughts, and when I did, it was to contradict my great friend.

"Wilkinson suffers from several of Mycroft's faults, I am afraid. He is arrogant and rather too full of himself for my liking. As for Green, he may seem slow but he gets there, and he is a solid chap."

Holmes laughed.

"Solid between the ears, perhaps?"

Despite my reticence of mere minutes before, I felt my temper rise; it appeared to me that Holmes was mocking, not just Lestrade's lad, but the very nature of our own relationship, and I am afraid my voice was rather raised when I replied.

"I am willing to bet that Green will ultimately achieve a better overall performance rating when we come to tally them up," I said.

"Why wait?" Holmes replied. If he had seen my annoyance, it certainly did not register in his tone or manner. "Let us pair them together and give them a case. I too am willing to bet on the fact that Wilkinson will emerge as the principal: the thinker ahead of the gatherer."

"Are you suggesting a wager, Holmes?"

"A small one only. Shall we say a pouch of Turkish tobacco from Helms in the Strand?"

That might be a small matter to Holmes, but it was several days' worth of wages for me. However, as I have intimated, my dander was up, and besides, I had meant what I said about young Green; so I rose, and shook Holmes's hand on the matter.

The wager was sealed.

The very next morning, it being a Monday and one of the set days for training, Holmes insisted that I accompany him to Russell Square for the case allocation. We had a smoke in the briefing room while we waited for the provost's man to fetch the lads. Holmes had gone quiet again, so I used the time to reflect on the two recruits we had chosen for our little experiment.

Wilkinson came to the school via Mycroft's personal preference for recruiting smart public schoolboys with Firsts in Classics. He was tall, lithe, sure of himself—a bit too much so for my liking—and obviously knew that he had been born to lead. I have met plenty of chaps just like him both on the rugger field and in the service; some you take to, others remain just that smidgen too aloof to allow any camaraderie to develop.

Wilkinson was of the latter variety, although I will grant that he was more than smart enough for the task at hand.

Green came up through police training, a young constable from the suburbs, eager to get on. He kept himself to himself mostly. I knew him to be industrious and studious, with an almost encyclopaedic knowledge of certain matters such as London railway timetables and batting statistics. He had a keen eye, was the best shot of all the current recruits and, having seen him box at middleweight for the Yard's team, I knew he was a stocky little beggar who could handle himself well in a tight spot.

Before they were shown into the room, I was feeling quite happy with my prospects for the outcome of the wager, but when they entered I began to wonder whether I had indeed chosen wisely. Wilkinson was as prim and proper as ever—starched white shirt, well-pressed black wool suit and shoes shined to a gleam. Green, on the other hand, had obviously been called away from a job at hand, and still wore the rubber apron used in the laboratory. His hands were dotted with purple spots where he'd been clumsy with the iodine, his eyes were red and rheumy—some chemical irritant that he'd allowed himself to get too close to—and there was a fresh acid burn on his left shoe. I noticed Holmes stifle a smirk as the lads stood in front of us.

"We have a case for you," Holmes began, and both the students smiled, then stiffened to attention. "You are to work together on this one, and you will be acting as representatives of Scotland Yard, so do try to at least act the part. You will proceed straight from here to 224 King's Road in Chelsea. There has been a burglary—that is all that is known at this stage. You will report back here in twenty-four hours. I expect the case to be completely resolved. Dismissed."

Having not said a word since entering, both departed. I noted a distance between them. There had been no eye contact, no acknowledgement of each other. My hopes of them working in tandem to reach a successful conclusion were receding rapidly, but it was early days yet. I waited until the door closed behind them before quizzing Holmes on the details of the case.

"I did not hear of a burglary. Is this a real case, or have you set up another of your surprises?"

"No, Watson, there will be no tricks this time. It is a simple enough matter, I am sure—a broken window, a neighbour's report of an intruder, and a few trinkets missing from a gentleman's London home. I suspect an opportunist thief, surprised in the act. The trinkets will be in the hands of a pawnbroker even now and should be quickly enough recovered—indeed, so should the perpetrator. I expect Wilkinson's report in a matter of hours."

"Then I shall expect the same of Green," I replied with a smile. "Are we to wait in Baker Street?"

"No, I think we might travel incognito to the King's Road, just to keep an eye on things. I am most curious as to how this will play out."

To travel incognito required us to don disguises. Fortunately the Russell Square wardrobe and stagecraft room was rather well appointed; there were several sturdy armoires filled with clothes. The accoutrements of various disguises lay scattered on a desk with a large mirror, and there was even a single armchair sitting beside a tall, well-stocked bookcase, should a wait be necessary.

"Which would you prefer?" Holmes asked. He held up a heavy overcoat in one hand and an older, tattered tweed jacket in the other. "A sailor home from the North Atlantic run? Or maybe an itinerant labourer looking for work? I think labourers today—the King's Road is a known short-cut for passing trade."

Holmes moved over to the mirror and started applying makeup to render his face darker and more unwashed. I then spent a most uncomfortable ten minutes allowing Holmes to apply some rather noxious-smelling gloop to my hands and face. After that, he got me to choose some clothing for my own disguise, which thankfully proved cleaner and less smelly than it looked to be. Lastly, he made me ditch my pipe and my cigarette case.

"All would betray us immediately, even to an untrained eye like Wilkinson—or Green—I'm afraid," he said. "But your faithful companions shall be safe enough here until our return. And, fear not, we shall not be short of smoking materials." He handed me a threadbare tobacco pouch and some rather rough papers. "An old soldier like you can surely roll his own, given the makings?"

I took my revolver from my discarded jacket and put it in the pocket of my new, rather more threadbare, apparel. Holmes, thankfully, did not try to dissuade me, and I felt more comfortable in the disguise knowing that the weapon was there should I need it.

By the time we were ready to face the city, Wilkinson and Green had a good head start on us; and that was made longer still by the fact that Holmes refused to take a carriage: men of reduced means would be walking, not riding. We had an enforced walk, almost a trot, down to Victoria then on to Chelsea, and I was quite relieved when we finally arrived on the pavement across the street from 224 King's Road.

We had a clear view into the front parlour. Wilkinson and Green were inside talking to a small, rather stout, man. He had his back to us, but I saw he was going grey and had a prominent bald patch on his crown. I took him to be the victim of the burglary. Green seemed to be doing most of the talking, and was more animated than I had ever seen him.

Holmes and I watched for several minutes, then Holmes seemed to come to a decision.

"They are taking too long over this part of the matter. Let us have a look around the back and see if we can find a clue to hurry them along somewhat."

I did not find this action at all unusual. It is often the case in such training exercises that we are required to move things along in order to ensure a conclusion. After all, this was a real burglary we were dealing with, and the poor victim should not have to suffer any further due to the inexperience of our investigators.

I followed Holmes to the rear of the property. We had to clamber over a tall brick wall, and then drop down into what was a most unkempt plot of garden, the grass having been left to its own devices for some years and the blackthorn threatening to overrun the area completely. But Holmes immediately started to pore over the ground.

"Our intruder came this way . . . remain behind me, Watson. And try not to step on anything important."

We had gone barely five steps before Holmes stopped completely, and bent over a barer patch of ground where it was more mud than grass. I saw a single footprint, clearly outlined. Holmes suddenly looked concerned.

"There is more to this than meets the eye, Watson. Our intruder was far too well shod to be a common criminal. Hurry. Our charges may already be in over their heads in this matter."

We made quickly for the rear door. To my great relief it opened when I turned the handle, and rushed inside, making rather a sudden appearance in the front parlour. Both the house owner and Wilkinson seemed startled at our entrance, but Green was not in the slightest bit taken in by our disguises.

"You are just in the nick of time, Mr Holmes, sir. We must arrest this man forthwith. I suspect him of being a German spy."

Of course, young Green's statement caused an outburst of indignation from the older gentleman, but to my surprise Holmes hushed him immediately to silence.

"I would like to hear the lad out, sir," Holmes said. "Unless you would rather explain down at Scotland Yard why you yourself did not report the crime—or, indeed, you could always tell me right now what you might have in your possession that would be valuable to a Russian military officer?"

The man reached for his pocket. At the same instant I reached for my revolver, but the blasted thing had got caught up in a torn lining in the old jacket, and the extra second it took me to free the weapon was almost fatal. The man had a small pistol—an American Derringer by the look of it—in his hand and, without hesitation or speaking a word, fired straight at Holmes, who went down in a heap.

Green was first to react, flinging himself forward and tackling the man around the knees, bringing him down—but the young policeman got a rap on the head with the butt of the pistol for his trouble and the man rolled away. I got off a shot but was slightly off balance, and only managed to take a chink out of the plaster of the wall, then he was off and away out through the front door.

Green was clambering groggily to his feet. Wilkinson still hadn't moved, having been rooted to the spot since our arrival, and Holmes groaned in pain as he tried to rise. I went immediately to his side. Blood ran down his sleeve, and he'd gone quite pale, but he would not let me minister to him.

"No time for that. I'll be fine, and will be along behind you when I can. Get after him, Watson. And ask Green what he knows—it seems your lad has taken the lead in our little game."

He grimaced again at that, and clutched his arm, then waved me away.

"Go, quickly. There's something of great import going on, and we need to find out what."

Green was already on the move towards the door and I followed, having to almost drag Wilkinson from his stupor to get him moving. Holmes was getting to his feet as the three of us went out through the front door, just in time to see our quarry turn a corner to the west and disappear from view.

We followed as quickly as we could manage, but he already had a good lead on us and we were hard pushed to keep him in sight. He almost eluded us when he leapt into a carriage in Cheyne Walk, and we were lucky to catch one that was coming up behind. The three of us squeezed into a seat made for two, I offered the driver a florin if he didn't lose our quarry, and then we were off and away, clattering over the cobbles.

I got the battered pouch of tobacco out and rolled a smoke for Green and myself—Wilkinson did not partake. The taller lad seemed most contrite, and attempted to apologize to me for his lack of action earlier. I patted him on the shoulder.

"Don't worry, lad, it happens to the best of us—once. Take it as a lesson."

He merely nodded in reply, then went back into his shell. I looked out of the carriage window. Our quarry was ahead of us, now proceeding along the Embankment, heading east into town. The man's carriage did not appear to be in any hurry, which convinced me that he thought he was no longer being followed. Hoping that I had time to get an answer, I asked Green to explain how he had marked the man as a wrong 'un.

"It was the books at first," he said, chewing on the cigarette as if it were a stick of liquorice. Wilkinson harrumphed, but Green went on, unperturbed. "The English books were neatly stacked, and dusty, but the German-language ones, several shelves of them, in fact, were all out of line and dust free, as if well handled. Then there was the footprint at the back door, the one left by the intruder—obviously military— Eastern European, I thought, and if Mr Holmes says they are Russian then I shall bally well take his word for it.

"So there was that, then the fact that the man himself was reticent about talking at all about what had been taken—and his accent, faint but unmistakable once you looked for it. And then there's this . . . I found it in the grate among a pile of ashes—this one didn't quite burn through."

It was a single sheet of paper, containing a word square—five letters by five letters. I had seen Holmes work on something similar in the past.

"A Playfair cipher?"

Green nodded.

"So I believe. But we don't have the means to decode it without the key—or more squares. But consider the calligraphy, Dr Watson; the overly black, heavy use of the Roman monumental lettering is distinctively Germanic."

"And this is all you have to go on?"

"One more thing; I found this in the book beside the fireside chair."

He took a ticket stub from his pocket and handed it to me. The destination was torn off, but there was a date and time—3.35 p.m. two days previously, out of Waterloo. "One of the three locomotives to leave Waterloo at that time is the Exeter train, stopping at Salisbury. And there is currently a large military training exercise going on in the area—the kind of exercise our continental friends would be most interested in. Taken as a whole with the rest, it is enough to give us a working theory, is it not?"

In that moment he sounded so like Holmes I was quite taken aback, but I had the presence of mind to congratulate him.

"Whether you have the truth of it or not, the mere act of accusation was enough to flush the man out, and sometimes, that is enough." I puffed at my cigarette before continuing. "So we have a German, possibly, perhaps even probably, a spy—being burgled by a Russian wearing military boots. What was he after?"

Wilkinson piped up, for we were now heading into areas where he was more comfortable: the shadowy world that was Mycroft's domain.

"It must be a secret of some worth, given that the German was willing to kill Mr Holmes to keep it so. But merely the details of our manpower and firepower on Salisbury Plain would be useful in the wrong hands."

That much I did agree with.

"We must catch our man, lads—catch him—and the Russian, too, if it can be managed."

"But we know next to nothing about either man," Green said.

"We know where our German is—that is a start," I replied, and ground my cigarette out in the ashtray on the carriage door, just as we came to a halt and the cabbie banged on the roof. He called down.

"St Paul's, sir. He's stopped at the cathedral steps."

I gave the driver an extra shilling for his trouble as we disembarked, and made sure the pistol would not become entangled in my pocket again should it be needed in a hurry. Using the carriage itself as cover, I peered around it and spotted our quarry immediately, standing on the steps of the old cathedral, lighting a pipe and clearly waiting for someone.

Of necessity, I had to think quickly, for our man had seen all three of us all too recently, so we would not be able to approach without being recognized, and we already knew he was armed, and more than ready to shoot if cornered. I did what I could to wipe the stage makeup from my face with a torn fragment of the jacket lining and swapped jackets with Wilkinson. I sent Green left and Wilkinson right, with orders to go wide to flank our quarry on both sides.

"Keep an eye open, chaps," I said. "There may be a veritable nest of vipers here. We need to see whom he meets and then follow them. If one turns up, you both tail him afterwards; if there are two, take one each and I'll take charge of watching our German. Report to Baker Street when you can. If neither Holmes nor I are there, then get to the provost's office back at the Square. Understood?"

They looked tense and slightly ashen, for this was rather closer to actual peril than they might have expected. But I saw in their eyes that they were both ready for action and, besides, with Holmes out of the game for an unknown amount of time, I had no other choice but to pursue my current course.

In the end, my caution was unwarranted. I had just finished another cigarette—still keeping myself hidden behind the carriage and being watched by an increasingly bemused driver—when the German was joined on the steps. The newcomer was as tall as Wilkinson, and from the same mould: straight-backed, assured and immaculately dressed, all the way down to his military-issue boots. The newcomer took something out of his jacket—a small book, leather bound, which was all I could make out at that distance, then put it away. The German spoke in reply, and put out a hand. I expected a deal to take place, but the Russian, for I was sure it was he, had other ideas. He reached forward, grabbed the proffered hand, and tugged the smaller man towards him.

In the same movement, the Russian flicked open a cut-throat razor—I saw it glint in the sunlight—and slit the German under the chin nearly from ear to ear. He dropped the body, bent over it briefly, apparently to slip a small object into the jacket of the motionless figure, then quickly walked away, as if he had not a care in the world. People in the vicinity were so shocked by this cold act of murder they simply stood and stared in horror.

I waited until the Russian turned his back on me, whereupon I waved Wilkinson and Green to follow him. As for myself, I went to see what might be done for the German but, judging by the blood already pooling below the body on the steps, I was too late. The German was quite dead. By this time, members of the public had recovered somewhat and began to cry out and point at both myself and the fallen man. A police whistle close by told me I did not have much time, so I quickly went through the cadaver's pockets and found the small notebook the Russian had given to him—the lure to get him here. I took it. I also found the small Derringer, which I left in place. Then the police arrived, and I had some explaining to do.

It was only when I invoked Holmes's, then Lestrade's names, and was recognized by one of the sergeants who had recently arrived, that I stopped being considered a possible suspect. And it was half an hour after that before—with my story, such as it was, told—I was allowed to be on my way.

I caught a hansom cab back to Baker Street. During the journey I managed a quick look at the notebook I'd lifted from the German's corpse, but could not make head nor tail of it. The pages were all covered in the five-by-five letter squares—thirty or more of them. But although I could not decipher it, such a profusion was good news, for I knew enough about Playfair ciphers to understand that having more of them greatly increased the chances of breaking the code, especially in the hands of a master code-cracker like Sherlock Holmes.

I found Holmes in his fireside chair. His left arm was in a sling, his colour pale and almost alabaster, apart from two high points of red on his cheeks. Nevertheless, he had his favourite pipe in hand and did not seem in undue discomfort. And he broke into a smile when I handed him the notebook and the charred piece of paper that had been retrieved from the fireplace grate in the house in Chelsea.

I joined him in a pipe, and we caught up with each other's deeds since our parting. He did not seem too surprised that the German was dead.

"Young Green had the right of it. Let me guess—he spotted the books, the footprint at the door, the ashes in the grate—and he found something incriminating. Am I right?"

I had to smile again at Holmes echoing Green, just as the younger man had echoed his mentor earlier.

"Right on all counts. Our man had been in Salisbury these two days past. Spying on our military was Green's guess."

"And it might have been mine, too," Holmes said, turning the notebook over, "had the Russian not given this back to us. He went to so much trouble to get it, then let it go again, far too easily. I smell a rat, Watson—a very big rat."

Holmes's attention was fully focused on the cipher for a while. I bathed, changed into more comfortable clothes, then sat by the fire, smoking and fretting as to the whereabouts of our charges. By then, I was rather regretting sending them after a man who had proved himself quite capable of cold-blooded murder. When a telegram arrived later that afternoon, I almost grabbed it from Mrs Hudson's hands before she was barely in the door.

WE HAVE HIM UNDER SURVEILLANCE. STOP.
25 VAUXHALL BR. ROAD. STOP
PLEASE ADVISE. STOP.
W&G. STOP.

"South side, next to the railway station," Holmes said as he read the note. "We had best get down there and see what's what."

He tried to rise, but the red at his cheeks spread to his whole face and his eyes fluttered, as if he might faint away at any moment.

"I'll go," I said. "You are not fit for duty, old chap. Solve the bally cipher. I'll be back before you're done with it—there is another wager for you."

I left Holmes by the fire and made my way out to hail a carriage.

Immediately on alighting in Vauxhall, I was approached by an urchin.

"They done given me a penny to tell you they is upstairs in the Queen's Arms," he said. "And they done said you'd 'ave a farthing for me, too."

I doubted they'd said any such thing, but I obliged the lad in his request and sent him on his way. It seemed that Holmes's methods were spreading even beyond the deductive process.

Green and Wilkinson were indeed set up in the room above the bar, keeping a watch on a tailor's shop across the road.

"He went in at two-thirty," Wilkinson said. "And he hasn't come out."

"Rear door?"

Green shook his head.

"The place backs on to the river, Doctor. A fifteen-foot drop to the waterline, and too shallow for a boat to come in close. I don't think he'd want to get his boots that muddy."

Once again I praised them for their work so far, and settled in to join them in the wait. As I had with Holmes, I brought them up to date on the matter in hand, and Green was most put out when I told him about the cipher, as he liked nothing better, he declared, than getting lost in a good puzzle.

We sat there until the light started going from the sky. I noted a certain warming of the relationship between the two students: there was none of the frosty aloofness from before. Moreover, they seemed to be working well in tandem, almost anticipating each other in conversation. I made a mental note to report this new-formed bond to Holmes.

Then I had to start paying attention, for there was a sudden flurry of activity at the door of the tailor's shop across the street.

I do not know what I had expected, but it was certainly not Lestrade, with a squad of officers, even now intent on breaking down the shop door. We gave up all pretence of hiding and went out into the street to join the men from the Yard.

"We had a tip-off," Lestrade's sergeant, Clarke, told me. "Anarchists making bombs, they said."

We went in with them. At first it looked to be exactly what it seemed, a small, reputable tailor's catering to city clerks, in the main. But the downstairs area was another matter. We did indeed find evidence of criminal activity—gunpowder, fuses and detonators, along with several rifles—but to my eye at least, it all looked far too neat; far too convenient. I started to smell Holmes's very big rat when we found two German passports next to the weapons, one of them belonging to the dead man I'd last seen on the steps of St Paul's Cathedral.

Wilkinson located a trapdoor to a sub-basement level that led out into a long wooden boardwalk that ran, hidden from the outside, beneath the southern embankment and away into the gloom as far as we could see. Our man could have been off and gone hours before. The only evidence he had ever been there was a metal cleat under the trap-door—the kind of thing a man who likes to take care of his boots might have attached to the heel to prevent them from wearing down too quickly.

Apart from that, there was no sign of our Russian.

We made our way back to Baker Street with our tails between our legs—at least three of us did: Lestrade, who accompanied us, was feeling rather pleased with himself, having, to his mind, foiled a plot before it could be properly born.

Holmes soon deflated any feeling of well-being our inspector might have had.

"I have solved the cipher," he said. "And made a thorough

investigation of the notebook the Russian was so keen to have us uncover. It seems there is a plot under way: the first part of which is to implicate the Germans, and the second is the part we now need to concern ourselves with most urgently. I believe there will be an assassination attempt on the queen—and I believe it will be tomorrow or the day after."

Of course that bald statement needed explanation, and Holmes, always pleased to have an audience, took his own good time in getting to it. Despite his movements being hampered because of his injured arm being cradled by the sling, he made a great show of cleaning out and lighting a fresh pipe before he finally explained the cipher. He showed us how it did indeed detail how the German had been watching troop and artillery movements on Salisbury Plain. Then he went on to explain why the Russian had both stolen it and given it back to us.

"It has been altered—or, at least, added to," Holmes said, turning to the rear of the notebook. "These last five pages are in a different hand: heavier on the pen stroke, less assured in the script. The Russian, having given us the German, wants us to believe that there is a plot against the queen's life. See here." He ran a finger over the last of the word squares. "This is a diary of the queen's movements over the last week, and for the next few days. She is due at Waterloo Station to name a new train tomorrow, then at Ascot for the races the day after. I believe our man will try to make his move at one or the other—then, news will spread that the Germans have killed the queen; the Empire will be in uproar and, as surely as I sit here now, war will follow. After which, Mother Russia can simply walk in and rule the ruins."

We all took this in in complete silence.

"Why would he tell us where he will make his move?" Lestrade asked.

"Because he believes we suspect the Germans—not him," Green replied before Holmes could. "He is confident that he is above us. Smarter, stronger, more cunning, and he cannot conceive that the likes of us could get the better of him. I know the type."

Holmes smiled at that. "As do I. We can only hope that his confidence shall be his undoing. There is only one matter I do not understand, and that is this last square—it is five pairs of numbers, and I cannot, for the life of me, construe any meaning from them. I do believe they have been put there just to taunt us."

"May I?" Green asked.

Holmes passed the lad the notebook. Green took one look and passed it straight back.

"It will be Ascot," he said. "They're not numbers, they're odds, and they are the odds of the past five winners of the Queen's Cup, which will be ridden at three-thirty precisely, the day after tomorrow. That's where we'll find our Russian."

Again the rest of us took this in in silence, until Holmes applauded softy.

"Well done, young Green. You have retained facts that I have discarded as of no import, and you have proved me wrong in having done so."

Green blushed.

"I merely look at things and I can remember them, Mr Holmes, sir," he said. "Any import therein is purely coincidental."

"Coincidental or not, you may just have saved the queen's life," Holmes said, and Green, still blushing, shook Wilkinson by the hand when it was offered.

Of course, the matter was far from settled. There was still the small business of actually catching the Russian and preventing a national disaster. Green and Wilkinson were both disappointed at being sent back to Russell Square for the duration.

"You've had quite enough excitement for a while, lads," Lestrade said. "And this is now a job for older, more experienced hands. I shall see that a commendation is written into your records, and you have the thanks of us all."

Holmes, whether through good manners or actual agreement, did not contradict the inspector on the matter. The lads left us, both of them looking rather hangdog, if not actually depressed at the turn of events.

But we had no time to consider their feelings. The next thirty-six hours were a whirl of activity, with sleep only taken when necessary or in a rare quiet moment; it was all I could do to get Holmes to rest. Lestrade had all the Yard's resources set on finding the Russian, to little avail. The queen herself was warned of the threat but refused to change her itinerary one jot, having survived numerous threats—and actual attempts—on her life during her long and illustrious reign. We could only endeavour to ensure her protection was adequate against any attack, and maintain the strongest possible vigilance at both Waterloo Station and Ascot racecourse.

I did allow myself a small snifter of brandy after the queen's trip to the railway station passed without incident. We had been there, of course. I could not keep Holmes away, although I insisted that he should keep movement to a minimum and that we took a carriage the full distance in both directions. In any case, the Russian did not show.

The next morning we rose early and made our way to Ascot for the final chapter.

I had been to the races before, of course, numerous times, but this was a first while on the job, and I took much more note of my surroundings. It was a bright, clear, early summer's day, and the great and the good were out in force. Ladies sashayed in new dresses, men wore tall hats and tails and smoked great thick cigars too big for their mouths, barkers hawked their wares and bookmakers took money from everyone, regardless of their social standing. And among the throng, men of the Yard, Mycroft's shadows and constables in uniform all mingled and kept a watchful eye.

Holmes and I sat together at the rear of the Royal Enclosure, with a clear view of everyone who might attempt to enter or leave. I knew Holmes had a small pistol inside his sling, and I had my service revolver in a shoulder holster, already loosened should rapid access be required. Holmes had quite lost all his colour again; the wound clearly pained him, but he refused all medication on the grounds that he needed a clear head should action be necessary.

We smoked in silence as the wealthier patrons started to fill the enclosure. Several races passed but I paid no attention to the winners or losers—all my attention was on the crowd, looking out for our tall Russian. Lestrade paced, chewing on a cigarillo, in the cordoned-off area in front of the grandstand—after the main race the queen herself would go down there to present the cup, and we were all agreed that was the moment when she would be at her most vulnerable. As the time for that presentation approached, I felt myself grow ever more tense, and even a smoke and a swig from a hip flask did little for my nervous disposition.

The race started on time. I will say one thing for racecourses, their organizational capabilities are second to none, and I have often thought they might do well given a chance at running the country. Neither Holmes nor I had an eye on the horses. I watched the crowd and noticed, when I turned, that Holmes was always watching the skyline. We had talked about the possibility of a sniper, and were both heartily glad that Sebastian Moran was no longer a problem, as this perfidious sharpshooter still languished in jail, for he might have caused us rather a lot of difficulty in such an open situation.

The race finished. The crowd cheered mightily. My nerves were as tense as they had been on any campaign in the Afghan hills as we rose from our seats to follow Her Majesty down from the Royal Enclosure towards the open ground where she would receive horse and jockey.

I saw Lestrade arrange his men in a tight ring around the queen—he'd chosen tall officers and they quite dwarfed our monarch, but also provided a great deal of extra protection, a wall of flesh between her and a possible assailant. Holmes and I followed close behind, and four of Mycroft's men followed behind us. At that moment I doubt anyone in the Empire was as well protected as our queen.

I was just starting to think that the event was going to pass without further excitement, when the first shot echoed around the course with a crack like thunder.

The Yard man immediately ahead of Holmes fell aside. The top half of his head had been taken apart by the shot—someone was using a high-velocity rifle, and I knew immediately that we were in deep trouble. Holmes reacted faster than I did. He stepped forward immediately, standing tall, filling the spot vacated by the dead officer and putting his frame directly in line of the next shot—one that surely had to come at any moment.

I turned and drew my pistol, already knowing that our sniper would be too far away for it to be of much use. My eye caught a movement high up on the roof of the grandstand.

Three figures were engaged in a tussle. The sniper had ensured the sun was at his back—as such, it was now in my eyes, obscuring my view. Another shot rang out, but nobody fell, so the bullet had obviously gone far and wide. Lestrade and his men scuttled away, taking the queen with them, back under the grandstand roof and into safety. Holmes came to my side and we watched as the three men continued to tussle overhead.

"It seems our lads were not content to take 'no' for an answer," Holmes said drily, and with some amazement I knew he must be right. Even as I realized it was indeed our recruits, the taller of the three, Wilkinson, threw a punch which the Russian—for it must be he—ducked, only for Green to throw an uppercut that fair took the man off his feet and sent him sailing into empty air.

The Russian assassin landed with a thud less than five yards from my feet, but he was already most certainly dead when I reached him.

We took Wilkinson and Green's report back at Baker Street over some rather excellent Scotch and some of Mrs Hudson's Scottish confection-ery. Neither of the lads seemed in the slightest bit contrite.

"We were not about to be overlooked like a pair of duty constables," Green declared. "After all, it was us that uncovered the German connection in the first place, was it not?"

I saw that Holmes had noted Green's use of the plural instead of the singular, as Wilkinson continued. "So when we left here, I suggested we have a look around some cobblers' shops, for surely the Russian would be looking to repair his boots?"

Green took up the tale. "And, right enough, we found his trail; he got his repairs done in a small place round the back of Chancery Lane."

Once again Wilkinson carried on seamlessly. "And after that, it was an easy matter to follow him and catch him in the act. Dashed sorry we weren't fast enough to stop that first shot. But we didn't want to get too close too early for fear of scaring him off completely."

"You did well, lads," Lestrade said, and both of them beamed, and gave each other a hearty handshake.

"Well, Watson," Holmes began drily, "it seems we were both wrong. It looks like the optimum number of crime fighters is two, after all. They make a good team."

"Just like the pair of us, Holmes."

He nodded. "Although I do believe the wager goes in your favour, Watson, if only for young Green's superior deductive technique."

I thought I had talked him out of that conclusion over several more glasses of Scotch, but the very next morning I found a fresh pouch of Turkish tobacco in my pocket that could only have come from one place, although Holmes never spoke of it again.

The Gargoyles of Killfellen House
Cate Gardner

—

Placing the magnifying glass to the crushed leaf, I attempted to discern who had stomped on it, and whether they had done so playfully or in anger. I had not yet determined the crime. Gravel dug into my knees, attempting to hamper my investigation. If I recalled correctly, the leaf belonged to a clump of trees near the Folly entrance where Victoria, Ted and I used to spend our summers. Laughter danced over the bushes. *Mother.*

As I gathered my things, the leaf broke beneath my clumsiness. Victoria turned the corner ahead of Mother and Mr James Hendrick (our cousin). If gaining a suitor turned you into a wilting flower, as it had done my sister, then I would settle for spinsterhood.

When we were younger, much younger, we would climb on to the roof and, along with the legendary gargoyles, would peer down at arriving guests. I named them Tweedledum and Tweedledee – the gargoyles that is, not the guests. As Victoria was six years older than me, I suspect she played along with my games rather than necessarily enjoying them. Sometimes our brother, Edward, would join us. Poor Ted.

Although I had not seen action, I could imagine the rage of guns and cannon fire. As a squirrel rushed by, the remains of the leaf catching in its tail, I imagined it a rat fattened by the flesh of fallen soldiers.

"I've found her. I've found Adrienne," Mr Hendrick said, as if Mother and Victoria hadn't already seen me.

Again, Mother laughed. As if I were an exhibit in their zoo, Mr Hendrick, my sister's prospective suitor, stood at the curve in the path and pointed at me. Although I'm not prone to thoughts of inflicting injury, I wanted to snap his fingers and remove them from my sister's arm.

Mr Hendrick is Mother's nephew. I should point out, as Victoria is Mother's stepdaughter, marriage between my sister and my cousin is legal. Mother emphasises Victoria's step-ness often. Victoria's mother was beautiful. She keeps a photograph of her (Father's first wife) beside her bed. I would not say my mother is ugly, but I tire of her determination to interfere.

Father dismissed the newspaper and the advertisement I had circled. This was my fifth attempt.

Pushing his glasses up his nose, he said, "It is not suitable employment for young ladies."

I shook both fists and newspaper. "The world is changing, Father."

He rubbed the top of his nose and yawned. When it seemed there was no dissuading me from my argument, he leaned forward in his chair and took my hands, stilling their frustration. "It is not suitable employment for my daughter."

Throwing the newspaper across the table, and almost dislodging the lamp, I stomped towards the mantelpiece and reached for the unopened telegram. I couldn't touch it, although I almost invoked my brother's name by saying he would allow Ted to go to the School for Detection, where the great Sherlock Holmes tutored. There was no truth to it, though. Although Ted was not Father's legitimate son – Mother had also previously been married – he'd wanted Ted to run the estate for Victoria. He wouldn't have allowed him to leave any more than he would me.

"Enough foolishness," he said.

Sometimes Father scares me. I push him too far. At least, that's what Mother says. Running from the room would have made me appear weak. Instead, I retrieved the newspaper, righted the lamp, and headed to the roof where I could rant and rage, and only the gargoyles would notice. Oh, to be taught by the great Sherlock Holmes!

Although Mother and James stood directly below me, due to the stillness of the day their voices did not carry to the roof, forcing me to lean far forward. Beside me, Tweedledum wobbled but I righted him. Time must have weathered the gargoyle's base. At that moment, my investigation into its instability ventured no further. Then James laughed, and he sounded so much like Ted that I wanted to cry. If only Father would open the telegram. I ached to know what had happened to my brother.

He's dead. Will knowing the cause ease the pain of that?

Across the garden, the edge of Victoria's yellow dress poked from behind the hedgerow. I was certain neither Mother nor James knew that she was there. Out by the Folly, someone moved amongst the trees. I could not make out who it was. Mother's hands waved and, for a moment, it seemed that she raised her fists. What were they chattering about? Mother hates to talk of the War and of the returning young men, of whom James is one. It's obvious the War has scarred him. He walks with a limp. He never mentions Ted.

Sometimes, Mother gets confused and calls him Ted. Then she hides in her room and cries.

Sobs pulsed through the wall dividing Victoria's bedroom and mine. I hugged my knees and rocked on the bed, causing the springs to complain. Victoria's mood had settled to low, Mother verged on hysteria, while Father was uninterested in all, and I . . . I just wanted to leave. I pressed my hands to my ears. Victoria had so much to cry about – her past was dissolving, her future would be set by others.

Getting out of bed, I knocked on the dividing door.

"Come in."

As I opened the door, Victoria wiped her eyes on the hem of her sleeve. If she attempted composure, she failed. I perched on the edge of her bed. I recalled the time when I used to climb under the covers with her, and she'd read me stories.

I said, "Tell Father you don't want to marry him."

"Ha! Father doesn't listen to us, Adrienne. And your mother is set on the marriage."

I pressed my hand to the folded newspaper article secreted in my pocket. "This is not Father and Mother's day. We have some freedoms."

I wanted to believe that.

"If we are free, why are you still here? You pester Father for permission to go to that school but you don't pack a suitcase." Victoria coughed into her sleeve; a cough that caught her throat and refused to let go. "I would rather die than marry your cousin."

"Take that back."

She sobbed then. Sobbed, coughed, and almost brought on a fever. I pulled her to me, her cries shaking through my body. It used to be that Victoria would sit with me until I slept; now it was my turn to do that for her.

As silence took over the house, I crept up into the attic and out through the window on to the roof. The night was clear and the moon full; a white handkerchief lay caught between roof tiles. Someone else had been here. I looked along the roof, expecting to find someone huddling behind a chimneystack. The roof belonged to me, to Victoria, to Ted. As I made to converse with the gargoyles, to ask playfully if they had seen anyone, I knew something was wrong. The tilt of the roof remained familiar, the vista brighter than usual perhaps, but that wasn't it.

The gargoyles were gone.

I must have lost my direction. I must have wandered to the wrong side of the roof. No, the driveway lay beneath me. Both Tweedledee and Tweedledum were gone. Family legend stated that if the gargoyles of Killfellen House flew away, the ladies of the house would wither and die.

I refused to do either.

Raising the alarm at eleven-thirty at night was perhaps a little excessive. In my defence, I didn't expect my sister to scream and prove said alarm. My intent had been for us to investigate this mystery together, so that she would find intrigue and forget her troubles. Instead, her wailing brought Father, three maids and James Hendrick. Soon, the entire household knew that the gargoyles were missing.

"Has anyone a handkerchief?" I asked, determining that whoever dropped the handkerchief on the roof would prove the culprit.

Several present readied handkerchiefs, and my examination of them proved no help at all. *If only Father would allow me to study under Mr Holmes.* Father, James, several maids and the butler, Andrews, headed into the front courtyard to investigate. I suppose they expected to find the gargoyles smashed on the ground. No one believed yet that they could have flown away.

It would be impertinent of me to ask if this was my cue to faint. Instead, a maid obliged. Her legs gave way beneath her. As far as I was aware, the curse didn't mention staff.

The butler said, "Apologies m'lord, but she's not been well this day long and we have two others in bed with this influenza. They say it's carried over from Spain."

"Why has no one informed . . ." Father started to say, but Andrews shooed the maids away and followed them.

With Father preoccupied with the mystery of the missing gargoyles, and Mother and Victoria having taken to their beds, I set about packing a bag. My sister would think herself into death just to prove the legend true. No one can prophesy such things.

This time I did not ask for my father's permission.

I hadn't been in London since before the outbreak of the Great War and, although I had been young and impressionable then, and intimidated by the city, it frightened me more now. Evidence of Zeppelin raids still ravaged the streets. Broken buildings – blackened bricks around glassless windows, like kohl smeared around blind eyes. A rat scuttled across the feet of a young man in a tattered uniform, one sleeve empty and pinned to his shoulder. He asked a passer-by to light his cigarette. Yet such ravages would be nothing in comparison to the horrors that my brother and other men saw.

Having lived at Killfellen House, grand buildings don't usually intimidate me, and yet I cowered before 1 Russell Square. The enormity of what I was about to endeavour, and how it might come to failure, almost caused me to turn around. I steadied my nerves, however, and pushed through the doors and into the building. For a moment, I feared they would turn me away, but sometimes being the daughter of a lord, even a minor one, has its advantages.

I would meet Mr Holmes. Mr Sherlock Holmes.

Short. That's how Holmes left me feeling. Short. Made all the worse by his gazing down his long nose at me, which meant I tried all the harder to look up, standing on tiptoes until I appeared ridiculous and almost wobbled forward. I think Holmes sneered at that, but I hoped he didn't.

"Your mother is living. Your sister is living," Holmes said. "You admit that their hysteria is the cause of this possible illness, if not this dreaded influenza. Mrs Hudson has contracted it and hasn't brought tea all week. Over the worst of it now, though, or so Watson insists. Silly woman was sleeping on the floor because she couldn't muster the energy to climb into bed. Well, until Watson moved her, that is. Yes, hysteria."

I nodded.

"Hmm! Yet, you wish me to investigate the disappearance of some ornamental features that are of no consequence—"

I interrupted. "Due to the legend attached to their disappearance, they are of great consequence. Especially if, whether it be a folly on the part of my mother and sister or not, it causes them to be very ill."

Holmes sat down upon a leather-backed chair and glanced at his colleague, Dr Watson. As Watson made to show me the door, and it seemed my interview was being terminated, Holmes leaned forward in the chair and tapped his fingers against his chin.

"What is it, Holmes?" Watson asked.

"If," Holmes said. "If I were to take you on as a pupil, Miss Killfellen, you must conduct any investigations in the manner I suggest and not—"

"Holmes," Watson said, with a touch of warning to his tone.

Holmes jumped up. "Let us convey ourselves to your residence, Miss Killfellen. There may be a crime here yet."

Dr Watson made a genial travelling companion, whereas Mr Holmes rested with his eyes closed and it appeared took no note of our conversation. However, I was certain Holmes listened, and thus I attempted to direct my answers in a manner that would interest and intrigue him. No doubt, Holmes was aware of my motives.

Having messaged ahead, there was a car to meet us at the station.

"Your father is mighty troubled," the chauffeur said. "He will not like it that you bring gentlemen with you."

"I am Sherlock Holmes and this is my esteemed friend Dr Watson, and we are more than mere gentlemen. No doubt your employer's troubles are weightier than our arrival."

We found Father in the library. All anger at my absconding had evaporated.

"They have taken to dying," Father said. "Your mother, your sister, and the curse is upon us."

I stooped before him and held his hands. "I am well, Father."

"That will not last. I thought the legend a foolish sideshow, a parlour trick, something to bring out when conversation grew stale, and to amuse and shock the women. I had not thought it true."

Holmes stalked the edges of the room, peering into glass cabinets and removing books from the shelves before placing them somewhere else. When he picked up the unopened telegram that concealed my brother's fate, I thought I'd stop breathing, but he did not open it. Instead, he held the envelope to the light and then placed it back on the mantel.

"Or that the ladies of your family would hold such stock in morbid prophecies. By the way, I am Dr Watson." He held out his hand, which Father shook. "Can I be of any assistance?"

"Yes, thank you."

"I must see my sister," I said.

Holmes caught my arm. "Watson and your father will attend to them. That is, if you wish to investigate this matter and bring about a suitable conclusion before your mother and sister find themselves in wooden boxes."

I did not wish to think of such things. "I'll show you the gargoyles. I mean, where the gargoyles were."

Dr Watson would, I know, give Victoria and my mother his expert attention.

"As the weather has been temperate," Holmes said, "with no rain or wind to sully evidence, I noted a pale portion of the stonework on either side of the entrance indicating missing structures. Also patches of dust on the ground at the base of the wall."

"From where they flew away," I said, because I'd put on a fool's head.

He ignored the comment.

"The wanderer returns with detectives in tow," James said, entering the room. For once Mother wasn't at his elbow. "We have a delightful mystery."

"That is to be evaluated," Holmes said.

Holmes walked more slowly than I'd expected him to. I assumed age and hoped investigation. After all, he has one of the greatest intellects of our time. As we reached the top of the stairs, about to enter the attic, he said, "Did you see anything untoward on the staircase?"

I was not to any degree nervous, and my mind was clear and focused, but it was evident that I'd missed something. I didn't want to disappoint him so, retracing my steps, I examined each rise.

Perhaps he was exasperated at my slowness or maybe he wanted to help, for he said, "Second stair from the top."

A-ha! Mortar dust of a colour I suspected akin with that found atop the roof and left by the missing gargoyles. I touched it, as if this would aid our investigation, and determined the maids would not have overlooked this; therefore, it had to have been left in the last few hours.

"The missing gargoyles came this way."

His lips seemed to twist at my comment, causing me to regret my choice of words. He did not give me a chance to rephrase my statement.

He said, "I hope by that you do not mean they flew, Miss Killfellen?"

As James was still at our heels, he added, "If you believe the legend, Mr Holmes, then they flapped their stubby wings. It is Mr Holmes?"

"That is indeed my name, Mr Hendrick."

"Is it not an inconvenience, having to deal with the whims of a fanciful female?" James asked.

I wanted to kick him.

"Should I meet such a person," Mr Holmes answered, "I shall let you know."

If I did not already admire the man, I would do so now. Crouching on the stairs, I removed a handkerchief from my pocket and gathered some of the mortar dust in it.

"For comparison," I said, because all great detectives do such things.

Holmes nodded. "Good, good. But, consider this, perhaps someone walked in the dust and carried it on their shoes. Do we have conclusive proof that the gargoyles were carried in this direction?"

I was wrong – that much was evident – but in what way? After all, the dust was clearly here. But, Holmes was right, that didn't mean the gargoyles were still in the house.

Despite my informing James that we were conducting a private investigation, he followed us into the attic and on to the roof. Ted would have done the same. In my weaker moments, I wished Ted had returned and that James had died in his stead. That is cruel of me.

I knelt at the edge of the roof, running my hand over the spot where Tweedledum should perch.

"They were purposefully removed," I said.

"And how do you deduce that?" Holmes asked.

"Apart from it's obvious," James said, rubbing his finger through loose, pale dust, brushing it on to his shoes. "Someone has taken a saw to this. Look how rough the edges are."

Like Victoria, I wanted James to go away. I wanted my world back to how it should be. "You seem to know a lot." It seemed I now investigated him.

I thrust my chin forward in defiance, drew my hands into fists, and looked James in the eye. If he had brought this disaster upon my family, I would tell Father, I would end his engagement.

James stepped back. "I shall leave you to your dalliances."

"Oh, we do not dally," Holmes said. "Do you often admire this view, sir?"

James pulled at his necktie; seemingly it had become unpleasantly tight all of a sudden. "It is my first time on the roof. I did not previously know of an entrance. In fact, it is very naughty of Adrienne to have kept it from me."

As if I would inform him of our hiding place! I looked down at the ground far below. Had the culprit pushed the gargoyles over the edge, then they would have smashed and left evidence other than dust.

Having being cornered as our suspect, James turned the evidence towards me. "I suspect Adrienne removed them and this is a double bluff. She wants to keep her sister here and thinks I will run away at any sign of weakness in my beloved. My dear, we will be living here. You will not lose your sister."

"Now you give her reason to steal them," Holmes said. "As to your never having been up here before, Mr Hendrick, I claim you are a liar. Prior to your conveniently knocking a weight of dust on to your shoes, I noted several specks caught within the weave of thread at the ridges and, as you walked, there was evidence underfoot as well. Plus, there was the handkerchief that you picked up and secreted in your jacket pocket, and the sure way you crossed the roof, when even someone as daring as myself took care with each step."

Mr Sherlock Holmes had solved the crime already! Although, to shine my own ego, I would have come to the same conclusion myself.

"A-ha! We have our culprit," I said. "Return the gargoyles and restore the health of my mother and sister." I grabbed James's arm and almost had us both tumbling from the roof.

"Unhand me," he cried.

Holmes intervened. "Alas, he is not the culprit and was unaware of the legend until someone told him. Your mother, evidently. She would delight in spilling all the family secrets to make herself and the house seem more interesting. She hoped to catch a fish who wished to be elsewhere."

"But you haven't met my mother."

"I already have the measure of her. She has taken to her bed but, unlike your sister, is enjoying a hearty meal, which I note the maid took to her room as we were entering the attic."

Screams echoed from within the house. I looked to Holmes but even he didn't seem to understand their cause.

I almost slipped down the attic stairs, feet tumbling over feet. Holmes followed, but James remained on the roof to contemplate Holmes's estimation of him. Two maids and a footman clustered outside Victoria's bedroom. The sight of them caused me to slow. Small steps that didn't want to discover the cause of the scream. One of the maids almost fainted at the sight of me, then rushed down the main staircase. It did not require a detective to know something was wrong. Holmes steadied my arm.

Within the room, Dr Watson stood by the window. Father knelt beside Victoria's bed. Father never knelt.

"She's dead," Dr Watson said. His pronouncement, though final, seemed a fairy tale.

He'd made a mistake. Sweet Victoria, so full of life, couldn't be dead. If this was the curse of the missing gargoyles, then perhaps Mother would be next and I would follow. No, such a stupid and self-ish thought. Somehow, I made it from the doorway to her bed and clasped her hand. Still warm; death had only recently visited. Not my sweet Victoria.

"It's a mistake," I said.

"I fear your powers of observation are lacking in this instance," Holmes said.

Again, Watson reprimanded, "Holmes."

I rubbed Victoria's hand, as if doing so would return her life.

"It may seem that Miss Victoria Killfellen succumbed to influenza or legend," Holmes said, almost dancing around the room. "However, this was born of foul play."

I gripped Victoria's hand. Who would hurt my sister? When Victoria was dying, the obvious suspect, James, had been on the roof with us. Of course, I wasn't certain at what point after death the body cooled. I had so much to learn and more reason to now.

"Out," Father said, his voice quiet at first, growing in crescendo. "Out!"

I didn't move. Father meant the others, and not me. Holmes also remained, conducting a quiet investigation. Father watched Holmes's movements, as if he couldn't believe the man hadn't left at his command. Before Father could again order him to leave, Holmes exited the room and appeared to follow a trail of some sort. I needed to discover who had done this to my sister. I could not utter the word *murder*.

"Wake up sleepyhead," I said, rubbing her unresponsive hand. "The act is over and the monster is gone."

Did my comment refer to James?

"You can wake up now; you don't have to marry him. We could hide on the roof and watch all the splendid guests arrive, or build a fresh den in the Folly, like we did when we were children."

Father placed his hand on Victoria's forehead. "I should tell Lady Killfellen."

Brushing his hand over mine, he left. A moment later, fresh screams filled the house. Mother. A sob caught in my throat. First Ted and now Victoria. Sherlock Holmes poked his head into the room.

"Tell me your impressions," he said.

My impressions? "My sister is dead and I do not know the cause."

"Sweep emotion aside. There is a case to be solved here, for the death is unnatural. See the dent in the pillow where your sister's head lay. If she has not stirred in some time, why is that indent still there? Also, the back of her hand is cut from where it slammed against the table. She fought her attacker."

I examined her hand. There was indeed a cut. I marvelled that I had not felt it when stroking her hand – and the fingernail of her middle finger was broken.

"I would not have thought to check for struggle." I'd been too blinded by the loss of my sister and at the disbelief that anyone could have wished her harm.

Watson stood in the doorway. "Play to his ego and you'll gain a great friend."

"There is deceit here, Watson. Deceit and murder and we will have an answer for it."

I traced the cut on Victoria's hand, the skin beginning to cool. If I had insisted on seeing her the moment I returned, then I could have saved her. Instead, I chased a thief. I never should have alerted the household about the missing gargoyles. I gave the murderer opportunity, motive.

"What else, Mr Holmes?" I asked. "Give me some clue so that I may detect my sister's murderer."

I would not have thought such a crime could occur at Killfellen House, our ancestral home for centuries. My father would cut down the culprit, if I didn't get to them first. Dear Victoria was the sweetest of us all.

"You always encouraged me to follow my heart; you reassured me that if I wished to be a detective, I could be. Now, I must honour that faith by finding your murderer." I kissed her cheek.

"Is anything out of place, alien to the room?" Holmes asked.

Apart from the visitation of death, I thought, but did not mention this. The photograph of Victoria's mother was lying face down, but that couldn't be a clue.

"Right," I said, wiping my hand under my nose. "Pillow and hand."

I looked at my sister's mouth. Even when ill, and although having no wish to attract our cousin, she still liked to look pretty. However, her lipstick was smudged. The sight sickened me. I lifted her head to remove the pillow. Dread caused my fingers to tremble as I turned it over. And there it was: a smear of lipstick on the reverse of the pillowcase. *No.* My knees gave way and someone caught me. Dr Watson. I mumbled my thanks.

"A chair, Holmes, bring a chair."

Holmes was too busy examining the pillow and its lipstick stain to bother with my fainting spell. Much more of my girlishness and he would refuse to tutor me. He removed a strand of red hair. One of mine, I thought.

As if reading my assumption, he said, "Different texture," and didn't elaborate further.

I regained my balance. If it would not mean tampering with the investigation, I would pull the sheet over my sister's face. This last image of her would haunt me.

"Are the crimes linked, Holmes?" Watson asked. "The missing gargoyles? This murder?"

Despite his advancing years, Holmes did a half-jump and clicked his heels together. I could find no jollity in this situation. Of course, to Holmes it was just another crime. Wood creaked as he opened the bedroom window and peered out across the garden. The day was too dreary for anyone to enjoy strolling out there, and besides, Mother lay in bed, and Victoria was . . . dead. Floorboards complained as I deserted Victoria and crossed the room.

"What do you see?" he asked, standing aside.

"This is not the time for tests."

"I disagree. This will prove the most important detection of your life."

Of that, I was aware. Let me not fail Victoria. At first, the scene was awash with my tears, but then I caught movement to the side of the hedgerow. Movement that appeared to me to be flying gargoyles.

Tweedledum and Tweedledee. Grief had unhinged me. Stone creatures could not take flight or climb from their parapets; a human hand was at work here. Again, the carvings gave the impression of moving within the greenery. Someone attempted to outfox the great detective Sherlock Holmes. By his reputation, I knew they would fail.

"We must give chase," Holmes said, unable to contain his childlike excitement.

Perhaps I shouldn't have abandoned Victoria. If trapped within their inert forms, the dead would require company, a soothing voice. In the end, I could offer little more than a final muttering of love and a kiss to her cheek. I hurried down the hallway, following Holmes and Watson, and I gave little thought to Mother's distress. My own pain threatened to become too weighty. Time enough to grieve later.

No one thought to stop us as we raced into the garden, chasing monsters. Only when our boots hit gravel did Holmes stop. He hushed us by placing his finger to his mouth. *Listen.* A rustle of leaves. Then we ran again, chasing our quarry. Holmes stepped aside to allow me to rush by. This was my investigation. This was my exam. If I passed this amidst my grief, he would oversee my studies, he would teach me to become almost as great as himself. Had I a weapon, I would bring the thief to harm.

If Holmes had not stopped me, I wouldn't have noted the cessation of sound. With the sudden silence there was no clue to chase, no hint of a ragged breath to match my own. At the base of the old water fountain lay a smashed gargoyle. I couldn't determine which.

As I stooped to examine the gargoyle, Holmes pulled at my arm.

"Do not disturb the scene until you have fully taken it in. Our killer hides within these pieces."

Did I exasperate Holmes as I do Father?

You will find your own way, Ted's parting words. I'd wanted to go to war in his stead and he'd laughed at that. *They do not send children. They do not send girls.* I'd kicked him in the shin for that latter comment and he'd laughed. We both had. Now all that remained of him were hidden words sealed within an envelope that no one dared open.

"Consider whether it broke here," Holmes said.

I looked at the scatter of stone against damp grass. "Yes."

"Your reasoning?"

I leant above the scene. "The spray of its pieces. They don't look placed."

Holmes stood beside me in order to make a more detailed examination of the ground. "You have a good eye, but you need more than that. Look again."

Now I felt under the magnifying glass. I could not take the responsibility for finding Victoria's murderer, and yet, I had asked for this. Whether or not I proved able, I thanked my will for bringing Mr Holmes here.

I said, "In their attempt to flee us they accidently dropped the gargoyle against the fountain edge. As we were at their heels, they did not have time to gather the evidence. They are afraid."

"They are afraid," Holmes repeated.

"Well of course they are," Watson said. "We will have them in our net. Which way, Holmes?"

Holmes picked up the gargoyle's nose, as if it held particular interest.

"We shouldn't have stopped," I insisted. "We should have continued the chase."

"They can still be caught," Holmes said.

Mr Holmes led us back to the house, while I was sure our villain lay ahead of us. I turned around intermittently, certain someone watched.

Despite having fallen into a supposed dead faint, Mother screamed for me. She held out her arms to embrace me, something she had not done in at least a decade, and offered sodden kisses to my cheeks as Father silently watched. I struggled against this new devotion. Besides, her hand smelled of Victoria's perfume and I could no longer bear its smell. I pulled away until she held only my fingers.

"Oh dear," Mother said, "I fear I shall follow my dear girl to the grave."

"Be quiet, woman," Holmes said.

Mother's spluttered response resulted in indignant gobbledegook. Even I thought him wrong to address her in such a brusque way.

"Please refrain from talking to Lady Killfellen in such a manner," Father said. "My wife is ill and distraught at the loss of our daughter."

"Your wife is a faker, sir. A faker and a murderer."

My mother dropped my hand at that, and drew up in the bed as if a rabid dog attacked her feet. For Holmes to throw such an accusation at her meant there would be some weight to it. Although I admired this man and thought him infallible, I wanted, in this instance, for him to be wrong.

Watson stood in the doorway, as if as a barrier to stop Mother from leaving should she attempt to flee. To me, she didn't look well enough to leave the bed.

"Who is this vile accuser?" Mother asked.

I replied, "It is Mr Sherlock Holmes, the great detective. He has come to help me solve the mystery of the missing gargoyles, and now, due to circumstances, Victoria's murder."

"Indeed. Well, find who stole the gargoyles and you'll find the murderer," Mother said. "I have been lying in bed the whole time and have witnesses to prove it so."

She glanced around the room. No witness declared themselves.

When Mrs Jenkinson, the housekeeper, was brought to give evidence as to whether a maid had accompanied Lady Killfellen all day, her reply proved damning.

"Maisie had to be called away, sir," Mrs Jenkinson said. "She was feeling poorly and madam said that," she glanced at Mother but looked sharply away again, "she couldn't sleep for the infernal racket – Maisie was coughing, sir – and to go away and clean something."

Sounded like Mother.

"Such nonsense," Mother said. "You all wish to force me into my grave. Oh, and what of their marriage? My poor James. He'll be heartbroken. I must find him."

Watson said, "Surely you are too weak?"

"Oh, dear Doctor, you are right, and yet in matters where I am . . . Well, I'm not certain of what I'm accused. Oh, and I have lost my daughter, and despite the risk to my health, I must visit with my nephew."

"The evidence," Holmes said, nodding to me as if he expected me to detail our findings.

"You cannot think Mother would have killed Victoria."

"The evidence," he insisted.

"Absolute nonsense," Father said.

"From the indent in the pillow and the smear of lipstick, we know that someone suffocated Victoria. There is also a cut on her hand and a broken fingernail indicating a struggle."

"What?" Father said. "You're saying someone murdered my daughter under my roof. This cannot be true. No one would dare."

Had he a shotgun, Father would have aimed it at us all.

"Someone did," I said. "I saw the evidence myself. Besides, people do not die because gargoyles are removed from a house, no matter how old the legend. You did not really believe that."

Father leant back against the wall. I'd never seen him look so defeated. Wearily, he said, "I believed that a woman could think herself to death due to superstition."

Holmes waved his hand. "Miss Killfellen, continue with the evidence."

"There was a red hair, the same as mine and . . . Mother's."

None of the maids had red hair.

A ridiculous notion to think that Mother would have killed Victoria. After all, the hair could be mine. It would not be evidence.

Mother snorted. "Then where is your proof that I murdered my dear daughter. If we are to go by a strand of hair, it could just have easily been Adrienne. You cannot convict me on such weak evidence;

besides, I have hugged my daughter and visited her many times to say goodnight. The hair, if proved to be mine, will have transferred then."

Mother never kissed Victoria goodnight. She turned away from my gaze because we both knew she lied.

What's more, her hands smell of Victoria's perfume. To speak of such things would be to condemn my mother. And yet what of the photograph placed face down on the nightstand?

Holmes took over. "Then there is the matter of the scratches on the back of your hand, brought about by Miss Killfellen's attempt to push you away. She fought you, Lady Killfellen. She fought as you suffocated her."

Mother sobbed then.

"Regarding the gargoyles . . ." Holmes began.

As if that crime was greater than murder!

I said, "But Mother would not have stolen them. Besides, the culprit was in the garden only moments before, and Mother was here."

It seemed I'd decided Mother capable of murder after all: something unthinkable to me just moments ago. What would become of her and of us? Did the world still turn in a way that we would be tarnished by her actions? Are reputations not so important, now that so many boys have been lost to war?

I ran. Dr Watson caught up with me in the library.

"I know this isn't the way a detective should react." I was close to weeping. "No wonder Father didn't want me to pursue the career."

"One would not expect to find that one's parent is the murderer. It is a rare occurrence indeed, although not as unusual as one would like."

"If she is the murderer."

"Holmes is convinced."

We would never recover from this. I looked to the unopened telegram on the mantelpiece. It would tell of how Ted had died in battle. It took an effort to cross the library and to pick up the weight of paper. Its heaviness was due to the news concealed and not to the paper's thickness. The mantel clock ticked in perfect rhythm, not missing a heartbeat.

"I could burn it and we'd never know," I said.

"Ah, that," Holmes said, for he'd entered the room without either of us noticing. "Open it. Open it."

Holmes struck me as dismissive in his tone. He already knew what it said. The how of it I couldn't figure.

"My brother is alive?" I asked, without opening the letter.

"I deduce that he is and I am never wrong."

As I tore into the envelope, aware that neither Father nor Mother would forgive me for doing so, I knew Holmes was right. Before I read the words, I knew Ted was alive, and yet I could not rejoice in it.

"He didn't die," I said.

Ted wouldn't be part of this conspiracy.

If I hadn't rushed off to London, if my ambition hadn't brought back Mr Holmes and Dr Watson, then Mother's crime would have gone undiscovered and I would not have opened the telegram. Victoria might not be dead. Could I have done something to change this outcome?

According to the telegram, after a bullet wound to the leg, they'd shipped Ted home to a sanatorium.

"Father knows."

Of course he did.

Holmes said, "The letter was steamed open and then resealed. See how the corner turns. Your mother is unaware, though. The tragedy of it is, because Lord Killfellen allowed Lady Killfellen to believe her son dead, she murdered his first-born when she refused to marry your cousin."

"Victoria said 'no'?" How had he come to this conclusion? "Victoria didn't refuse. She'd never refuse."

The great Sherlock Holmes had made a mistake.

"I repeat that she did refuse matrimony and as a consequence your mother suffocated her to ensure that her daughter – your good self

– would inherit the house. Unfortunately for your mother, you cannot marry your first cousin, so she had to abandon that part of the plan."

"So James stole the gargoyles to get back at Victoria?"

"I'm afraid that Mr James Hendrick is innocent."

What other explanation could there be? I placed the opened telegram on the mantelpiece, yet I was tempted to drop it into the fire. If Victoria had to be dead, then let it be someone other than Mother who murdered her. I still feared that the stigma of such a crime would ruin my family.

"You must follow the trail," Holmes said.

I had gained a brother and lost a sister. Further screams emanated from upstairs. They echoed within my chest. The fact that they were injected with hate proved pain enough. I had to find the gargoyle thief. They were the start of this.

"Does it matter who stole the gargoyles?" Watson asked.

Both Holmes and I spoke as one: "They are the catalyst in all this."

Outside, the air had cooled. First, I returned to the scene of the broken gargoyle; from the spray of stone, I determined in which direction the thief had run. The entire time one place nagged – the Folly. I could not speak of it to Holmes yet. My brother would hide there. If he had stolen the gargoyles, if he had caused the landslide that ended with Victoria's murder, he would not have expected Mother's reaction.

Not Ted.

No one could have foreseen that outcome.

A freshly trod path wound through the nettles and bushes that concealed the long-forgotten Folly. As children, we'd laughed at the gargoyle legend. We'd thought it no more terrifying a fate than becoming Sleeping Beauty.

"I believe we will find the culprit in there," I said, a weight on my tongue.

It did not matter if I revealed Ted, for Holmes would know the truth of it. How clever of me to bring the world's greatest detective to help me solve the crime that would destroy my family. No one would care if

I joined the police force or became a spy now. Actually, I would probably be too notorious to become a spy.

Holmes placed his hand on my arm as I brushed aside broken foliage and made to push open the Folly door. "Perhaps you should turn back, Miss Killfellen. Leave those better equipped to deal with it."

I shook my head. "A good detective does not retreat from the crime, especially at the reveal, no matter how harmful it proves to them."

Holmes did not contradict me. Nor did he say that act would bring no further injury. Even Watson did not insist that I turn back. It seemed all of us knew whom we would find in here.

He cowered in the corner, a mad thing. This was not my brother, not the boy with the infectious grin who had gone off to war in a crisp new uniform. This boy had dull eyes and torn and dirty clothing. The Folly walls filled with ragged laughter. I recalled all the times we'd laughed in here and how we used to hide from Mother and Father and thought the world a much better place than it was.

I knelt before him. "You've been waiting for me."

For a moment, I thought this version of Ted didn't recognise me. He held out the remaining gargoyle – Tweedledum. I took it from his hands and curled beside him, resting my head on his shoulder. He'd meant no harm.

Holmes sat on the floor before us, cross-legged, waiting for the moment when both Ted and I would master the courage to move.

Holmes telephoned the constabulary and they took Mother away. She confessed in the end, breaking down at the sight of her poor, broken boy. Father didn't admonish me for opening the telegram, for finding Ted alive, despite the fact that he didn't know what to do with a boy who could not run the estate or even dress himself.

Between us, we changed the future of Killfellen House and of the Killfellen family.

We've opened the house as a respite home for those suffering the effects of that bloody War. Ted's improving. He's mostly in his room, and only twice over the past month have I had to go to the Folly and bring him home. The gargoyle is still there, though – Tweedledum, peering from the shadows to create fresh legend. Mr Holmes has assured me of a place in his School for Detection and, once my brother is well, and the estate running smoothly, I shall take him up on that offer.

The Bell Rock Light
Guy Haley

———

In these latter years of my life I have come often to cast an eye over my notes taken during the many years I spent with my friend, the celebrated Sherlock Holmes.

Of the hundreds of incidents in which we participated, there are many investigations that I decided – for one reason or another – were not suitable for publication in *The Strand*, that fine paper which ensured the preservation of Holmes's record for posterity. Discretion was my chief motivation for holding back the majority, and remains so. The principal actors in these particular cases are for the most part long dead as this century wears on and ceases to be so new, but I balk still at publishing. One or two are so strange, so shocking, that I am reluctant yet to inflict them upon the world, however bold social convention has become.

From time to time, I come across an investigation which might have made it to the pages of *The Strand* had I ever transcribed them into fuller versions, or perhaps I began the work but never completed the piece, for in our prime years our time was quite thick with adventure, and often plans made had to be set aside, most frequently owing to the sometimes mercurial nature of my friend and his feverish desire for occupation for his formidable mind. There was little time for rest or recollection. The heights of one adventure might be surmounted by another, and an account ready for Holmes's followers overshadowed by a successor yet more thrilling.

This incident of the Bell Rock light was one of those incomplete stories. Upon re-examination I have judged it suitable for publication, being intriguing, and noting now as ever the insatiable hunger the reading public appears to have for the investigations of Holmes, who to me shall forever remain the world's first and greatest consulting detective; therefore, it should be of interest to many people.

Looking at my notes, I see that this was a rare escapade set in motion by my hand. It was in the June of 1907, some time before Holmes retired to Sussex, and still more years before the terrible business of the Great War reinvigorated my friend's enthusiasm for physical investigation and called him into the service of his country.

Holmes had lapsed into one of his uncommunicative periods of introspection, occasioned by the lack of what he referred to as "challenging stimuli". He was as apt to neglect himself at these times as when he was most highly motivated, spending long days of that dreary late spring inside with the curtains drawn, eating insufficiently and indulging himself to ruin his lungs with that pipe of his. Wishing more than anything for my friend to divest himself of this gloomy state of mind before he strayed towards cocaine, I decided it would do us both a measure of good to leave the city upon something of a holiday.

Holmes would never acquiesce to a trip away for the sake of relaxation, so I was forced to commit a small act of subterfuge. I asked the school that they might request he perform a tour of the country, on the pretext of visiting various of his old students, in order to assess their work, judge how much of his own deductive method they had managed to absorb, and thus, by feeding his findings back to the school, the manner of instruction might be adjusted to favour better results. At this time the school was well into its second decade, and the number of skilled men and women to have graduated from its halls was pleasingly considerable. The provost at the time thought it a worthwhile endeavour, and thankfully I had to engage in minimal deception. Naturally all this had to be conducted in the utmost secrecy and discretion. Sherlock Holmes, as ever, was a very difficult man to surprise.

Holmes agreed, albeit reluctantly at first. He bore a great affection for the school and his students, the more gifted of them at the least, and I was relieved to see his spirits lift, if but a little. I constructed our itinerary to take us as far away from the brume of the capital as possible. We ventured to the north first, to Yorkshire, then over the Pennine hills to the grim town of Manchester, thereafter north to Carlisle, Berwick, and on to Edinburgh, where we were the subject of much celebration, to Holmes's annoyance, thence onward to St Andrews. It was in this most charming of cities that the incident took place.

One of Holmes's students, a James Leslie, had taken up residence and a role with the local police there, rising by that time in his career to the rank of inspector. Holmes remembered him well, and looked forward to seeing him again, although it had been well over ten years since Leslie's graduation from the school.

Leslie greeted us cordially at the station. He was a genial if unkempt young man who had grown into a genial if unkempt adult. Time had had its way with him. There was grey around the temples, he was a little fatter than he had been, and sported a large moustache the callow youth under Holmes's tuition could only have dreamed of. He had exchanged the threadbare garb of his student days for a well-made suit, baggy with long use, over which he wore an overcoat in similar condition.

"Young Leslie!" said Holmes, shaking his hand warmly. "Or perhaps I should call you inspector?"

"I'll be happy to be named as either by you, though I'm not so young any more," said Leslie.

"Yes," said Holmes, peering at the man's greying hair.

"It's a pleasure and an honour to see you again, Mr Holmes."

"Well then, well then, let us have a look at you and see what we can see," he said, and looked Inspector Leslie up and down. "From the worn nature of the toes of your shoes and the stretch in your overcoat pockets, I see you are still in the habit of pacing while thinking, hunching, as you did as a youth, with your fists thrust into your pockets and scuffing at the floor with your feet."

"You suppose correctly," said Leslie.

Holmes shrugged away his comment. "Not at all difficult to deduce. I remember your habits. What is new, that is the question?" He gave his one-time pupil a bright grin, the first I had seen him essay in weeks. "You sustained an injury to your left leg, not longer than a year ago, no sooner than six months since. You habitually smoked a pipe for a number of years, probably in imitation of my own custom, but gave it up some time ago. You spend a good time at the shore, fishing. You are divorced."

Leslie and I shared an amused glance.

"You must tell me how you reached your conclusions," said Leslie.

"Can you not determine for yourself?" said Holmes.

"I am sure you recall, as you recall everything, Mr Holmes, that I never had the same facility for observational deduction that you possess."

"Very few do," said Holmes. "But you had other talents."

"You tell me your theory, and I shall tell you if you are right."

"Right?" said Holmes with a small frown. "The inside of your left shoe is worn more than that of your right, suggesting a dragging of the leg which you no longer exhibit. A splinted leg would not produce the same pattern, so I suggest a problem with the tendon in your knee that has since healed, somewhat to your surprise. It cannot have been long ago, because you are still wearing the same shoes, and have not had them resoled. The breaking of your marriage is easily observable by the thinning of your ring finger. Doubtless you were married while slimmer, and did not have the ring enlarged, which has trained the shape into your finger at the root. There is no line in the colour of the skin, so this must have occurred at least a year ago, enough time for the colour to equalise, or it should be whiter than the surrounding area. There are faint salt splatters on your trousers, and your hands and face are weather-beaten by long exposure to the outdoors. I expect fishing, a way for you to put aside the cares of the day, and eagerly rushed to, for you do not change your clothes. Finally, the smoking. You have a gap in your teeth not present while you were a pupil at the school, the mark of a pipe smoker of some years who gnaws at the stem."

"And the desire to emulate you, sir?" said Leslie.

"You have chosen a small city to work in. You have been away to London, and studied under Sherlock Holmes. It will have done you no harm to advertise the fact. I see no yellow staining on your moustache, and detect no odour of tobacco. Your wife told you to cease the habit."

"She urged me to give up the vice," he said. "It did not save relations between us."

"Vice? A harmless aid to thought! You sound like Watson here."

Leslie tipped his hat. "Well done, Mr Holmes. All correct."

"Naturally."

Leslie finally greeted me, took our bags and led us to a car. "Seeing as you are here, Mr Holmes, and your faculties are undimmed," he said, climbing into the driver's seat, "I have a case that you might apply yourself to."

"Oh?" said Holmes, his interest immediately piqued. "If you are asking for help, it is probably not a trifle. I expect you to be more than capable."

"Not a trifle at all, Mr Holmes," he said. "A murder." He paused. "You are here to assess my abilities in my professional role, and I would not wish to tarnish my own reputation by bringing to your attention one of my failures, but I feel I have no choice, and not from a desire for completeness or honesty."

Holmes leaned forward, the better to speak into Leslie's ear as he engaged the engine. "As there is no urgency to this matter, you must be referring to something past. Most likely a miscarriage of justice. You always were a moral man, Mr Leslie."

"Exactly so, Mr Holmes."

We had a fine dinner at the local hotel, within sight of the magnificent castle. Both these things Holmes approved of. He most certainly did not approve of the prevalence of golfing images and associated items, which were the dominant decoration of the hotel. In terms of sports, Holmes had tolerance only for those of practical use, and he found golf to be no use whatsoever. To his credit, he voiced his disapproval only once.

Neither Holmes nor I pressed Leslie for his account of the case that so troubled him; instead we dwelt on other matters over dinner. Leslie had done well for himself; so well that his reputation would remain untarnished, no matter what mistake he revealed to us, and it was obvious from his prematurely greying hair – Leslie was no older than thirty-two years – that he worked himself hard. Holmes was difficult to read. Many people who met him ascribed a certain aloofness, even arrogance to him, and consequently a cold heart. However, to me, who knew him well, it was evident that Holmes took satisfaction in Leslie's tales of this blackmail thwarted and that thief apprehended, all the more so at the ingeniousness of some of his resolutions.

When the last of the plates were cleared away we retired to a quiet room. A fire burned there, for the year had been unseasonably cool in London and was colder in Scotland, as is to be expected. When seated comfortably, Holmes produced his own infernal pipe, and at last asked Leslie to relate his story.

"I should be interested to hear your version of events first," said Holmes, filling the air with his fumes. "We might then proceed to a solution."

Leslie took a large glass of whisky and sat himself opposite my friend. The expression on his broad, open face became somewhat rueful. "I must apologise for taking up your time with this, Mr Holmes. The truth of the matter is that any light you might shed on the events will be for my own benefit. You see, a man hanged for the crime of murder, and it is my conviction that he was innocent."

"A shame, and a heavy burden for you to bear," said Holmes. "But so long as the puzzle engages the mind, you have my attention. Either we shall solve it swiftly, and that will be that, and we shall be content with your account as a story and with the satisfaction of setting your mind at rest. Or it shall prove a knottier problem and you will provide us with more than after-dinner entertainment."

"I fear it is a weightier affair than that," said Leslie.

Holmes sat forward. "Then continue."

This is the story that James Leslie related to us.

"There is a lighthouse some fourteen miles offshore upon the Inchcape rock," he began. "A reef hidden only feet below most tides, and deadly for it. The rocks claimed so many ships that even so far back as ancient times, the abbot hereabouts set a bell upon it, hence the reef's other name of the Bell Rock. However, it was not until the beginning of the last century that the problem was finally addressed properly by the construction of a lighthouse by the Stevenson family, whose most famous son is the author, Robert Louis Stevenson."

"I am aware of his ancestry, although not his work. I've little time for the scribblers of fictional tales." Holmes gave me a look of pure impish provocation over his pipe. "Fact is so much more satisfying than fiction. The Stevensons adapted pioneering techniques first employed by John Smeaton in Cornwall at the Eddystone Rock, if I am not mistaken, that have since become used all over the world."

As always, Holmes's ability to produce the most recondite information astounded me. Once I had thought his capacity for such limitless, but I had known him long enough by then to realise he must have been reading ahead of our trip, for that kind of detail my friend kept in his mind only so long as it were useful to him. By extrapolation, I suspect he was probably well aware of the crime that Leslie was about to relate to us. As I said, Sherlock Holmes was a very difficult man to surprise.

"Aye, sir, you are never mistaken," said Leslie. "Concentric rings of linked masonry, so carefully cut and laid that the pressure of the stone keeps the whole in place, even in the highest seas. An Englishman conceived the idea, but it took a Scotsman to perfect it. Before the lighthouse's construction, the Bell Rock claimed dozens of ships a year bound for port in Aberdeen. Its building was nothing short of a triumph of human ingenuity and compassion for his fellows."

"The incident that concerns you must involve the lighthouse keepers. There would be two, is that correct?" said Holmes.

"It does, and there are."

"And one murdered the other."

"So it was judged in court."

"Go on," said Holmes. He puffed on his pipe, eyes bright as the coal of tobacco glowing in the bowl.

"There are two men stationed in the lighthouse at all times to tend the light. The men in question were William MacGregor, a man from the west of the country, and Donald Leslie."

"No relation of yours," said Holmes.

"A distant clansman, perhaps."

"So Sir Walter Scott would have insisted, no doubt," said Holmes.

"It is a common enough surname in these parts," said Leslie. "Donald was a quiet man, some would say secretive, and those who did not know him well thought him unfriendly. He had been a lighthouse keeper for many years and was shortly due to retire. The Northern Lighthouse Board pays a pension to those who leave the service. He had plans to establish a small business as a stonemason, the profession he was instructed in as a youth. He had a wife, Annabelle, who lives still not far up the coast. They were fond of each other."

"He was well liked?"

"By those few he permitted to know him, yes. He was more respected than liked. There were a few who took against him on account of his reluctance to attend church."

"He was an atheist?"

"So they say."

"And the other keeper present at the time?"

Leslie's expression darkened. "MacGregor was not well liked. He was opinionated, and had a cruel sense of humour. He was of that breed of men who seem to carry a special loathing for themselves, and seek to justify their low opinion of their own character by provoking others to provide the proof of it. He stayed to the right side of the law, most of the time. I had reason to detain him twice: one account of a maliciously broken window; secondly, a prank that scared a poor woman half to death."

"You always were a percipient judge of a man's thoughts, Leslie," said Holmes. "That is where your talents are."

"To have you say that to me is worth a year's pay," said Leslie, and his face lifted a little.

"So MacGregor was convicted of killing this other Leslie," said Holmes. "Describe to me the circumstances of the crime."

"A storm blew up – a common occurrence at that time of year."

"Which was?" asked Holmes. "Remember to include all facts, please, Mr Leslie."

"October, 1905. A gale that lasted two weeks. We had snow early. I remember it clearly."

"For the duration of the storm, the lighthouse would have been cut off from communication?"

"Yes sir. There is no telegraph or telephone line run out to the light. The relief ship goes out after every major storm to check upon the keepers. When the boat arrived, the crew found a terrible scene. There had been a fire in the lighthouse quarters, burning one room severely. Within that room, the body of Leslie was discovered, blackened by fire, his heart pierced with a fisherman's knife belonging to MacGregor. At first, there was no sign of MacGregor, until upon searching the lighthouse he was found in the lamp room. He had barred himself in. The relief crew had already made up their minds as to the nature of the events and went in quite heavily, expecting resistance. MacGregor threw himself on their mercy. He insisted he had been camping in the lamp room ever since the day of Leslie's death out of fear that he would be accused of his murder. Of which he was in due course convicted, and then hanged for."

"You do not agree with the verdict, Leslie."

"No, Mr Holmes, I do not," said young Leslie with surprising passion. "I interviewed MacGregor when he was returned to land. He told me that on the day of the fire, the second of October, he had gone out to check on his creels – he was in the habit of fishing the reef around the lighthouse for crab. His pots were accessible that day by foot, as it was a spring tide, and much of the reef that is usually covered was exposed to the air. While retrieving one of his pots, MacGregor said his attention was drawn back to the lighthouse by a flash behind one of the windows there in the keepers' quarters, followed soon after by smoke. As he scrambled back over the rock, he saw the lighthouse rowing boat drawing away in the gloom, the lantern lit, the silhouette of a man at the oars, it being close to dark at that time. When he returned, he found the keepers' kitchen in conflagration and he spent some thirty minutes extinguishing it fully, at risk to his life. There he found Leslie's body, stabbed through the heart and horribly burnt. He ran immediately to the lamp room, the highest part of the light, seeking any sign of a ship that he might signal, but to his dismay there was none. The next day, the gale blew up, a day before the forecast, and he was cut off for two weeks with poor Leslie's corpse."

"And the boat? Did he say where the boat was at this point?"

"Far out, lantern lit, heading inland. Its final resting place was never found. It is a long way for one or even two men to row from the rock, and he saw only one. He said he saw the man was wearing a hat – his hat, he thought, as he had mislaid it, along with his knife. He was convinced the murderer had taken both."

"It may prove to be so," said Holmes. "MacGregor's story was that there was an intruder within the light whom Leslie discovered in MacGregror's absence; and that the intruder murdered Leslie in a panic, then used the boat to flee, whereupon this self-same intruder had been swallowed by the sea. A convenient story."

"That is what the jury thought. It was based only on MacGregor's supposition, and the court denounced it as fabrication. The judge used that opinion as grounds for his hanging, for it was obvious to him the crime was premeditated and a plan coldly enacted in its aftermath, covered with a wicked lie. I do not agree. But the important question is, what do you think, Mr Holmes?"

Holmes tapped out the bowl of his pipe, laid it to one side, and steepled his fingers before his nose. Through this cage he eyed Leslie.

"Be sporting, Leslie, let's see what you retain from your lessons. Tell me what you think."

"I don't think he did it, sir," said Leslie. "Not for any evidence. That was damning, if I am entirely honest. But I am sure he did not."

"And a motive?"

"MacGregor often argued with Leslie. He wanted him to retire sooner so that MacGregor might become head keeper. A question of money – MacGregor was often short. Leslie resented him. They never saw eye to eye."

"And yet the Northern Lighthouse Board kept them working together?"

"The cogs in the mechanisms of these large institutions turn slowly. There was also a rumour that MacGregor had a sponsor in the board: that was how a man of such unsuitable temperament retained his position as an assistant keeper. When I looked into it, I found it to be correct. MacGregor's cousin is a man of some influence."

"Yet you still think MacGregor innocent?"

"He was not an innocent man, but this crime was not his doing. I could see that in his eyes. He went to the gallows in Aberdeen gaol with the same look. It haunts me still."

"There were no witnesses to this crime other than the keepers?"

"Only one. Andrew Aldburgh, a close-mouthed lobsterman of low character. He keeps creels out by the rock. He said he saw lights there, but cannot recall the timing. This one detail troubled me, because Aldburgh is of that rare sort of men who have a fine – some might say photographic – memory. But he is taciturn when not in drink. When I challenged him, he told me he had only noticed the lights briefly, but became concerned with retrieving his own pots."

"His relationship with the men?"

"If you are asking, Mr Holmes, if he were the murderer, then I do not believe so. He and Leslie had no quarrel. MacGregor, on the other hand, he despised, accusing the other man of wrecking his pots on more than one occasion."

"A-ha!" said Holmes, sitting forward. "Did you investigate these claims?"

"My work here has engaged me with all manner of crime, from the inconsequential to the abhorrent. Nothing could be proved regarding the matter of the pots."

"So Aldburgh thinks poorly of you?"

"You might say so," said Leslie.

"Do you have an idea, Holmes?" I asked.

"I do, I do. All that is needed to solve this affair is contained within the words of our host here. Proof is another matter."

"You think young Leslie may be on to something?"

"I believe he is right that MacGregor did not kill Donald Leslie. I shall save my hypothesis until we have gathered sufficient proof. You will aid us, James?"

"Without hesitation. To have resolution of my doubts one way or the other would be the finest gift any man could give me." He was sincere. I remember Leslie being a lively lad, and our dinner together suggested he retained his good humour. But throughout his tale he had remained subdued, only brightening at this prospect of a conclusion to his worries.

"Then we shall see what we can do. Let us talk no more on this until tomorrow. Pour us all some whisky, there's a good fellow, and tell us more of your work here. I should not want to return to London without adequate notes."

Holmes meant that I should take them. As my jotter was already out for the purposes of recording young Leslie's account of the murder, I obliged, though not until I had my whisky in hand.

We spent the next day under chilly skies seeking out acquaintances of the lighthouse keepers. Both men were known in town, but though St Andrews is small for a city, it is still a sizeable settlement, and the familiarity the populace had for the names was more for the notoriety of MacGregor's crime than through any personal affection or animosity held for the two.

Much of the intelligence we gleaned was useless, sensational, worn reports of the incident. The few men we spoke to who had known the keepers personally were damning as regards the case for MacGregor's innocence. Their appraisal of Leslie was that he had been a good man, respected for his knowledge of the local weather and sea, of which he had been an ardent student, albeit in an amateur capacity. Contrarily, MacGregor was widely thought of as being an annoyance at best, and a blackguard at the worst. There were several men who claimed he owed them money from gambling, a habit he pursued as avidly as Leslie had his study of the weather, but with far less success.

The woman whom MacGregor had frightened with his drunken prank – he covered himself up in a white sheet, affecting to be a ghost – was particularly scathing of him. The composite impression that arose of his character from these interviews was of idle cruelties, bullying behaviour, puerile humour and occasional dishonest conduct.

"As you can see, Mr Holmes," said young Leslie while we took a beer and a rest from the rain in our hotel bar, "MacGregor had ample motive. He needed the money and craved the respect of the position."

Holmes fidgeted, deep in thought, his beer untouched. As he often did when deeply invested in a problem, he took little sustenance. In this case, I do not think from the effort of the solving of the crime. He would almost certainly have accomplished that himself already, but from his desire to steer Leslie in the right direction so as to further the young man's improvement as a detective. I was witness in that hotel bar to Holmes being at once detective and tutor.

"Watson?" Holmes asked, "what do you think?"

"It appears that he did it, lighting the fire to cover the evidence of his deed, as the court ruled." I did not see how it could be any other way, and anticipated Holmes's own expert deductions.

"Do you still think MacGregor is innocent of the murder?" Holmes asked Leslie.

"I am certain he is," said young Leslie. "But I cannot fathom how to show it."

"In that case, we have more work to do," said Holmes. He abruptly ceased his fidgeting, got up and plucked his coat from the stand. "Back into the rain!"

Four further discussions yielded nothing more of note. Leslie was a good man, if quiet. MacGregor was a bad one, and loud.

As the morning drew to a close, my thoughts wandered regretfully to a lunch I knew would be deferred when Holmes asked of Leslie where Aldburgh might be found.

"Do you think he might have something to tell?"

"I do," said Holmes.

"He will not speak with you. He has a rabid mistrust of Englishmen," warned Leslie.

"I intend to go alone. He will talk to me."

Leslie looked doubtful, but told Holmes what he wished to know.

"He drinks heavily. At this time of day I expect him to be firmly quartered at the Ship – his favoured inn, when he is not barred from entry."

"There are a few questions I have to answer here in town before approaching him," said Holmes. "With a little luck I will be finished quickly and will then proceed to interview Aldburgh. Watson, if you would accompany young Leslie here to the widow's cottage and question her, it would save valuable time and effort."

I agreed readily. Tomorrow we were due to leave for Glasgow. Besides the pressures of our itinerary, I learnt a very long time ago that there was little point in arguing with Sherlock Holmes when his mind was set.

The widow Leslie lived in somewhat straitened circumstances, miles out of town on the way to Dundee, down an intolerably rough track within sound of the sea. The road was appalling. Young Leslie's car broke a wheel on the way and we were obliged to change it. We arrived later than we intended, smirched with mud and soaked by the rain. Despite the time of year, the louring clouds dimmed the evening considerably, casting a gloom over everything that, I remember remarking, was appropriate to our grim business.

The widow's cottage was small and mean by modern standards. That sort of longhouse one finds all over Scotland, built of stone and turves. A full single storey on the ground floor divided into a kitchen and parlour, a ladder leading to cramped sleeping quarters above in the eaves. Nevertheless, in comparison to the crammed tenements occupied by the poor of London, it was a fine abode, and was kept with a fastidious eye for cleanliness.

A small woman in black had opened the door, seemingly for the express purpose of frowning at the dirt on our clothes, so pronounced were the furrows on her brow, but she recognised young Leslie without presentation of his card and grudgingly let us in. Her disapproval was quickly replaced with a concern for our well-being once she had a good look at us in the lighter environs of her cottage, and in no time had bustled us over to the fireplace to warm ourselves through and furnished us with hot tea.

Gently, I began my questioning of her. As Mr Holmes's closest companion, interviewing the bereaved is a sad task I have undertaken on many occasions. It never became any easier. I commented favourably on her small collection of books in order to put the woman at her ease. Sadly, it had the opposite effect.

"They were all Donald's," she said. "My late husband was very fond of reading natural history. Meteorology was his favourite subject. He had a fine knack with the weather, people from all around these parts would ask him for forecasts, and they were often right. Better than those in the *Advertiser* and *Herald*," she said with faint, sorrowful pride. "I do hope you will not keep me, Dr Watson. I am to be away to bed soon. Old bones need much rest."

"Of course," I said. "We will not delay you for long. May I ask you some questions? I understand it is not easy to revisit such a profound personal tragedy."

She glanced at Leslie, standing gravely by the fire and trying his hardest not to drip on the widow's worn rug. "I have answered everything the police have put to me. I do not know what more you can learn. That man hanged for his crime, justly." She spoke shrewdly. I suspect she guessed we were unsure as to the fatal verdict. "Let me tell you, Dr Watson, MacGregor was an oafish bully. My husband hated working with him, and his hatred was made no better by the board's insistence they work together. As head keeper, he should have had the authority to remove MacGregor from his post, but he was put off and his concerns dismissed. It wore at him badly. Forty years he gave the light, and at the end they treated him so poorly. MacGregor's cousin, I hear, is on the board. A disgraceful turn of events, that a man's place be bought so. MacGregor harangued my Donald day and night to retire. Saying he was too sick to do it, and he never missing a day to illness in all his life. He'd go out no matter how he felt. 'There's them that depend on the lights, Annie,' he'd say to me. 'No cold or flux will stop me lighting it.' He was devoted to his job. He took it truly seriously, not like MacGregor, to whom tending the light was a burden, done unwillingly solely to earn coins for the card table."

"I had heard of his habit. You say MacGregor said Mr Leslie was sick?"

"And what bearing on his death does that have?"

"As my friend Mr Holmes says, all details, however small, must be examined. I am sorry."

"My Donald had a cough, that is all. I pressed him to go to the doctor. But only after weeks of repeated asking did he relent, and saw the man here in town. When he returned I asked him what ailed him, but he would not tell me what he had learnt there."

"He would not answer?"

"He answered all right. He said it was naught grave, but he did not tell me all; that is my meaning. Married thirty-two years, a woman can tell. Especially when married to a man like Donald, who did not like to speak if it could be helped. He had medicine – he did not tell me about that at first, until I found it. His cough eased, and a month later, he was dead, so I paid it no more mind. Really, Doctor, this is a shameful visit. MacGregor murdered my husband and made up this ridiculous tale of another man. I thank you not to revisit me, or this crime."

We talked a little while longer. I spoke with the widow of her own health and gave her some small measure of advice before departing. She was grateful for this free consultation, and we left on better terms.

"Did you learn anything?" asked young Leslie.

"A little, maybe," I said. I had an inkling of what Holmes might make of it, but decided to keep my opinion close until we had made more progress. For once, I felt as Holmes must, harbouring secrets until the final revelation. The feeling was delightful. No wonder my friend made such a show of his solutions.

We arrived back past ten o'clock, whereupon the evening's grey gave way to night with surprising speed. No sooner had young Leslie put his car away than a uniformed constable came running, out of breath and excited, to inform him there had been an altercation at the Ship Inn, and that he should come immediately to the police station. My tiredness and hunger were overcome at once by concern for my friend, who had been due to go there after we departed to speak with the widow. Although I was certain he would not have been present at so late an hour, I thought it wise to make sure, and – after asking the constable's permission – hastened after Leslie to the police station. The constable took me down into the cells beneath the station offices. One of the detained men was making the most awful racket, singing and shouting with some of the most profane language I have heard for a time, delivered in an impenetrable Scots brogue.

Leslie paused by a cell door. "That there is Mr Aldburgh," he said, pointing at a huddled figure snoring loudly in the corner. The constable took us to the last cell whose occupant was making the din. The man inside sang out his heart, none too tunefully.

"He and Aldburgh got drunk, and this one here picked a fight with me when I was summoned to remonstrate with them on account of their rowdiness. The impudent sot knocked off my helmet, and I arrested them both, and was obliged to land several blows on this one when he became violent."

"He seems all right now," said young Leslie. "You there, you! Stop singing."

I was about to ask the constable if he had seen Holmes, and whether he had been drawn into all this unpleasantness, when the man ended his clamour and came to the barred door.

"Ah! Inspector Leslie, Watson, about time you got here."

With a shift of his back and the removal of his wig, some contortions of the expression on his face, the drunk was gone. In his place was Sherlock Holmes. He chuckled at the success of his disguise and grinned wolfishly through the bruises on his face. The poor constable went deathly pale, and I feared he might faint.

"I . . . I . . .?" said the constable.

"This is Sherlock Holmes!" bellowed Leslie.

"I know who he is," said the constable in a small voice.

"Evidently not! By God, Holmes," said Leslie. "How do you do it?"

"Do not ask him that," I said. "I have never received a satisfactory answer."

"Constable Kilmore, let him out. You've some questions to answer, Mr Holmes," said Leslie, attempting to be stern but failing to hide his amazement.

"You shall be glad to hear that I have a great many answers for you," said Holmes.

"Come on man, get him out!" said Leslie to Kilmore, who was standing stock-still.

Constable Kilmore fumbled the keys three times before he found the right one.

We hastened to Leslie's office, and Leslie sent Kilmore away, suitably chastened, for soup. Once Holmes had cleaned himself up, I attempted to inspect his bruising. He waved me away impatiently.

"It is superficial damage, Watson, superficial! A little suffering must be endured for the attainment of any worthy goal."

"At least allow me to put a little arnica on the bruises," I said. He acquiesced poorly, and tutted all the way through my ministrations.

When I was done, he smiled widely again.

"Do tell your man Kilmore not to take my fooling him to heart. Nor to worry over the blows done; they were, in fact an essential part of my ploy. Without them, I should not have managed to win Aldburgh over to my trust."

"You got him to talk?" said Leslie, amazed anew.

"I did," said Holmes. His pleasure at his own cleverness would have been insufferable in any other, I often thought.

"What did you learn?"

"You first, Watson."

I told him of our visit with the widow. He pursed his lips and nodded. "You did well."

I puffed up at his praise.

"Although you did not learn anything I did not already know or suspect," he said, which rather undid the effects of his approval.

"And what did Aldburgh have to say?" I said.

"In order to get him to talk, it was essential I present myself in a fashion that would ignite sympathy in his breast. Any man will speak with one he thinks understands him, and so I presented myself as a heavy drinker tormented by memories of the Boer War, which proved more than adequate to forge a bond between us. Your comments, Leslie, on his ability to recall obscure facts suggested to me that this man abuses alcohol for a very specific reason. I deduced that he has, in fact, what is properly referred to as an eidetic memory, and is dogged by an inability to forget."

"Then surely, Holmes, he is like you!" said Leslie.

Holmes shook his head. "I do not have so fine a memory. What skill I have is trained. Any man might learn the technique, it being pioneered centuries ago by the early Humanists. His is an innate ability, and without superior intelligence to direct such a gift, it has done him more harm than good – witness his fondness for drink, taken to dull his remarkable faculties."

"He would forget no insult, slight or failure," I said. "The poor soul."

"Quite, and the point you make there, Watson, is apposite to our narrative. He and I spoke for some time, establishing a rapport. I offered the information that my exploits with the Highlanders in that awful war could not be forgotten. He rejoined with greater suffering, that he could forget nothing. However, I did not dare press him to tell me what he had seen that night until he had imbibed a great quantity of drink, and developed a certainty that I was in the same dire straits as he. He is a taciturn fellow, and suspicious. Hence all that business with Kilmore's helmet, for which I shall apologise. When we arrived at the cells, we spoke longer. I turned the conversation to the murder, giving the suggestion that I had heard it where I hailed from."

"Which was?"

"I chose Inverary. Far enough away so that there would be little chance of him knowing me. I also have an ear for that particular accent, and mimic it convincingly." Kilmore returned with mugs of soup for us all. Holmes took a single sip before continuing his story. "Two days before the killing, Aldburgh went to confer with Leslie about the weather. As we have learnt from Mrs Leslie's testimony, the locals often did. Having been informed that the storm would break two days earlier than the official forecasts, Aldburgh went out the next day to retrieve his crab pots, beginning close to the Bell Rock reef. And now comes the meat of my new knowledge. He did see lights, as he told you, Leslie, but he remembered full well the exact circumstances, being anchored only two hundred yards from the rock. He saw a lantern proceed along the exposed reef, and set up at the end where MacGregor liked to drop his own pots. He noted this well because, as you told us and he told me, in great detail, he believed MacGregor to be the agent of his own pots' destruction. The light remained on the rock for a long time. The boat departed the island, lamp burning. MacGregor's lantern was still lit at the end of the reef when the fire started. Now, it is feasible that MacGregor had hastened back to the lighthouse, untied the boat, killed Donald Leslie, set the fire and hurried back to his own lantern to give the impression he had been in a static position throughout the murder. But we have to ask ourselves, why would he do this? He would not have expected witnesses. Why not wait until there were assuredly none? Furthermore, Aldburgh noted that MacGregor's lantern left the end of the reef immediately when the fire began. There was not enough time for MacGregor to traverse such treacherous rocks, there and back, to put his play into action. He heard a cry 'Leslie's dead!' from the rock, and knew it for MacGregor's voice."

"MacGregor said he went to the tower's summit and looked about for help, but did not see anyone," I said.

"A fact that troubled me. But I have the answer to that as well," said Holmes. "Hearing MacGregor shouting, Aldburgh did not wish to become entangled in whatever had happened at the rock, doused his lamps and sailed away."

"This is an action of a friend of Leslie's?" I said, aghast.

"Aldburgh's motives are his own. Uncharitable, but at that moment his hatred of MacGregor overrode any feeling of morality he might have in regard to aiding his fellow man. He is a troubled soul, much given to rumination on ill-favoured thought. You have noticed that since the murder he has been drinking and in trouble more frequently, Inspector Leslie."

"Did he tell you that too?"

"That is a deduction. His memories cannot be silenced. For that reason he left the scene. He was so overcome with every petty grievance he had had with MacGregor that he went, for want of a better word, out of his mind. He calmed on the voyage home and resolved to return the next day but, by then, true to Leslie's forecast, the storm had blown up. The next he heard the supply ship had set out. His poor judgement gnaws at him. We should feel pity for him, not condemn him. He is afflicted by a memory he cannot control."

"You believe MacGregor is innocent."

"It is obvious that he is," said Holmes.

"Do you credit MacGregor's story then, Holmes?" I asked. "I for one do not."

"You are right not to, Watson. It is, as the jury supposed, a fabrication." Holmes leaned in, daring me to finish the puzzle. I believed I had a firm grip on it by that point, but said nothing for Leslie's benefit.

"So MacGregor lied about that," said Leslie, looking more baffled than ever.

Holmes smiled. "I did not say it was MacGregor's lie."

"What about the boat?" said young Leslie.

"While you two were playing mechanics in the mud of the roadside . . ."

I looked down at my dirty clothes. We had, of course, not told Holmes of our mishap.

". . . I went to the library and there examined all the data I could on tides and currents in the vicinity. At the time of a low spring tide, as the water turns to come back in, there is a powerful current away from the rock towards the coast. MacGregor was out at his pots at this time, by his own statements and Aldburgh's attestation. It is clear that the boat MacGregor saw was empty, carried off by the action of the sea, not under power of oars. The silhouette could have been sacking or something similar dressed to look like a man. You recall MacGregor mentioned that his hat had been taken. That had been placed atop the sacks. Nothing more complicated than that."

"Then who did it, if not MacGregor?" said young Leslie. "There is no other man."

"But there is. What is one of my favoured phrases, one that I used often during your time at the school?"

"When you have eliminated the impossible, whatever remains, however improbable, must be the truth," quoted Leslie. "So it was Aldburgh? MacGregor did not mention his coming to the reef.

Indeed, you say he deliberately concealed his presence and turned away. Were they in it together?" He frowned. "No, that cannot be it. But that leaves . . ." Realisation broke over his face like the dawn.

Holmes held up his hand. "We will wait before we name the culprit, even just among us three. One must never present a conclusion before the evidence is complete. There is one final link to this chain that must be closed. I am afraid we have a rather grim duty ahead of us, gentlemen."

We were furnished with an order of exhumation by the sheriff only hours before our train was due to depart, in the darkest time of early morning. The process of application ordinarily took days, but Holmes's name was enough to shorten that period considerably. Under Holmes's urging, Leslie rousted out two gravediggers, their grumblings silenced with the promise of double pay for the work, and headed to the grave-yard of the Church of the Holy Trinity, a handsome building whose core dated to the twelfth century. Leslie had a surprisingly impressive head-stone for a man of modest means, another sign of the regard in which the town held him.

The diggers were quick about their job. Within the hour, the grave was opened, and Leslie's coffin carefully removed. Holmes bid them prise off the lid and he fell upon the corpse. I am glad to report Widow Leslie was not there to see this disturbing display of avidity. Holmes's actions were easy to misinterpret. He ignored the stench of decay as if it were the scent of flowers. He was intent upon his solution, and noth-ing would stop him.

Of Leslie's mortal remains, little – thankfully – was left. Two years is no time at all for a body to decompose six feet under the earth, but owing to the ravages of the fire, all that had been interred was a black-ened skeleton. The little remaining flesh had been reduced to scraps. Even so, exhumation is an unpleasant business, and I will save the reader from further detail.

"Watson! Come here!"

Holmes drew aside the deceased's suit of clothes, exposing his blackened ribs.

"We are looking for the terminal wound," I said.

"Exactly. Here!" We found it, directly over the position of the heart. Holmes shone a bull's-eye lantern at the chest. Holmes favoured those right up to the Great War, and it was a few years before the electrical invention of David Misell succeeded in replacing such devices.

"Now then. Tell me, young Leslie, what your deductions are."

The graveyard filled with the scent of cigarette smoke as the grave-diggers took the chance for a rest. They crowded in, keen to hear what this famous London detective might say. Holmes gave them a severe look. "Away with you – this is a matter of great sensitivity."

The men grumbled. The offer of an extra shilling mollified them and they shuffled off. I was sorry to see them go. Their tobacco smoke did a great deal of good in masking the scent of death.

"So then," said Holmes, when he was sure they were no longer listening.

"Donald Leslie did it," said young Leslie. "He released the boat, set the fire, and while it took, pierced his own heart with MacGregor's fishing knife which, along with the hat, he had taken earlier."

"Well done. Now, why?" asked Holmes. "What is your proof?"

"The pension for widows is higher than the pension given retired men. His animosity towards MacGregor was well known. The story of an intruder, which he was sure to plant in the other's mind, was improbable, and helped secure MacGregor's conviction, he being a known liar."

"Now, anything more? How do we prove it?"

Leslie shook his head. Holmes sat back on his haunches by the corpse. With his coat around his ankles like wings, and that proud aquiline nose thrust out, I was put in mind of a vulture.

"Never mind, never mind, you have done tolerably well."

"You knew from the beginning."

"I suspected, but I never theorise before all the evidence is in place.

I was first alerted to the possibility of this conclusion by your mention of Leslie's supposed atheism. The Scots here are a pious lot, and I hear will not work on a Sabbath. But Leslie, being a lighthouse keeper, would have to break such a ban, so the claim of his atheism is easy to credit. To take one's own life, one would have to be less than convinced of the hereafter. The issue of the larger pension provides us with a motive. The widow revealed that her husband was ill. I am sure if we were to contact the local doctor, he would tell us that Leslie had a cancer on the lung and would not have lived long – note his cough, and reluctance to share the diagnosis with his beloved Annie. The medicine was a palliative, not a cure. His expertise in reading the weather and tides of the sea was a further indication that this line of reasoning might bear fruit. He planned his crime perfectly, setting the scene and taking his own life the day before a powerful storm that would keep MacGregor isolated, and further obfuscate the truth of the matter. Leslie set the lighthouse alight to hide his suicide, not MacGregor to hide his crime. But the final proof is here. Watson, you have been following?"

"I have, Holmes. I believe I know to what you refer."

"Then enlighten young Leslie here."

"The coroner said Donald Leslie had been stabbed but once."

"Yes," said young Leslie.

"Then look here at the rib. You see these grooves in the bone?"

He bent down to squint at the marks there, barely visible even in the glare of the lamp.

"He has been stabbed not once, but three times, the first two very shallowly and into the same wound, but the knife has marked the bone separately."

Here Holmes took up the lesson again. "No man would stab so delicately when aiming for another's heart. Such wounds would be deep, and penetrating, scarring the bone very noticeably, and not so closely together. What we have here is a man hesitating before driving home the final plunge of the knife that would end his life. This proof, I believe, will be sufficient to exonerate MacGregor."

Leslie stepped back from the coffin, took off his hat, and ran his hand through his hair. "I was right, then?"

"In the broadest terms, yes. Well done. I shall pass on a good report of your work here," said Holmes.

"But I solved nothing. You led me by the hand!" said Leslie.

"That you noticed something amiss at all is a great credit to you. But now, you must consider not what you failed to see, but what you will do next."

"The widow," said young Leslie.

"If Leslie's suicide is made public, she shall lose her husband's pension. A special case might be put, but MacGregor's cousin is on the board and it will surely fail. You must decide what to do with this information, Inspector Leslie. Salvage the reputation of a wrongfully hanged man who was universally disliked and of criminal persuasion, and cast a blameless woman into penury, or leave a miscarriage of justice unchallenged. I am sorry." Holmes rose. "You asked me to help you ease your conscience, but in solving the problem I have exchanged it for one worse still."

"Thank you Mr Holmes. Thank you," said young Leslie, grave with his responsibility. "I must think on it. Thank you for sending the grave-diggers away, I am not sure I would have thought to."

Holmes bowed. Leslie stepped away from the grave, and walked a few paces, dazed by the intractability of his new problem.

"He will be fine, I am sure," said Holmes.

"I hope that is the case," said I.

"'But even in his dying fear, One dreadful sound could the Rover hear; A sound as if with the Inchcape Bell, The Devil below was ringing his knell.'"

"What's that, Watson?" said Holmes.

"The last stanza of Robert Southey's poem, 'The Inchcape Rock'." I was rather tired by then, but pleased to share some knowledge with my friend. "The abbot's bell was cut loose, legend has it, by Ralph the Rover, a pirate who the following year foundered on the Inchcape Rock and died for lack of the bell's warning. That is the subject of the poem. I only feel it appropriate in these sorry circumstances. Even with a light upon it, the rock is still claiming lives."

"Quite so, Watson, quite so," Holmes said. I could tell he was not listening, but was already anticipating what might await us in Glasgow. That was Holmes's way, always looking forward.

The Case of the Cannibal Club
Carole Johnstone

——

On an afternoon in January 1891, the exact date I now forget, the dank and Stygian drear of London lifted suddenly like a shroud, and so I abandoned my letters to take a walk across town. It was as I was heading towards Hyde Park that I remembered Holmes was giving a lecture to a new class of students at the Assembly Rooms. I was still not long married, and had certainly been neglecting my good friend's company; thus, I changed both mind and direction, turning east towards Soho.

I certainly dawdled; though the sun was bright and the air quite dry, my old war wound still objected to the midwinter chill. By the time I arrived at the Assembly Rooms, the lecture had finished and only two students remained in the theatre. Holmes was deep in conversation with both.

"Watson, my dear fellow!" shouted Holmes, just as I was retreating back into the corridor. "Come in, come in!" On a large chalkboard behind his lectern, the words The Methods and Philosophy of Deduction were written in his familiar scrawl. "Would you believe, it seems these gentlemen have brought me a case!"

I was tentatively glad, for Scotland Yard had allocated the School for Detection none for many weeks, and latterly, I'd recognised in my friend the ill-temper and lethargy that too often precipitated periods of black reaction. It had perhaps been this grim concern that had turned me towards Soho in the first place.

"This is Edward James Hardacre from Green Park, Piccadilly."

"Arlington Street," said Hardacre, extending his hand. A more English young gentleman it might be hard to imagine: tall and fair and dressed in the finest lambswool. "Have you heard of it?"

"Indeed I have," said I. "A most desirable address."

"And I am Hamid Khan," said his companion, through a smile so wide it was quite impossible not to return it. "A very great pleasure to meet you, Doctor."

"The pleasure is all mine," I replied. "I'm sorry, but I cannot place your accent."

"My family are Pashtun, Doctor. My father is a merchant, who also fought alongside the British against the Uzbeks. I am recently arrived from the Swat province in Khyber-Pakhtunkhwa."

"Ah, a most beautiful place! After I was wounded in Afghanistan, I visited very briefly. The Switzerland of the East."

Khan bowed his head. "So they say. And it is indeed most beautiful. I am only sorry that you found yourself there in such unfortunate circumstances. I hope very much that—"

"Why do you think we bring you a case, Mr Holmes?" Hardacre interrupted.

"Because," said Holmes, "you have been whispering together for days, and given that Khan here is a new addition to the class and you have only just been paired up in study, this can hardly be because you are friends. Every student will seek to secure himself a case until such time as one is handed to the school by the provost. How else to work alongside the great Sherlock Holmes?"

"Will you not then guess what the case is?" Hardacre enquired. Somewhat ill-advisedly.

Holmes clasped his fingers together. "I am neither performing pony, nor travelling magician, Hardacre. I hazard no judgement at all until I have sufficient information. And I never *guess*."

"Our apologies, Mr Holmes," said Khan. "No offence was intended. Our case is concerning the death, in Trieste, of Sir Richard Francis Burton."

"Ah!" said Holmes. "The great British explorer, soldier, writer, geographer, cartographer, ethnologist, linguist, translator, poet, fencer, diplomat and spy!" His sudden clap made all of us flinch. "Watson! Your disapproval is as silent as a clock in a Gladstone bag!"

"I have heard a great many less palatable nouns attributed to him, that is all." As had the whole of London. Brilliant and courageous Burton had doubtless been, but scandal and disgrace had been his better bedfellows. He was a gentleman who had squandered all worthy advantage; a hedonist who had sought only to eschew both tradition and modern convention. His licentious lifestyle and illegal publications were likely only the tip of a far larger iceberg. Dark rumours of his time in Africa and the Middle East were legion.

"Ha!" Holmes laughed. "But one can and does hear many things. The trick is to listen with more than just our ears." He reached behind his lectern and brought out a leather-bound notebook. "Well, I must confess that Burton's death was number two on my list. I had rather thought a student might first ask me to investigate the Tranby Croft affair. A royal scandal seems always to be the more irresistible."

"Why was Burton's death on your list at all?" Hardacre scowled.

"Why? His death was in all the papers last October, and there was some mystery to it, was there not? Inevitable, perhaps, considering his colourful life, but I have found that rarely is there smoke without a fire. Were there not rumours of necromancy and secrecy surrounding his death; that he had in fact died a full day before the Last Rites were performed upon him? And did not Lady Burton that very night burn all of his secret papers and journals? I assume that you both do not believe that Sir Richard died of a heart attack, as reported?"

"I believe that he was murdered," said Hardacre. "He had a great many enemies, that cannot be disputed. And his home in Trieste was rumoured to be full of vile native antiquities: sacrificial bowls and altars, human bones, and the like. His servant for many years was a savage African giant who would tolerate no other. And, as you say, the behaviour of Burton's wife upon his death was most peculiar. I took it upon myself to visit with Lady Burton and, in an unguarded moment, she let slip that she had found a mysterious calling card upon her husband's body. When I mentioned who I had been accepted to study under, she insisted on speaking not a further word to anyone but you."

"Very well," said Holmes with a shrug, although I could see that both his vanity and curiosity had been very surely piqued. I was rather gladder to see that the darkness over his head had lifted as swiftly as the winter's pall over London. "Then I shall, of course, investigate."

"Alongside Khan and myself," said Hardacre. "For it is our case, is it not? I have made a methodical study of proven murders disguised as pathologies of the heart. In fact, I have written a lengthy monograph on the—"

"And I should be glad to appraise it," said Holmes, already marching towards the exit.

St Mary Magdalen's churchyard in the village of Mortlake, some ten miles outside the city, was an entirely unassuming place. Save perhaps the incongruent mausoleum at its centre: an uncannily drawn Arab tent, with sculpted sandstone walls, rippling as if against a desert storm. Upon the roof, there was a foot-high crucifix, surrounded by gilded Islamic crescents and star motifs. There is naught, I have come to realise, that money cannot buy. Nor permit.

Lady Isabel Arundell Burton stood ahead of the tomb: straight-backed and solemnly handsome in black dress and coat, the long white streamers of her widow's cap seeming to catch the same unearthly breeze. To her left, and casting an imposing shadow nearly the length of our path, stood the largest African I had ever seen, his black frock coat reaching to his calves, his expression thunderously hostile.

"Many thanks for agreeing to meet with me, Lady Burton," said Holmes. "May I introduce you to my good friend, Doctor Watson?"

Lady Burton inclined her head towards us both. If Holmes has an instinct for the criminal, then I have an instinct for the sick. Lady Burton's pallor was unmistakable, her bearing too obviously and carefully stiff.

"Also, Mr Khan. And, of course, you must already know Mr Hardacre."

She looked at neither, waving the flat of her palm towards her intimidating companion instead. "Joseph is a Rwandan Hutu. By the finish of the rather hopeless Nile expedition in '58, alongside the rather more hopeless John Speke, my husband was quite a broken man. Joseph returned from East Africa with him, and he has remained with us these long years since."

"Indeed?" said Holmes, nodding briefly towards him before returning his attention to Lady Burton.

"I hope that you don't object to us meeting in such surroundings, Mr Holmes," she said, her smile thin. "But I had been expecting your telegram, and if we are to discuss my husband, then he should at least be present."

"Lady Burton," said Hardacre, with a winning smile that smacked of practice. "Would you be so kind as to answer—"

"It is quite lovely, is it not?" she said, turning suddenly back to the tomb, and I realised, with a start, that she wore no jewels whatsoever, not even a mourning brooch. I wondered if the rumours of Burton's squandered fortune might not be exaggerated after all. "More than five hundred attended the funeral last month; it would perhaps have been closer to a thousand were it not for influenza refusals. I shall be buried here too, of course. It was Dick's dearest wish that we should lie side by side for all eternity."

"It is a marvel, madam," Khan said gently, and only then did I notice the harder strain of Lady Burton's spine, the tremble in her hands.

"A kindness," she said, and the smile that she offered him was so warm that suddenly I could imagine what an extraordinary libertine such as Burton might have seen in her more than thirty years before. "Though few others have been so generous. Even his niece called it 'an eccentric tomb' in a 'shabby sectarian cemetery'. Might any of you perhaps have read Georgiana's book, *The True Life of Capt. Sir Richard F. Burton*?"

"No, indeed not," said I, before any others could reply more honestly. I had read serials in the Temple Bar, and as prurient and sensational as those excerpts had doubtless been, the pious tone of their author had promised little else than more condemnation of the same.

"I too am writing a book on his life," she said, pressing a thin hand to her chest. "Though I fear I shall not finish it."

From Holmes, I have caught the unpleasant disease of taking nothing at face value. Even my own motives I examine to a ludicrous degree. And, in Lady Burton, I detected invention; a reluctant insincerity that was extraneous to her badly disguised poverty and ill-health.

"Lady Burton," said Holmes. "Would you be so kind as—"

"Contrary to rumour, Mr Holmes, I did not burn all of his papers when he died." Her gaze was suddenly defiant. "Many more yet remain."

"Then may I ask why you burned those that you did?"

She looked hard at Holmes, and then sighed. "Dick was never happy in Trieste. It was an exile really, an enforced retirement after his consular position in Damascus. Our happiest times were spent in that wonderful city. I know my husband could be a difficult man, Mr Holmes, sometimes even a wild man, but he was forced out of Africa by jealous, petty men hardly fit to lick his boots, and it left him a broken shell with nothing to do but shock the London establishment with his salacious publications. I burned those papers because they demeaned his intellect. And because I wanted to some day be able to refute all of the vile calumnies set against him."

"And what of the rumour that Doctor Grenfell-Baker had declared your husband dead a full day before you had a young priest give him his rites?"

"I did that for the same reason that I burned those deviant translations," she said, and not without some measure of weary scorn. "Because my husband was one of the greatest, noblest, and most fearless of Englishmen, and I was determined that he be buried as a good Catholic." She looked rather more softly upon both Khan and me, before returning her hard gaze to Holmes. "I was determined to save his immortal soul."

"Was your husband murdered?" Hardacre asked.

When she offered no reply, Holmes stepped forward and took hold of her gloved hand. "Lady Burton, do you believe that your husband was murdered?"

"I have come to suspect it," she said, though she looked only at the ground. "Our homes were always full of a great many unusual artefacts, but on the night he died I found two objects lying upon his lifeless chest." She closed her eyes suddenly, as if bracing herself for a fall. "One was a necklace of human bones that King Gelele of Dahomey had gifted to him in 1861, and the other was a watermarked envelope with the letters CC writ large in black ink and scored through with red. There were large, muddy footprints stamped in a counter-clockwise circle around his bed, ending at the headboard."

"And inside the envelope?"

"A single small written page," said Lady Burton. "'*Of thy sweet mercy, damn their eyes; And damn their souls!* The Cannibal Club'."

"Ah," said Holmes, letting go of her hand.

Lady Burton exhaled, pressing her palms once more against her chest as she closed her eyes. "If my husband was murdered, Mr Holmes, no one more than I would wish to know by whom."

"Think no more on it," replied Holmes. "I shall investigate entirely free of charge or contract. My only proviso is that both Khan and Hardacre should be my mentees, although they will be no less discreet or thorough than me, I can promise you that."

At Holmes's words, Lady Burton's tension seemed nearly to vanish. She turned upon us all a wide and dazzling smile. "I am shortly to take rooms on Baker Street."

"Indeed?" said Holmes.

"Number Sixty-Seven."

"Portman Square," Holmes smiled. "Well, it is to be recommended as a fine neighbourhood."

She looked to the African, and then back at Holmes. "And we shall be in fine company."

"Well," said I, as all four of us sat inside a short stage, heading back towards the city. "What do you make of it? What the devil is the Cannibal Club?"

Holmes turned from the window. "You have never heard of it?"

"I have not. I think I'd have certainly remembered hearing of such a devilish-sounding place."

Holmes chuckled. "I had thought it the worst-kept secret in London." He leaned suddenly forwards. "And what say both of you?"

When Khan merely shook his head and Hardacre carried on scribbling inside the leather-bound notebook that he appeared to carry everywhere, Holmes snatched the latter out of Hardacre's hands and frowned down at its pages.

"What is this?"

"It's nothing," said Hardacre, though his face had flushed pink. "A doodle."

"A *doodle?*" Holmes scowled as if something foul-smelling had been held under his nose. "Do you often feel the need to doodle? It shows an untamed, untrained, ill-organised mind. I have had neither cause nor pause to doodle even once in my life."

Hardacre's flush darkened. "And yet, I hear that you play the violin whenever it is you need to think."

"Is that what you are doing, Hardacre? Are you trying to think?"

"Holmes," I muttered, taking back the notebook and handing it across to Hardacre.

Holmes cast me an inscrutable look before straightening his spine and seeming to cast off his cruel mood. "Very well. A teaching exercise. Do you perhaps remember my lecture on the principal skills of Observed Deduction?"

When they both nodded, Holmes turned again to Hardacre. "Then, what were your observed deductions of our meeting in Mortlake, sir? Remember, always present the most significant and pertinent first, and then work your way backwards."

"The African, Joseph, seemed violently disinclined to tolerate our—"

"That is neither significant nor pertinent." He turned towards Khan. "Next!"

Khan seemed uncomfortable. "The Lady Burton is dying, sir. And she also told to us a number of lies. She—"

Holmes clapped his hands together loudly enough to make me jump. "Khan! A good detective never – *ever* – allows either sensibility or association to cloud his judgement for even a moment. The truth, the solution, is all! So, I will ask you just once more. What was your most pertinent observed deduction of our meeting in Mortlake, sir?"

Khan let out a breath, and then closed his eyes, and I must confess to feeling great pity for him, despite having no clue at all as to what he was supposed to be revealing. "That Hardacre is an imposter, sir."

"Ha!" shouted Holmes, sounding quite delighted. "How so?"

Khan opened his eyes, but only looked across at Holmes. "The Lady Burton ignored him entirely. She never once acknowledged him, spoke to him, or even looked at him, which would suggest over-familiarity, or the specific attempt to hide it – neither of which makes sense if they have, as he has informed us, met only once as strangers, in order to engage your services." He paused, swallowed. "And Hardacre Street runs parallel to our rooms on Arlington."

"Bravo!" said Holmes. "My sentiments exactly." The stage rattled over a bad patch of road, and Holmes lurched towards Hardacre. "Before we go any further, I need to know exactly who you are."

Hardacre looked hardly perturbed at all. "Very well. I am John Stisted. My mother is Georgiana Stisted; my grandfather was Sir Henry William, Lieutenant Governor of Ontario, and my grandmother, Maria Katherine Elizabeth Burton."

"You are the great-nephew of Sir Richard Burton."

"I am."

"And, like the Lady Isabel, you do not approve of your mother's biography of Burton?"

"No, I do not. It is pious and inaccurate."

Holmes smiled. "You approved of your great-uncle."

"In most part. He was certainly extraordinary, would you not agree? Just as you are, Mr Holmes. Why, he was a brilliant linguist; a studier of men, and of human behaviour. And the challenges he set himself! Even before all his well-documented African expeditions, he had enjoyed untold dangerous adventures, first as a soldier in the East India Company, and then as a Hindu spy under General Napier. You yourself cannot possibly fail to be impressed by his legendary powers of disguise: as Mirza Abdullah, he became the first non-Muslim European to make the Hajj and survive undiscovered and, not long after that, he sought out the forbidden East African city of Harar dressed as a—"

"Yes, yes," interrupted Holmes, and not without some measure of irritation. "I assume therefore that you do not desire to become a police officer should you graduate Lestrade's school?"

"Not for a minute! I believe that I have inherited much of Burton's traits, and as such I would be a detective – perhaps even a spy."

"Then you need to become rather more adept at subterfuge," Holmes observed drily, as we left behind the Thames for Camberwell.

"I asked Lady Burton to pretend that we were strangers only because I thought it might force your hand or prejudice the case, that is all. I would have told you myself had Khan not told you for me. But now that all is out in the open, I wish to propose a wager."

Holmes leaned back against his seat and pinched the bridge of his nose hard enough to turn it white. "A wager?"

"Why not? A learned challenge between two gentlemen. I have made a study of all your cases, and so I have brought you this one. At the finish of our investigations, whenever that might be, we shall both present each other with an envelope containing the name of Sir Richard's murderer. And the prize to the victor shall only be the knowledge that he has beaten the other, no more – save perhaps Doctor Watson's written attestation, should it officially be proved true. What do you say, Mr Holmes?"

"Hardacre, Stisted, whatever your name is," said I, quite infuriated by his heedless arrogance, "I hardly think—"

"He will be Hardacre in public," said Holmes mildly. He turned back towards Khan and then me with a smile. "The Cannibal Club is a darkly secretive gentlemen's dining club, closely affiliated with the Anthropological Society of London."

"The Anthropological Society of London?" said I. "But, Holmes, that concerns itself with pseudo-medicine and phrenology. I fail to see how—"

"That is an altogether different Anthropological Society, Watson, founded in 1836 by John Isaac Hawkins. And neither to be confused with the Ethnological Society of London, founded in 1843. The Anthropological Society of London broke away from the latter in 1863, in the very same year, in fact, that the Cannibal Club was formed. And Burton was the co-founder of both." The short stage ground to a sudden and shuddering halt. "I will take your wager, Hardacre. Though I must insist upon full disclosure from this moment on, do you agree?"

Hardacre's smile was too wide and too easy. "I do."

"Anthropology," said Holmes, as the door was opened on to a city that had once more returned to the dark gloom of midwinter. "The study of humanity. Obviously, we have no body to examine, no crime scene to catalogue. So, studying our fellow man is all that is left to us. Tonight, gentlemen, we go to an Anthropological Society meeting."

For the entirety of the hansom journey between Marylebone and St James's Hall, I felt ridiculously – and acutely – certain that Holmes and I were being followed. Even after we alighted, and our cab had disappeared into the night, I felt no less watched – although if I am truly honest, *stalked* was the word that I first thought of, and it raised the hairs on the back of my neck.

"Holmes," I whispered, as we were ushered through a side door on Regent Street, rather than via the main entrance on Piccadilly, and then down a set of narrow stairs, "I believe someone is following us."

He flashed me a brief smile over his shoulder – "I have no doubt at all of it, Watson" – before we found ourselves inside a room about sixty feet square, furnished with long, narrow, green-upholstered benches, plain walls, and a low platform with an empty lectern.

"What the devil do you mean?" I muttered, still horribly unsettled, though now somewhat angry too. "Holmes! What—"

"Ah," said Holmes, looking over my shoulder. "And here arrive our mentees. Good evening, Khan, Hardacre."

On the floor above us, the orchestra were tuning up, presumably for a rehearsal rather than a performance because Piccadilly Circus had been almost empty. The discordant strings, woodwind, brass and percussion called to mind the concert hall's rather more grandiose pretensions: its Florentine arches and arabesque columns; its wonderfully Gothic restaurants.

"They say that St James's is based upon the Alhambra in Granada," Hardacre observed, as a rather less musical bell sounded the start of closer proceedings. "Sir Richard visited the palace in '41. He said it was quite incredible: a pearl set in emeralds. I have made many lithographs of Moorish *muqarnas* and screens. In Nasrid palaces, the arabesques and calligraphy are said to hide codes of great import—"

"Your seats are over there," Holmes said, pointing back towards the exit as he moved closer to the stage.

"Why, Khan," Hardacre drily observed, "we are to be almost street Arabs."

Holmes said nothing until we were both sitting in our rather more comfortable seats. "Ye Gods, I find him insufferable!"

"He is certainly an acquired taste," I smiled.

Holmes turned to me with narrowed eyes as the first guest speaker began walking towards the lectern to enthusiastic applause. "Was that a witticism, John?"

Holmes and I had known each other nearly a decade by then, and amid everything that I had observed of and learned from him, the most significant – the most pertinent – was knowing very definitely when a fight was not worth the fighting.

"Look," I said, "I do not think—"

"Perhaps you, too, are dunderheaded enough to fall in with his crudely imagined belief that he is just like his great-uncle, and so, therefore, by further illogical and ill-founded implication, just like me?"

"Of course not," said I placatingly, for it was most unlike Holmes to allow himself to be so rattled. "And yet, you accepted his wager."

"The *case* interests me, Watson. That is all," he muttered. "He wanted me to know that he was Burton's great-nephew – of course, that is not in any doubt. He is a buffoon, a tiresome know-it-all."

"He is a boy, Holmes. And one most likely used to getting what he wants."

"Certainly one who thinks himself altogether cleverer than he is."

When an angry fellow spun around in his seat to glare at us, Holmes returned a stare so deadly that the gentleman audibly swallowed and turned back towards the stage without so much as a tut.

"A brandy, Watson. You look as though you have need of it."

The lounge was loud and too hot, but I hardly cared; the intermission could not have come soon enough.

"I can hardly believe that such supposedly learned men can so staunchly and imprudently defend such a ludicrous idea as polygenesis!" I protested. "To imagine that one race of people is more mentally and morally developed than another; or, furthermore, that there is more than one kind of human at all, is preposterous!"

Holmes merely smiled and waved towards Hardacre and Khan as they pushed their way towards the bar.

"And what exactly was the wisdom behind subjecting poor Khan to such ignorant *enlightenment*?" I asked, for in truth I was altogether incensed enough to believe that my friend had sought to use him only as an inflammatory device.

"He wanted the case," said Holmes. "That is all. I fail to understand what has you so furious, Watson."

"Holmes!" I exclaimed. "What is wrong with you? You surely do not believe all those—"

"Khan, Hardacre, well met again," Holmes said. "Might I also buy you both a drink before the infernal little bell calls us once more back to duty?"

"I am heartily sorry for all of this, Khan," said I, as Holmes snapped loud fingers towards a passing waiter.

Khan smiled his wide, warm smile, though his face belied the strain of doing so. "It is quite all right, Doctor. I am long used to such . . . ideology. And thank you, no, Mr Holmes. I do not drink."

"A Scotch," Hardacre said, and the waiter vanished back into the crowd.

"If I am finally permitted to answer your hysterical question, Watson," Holmes said. "I believe in that which is always the most logical, and nothing more. I am swayed neither by jaundiced doggerel nor by liberal idealism. Clearly, you are for monogenesis—"

"Of course I am!" I exclaimed. "As is anyone of a sane mind. *On the Origin of Species* is a remarkable piece of—"

"You would do well not to say so quite so passionately within these walls," said Holmes. "Though I do not disagree with you. In my studies of cadavers, I have had cause to document and measure all manner of men, and there is little or no anatomical difference between races that cannot be explained either by environment or Darwin's own extensive studies." He gave a humourless smile. "And the morals of men seem predictably monotonous the world over. The evidence for polygenesis is neither sound nor sensible." His gaze landed upon Hardacre. "Superiority is not passed on like a Roman nose or a disease of the liver. It is entirely in the realm of the individual."

As the bell sounded, calling us back to doubtless more hours of stoic nonsense and the apt disharmony of the rehearsing orchestra on the floor above, Holmes bade us wait at the back of the jostling crowd.

"Two things to always remember," he said to Khan and Hardacre. "As a detective, you must distinguish yourself from common ways of thinking. One must learn to be impartial, to put one's own views out of sight. Khan here has admirably managed it, and under considerable external duress. Watson, you have not."

"Well, I—"

"Another thing that you are also rather guilty of, Doctor – although in that, too, you are far from alone – is that you only ever reason forwards. For example, if I were to describe to you a series of simple events, you would be able to draw a likely conclusion to them; although it is also worth bearing in mind that your conclusion would be rather influenced by what I had and had not told you." He steepled his fingers. "But, if I were instead to present you with only the conclusion, you would be quite unable to reason backwards; that is, to deduce both logically and objectively those events leading up to that conclusion."

"Holmes," said I, as confused as I was put out, "I have no idea what—"

"You assume, Watson, that all of these gentlemen believe in polygenesis only because they have said so, and because you yourself are so vehemently against it. But, a man may posit anything at all; it is his motive that is the more important – what will be the result? For example, I know of at least two men in this room who were once paid agents acting on the behalf of the Confederate States of America, their sole purpose to convince men of means that the abolitionists were wrong, and that the 'Negro' was fit only to be a slave. Belief is irrelevant. Cause, motive, and effect are all. Do you see?"

"I am sorry," said Khan, "but I do not."

"Very well. To put it in plainer terms, in order to understand the crime, we must think like the victim. And Burton must have been very much for polygenesis; why else would he have broken away from the liberal, Darwin-supporting Ethnological Society in the first place to form this one? But the question that we must ask ourselves is why? To what end? And where does his Cannibal Club fit in?"

"This is a pointless discussion!" Hardacre suddenly cried, attracting some attention. His face was quite puce. "What does it matter what Burton did or did not believe? Why are you not looking instead for his enemies? At the muddy footprints around his bed and the bone necklace on his chest? The card that—"

"Sherlock Holmes, as I live and breathe!" said a loud voice from behind my shoulder, and I spun around to see a stout gentleman in formal evening dress, his nose and cheeks flushed red with what we in the profession call 'a king's corollary'. He grasped hold of Holmes's hand between both of his. "How wonderful to have such esteemed support."

"I am merely an impartial observer," Holmes said, taking back his hand as soon as he was able. "This is Edward Hardacre, Hamid Khan, and my friend and colleague, Doctor Watson."

"Well met, well met! And I am George Hope Henley. I must confess that I too am somewhat ambivalent. I come here for the diversion and the port." He drained his wine glass with a grimace. "If not the claret." He nodded towards the still-crowded exit. "You do well to wait. It will be at least another quarter of an hour before everyone is settled down to a new, dry talk. Burton should be turning in his grave, eh?" His laugh was loud and booming, but Holmes seemed hardly concerned when yet more gentlemen looked our way.

"So, you knew Sir Richard Burton?" Holmes enquired, after Henley had ordered some port and we had settled ourselves at an empty table.

"Indeed so! I was attached to the Foreign Office in Damascus when he was consul, though I met him on only a few occasions. Oh, he was quite the intimidating fellow: nut brown and tall as a native, with a vast moustache and piercing, furious eyes – one was blue and the other quite dark, you know – and he had a huge, grisly scar on both cheeks, where a Somali spear had passed clean through his mouth and out the other side.

"He was already something of a legend by then, of course; marriage had not tamed him one iota. I heard such tales from colleagues who had worked alongside him on Fernando Po, his first diplomatic posting after his army years and Nile expeditions. Of trips up mountains searching for cannibals and gorillas; of drug-induced atrocities and perversions. Certainly, he made great study of juju and ritual murder and the more peculiar sexual practices of the natives. It is said that he even lived awhile among the Amazonian warrior women of Dahomey, a kingdom famous for human sacrifice. There cannot have been a man in Damascus who did not think Burton mad or bad or both." Henley grinned and made much pantomime of winking. "Which isn't to say that any one of us would not have sacrificed our right arm to be him just for a day."

Holmes laughed long and loud.

"And, of course," said Henley, leaning closer to the table, "Burton was a man of many contradictions. Take, for example, his Rwandan companion."

Holmes raised his eyebrows. "What of him?"

"Well, Burton was always somewhat removed from the typical gentleman explorer. For every anthropological paper on the Hamitic theory that the White man is superior to the Negroid man, he would write another on the intricacies of ancient ritual or language. He rather immersed himself in every culture that he encountered." Henley gave another obvious wink. "And the Rwandan was a Hutu tribesman. The Hutu were seen, even among the natives, as being inferior to other regional tribes, such as the Tutsi and the Twa."

"But the Hutu was his slave!" Hardacre protested.

"Begging your pardon, young man, but the Hutu was neither his slave nor even his servant, but his willing companion."

"And so, your point must be why, then, should Sir Richard have chosen such a man as a companion?" said Holmes.

Henley nodded. "Indeed. Although if you ask me, much of the scandal and rumour that plagued Burton came not from his own ill-advised *experiments* – for want of a better word – but rather from the sanctimonious envy of his rather less successful contemporaries. Not least, his ill-fated Nile companion, John Hanning Speke."

"Speke!" I exclaimed. "Why, Holmes, did not the Lady Burton mention him when—" Too late, I noticed Holmes's glare of censure.

"See those two fellows over there?" Henley said, quite oblivious. "The ones that have been giving us the evil eye since we sat ourselves down?"

I followed his gaze to two men standing alongside the bar. One was tall and grey and of a military bearing; the other was the angry gentleman who had sat ahead of us in the lecture hall.

"They are Major Thomas Rowlands and Lord John Bowles, longtime friends of both Speke and Henry Stanley – incidentally, I have it on good authority that General Gordon once received a letter from Burton insisting that, 'Stanley shoots Negroes as if they were monkeys.' Imagine! *The* Henry Morton Stanley!" Henley drained his glass, and then seemed to make a concerted effort to sober himself. "My point is that Burton was something of an anathema to these kinds of men; he collected enemies as enthusiastically as native artefacts. Upon their return to London, Speke made it known that Burton had gone to the devil in Africa, and a terrible hoo-ha ensued."

"Yes, I think I remember reading about this," said I. "Some dispute over who had discovered the source of the Nile?"

"A dispute!" Henley snorted. "Well, yes. Court cases, slander, libel, the lot." He leaned close to the table again, and all four of us followed suit. "The day before Speke and Burton were scheduled to debate the topic at a meeting of the British Association for the Advancement of Science, Speke went hunting on the nearby estate of a relative. He was discovered next to a stone wall, felled by a fatal chest wound from his own shotgun. There was talk at the time of suicide, of course. Even murder. Though it was ruled an accident."

"Gentlemen," boomed a voice rather too close to my ear for comfort.

"Major Rowlands," said Henley, in a higher-pitched tone.

The major stood tall and impassive, several men, including Lord Bowles, close behind him. "I believe that the next lecture is about to begin. Perhaps you might wish to save further conversation until later?"

Holmes stood. "Indeed. And many thanks for the warning." He grinned fast and fleetingly, every one of his teeth visible. "We should not wish to miss one moment."

Only when those men had disappeared back into the corridor did

Holmes urge us all to follow. "Henley, I must thank you most profusely for so enlightening a conversation." He pressed a card into the delighted man's palm before shaking his other. "Should you ever find yourself in Marylebone, please do not hesitate to call upon us, you shall be most welcome. I have just one more question for you: might you have heard of the Cannibal Club?"

"Indeed I have, Mr Holmes, although, of course, I have never been invited to attend, and have no clue at all as to where or when it is held. I hear it is still quite outrageously wild, even with Burton no longer at the helm."

Holmes smiled and clapped him hard upon the shoulder. "Good man." He waited until Henley too had gone the way of the rest before turning back to us. "Watson, can you stand to suffer the final instalments of this night alongside me, while these two gentlemen interview the waiting staff and doormen? I fear we will not learn much more here tonight, but we must never squander either opportunity or the advantage of numbers. We shall regroup at the main entrance on Piccadilly at midnight. Agreed?"

Due to our delay, Holmes and I found ourselves having to sit on the rather uncomfortable wooden stools close to the exit – Hardacre's "street Arab" seats. This proved fortunate when, less than half an hour later, a white-faced waiter tapped Holmes on the shoulder and leaned close to our ears.

"Mr Holmes, there has been . . . an incident, sir. We have already sent for Scotland Yard, but perhaps you might—"

"Indeed, indeed!" said Holmes, standing immediately. "Come, Watson."

We followed the waiter back out into the narrow corridor and stairwell that led to the private Regent Street entrance. Around the open door crowded perhaps a dozen men and women, jostling and gasping and exclaiming. Such symptoms I am always able to diagnose before any other: the excited dismay of discovered death.

"There are altogether too many people here!" Holmes boomed, scattering them like spindrift.

Once we were alone, he made no move to step through the door, but instead ushered me ahead of him. "Doctor."

The body lay spread-eagled upon the wet ground, its eyes staring up into the moonless night. Blood pooled around him and inside the ruin of his torso; it speckled his waxy face.

"Oh, Lord, Holmes, it is George Hope Henley!"

Holmes stepped out of the doorway and on to the street. His face was quite set in stone, but his eyes were bright, dark marbles.

"Holmes, this is not your fault. This *cannot* be your fault." When I took a step towards him, he retreated two.

Luckily, or unluckily – I still cannot decide which – both Hardacre and Khan then rushed out into the space behind him.

"Oh no!" exclaimed Khan, trying and failing to catch his breath. "It is Hope Henley!"

Hardacre said nothing at all. He stood in the street and looked down upon the body with an ashen face and tight-pressed lips.

"Are you quite well?" Holmes snapped. "I understand that it can be unsettling to be faced with a corpse, but in your proposed profession—"

"Yes, yes," muttered Hardacre. "I am quite well."

"Then what, pray, is your preliminary assessment of the crime scene? It is raining, Hardacre. Need I remind you how transient much evidence can be?"

"No, indeed," Hardacre muttered, dropping quickly to a crouch next to the body.

"I shall scout for secondary evidence and eyewitness accounts," Khan announced rather grandly before running off towards Piccadilly, and I noticed, with the inapt humour that so often accompanies shock that, although he had on his hat and his scarf, he had managed to quite forget his coat.

"There are footprints," Hardacre said. "Leading up to and then away from the body. The same size and tread. Large, low-soled. Shoes rather than boots."

"What else?"

Hardacre continued to quail under Holmes's disdain, where it had previously served only to bolster his resolve. "The stride is wide, perhaps eighteen inches. Which must mean a man of at least six and a half foot or taller."

"Very well. Doctor, how did he die?"

I sighed, dropping back down on to my haunches. The rain was growing heavier; it began to soak through my coat. "He exsanguinated. He was stabbed repeatedly. Though filleted might be a better description. At a rudimentary glance, I'd hazard that the stomach, liver, and perhaps the kidneys, have been excised."

"Indeed?" said Holmes. Some of the colour had returned to his face, though he looked no healthier. His smile was thin. "The internal edibles, as Mrs Hudson would say."

He turned away as Khan splashed noisily back along the street. The fellow was quite breathless, with twin spots of red high on his cheeks. "I found a couple on the Duke of York Street," he gasped. "They said a man, dressed head to toe in black, rushed past them not five minutes ago, heading towards St James's Square and Pall Mall. They said he was *barhaa* – " he waved his hands in frustrated agitation – "big, large." He looked down at the body again before closing his eyes and turning his head.

"But there is something missing here, is there not?" Holmes said, and his voice was so coldly furious that I could only bring myself to look at him when there sounded a bang loud enough to make both Hardacre and Khan yelp. Holmes kept his gloved hands pressed hard against the slammed-shut door to the stairwell long after the panicked cries and thuds began from within.

On the back of the door were painted the letters "CC" in thick, arterial blood.

Holmes glanced first at us, and then at poor, dead Hope Henley.

"The Cannibal Club," he said, wrenching open the door again with force enough to make me wince.

When three days passed, and I had heard not a word from Holmes, I called upon 221b Baker Street out of concern as much as curiosity. Mrs Hudson ushered me in with some measure of relief.

"He has had no visitors at all, Doctor, save a rather angry Lestrade on Monday. Although he himself is in and out at all times of the day; I never know when I'm supposed to feed or water him—"

"Calm yourself, Mrs Hudson, he is quite immersed in a case, that is all."

"Well, this day he is quite immersed in his room, if you please, and is quite refusing to come out!"

She was right. When Holmes would neither acknowledge nor answer my repeated knocks at his door, I settled down to tea in the sitting room. I had been waiting there less than half an hour, when Mrs Hudson reappeared, looking even more harried than before.

"Doctor Watson! This man is quite insist—"

"This man" was a near hysterical Khan and, while I was trying to calm both him and poor Mrs Hudson down, Holmes abruptly barged out of his room. He looked as if he had only just woken up: his eyes were bloodshot, his hair wild, and he was still dressed in his nightclothes.

"Hardacre is missing, Mr Holmes!" Khan cried. "Yesterday, we were supposed to meet up to discuss our theories as to the case, but he never appeared, and today I gained access to his room, and it has been turned over just as thoroughly as if Scotland Yard had exercised a warrant."

"Then there is no time to lose," Holmes said. "Khan, go back to the school. Ask every fellow student if Hardacre mentioned what he was doing, or where he was going. Do you still have the key to his room on Arlington Street?"

When Khan nodded and then handed it over, Holmes ushered him back towards the door. "Watson and I shall investigate his room. And we shall all meet up again," he said, wafting his arms about quite uncharacteristically, "at some point. To discuss the findings."

"But, Holmes," protested Khan. "How—"

"Mrs Hudson!" Holmes bellowed, casting off his heavy dressing gown. "Some clothes, if you please!"

As soon as Khan had gone, Holmes sagged, groping his way to the nearest armchair. "Gods, John, I fear that I have made a very terrible mistake. I fear that I have done everything wrong."

"You?" said I. "*How?*"

"Because I have done nothing at all *right*," Holmes said, just as Mrs Hudson re-entered, carrying both his suit and coat. He sprang up from the chair like an uncoiled snake. "But it might not yet be too late. I cannot undo what has already been done to poor George Hope Henley, but perhaps I can prevent what must come next. Come, Watson – to Arlington Street!"

"Well, Khan was not wrong about the mess," said I, as we picked our way through it. Hardacre's room was small, and every inch of its space had been covered in books and clothes and crumpled papers.

"Start looking!" Holmes barked.

"But what are we looking for?"

Holmes gave me an exasperated glare. "We shall know when we find it." He began tossing the larger books on to Hardacre's bed, and then paused. "Also, an envelope. Small, sealed."

For perhaps twenty minutes or more, we sorted through Hardacre's disturbed possessions – I rather more thoroughly than Holmes, as I was too afraid I might discard something of vital importance and never know it. From time to time, Holmes would sift out objects significant enough to elicit a sharp *Ha!*, although I knew better than to stop what I was doing to enquire as to what these might be.

When I was rifling through a pile of Hardacre's clothes, I felt something inside a coat pocket. "Holmes, an envelope!" I took it out. "Small, sealed!"

"Well done, Watson!" Holmes said, although he did not turn around.

"Why, it has your name on it! What—" And then, of course, I remembered. Hardacre's wager with Holmes. Inside this envelope, Hardacre had written the name of Burton's killer.

"Open it," said Holmes.

I did so, although I must confess that my fingers fumbled as I tore through the envelope and plucked out the card. "Wait. This can't be right—"

I looked up just as Holmes's shoulders slumped. Finally, he turned to look at me. "It is blank, is it not?"

"Yes it is. But why? And how could you possibly have known?"

"Why indeed?" said Holmes, sitting heavily down on Hardacre's bed.

"Perhaps Hardacre has not yet made his decision regarding the killer. Perhaps—"

"Watson, sometimes you can be altogether too inclined towards the obtuse," Holmes snapped. I chose to let the insult pass, as it was obvious that he was rather more furious with himself than with me. "The envelope was sealed, was it not? And isn't it also rather more logical to assume that a man such as Hardacre would be very unlikely to suggest a wager of any sort without first being certain of the answer?"

"Well, yes, that does make better sense, I admit. But why, then, is it blank?"

"We are too late," Holmes muttered. "I am too late. But how could I have done anything else? It is always a grave error to theorise in defiance of all the evidence. It biases the judgement." He covered his face with both hands. "Though Lord knows, I have been biased enough."

My friend's agitation was nearly too much to bear. "Holmes—"

"I should not have called Hardacre a know-it-all. I am a know-it-all because *I know it all* – as much as matters anyway. And what I do not know, I have the means to discover. But this boy – this rather foolish, rather too pleased with himself boy – was very, very far from knowing it all."

"As am I," said I, knowing that the only way to draw him out of this fug was to play to the very greatest of his strengths. I waved my hand holding the card and envelope over the mess of papers on the floor, and the rather more organised stack that Holmes had made upon the writing desk. "What does this blank card mean? What in all of this detritus confirms anything at all?"

Holmes's smile was wearily resigned. "This room is a rather perfect textbook example of observed deduction. It would have been quite the teaching exercise." He gave a long, low sigh. "Very well, sit down, Watson, and I shall explain. There is no great hurry now, after all."

He began to pile journals in the space between us. I picked up the last: *Anthropologia*, with Sir Richard Francis Burton's by-line.

"Every edition since 1863," Holmes said, "I've checked." He added more and more papers to the pile. "Texts on polygenesis, Hamitic theory, the Atlantic slave trade. A few magazines, most likely for distribution; bad satire and cartoons against the church and the Society for the Suppression of Vice; Mrs Grundy caricatures and the like. All six volumes of *Anthropologie der Naturvölker*—"

"Holmes!" I protested, as the heavy hardbacks began toppling everything before them. "So, Hardacre was a supporter of the Anthropological Society? A member?"

"He fancied himself equal to Burton, did he not? Or perhaps, instead, his rightful successor. Did you never notice that he always stood ahead of Khan, spoke ahead of him, interrupted him at every opportunity? And he had little or no regard for Burton's artefacts and cultural writings, nor his Hutu companion." Holmes's smile was thin. "*We are to be street Arabs*," he said, in startling imitation of Hardacre.

"I feel that you are accusing Hardacre of something, but if being an ill-informed bigot was a crime, Holmes, then surely half of London would be locked up in Newgate."

"Peas, Watson."

"What?"

"There was a Moravian scientist and friar named Gregor Johann Mendel. He was quite a genius; I'll wager more than I will come to realise so in years to come. He made a great study of peas. When a yellow pea and a green pea were bred together, their offspring were always yellow. But, in the next generation, one in three peas was once more green. Mendel categorised the phenomenon by using the terms 'recessive' and 'dominant' to describe the predictive outcome of future generations of peas."

"Yes," said I, now beginning to lose patience. "I am familiar with recessive and dominant factors. I do read medical journals, Holmes. I just didn't realise that they were anything to do with peas."

"And have you also heard of heterochromia iridis?"

"Of course. It occurs when one is born with one iris a different colour from the other."

"Quite so," said Holmes. "Hardacre has heterochromia iridis. Did you not notice? One eye was blue, the other hazel."

"I did not notice, but—"

"And you will also know, no doubt, that hereditary heterochromia is dominant factor led rather than recessive; thus, in other words, the next generation of affected peas would have a one in two chance of being green instead of yellow."

"Will you please just tell me what you're getting at, Holmes?"

"I have been rather busy these past three days," he said. "In 1845, Burton's sister, Maria Katherine Elizabeth Burton, married Sir Henry William Stisted, the Lieutenant Governor of Ontario. They had one daughter, Georgiana Martha Stisted – she of *The True Life of Capt. Sir Richard F. Burton* fame – who, rather obviously, given her surname, never married and therefore could never have had a son called John Stisted."

When I offered Holmes's raised brows only a bewildered shrug, he threw up his hands in exasperation. "Good grief, Watson! Burton had heterochromia entire! It was much talked about and written about

– further evidence, were it needed, that Burton had indeed gone to the devil! Did you not listen to a word that George Hope Henley said to us in the bar of St James's Hall?"

"Holmes, rather a lot has happened since then! How can I possibly be expected to . . . Wait a minute, do you mean to say that Hardacre – or whatever his name is – is actually Burton's own son?"

"Bravo, Watson," exclaimed Holmes. "I knew you'd get there eventually." He glanced across the ruined room. "And it must be said that while it is prudent, and often necessary, to employ one alter ego, to simultaneously require two implies only an excess of incompetence."

"I still don't understand. When and where did—"

"Well, that is rather more down to deduction than acquired knowledge. He was illegitimate, of course. Judging by his age, he was most probably conceived while Burton was consul in Damascus. Perhaps it was one of the reasons for his rather abrupt exile to Trieste. Hardacre is white, so his mother was doubtless the wife of one of Burton's Foreign Office colleagues." Holmes abruptly stood. "Of course, there is far more to it than that, but now we have run out of time. Watson, I must embark upon an errand, and you must return home to your wife." He flashed his teeth. "And then I must away to the Cannibal Club."

"The Cannibal Club? You mean to say that you have known of its whereabouts all along?"

"Yes, I regret to say. I have been there many times."

"Well then, why the devil didn't you ever say so?"

"I am supposed to be fulfilling the role of teacher and mentor, Watson! What lesson would there be in answering every question before it is even asked?" He stopped at the door, and then punched once at its frame with the heel of a fist. "Though a pox on that! A pox on tempering my mind to match everyone else's. Look at where it has landed us!"

"Then you don't intend to ask Khan along? Is it not still his case?"

"No, it is not. Lestrade's School for Detection is all well and good, but here this particular lesson must stop."

"Very well," I agreed. "Then where *is* the Cannibal Club?"

"Bertolini's Italian and French restaurant on Leicester Square," Holmes said, as if that, too, should all along have been obvious. "It is held every Tuesday."

It was only once Holmes had gone that I realised in baiting him out of his despair, I had filled the role of simpleton rather too well. For I still had not a clue as to what the blank card inside the envelope meant at all.

Leicester Square was most definitely not a place one would expect to find a gentlemen's club, secret or no. In recent years, it had gone further downhill, and was frequented only by gamblers and sharks and women of a certain vocation. Nevertheless, Holmes and I arrived there by hansom at seven o'clock, and walked a short distance to Bertolini's off St Martin's Lane, whereupon he turned quite abruptly into a neighbouring alleyway.

I was wearing a pinstriped Chadwick suit and frock coat, which was most uncomfortable, not least because it belonged to Holmes who was far leaner and taller than I, but also because it was far more flamboyant than I was accustomed to. Holmes himself was rather more conservatively dressed, but he had on a wig, a moustache, and a false nose, whereas I, other than the suit, had been let off lightly; he had insisted on my wearing only a big, bushy beard.

The alleyway terminated in a high wall, next to which was a red wooden door. Holmes knocked thrice upon it, and a morose, thin-haired gentleman thrust his head through a creaking and narrow gap, eyes sharp.

"Ah, Mr Basil!" he exclaimed, revealing horrible teeth. "We have not seen you here for many months!"

"A great regret," Holmes replied. "I am just returned from Upper Guinea."

"Then come in, come in, a return to the London winter must be quite disagreeable – and who might this be?"

"This is my friend and colleague, Captain Beatson," smiled Holmes. "I am permitted one guest, am I not?"

"Indeed so," said the man, though he peered at me quite disconcertingly with those still-sharp eyes. "Any guest vouched for by Mr Algernon Basil is most welcome, of course."

He ushered us in through the narrow door, and then along a barely wider corridor. I could hear the loud bustle of the kitchen and the restaurant beyond, but we were heading further from both.

"Who is that gentleman?" I whispered to Holmes.

"Giovanni Dominico Bertolini Junior," Holmes whispered back before stopping briefly to sniff the air. "No, I am mistaken. Tonight: Jean-Dominique Bertolini Junior."

"Come, gentlemen," Bertolini said over his shoulder. "You must hurry."

We obeyed, and presently came upon a closed set of large oak doors, above which there was a tarnished plaque bearing the words "Banqueting Rooms".

"Now, remember, Beatson," said Holmes, as Bertolini began unlocking one door. "Follow my lead at all times."

The doors opened upon such a wall of sudden noise that I was quite taken aback. The room, although very large, was packed full of gentlemen, some sitting in scruffy hard-backed chairs and couches set against its walls; most standing in huddled, tight groups in its centre. Everyone, it seemed, was speaking at once, and loudly; the frenzied chatter was eclipsed only by raucous booms of laughter.

Once Bertolini had left us with a curt nod, Holmes turned to me as swiftly. "I must get my bearings. Meet me back here in quarter of an hour. Explore. Observe."

And then he was gone.

I did as he bade me, of course, although I felt quite conspicuous as I picked my way through those loudly bombastic fellows. I felt certain that they would be able to see through my bad disguise to the disdain beneath. For how scornful I was! I didn't doubt that these were the same gentlemen as had attended those interminable lectures in St James's Hall, but in private and in drink – as is so often the case – their true motives and proclivities were revealed to repellent effect. Such self-serving bigotry; such dissolute and primitive baseness in a roomful of so purportedly learned gentlemen, I have never again had the misfortune to come across. By the time Holmes returned with one large glass of wine, I was so appalled, it was all I could do to begin drinking it.

"Well," Holmes said, "what do you say?"

"I say this is no Diogenes," I muttered.

"Ha!" Holmes laughed. "Indeed not. It is its antithesis in rather many more ways than one."

"Holm . . . Basil," I muttered, though scarcely anyone could have heard us in the din. "All I see are rich, debauched men titillating themselves by reading aloud from banned texts, and whispering about pederasty and algolagnia in dark corners." I put down the wine. "And rather a lot of bad burgundy. There is nothing either learned or mysterious about any of it."

At that, there sounded another burst of lurid laughter.

"Well," said Holmes mildly, "I have, as you know, only a passing interest in literature of any sort, but I do hear that the *Kama Sutra* and Burton's abridged *Arabian Nights* are at least accomplished works. What is of rather more import, however—"

"Good God," I exclaimed. "Is that not Lord Penzance QC? And over there! Charles Bradlaugh, the Liberal MP for—" Holmes's sharp elbow between two of my ribs silenced me better than his furious glare.

"We are supposed to be incognito, and that requires rather more than just a bad suit and a false beard. Please do not make me regret asking you along."

"You did not ask me along," said I. "I threatened to go to Lestrade if you came here alone. By Jove, and this beard itches abominably."

"For someone so desperate to come, you do not seem to be having a good time."

"Yes, well," said I, still angry – and perhaps more than a little apprehensive, "we are not here to have a good time, are we?"

"No," said Holmes, rather more soberly than I liked. "We are not." Perhaps sensing my consternation, he gave a thin smile. "Although this might appeal to your need for titillation: Tennyson used to come here twice a month."

"Lord Tennyson?" said I.

"He called the place 'Dirtolini's'."

"Look there!" I exclaimed. "Is that not John Hanning Speke's friend from St James's Hall – the major?"

"Major Thomas Rowlands," Holmes muttered. At once, he was as tense as he had been in Hardacre's room. "And alongside him, Lord John Bowles, if I'm not mistaken."

"Are they something to do with Hope Henley's death and Hardacre's disappearance? You must surely share with me that at least—"

"If one wishes to give both voice and life to long-cherished beliefs or prejudices or perversions," said Holmes, in a low, careful voice quite unlike his own, "then all that is ever required are like minds and a righteous fight for false freedoms. You may call it intellectual inquiry; better still, you may call yourselves learned or cultural warriors against an enemy that does not exist. Men like these – " he threw out an arm towards the packed room, its fist clenched – "powerful men, bored senseless by their own privilege, have been doing just that since the beginning of time. And yet, never once – despite their expensive educations – do they ever glimpse their own ignorance. These, Watson, are the very epitome of men incapable of reasoning backwards; it is not in them to ever see what monsters they might be creating – monsters far worse than even them." He suddenly turned his sharp gaze on to me. "Have you your revolver?"

"Of course I have. You instructed me to bring it. Look here," I whispered, because Holmes's nervousness had become an uncommon tension obvious enough as to be palpable. Although hindsight can often blur recollection, I'm certain that I knew then that something terrible was about to happen. "You are making no sense at all. I do not—"

"Ah," said Holmes, at the sound of a gong. "The call to dine."

He spared me no more room to object, weaving his way through the crowds towards an adjoining opened door. I followed, finding myself in another large, windowless room, filled to capacity with long benches and trestle tables, a raised wooden dais at its end. I spotted Holmes and hurried over to sit alongside him. He offered me not the slightest acknowledgment as a slim and ginger-bearded gentleman mounted the dais and then banged hard on the table with a carved wooden mace before launching into the strangest of speeches, which I only latterly recognised as a blasphemous mockery of the Eucharist.

"Preserve us from our enemies,
Thou who art Lord of suns and skies,
Whose meat and drink is flesh in pies,
And blood in bowls!
Of thy sweet mercy, damn their eyes,
And damn their souls!"

"Good God," said I into Holmes's ear. "Those were the words on the card left next to Burton's body!"

"Indeed," said Holmes dismissively, and, when I followed his gaze, I recognised the broad figure of Major Thomas Rowlands sitting at the table furthest from our own. "The Cannibal Catechism. An infantile jeer."

When the ginger-bearded man set the mace down upon the high table, I was better able to see it, and was further appalled to realise that it was a rudimentary depiction of an African native gnawing on a human thighbone. I suffered the uncanny prickle of déjà vu, until at once I remembered where I had seen it before, and grabbed hold of Holmes's arm in startled reflex.

"Hardacre's doodle," Holmes pre-empted, taking back his arm with a frown. "Mistake rather than design, I suspect. Hardacre was altogether too excited by his own deception – very few men are able to maintain the proper restraint when inhabiting a disguise." He shot me a look that I interpreted only too well.

But as the food and wine were served by silent, white-shirted waiters, and the dining room returned to the same loud chaos as the lounge before it, I found that I cared less for Holmes's scorn than I did for that terrible sense of impending doom.

"I am no longer *prepared* to maintain the proper restraint," I whispered, leaning close enough to exclude any possibility of being overheard. "And I care little what your opinion is of that. If you do not explain to me exactly what is going on, I shall announce us both to everyone here."

"Be assured, that would be a most ill-advised path to take," muttered Holmes, as two bowls of blood-red soup were set before us. "But I suppose I must tell you some of it, for I fear very much where the events of this night might be leading, and you have always been, of course, the very best of my allies. Ask me one question, and I shall answer it entirely truthfully."

I took some time to consider, but only one stood the tallest. "The blank card inside the sealed envelope. What was its meaning?"

Despite his obvious consternation, Holmes smiled. "Bravo – by far the wisest choice! Very well: we already know that Hardacre was Burton's illegitimate son; that he was aware of the Anthropological Society and, by his doodle, the Cannibal Club, and that he undoubtedly held and supported the very same views. We know also that he and Lady Burton were familiar with one another, and that he fancied himself rather resourcefully clever and something of a master of disguise.

"In Mortlake, it was obvious how penurious Lady Burton appeared next to so grand a mausoleum; it is not therefore so great a leap to assume that Hardacre had been blackmailing her for some time. He doubtless had some proof of his own provenance: letters, perhaps even photographs, and we know, too, that Isabel was so averse to scandal that she burned all of Burton's papers and even had a priest collude with her in a lie over the timing of his death, only to ensure that he be buried a Catholic. I imagine that when she eventually ran dry of funds, Hardacre forced her instead to engage my services in the discovery of her husband's murderer."

"But why?"

Holmes leaned back as a loud group of men barged past our table. I was dismayed to recognise a captain of the Fifth Northumberland Fusiliers among them, though not because I thought he might recognise me; that only occurred to me much later.

"We are supposed to think that the murderer of Burton is also the murderer of poor George Hope Henley," said Holmes.

"Then it is not the same man?"

Holmes shook his head. "It is not. Whom do you believe killed Burton?"

"I have no—"

"Come, be bold!" Holmes bellowed, his eyes shining too brightly. His shout was lost in the cacophonous melee, although when he banged his fist against the table, a few neighbouring fellows gave a drunken cheer. "The large, muddy footprints circling counter-clockwise around the bed; the Amazonian necklace of human bones upon his chest!"

"Very well," I snapped, my patience quite at an end. "Burton's companion, Joseph, the Hutu. It is rather obvious."

"Indeed it is," Holmes said, as our soup plates were taken away, to be replaced with larger dishes of still spitting beef entrecote, accompanied by gratin dauphinois. Holmes poured me a rather conservative glass of burgundy and none for himself. "And Hope Henley's murderer?"

"The same," I muttered. "I supposed the same."

"Because of the savage defiling of the body and the second Cannibal Club calling card. And Hardacre's assessment of the crime scene: of a perpetrator at least six and a half foot or taller, and the summation of eyewitness accounts of a giant man dressed head to toe in black running towards Pall Mall."

"Are you implying that Joseph did not murder Henley?"

"Given that I have just told you that the murderer of George Hope Henley cannot also be the murderer of Burton, I am certainly implying something."

I swallowed what there was of my wine. "He was following us that night," I said. "From Marylebone to St James's Hall, I am certain of that. And then again on Regent Street as we examined Henley's body."

"Yes, you are quite correct," said Holmes. When he cut through his beef, red bloody juices spilled on to the plate. "But to what end? And what of Hardacre's grand deception?"

"I do not know," said I. "The blank card inside the sealed envelope. What was its meaning?"

"Single-minded as ever, Beatson." Holmes smiled an ugly smile, and then put down his cutlery. "Very well. The card was blank because Hardacre knew just as well as I that Burton did indeed die of a heart attack in Trieste on October the twentieth, 1890."

"Do you mean that Burton was not murdered at all?"

"Hardacre's mission was three-fold: by making his father a false martyr, he could bring back into public consciousness the polygenist ideologies of the Anthropological Society; by the same token he could ensure that Joseph was declared his murderer by none other than Sherlock Holmes himself – for who would disbelieve it? Who, in all of England, would favour the crude savagery of an imported African *Negro* over and above my own testimony? Last, and doubtless most important of all: despite his clumsy, obvious, and entirely amateur machinations, Hardacre truly believed that he was cleverer than I, and set out to prove it – had my mistake been his only success, and had only he and I been the ones to know it, I still feel certain that he would have considered himself the victor. That little blank card inside that sealed envelope screamed such hubris, such self-aggrandisement! Although, of course, I must confess to some hubris of my own, for I feel certain that I would not have been so long blind had not my own ego been so easily goaded by his."

Of everything, this admission worried me most of all, for its self-deprecation was so out of character as to be extraordinary. "I still do not understand," I muttered. "Not one bit. Nor do I like the way you are always talking of Hardacre in the past tense. Do you believe that something untoward has happened to him?"

"It is rather worse than that," Holmes said. "I believe that he is dead. Murdered by the same hand as George Hope Henley."

"Good Lord! Surely not! Is that why we are here?"

"I believe that the murderer is here tonight, yes. Stalking his next victim."

"Do you know who the murderer is?" When he refused to answer, or even to look my way, my agitation became too much to bear, and I leaned forward to grasp his arm. "Holmes! Do you—"

"Silence!" When he turned back to me, his eyes were dark. "Yes. Of course I know."

"You will not tell me."

"I will not put you at further risk, no." He reached into his waistcoat pocket and brought out a sealed envelope, which he handed to me without further comment.

"This is not a game," said I, because dread permitted me to say nothing else. The envelope was of the same size and type as Hardacre's had been.

"Indeed it is not," Holmes said, carefully excising another square of beef. "Keep it safe. In case something happens to me, Scotland Yard need to know who they are looking for."

"This is intolerable! Can you not at least tell me how we can stop it? Or even how the victims are being chosen?"

"By natural selection," said Holmes rather too grimly, but before I could protest any further there sounded a scream from outside the dining room – long and drawn out and agonised; inhuman enough to raise the hairs on the back of my neck. Holmes was up and away before anyone else had even thought to put down their knife or fork.

By the time I managed to battle my way through the jostling, shouting men already in fast retreat from the lounge – although there was scarcely anywhere else to go except back into the more crowded dining room – I could already smell the copper tang of spilled blood and the sharper sweat of combat. Two men were grappling over an unmoving body ahead of the exit into the restaurant, with Holmes circling along-side, his cane held at chest-height as he drew closer. Major Rowlands stood between me and all three men, his eyes as glassy as they were thunderous.

The Hutu I recognised immediately, of course, for who wouldn't; his bulk and height and hostility were, at first, all I could see. His combatant – holding what appeared to be a knife, although he was too quick for me to be sure of it – seemed hardly matched at all, dodging in and out of the Hutu's enraged reach and swing. I was horrified to realise that the body on the floor was that of Lord John Bowles, and when I recovered enough to realise that the fellow defending himself against the Hutu was none other than Khan, I was freshly horrified again.

"Stay back, Watson!" Holmes shouted, when I rushed towards the major. "Stay back!" He looked as dismayed as he did furious, as if all of his plans had gone awry, and I cannot describe what fear that uncom-mon look provoked in me. What dread.

Although, of course, I could not obey. I knew that Holmes was an expert in singlestick, but as his friend, I could neither dismiss his obvi-ous distress nor the bellowing rage of the Hutu, any more than the likely fate of yet another of Holmes's students. And while I might have greatly liked Khan, most of that fear, I must admit, was not for him but for the condemnation that my friend would surely face when Lestrade learned to what lengths Holmes had gone in the instruction of his students.

I took out my revolver, and Holmes immediately spun around again, pointing his cane my way instead. "Put away your gun!"

"What?" I kept it trained on the fight, which was still little more than attack on one side and feeble defence on the other, and while I didn't see how I might be able to put a stop to it safely, neither did I see how putting away my gun would be of any help either. My skin prickled as I sensed the major edging closer to my flank.

All at once, the Hutu gave a low, ominous roar, and lunged so menacingly towards the sweating, exhausted Khan that I had little option but to try to aim for his larger bulk.

"Peas, Watson!" shouted Holmes. "Peas!"

And then – to use a rather indecorous metaphor – all became blindingly clear. As Holmes steeled himself again to enter and end the fight, I was finally the quicker. I raised my gun and pulled fast on its trigger.

Naturally, Holmes was the first of us to recover his wits. When Bertolini barged back through the banqueting-room doors, Holmes grasped him firmly by his collar and ordered him to call for Scotland Yard.

"Make sure that you ask for Inspector Gregson," he barked. "Major Rowlands! Would you be so kind as to keep everyone away from the crime scene?"

I was altogether less calm as I approached the Hutu and Khan. I knelt by the latter and pressed the pads of my fingers around the blossoming wound in his thigh. It was a match for my own: grievous but not mortal. He screeched and tried to bat me away.

"Enough!" said Holmes. "You know he's a doctor, Khan. Let him help you."

"It's just a soft tissue wound," I muttered, the tremor in my voice betraying my relief.

"A thousand pardons, Mr Holmes," the Hutu said from behind my shoulder, and still I flinched, for his voice seemed to shift the very boards underneath my knees.

"It is quite all right, Joseph," Holmes replied, with an air of too-easy familiarity. "Of course you had no other choice but to act, and you have my grateful thanks. It was my fault entirely. I had determined that the next victim would almost certainly be the major."

After dousing it in whisky and fashioning a pressure pad out of a cushion's stuffing, I bound Khan's wound tight with swathes of ripped tablecloth. He groaned, and clutched at his chest, eyes squeezed shut.

"I am sorry, Watson," said Holmes, removing his false nose, wig and moustache. "But I couldn't be certain that he didn't have a gun, and I trusted that you would recognise his guilt. Sometimes the element of surprise is all that a detective can employ when the burden of proof is always greater than his own absolute certainty."

"You *wanted* this to happen?" I asked, one hand still pressed hard against Khan's thigh.

"I sought to draw him out, and that is all. There was no alternative, Watson! I could not tell you what I suspected, because I could not prove it. And because you liked him just as much as I did, I knew that if I told you anything at all, you would be quite unable to hide it."

"Help me lift him on to the couch," I muttered and, once that was accomplished, and I had stacked some cushions under his wounded leg, I returned to the body of Lord John Bowles. "His throat has been slit," I said, somewhat unnecessarily, looking at Khan's abandoned and bloody knife. I sat heavily down on a leather armchair. "Tell me how you knew."

"Khan had calloused hands and a sinewy build, which belied his claim that he was the son of a merchant," said Holmes. "Always, there were faint black lines against the front of his trousers between knee and mid-calf; a telltale sign of climbing the ladder on to a knifeboard omnibus, and what gentleman takes anything less than a hansom or stage? On the night of Hope Henley's murder, Khan reported eyewitness accounts of a man, dressed head to toe in black, running towards Pall Mall. A man who was big, large – a giant. But the word that he initially used was *barhaa*, and that, Watson, is Urdu, not Pashto. So, then, Khan had lied about what he was and who he was. And yet he had displayed genuine sentiment for the Swat province in north Pakistan when he first met you in the Assembly Rooms."

"The Switzerland of the East," I said.

"Indeed," replied Holmes. "One of the simplest and so rarely adhered to rules of deception is to invent nothing more than is absolutely necessary. But if Khan was indeed from the Swat province, why then lie about being Pashtun? I have made some study of indigenous language and traditions – certainly nothing to rival Sir Richard Burton's rather more intimate efforts—"

"Holmes," I warned.

"Pashtuns live by *Pashtunwali*: an ancient code of eleven principles. The third of these is *Nyaw aw Badal*. Justice and revenge."

Khan groaned and tried to move.

"You must stay still, Khan," said I, moving forward to restrain him.

"All of this," said Holmes grimly, looking across at the struggling Khan, "has been about revenge."

"Let me up," Khan spat, arms flailing as he sought to pull himself up from the couch. "I will speak!"

"You should *not* speak," said I, and meant it as both his doctor and the man who had shot a bullet into his thigh. Murderer or not, it would surely do Khan no good to say anything at all.

He groaned again, and when I realised that he was not going to stop trying to get up, I helped him into a sitting position instead. The eyes that turned on Holmes were full of pain and fury: one brown, the other hazel. "Then speak *to* me."

"Very well," said Holmes. "When you claimed to have returned from the Duke of York Street, your clothes were far too dry. I imagine that you had sheltered under a rooftop or awning instead, and waited until such time as you could return with your incriminating eyewitness accounts. Naturally, you assumed I was already predisposed to think that the perpetrator was Joseph, because, of course, you already knew of Hardacre's own plot, and it served your purpose to encourage the same suspicion. And you wore no coat, only a hat." Holmes's lips thinned almost to nothing. "I imagine that there must have been a lot of blood while you were butchering poor George Hope Henley."

When Khan offered neither confession nor rebuttal, Holmes carried on. "You, too, were blackmailing Lady Burton, but unlike Hardacre, it was only ever by written correspondence. Lady Burton did not know your name, or what you looked like. But it seems you must be rather more skilled in the art of extortion, for it was through Lady Burton that you found out about the existence of Hardacre, and then subsequently of his plan to stir up doubts about Burton's natural death: the fabricated murder scene and the Cannibal Club card, the framing of Joseph. Seeing an opportunity for revenge that was far better than the mere blackmail of Burton's widow, you then used the money that she had sent you to travel to London, where you enrolled as a student of the School for Detection and rented a room in the same building as Hardacre. And, of course, you made certain to be partnered up with him as soon as you could."

"But why?" I protested, turning back to Khan. "And how can you be—"

"You are right, Mr Holmes," Khan said, ignoring me entirely. "I am not Pashtun. I am Guijar. In 1853, my grandmother undertook the Hajj to Mecca, with her brother as *mahram*. When he became ill with a fever outside Medina, my grandmother carried on alone against his wishes. A week later, she met a Pashtun named Mirza Abdullah. And nine months after that, she gave birth to my mother. Nani was found guilty of *zin* under Sharia Law; both she and my mother then endured lives of poverty and shame. And when I was born – with no father willing to acknowledge my birthright either – it was then the same for me."

"Mirza Abdullah was Burton," said I, beginning to understand the terrible truth. I remembered Hardacre's boasts inside that carriage; his smug recounting of Burton's Eastern adventures. Holmes had been right: my skills of deception, of appearing indifferent to even the most offensive points of view, had certainly never been any match at all for Khan's.

"Men like Burton think that they can crash their way around the world like cosseted children," Khan growled. "They think that they can just take and take and take."

"And yet," said Holmes, "you had to wait until Burton was dead before putting into motion your plan of blackmail and then revenge."

"Burton was amoral. He had no sense of right or wrong. He cared nothing for what others thought of him. And I could go nowhere, could do nothing, until I had the money and means to leave India." He winced, and clutched too hard at his bloodied leg before I was able to prise his fingers free. When he spoke again, his voice had become hoarse with pain. "I had letters. And a photograph. When my grandmother realised that she was with child, she wrote to Burton and initially he wrote back." His smile was bitter. "Although I imagine that her letters were among the first papers that Lady Burton burned upon his death."

"But what about Hardacre?" I protested. "Surely you were both in the same unfortunate boat?"

"The same boat?" Khan snarled. "He is just as much a *haramzada* – a bastard – as I, and yet if all of London knew it, they would not care! His life was destined never to be as mine: one of shame and penury. He had money; he had a family and respectability, and yet still he felt as if the world had done him a disservice." His snarl became a crueller grin. "So, I decided to play him at his own game – to expose the Cannibal Club before exposing him. Ha! Did you see his face when Hope Henley's body was discovered?"

"But what does Joseph have to do with any of this?" said I, and I had to raise my voice, for the crowd at the dining-room door was growing impatient and angry, despite the major's best efforts to keep them in check. "Why, indeed, is he here at all?"

"Because I asked him to be," said Holmes. "Once I was certain that he was not the killer of Burton or Hope Henley, I could see no other logical explanation for his following us other than that it must be at Lady Burton's behest; that it was not us he was following at all, but Hardacre. Keeping your enemies close is always the wisest recourse. And perhaps they sought to find some weakness, some indiscretion with which to counter-attack. When I realised that the killer was Khan, and understood what rage there was in him – a rage that would only build and never recede – I realised, too, that I had no option but to allow him to expose and incriminate himself. And so, this afternoon, I visited Lady Burton and Joseph, and asked the latter to serve as added protection; a rear-guard, so to speak, with the promise of their release from all extortion."

"You are a fool," Khan spat at Joseph, "if you think further serving your masters like the obedient dog they demand you to be will win you anything more than their continued contempt." But when Joseph made a sudden lunge towards him, flashing white teeth, Khan shrank back against the couch and said no more.

"Where is Hardacre?" I asked him, certain now that I didn't want to know the answer.

Holmes looked first to Khan and then to me. "*Pashtunwali* dictates that if you cannot spill the blood of the man who has wronged you, then you should seek to spill the blood of his son."

"Do you know what name my mother gave me, Mr Holmes?" said Khan. "Abuzar. It means owner of wealth and power and beauty. She died before she was forty years old, crying and begging in the dirt."

"Where is Hardacre?" said Holmes, appearing entirely unmoved.

Khan laughed – it was an ugly, raw sound – and then he turned that furious gaze upon all those men crowded around the entrance to the dining room. "What do you suppose you have been enjoying with your fine wine and port tonight, good gentlemen?"

The scuffling impatience became hysterical uproar, and Joseph was forced to join the major in his efforts to keep the crowd out of the lounge room. The racket swiftly became deafening. With horror, I recalled that still spitting entrecote and its bloody juices.

Holmes raised his hands. "Gentlemen, gentlemen. I, Sherlock Holmes, can categorically assure you that you have not this night lived up to your club's odious name. All on your plates that was once alive did nothing more than moo and chew cud."

Khan shot Holmes a scornful glare. "He is at the bottom of the Thames. Weighed down by his stupidity and his belief in the white man's superiority. They think we are savages, and so I gave them a savage. I gave them a cannibal. And you may believe that if I had the means, I would have made them cannibals, too."

When the main banqueting doors were unlocked again and Bertolini ushered in perhaps as many as a dozen Scotland Yard officers, Khan's pallor grew more pronounced.

"Mr Holmes! Did I not successfully disguise both my identity and my motive? Did I not reason backwards? Did I not employ meticulous patience? In the end, was I not cleverer and more erudite than Hardacre, or any of these supposedly worthier gentlemen?"

"Yes, you were," said Holmes, and there was indeed some admiration in his voice; certainly far more than he had ever reserved for Hardacre. When some of the officers brought forward a stretcher to take Khan away, Holmes even offered a sympathetic smile. "But you were not cleverer than me."

As I sat at my old desk, writing up the notes that would eventually become this account, a new question occurred to me, and I put down my pen. "Holmes, if revenge was his only motive, why then did Khan not just kill Hardacre? Why go to all that effort and subterfuge?"

Holmes looked up from his newspaper and shrugged. "I imagine that he wanted Hardacre to flounder, to suffer, to feel fear in the face of a greater foe. Or perhaps the temptation to turn the tables on Hardacre's plan, and destroy the Anthropological Society and the Cannibal Club at the same time, became too great to ignore. As I told you in Bertolini's, monsters are created from monsters, and the latter must bear the consequence. There is a very fine line, Watson, between heroism and infamy; the distinction is nearly always a matter of perspective." He smiled. "And, of course, written account."

When I made no move to pick up my pen, Holmes smiled again. "Perhaps this will be more to your liking then. It is said that the phrase 'revenge is a dish best served cold' is of Pashtun origin, perhaps even derived from the *Pashtunwali* itself. That is the kind of frivolous titbit that you enjoy, is it not?"

That was true enough. But what is true is not always wise to admit. I had been made too uneasy by the whole sordid affair, and its retelling was proving difficult; there were many things that I had no desire to re-examine or acknowledge. The worst of these was admitting that in the lounge room of Bertolini's I had no more noticed Khan's hazel eye than I had the faint black lines against his trousers, nor the *Pashtunwali badal* inside his heart. Without ever seeing or understanding anything at all, I had trusted only that my instincts and the uncommon bond between Holmes and myself would guide my hand. My gun. A deduction of sorts, but never one that would have sat easily with Holmes. And nor, indeed, with me.

"I'm not sure, Watson," Holmes said, carefully folding his paper, "what this case has to contribute to the study of anthropology, save to further muddy the waters. At first glance, it would seem perhaps a nearly perfect test for monogenesis versus polygenesis, but who could possibly separate the roots of a man's origin from his environment? I rather think it an example of that other fine line between madness and genius."

"And am I to quote you on that also?"

"You are not!" said Holmes. "All of London will believe that I am speaking of myself!" He stood, walked over to the dining table, and began pouring two glasses of wine. "Although, in my research of Burton, I have come to realise that he and I were indeed similar in a great many ways."

"There is no denying that he was a great man," I agreed, "who had but one enemy."

Holmes smiled and lifted his half-full glass. "Discipline is the key, Watson. Indulge some vices but never all of them at the same time." Although he knew my real meaning well enough to avoid my eye, looking instead at his violin case, propped up against the wall.

"Darwin has much to say about music, you know. He believes that the human race evolved an understanding of music before even speech, and that whenever we hear a whistle or a concerto, our ancient souls remember those days when we were just beginning." He sat down and closed his eyes. "I do not berate myself for either Hardacre or Khan, for they set themselves upon their own dark paths. But Hope Henley and Lord Bowles I might have saved."

To answer or argue with him was to indulge his melancholy, and so I did neither. "I read somewhere, perhaps it was in the Temple Bar, that as a schoolboy, Burton smashed a violin over his teacher's head and knocked him quite unconscious."

Holmes paused, and then turned back to the wall, where his own violin case was propped, before throwing back his head to laugh long and loud: that uncommon strident staccato that he indulged in so rarely. Once recovered, he regarded me warmly and with clearer eyes.

"Come, Watson, let us sit as old friends and enjoy this burgundy. And afterwards," he smiled, "we shall draw straws to decide who is to answer Lestrade's hysterical summons. Are we agreed?"

An addendum:

It may be of some interest, for those of a synchronic persuasion – Holmes, of course, believed not at all in coincidence – to learn that Hamid Khan was executed on the gallows at Newgate on the very day that my dear friend met his own untimely death on the Reichenbach Falls.

I realised this only with hindsight many months later. Though I had made little or no peace with the loss of Holmes, I had begun writing about him again, and one afternoon, as I was searching in my wardrobe for the details of a previous case, I came upon the pinstriped Chadwick suit and frock coat that he had made me wear to Bertolini's. At once, I remembered the sealed envelope that he had handed to me as we had been sitting in the dining hall, and I began rifling through the pockets.

I found it and drew out the card inside, and my heart was as heavy as it was light when I saw Holmes's familiar handwriting.

On the card he had printed, carefully and all in upper case: HAMID KHAN.

And upon its other side: ABUZAR KUMAR.

Sherlock Holmes and the Four Kings of Sweden
Steven Savile

———

The Bernadotte Chambers, The Old Town, Stockholm, Sweden, 1930

It was a lonely walk into the spotlight at the centre of the auditorium. The room was filled with ghosts and draughts, though it was impossible to tell which was which as they brushed up against me. To amuse myself I tapped out a message with the tip of my cane as I crossed the bare boards. It was short and sweet. I wondered if any of the brilliant minds gathered to listen would notice I'd just given them a clue to the real secret of the lecture?

Holmes had decided against attending. Something far more interesting, he assured me, had caught his attention just an hour before he was meant to join me on stage, and it simply could not wait. He refused to enlighten me, promising I would find out in good time.

"It is with great pleasure, I present to you, Mister Sherlock Holmes and his associate, Doctor John Watson."

I gave them a moment for the polite ripple of applause to subside. My hosts were nothing if not polite, which I am assured is a Swedish trait.

I set my cane down beside the lectern and nervously shuffled the sheaf of papers I'd meticulously prepared for my talk. Even after all this time I felt uncomfortable addressing an assembly, though, in this case, I confess, my nerves were due in equal measure to who was listening in the banked seating and the fact that a good many of them would not be able to understand a word that came out of my mouth.

"Thank you," I said, "Thank you. As you can see, I am . . . ah . . . diminished. That is to say only half here or, as we British are wont to say, 'not all there'," I offered a self-deprecating smile to the gallery. "My name is Doctor John Watson. Some of you may be familiar with my stories." I paused, allowing for a few murmurs of agreement to return to me. "Though I suspect you are here out of curiosity rather than any great desire to listen to an old man talk about his famous friend."

Holmes had picked some thirty names to attend our first lecture here in the icy north—at the invitation of the Justice Minister, Georg Bissmark himself, who was seeking to establish a School for Detection much like the many we had lectured at across the world, sharing Holmes's methods with the most promising minds of two generations now—and had dispatched a plain black invitation to each of them with the address and time of my lecture embossed in gold foil on the front and an individual message to each on the reverse. There was nothing random about their selection. Each of the thirty men had come to our attention during our investigation into a curious fellow who called himself the Magister, which loosely translated to "Master of Science", and was derived from a form of the word "teacher". It was a curious name befitting a most curious investigation. One most worthy of study, and hence the subject of my inaugural lecture.

A disembodied voice up in the gods said something I didn't catch. Swedish is a most peculiar language, more fitting to the trill of a mynah bird than the mouth of a man.

"If you would humour me, beneath your seats you will find an envelope; would you be so kind as to open it?" I gave them a few seconds to retrieve the envelope and empty its contents. There were several reproductions of key evidence and testimony inside, but for now I wanted to focus on the newspaper. "The Riddle of the Four Kings," I said, giving the signal for the lights to come up. A few confused murmurs greeted the sight of last month's *Svenska Dagbladet* headline.

"We have all read the papers, Doctor Watson," another voice heckled.

"Why are we wasting our time with this? It is just a stupid story, nothing more," another said.

"On the contrary," I opined. "On the face of it, what we have here is a curiosity, one in which the king has been sighted in four different cities, each of them several hundreds of miles apart, from Lund in the south, to Gothenburg on the west coast, Stockholm itself, and moving north, Uppsala, on the same day; an undoubted physical impossibility and yet in each instance crowds of people attest to having seen His Majesty acting distinctly out of character. One eyewitness we could assume to be mistaken, but fifty? Five hundred? We cannot merely dismiss the phenomenon as either mistake or prank. We could, of course, ask His Majesty," I said, looking up towards the Royal Box, letting his royal presence sink in, "but, for now, humour me. Let us consider, how could such a thing happen?"

"It can't," the same speaker said, adamant in his refusal to believe the impossible.

"Good. Yes, you are of course absolutely correct. It cannot happen. The principles of the physical universe stand. An object cannot exist in multiple locations simultaneously. So we eliminate that from our thinking and evaluate the remaining alternatives to deduce the truth. One obvious possibility is that the reports are false. Lies. But for that to be true we must consider upwards of a thousand eyewitnesses across the country being complicit in the same lie, which is unlikely to say the least."

"Actors?" someone asked.

"Excellent, now you are thinking. Indeed, some form of paid shill is indeed a viable solution. It would mean locating seven men bearing a passing resemblance to the king, and each putting on a performance, deliberately wanting to be seen. To be remembered. Worthy of note, too, is the fact that these reports all make reference to the king behaving out of character. For a student of deductive reasoning, an answer like this begets more questions. First and foremost: why? Motivation is a fundamental aspect in understanding the criminal mind. Without it, we lack a clear picture of the crime. So, why would seven kings all act out of character? What possible reason could they have to be seen acting out?"

"To discredit His Majesty," a voice called.

And there it was, the underlying reason for our visit to this inhospitable land.

"Very good, yes, to discredit the king," I agreed. "And the moment that kind of thinking becomes a part of our deductive process, it changes everything. That story ceases to be tomfoolery and becomes something entirely more sinister because there must be a grander—darker—scheme at play."

There were grudging murmurs of assent from around the chamber.

There was a nugget of something there that defied easy understanding.

It was precisely the kind of thing that attracted my friend to a case and why he had been so keen to take up Bissmark's invitation.

We had only been in the country for a fortnight, and in that time I had marvelled at the culinary horrors the locals called food—mainly fish, preserved in a manner that doesn't bear thinking about, and the distinct lack of fresh vegetables, something I must admit I took for granted thanks to the easy abundance of them back home—and the sheer cold. The lodgings we had been afforded included a quite ingenious use of one to help preserve the other; the pantry, or *skafferi* as they called it, was constructed in such a way that there was an air vent built into the outside wall allowing the sub-zero air to fill it, keeping the food cool, extending its life. It was so simple in its logic and construction you could not help but admire the Swedes their industry.

"As I am sure you have surmised by this point, your invitation to this inaugural lecture was no mere coincidence. Each and every one of you is vital in some way to the solution of this most vexatious plot. Indeed, over the next few hours, with your help, I intend to unmask the criminal mastermind hidden within our ranks. What better way to prove the value of deductive reasoning and underline the importance of our techniques to truly understanding the criminal mind."

There were gasps of astonishment, which I had expected. I made a study of their faces, but not a man betrayed anything that might have been read as guilt.

"We should begin, I think, at the beginning, which would be our first encounter with the name the Magister."

The snow was deep but far from crisp, and decidedly uneven, the ruts in the slush caused by the constant flow of foot traffic.

A tram rumbled away around a distant curve in the road, unperturbed.

I followed my companion on a circuitous path around the spreading puddles of slush. Holmes walked with singular purpose, eyes fixed on some invisible point in the middle distance. He did not stop for man nor beast until we arrived at the door of the theatre. The bill posted beside the door promised mind-bending feats of illusion and mentalism from the Danish mystic, The Great Andersen. I was unfamiliar with his name.

"What in the blue blazes are we doing here, Holmes?"

"Following the crime," he said.

"What crime?" I asked, feeling, as I did so often, about a dozen steps behind my companion.

"All in good time, my dear Watson. All in good time."

He paid with a crisp five-kroner note, purchasing two seats towards the back of the house. As we followed the usher's torch to our seats I noticed a peculiarity of the seating arrangement that in retrospect I think wonderfully illustrates the Swedish personality. The audience gathered in seats around the middle of the house, leaving plenty of spaces at both the front (where the view was restricted but you were close enough for the actors to spit on as they enunciated) and the back (where the view was panoramic, but the sound was less than ideal). They were the Goldilocks People. The word they used to describe this phenomenon, *lagom*, has no literal translation into the King's English. It is "sufficient", or "satisfactory", or any such Latin derivative, and dates back to the time when their ancestors passed the drinking horn around the fire, each man supping the perfect amount for the horn to make it all the way around the fire. As an ethos it was deep-rooted in the

Swedish psyche. In every situation there was a Goldilocks solution that was just right. Feeling rather pleased with my deduction, I took my seat. There was no one in any of the three rows immediately in front of us, which afforded us a wonderful view of the stage.

I waited, wondering what point Holmes was trying to prove, through a series of tricks that were competent if not awe-inspiring, and more often than not included some rather obvious gimmick if one took a moment to consider what you were being shown as opposed to what you were seeing. Finally, Andersen called for volunteers and three men took to the stage. I watched with fascination as he proceeded to hypnotise them and by turns planted trigger words and suggestions in their minds that had them participating in all manner of parlour tricks. "This is what you wanted me to see?"

"Indeed, Watson. What did you make of it?"

I wasn't immediately sure how to answer that. "You believe we have stumbled upon a crime involving mesmerism?"

"There is a very strong probability, yes."

"A crime in which weak-minded fools are put into some sleep state and made to act against their moral compass? I'm not sure I believe it."

"Did I say anything about a weak mind? I did not. In fact, the reverse is far closer to the truth—the fiercer the intellect, the greater the self-control, the more susceptible a subject is likely to be to mesmerism. Entering a hypnotic trance requires intense concentration. Note I said trance—it is not sleep, another great fallacy. The subject is actually in a heightened state of concentration, again quite the reverse of slumber."

"And this has some bearing on a case I know nothing about?"

"It does indeed, Watson."

He presented me with a folded-up front page from a week-old broadsheet. Above the fold the headline read: *The Riddle of the Four Kings*. I read through it quickly, my initial instinct to dismiss it as rubbish, but as I folded the page again, I said to my companion, "And this is the true reason for our presence here, not the opening of a School for Detection?"

"Our visit has a dual purpose, my friend. Note the four locations in which Gustav was allegedly sighted. What does each of them have in common?"

"Aside from the fact they played host to a monarch who was noted to act most peculiarly?"

"Yes."

"I must confess, my knowledge of our host country is wanting. Enlighten me."

"Each city is well known for its academia. For example, Lund is the site of one of the country's oldest educational establishments—its beginnings can be traced back to 1425—whilst Stockholm hosts three of Sweden's most prestigious schools, Kunliga Tekniska Högskolan, the Karolinska Institute, and of course the university college."

"Strong minds," I said, seeing the link, as tenuous as it currently was, "but what on earth makes you think there is a crime here?"

Holmes handed me a second item. It appeared to be a ransom note, words cut from articles from the same newspaper to spell out some threatening message I could not read. "What does it say?"

"'We know your secrets. Do you want the world to know them?'"

"And this was addressed to the king?"

Holmes nodded.

"Someone is blackmailing the king? That is hard to fathom. I cannot begin to imagine what manner of secrets these must be."

"Bissmark was not forthcoming when I asked about their nature, other than to say they are most personal, and scurrilous lies with it. Whatever they are they run deeply enough to have caused genuine concern at the Royal Palace, though. Initially I was inclined to dismiss it, as all people of power and influence attract those of a troubled disposition at some time during their lives, but coupled with the sightings of these faux kings, I believe we are seeing the opening gambit in what will be a greater crime to come."

"And you have a plan?"

"We must find ourselves one of these imposter kings. Without proof of wrongdoing we are merely clutching at broken straws and hoping to stumble upon a whole one."

"Then that is what we must do. But where to begin?"

"We have already begun, my friend," said Holmes. "Mister Andersen here has performed several engagements across the country, first in Lund, then Gothenburg, Stockholm and Uppsala."

"That is an eerily familiar route," I observed with a wry smile. My friend, as ever, was one step ahead of the game. "Where should we be looking next?"

"He has been invited to one final engagement in Sweden, a private function. One might go so far as to call it by Royal Command."

"Oh, now that is interesting," said I.

I picked Karl Andersen's face out in the audience.

The mystic looked nonplussed. He would, I believe, prove to be a worthy opponent across the gaming table. He studied me with quiet fascination.

I was more than a little interested in watching his face as I presented my first surprise of the evening.

"The mind is a curious thing," I told my audience. "One would not think it possible to so influence a soul that he would completely lose inhibitions and all sense of self but, with the right skills, such trickery is akin to magic," I said. "Kent Nylander? Would you be so good as to make yourself known?" My request was greeted by a shuffle of feet and the scrape of the man's chair going back. Even now, Nylander bore a striking similarity to the man up in the Royal Box. It really was uncanny but, even so, there were many subtle differences that marked the two men as different, some as simple as posture and bearing, others ingrained from lives lived most differently. But for a moment his appearance was enough to fool the audience into thinking that they were seeing double that there were audible gasps from a few. "Now, as you can see, Kent is a fairly unremarkable man, save for his passing resemblance to His Majesty. In fact, Kent is one of our faux kings. He was responsible for the reports generated in Uppsala."

I watched Andersen's face most closely, but if there was guilt within his mind, he did well to hide it.

The next few minutes promised to be most interesting if Holmes's supposition was correct. We had watched the mesmerist's show and made specific note of some of the cues he used to trigger the more peculiar behaviour. I crossed the floor to the front row, dealing out a number of small cards, each with a statement from Andersen's show written neatly upon it. I did not trust my grasp of phonetics to do anything other than mangle the language, so I asked, "Would you be so kind as to read out the line written on your card?" to the first man. He looked puzzled by it, but did as he was asked.

"*Som är vid dorren?*"

Who is at the door?

Immediately Nylander's head whipped around and, tongue lolling slackly, he began to bark. His barking lasted a full twenty seconds. It was a cheap parlour trick but, given our surroundings, a powerful example of just how easily a man's mind could be influenced if you knew how.

"And now you," I said to the second man.

"*Du är i brand.*"

You are on fire.

Nylander greeted this one by slapping his arms and chest vigorously, trying to beat the invisible flames into submission.

No one was laughing this time.

The man fell to his knees, seemingly trying to pull the hair from his scalp.

"*Tillräckligt,*" I said, the one word I had committed to heart. *Enough.* That was how Andersen had ended the theatrics on stage, and it worked here. I nodded to the third man in the front row, who got Nylander hopping on one foot for half a minute, then dancing an uncontrollable dance, believing the floor beneath his feet to be quicksand. And on it went down the line, each new humiliation reinforcing the point that Kent Nylander was not in control of his own actions. "Now, I don't believe it is as simple as saying, 'Kent, behave like a king,' and him doing it, but as I hope I've just demonstrated, such an imperative would account for the reports of the king acting out of character, as each and every one of us has a different idea of what it takes to be a king. But it does nothing to answer the question of: *why?*"

"Curious," Holmes said.

Something had obviously caught his attention. "There is a story here of a day before the four sightings of the faux kings, which suggests Gustav was seen in a small mining town north of Uppsala—Sala. I had thought nothing of it as there were no conflicting reports that day, but I believe we may be looking at our mesmerist's first attempt at manipulation, a dress rehearsal for the main event. Look."

He handed me a copy of the newspaper that I could not read beyond picking out key words like king and Sala. "What am I looking at?" I asked.

"A throwaway line, Watson, nothing more, but I believe it to be telling. Gustav, like most Nordic nobles, is an accomplished hunter, that is well documented, but the final line suggests the elk evaded its hunters and the royal party returned home empty-handed."

"That is tenuous, Holmes. Perhaps it merely knew the land better than the hunting party?"

"Perhaps, but what better way to test your deceit than to replace your subject in the most familiar of environments and see if any note his sudden loss of skill?"

He had a point; it would have been a most efficacious test of the mesmerist's substitution, if that was truly what was happening here. What better dry run than that?

"I still don't see what Andersen stands to gain from this game of kings?"

"Power, inevitably," Holmes said. "Wealth more immediately. You control a monarch, you control more than merely the trappings of royalty. This land is not like our own, my friend, far from it. Here there is a groundswell of distaste for the blue bloods, a growth of social democrats and liberals who would be free from the tyranny of kings."

"You think this is an attempt to bring down the monarchy?" I said, aghast.

"It is not so long ago that a peasant uprising saw the nation teetering on the brink of outright revolution, akin to the events in Russia. The conservative government fell to a coalition of socialist and liberal parties greatly influenced by the teachings of Marx and Engels. The situation called for desperate and radical changes to stave off the collapse of a way of life, and the upshot was a huge reduction in political powers from the absolute authority of the king, effectively transforming the monarch into a figurehead. It is a small step from that to a Republic."

"All it would take is a disgraced king," I agreed, following his inescapable logic.

"And here we find ourselves with a king harbouring secrets."

"Secrets," I added, "that are known to others—"

"—Are barely secrets at all," Holmes finished. "It behoves us to travel north, my friend. I believe we will find at least one solution to this sorry affair in the mining town."

"Who in their right mind would want to be a king in days like these?"

"Indeed," said Holmes, thinking.

It was in Sala that we first stumbled across the Magic Circle and a man who called himself Thurneman.

It wasn't his given name; indeed, it did not take long for my friend to deduce that it was in point of fact an anagram, a clue to his true nature: manhunter.

Between the capital and the mining town the landscape was one of trees, trees and more trees – every genus of hardy evergreen clinging to their colour as they battled the elements to live up to their name.

Our train pulled into the station an hour before midday. The sun was bright on the snow, the air several degrees colder than it had been back in Stockholm when we'd embarked upon our journey a few hours earlier. My first impression of the town was one of almost fairytale cuteness, the architecture in keeping with my imaginings of Grimm's Bavaria. We moved slowly, neither of us young men any more. The locals were wrapped up against the cold, features hidden behind layers of scarves and thick woollen coats. Even so, they left a trail of foggy breath in the air behind them as they went about their business.

Our first port of call was with the hunt master who had arranged for the king's unsuccessful outing in the local forests. His house was a crooked blue building where the old timbers had twisted so far out of skew that the only thing holding it upright were the buildings on either side. The narrow cobbled street was one of a few survivors from a huge fire that had scoured the area around the town square, laying waste to three hundred years' worth of history in a huge blaze. We opened the gate which, in turn, opened on to a courtyard where the man's horse grazed beneath a barren apple tree. The poor animal looked wretched. Our intrusion was greeted by the manic bark of a terrier intent on making sure we came no further. The hunt master followed the baying chorus to greet us on the threshold. He babbled something at us that was frankly unintelligible, but Holmes took it in his stride and countered with a slow, precise phrase he'd committed to memory. I heard the word "English", or something very much like it, in there, and assumed he was asking the man if he spoke the language.

The hunt master shook his head and proceeded to say something, but it sounded different to my ear. Louder, slower, as though by talking to us like children—or simpletons—we'd suddenly grasp what he was saying simply because it was loud enough and slow enough to make sense to us. Holmes was adept with languages, and had a good grasp of Latin and a smattering of German and French. I had even heard him utter a few words of Mandarin. There were, as so often, no limits to my friend's ferocious intellect. He repeated the same question, though this time there was no mention of English. He was asking the man if he spoke German, earning a slight shrug as though to say "a little". It was enough for Holmes to work with. They proceeded to mime and mumble question and answer, somehow making each other understood. It was quite a performance.

I found my concentration drifting, and my gaze moving around the cramped room. It was surprisingly warm, given the chill outside. A log fire was banked up in the corner; combined with a ceiling so low that Holmes had to stoop, it generated considerable heat. I noted a photograph of the royal hunt on the windowsill and crossed the room to study it. The man in the picture, I realised quickly, was a southpaw, while Gustav himself was very much right-handed. Little things betray so much, I thought. A riding crop, in this case. The man in the picture wore a tartan scarf over his mouth and nose to shield him from the elements. I noticed the same tartan scarf hung on a hook behind the door. Through the window I saw a second building across the inner courtyard that looked to be a mirror of this one: single storey, with a cellar arrangement and low sloping red clay roof. It appeared to be some sort of workshop.

After a lull in the interrogation, the hunt master led us across the narrow yard to the second house, and inside to a room where all of the accoutrements of the hunt were stored, including, I noted, the brass horn the king would have used to sound the charge.

Holmes studied the instrument for a moment before hanging it back on the hook and turning his attention to something else. If I hadn't been paying attention I would have missed him palming the brass mouthpiece and slipping it into his pocket. He made a show of asking a handful of questions, but I could tell he wasn't particularly interested in the answers. He'd found whatever it was he'd come for.

We left the hunt master with directions to a public house two streets over, but not before my companion asked whether he might borrow the scarf to protect himself from the biting wind. He had noticed it, too.

There is no better indicator that you are a visitor in a strange land than the sky above your head, with its familiar constellations of stars in unfamiliar positions. I noticed the distinctive arrangements of Ursa Major and Minor, which back home would have been a little above my right shoulder, were away over my left. It was the most disconcerting change the world could ever offer. I remember still the confusion the first time I looked up at the utterly wrong skies above Afghanistan.

What I wouldn't have done for a little of that desert heat now. Despite the fact that the walk took less than three minutes, the temperature dropped to the point where I felt sure the blood would freeze in our veins. The tavern was a welcome respite. We made something of a grand entrance, trying to beat the warmth back into our bodies as we crossed the threshold and took up seats beside the fire. We were approached by a lithe blonde serving girl who, I assume, asked us what our fancy was. Holmes answered in German. After a moment's hesitation she nodded, mentally moving tracks to the unfamiliar second language, and left us to settle in beside the warm fire while we waited for our food.

There were half a dozen diners in the taproom; men with calloused hands from physical labour. My first thought was that there was nothing menial about such tasks in a hostile clime such as this.

Holmes put the mouthpiece on the table-top between us.

"What am I looking at?"

"See for yourself."

I picked up the fluted piece of brass and turned it over in my hand, back and forth several times. I noticed some obvious wear around the edge where lips and teeth would have come up against the metal, and was about to dismiss it once again as something I wasn't seeing, until I noticed the thin traces of white powder-like dust on the inside of the hole. I raised it to my nose and sniffed, but there was no discernible scent, and then proceeded to lick the tip of my finger and went to dab the tiniest sample of the white dust on the tip of my tongue.

"I wouldn't do that if I were you," Holmes stopped me short.

I looked at him askance.

"What is it?" I asked.

"Proof that our king was not who he purported to be," Holmes said. "A sulfosalt. I thought that perhaps, given our proximity to a silver mine, it was evidence that our imposter spent some time in the mine shafts beneath us, some sort of residual from the mining process, but the hunt master assured me the mines have been disused for the better part of twenty years. Now I believe it to be a trace residue from the arsenic that was used to poison him. Dead men do not make the most reliable of witnesses," said he.

"If he was poisoned, where is the body?"

"We have an endless expanse of forest out there," Holmes said. "Acres upon acres upon acres. Plenty of room in which to dispose of a corpse."

"What now then?"

"Now, like our investigation thus far, we go to the dogs." He held up the tartan scarf. I understood immediately what he had in mind, but I must confess I was in no great rush to go back outside.

We could not very well hunt by night, so we resigned ourselves to a long evening of inactivity.

We could not have been more wrong in our assumptions.

Holmes used the Riksteleverket phone booth in the main square to place two calls through the operator, one back to the police headquarters in Stockholm, summoning urgent assistance—including a translator—and the other to the master of the hunt, informing him that we would like to book a private hunt for first light.

I watched him through the window, listening to the singsong conversation of others in the pub while not understanding a word. I had never felt so isolated in my life, if I'm honest. The logo on the telephone kiosk was of a lightning bolt or, more precisely, two lightning bolts, contradicting the notion that lightning did not strike the same place twice. The girl brought our food, fairly basic fare of meat and potatoes, overly salty, but a marked improvement on the sour herring we'd had the day before. Holmes looked most frustrated as he strode back across the gravelled square to join me. Without a word he withdrew his pipe from the folds of his coat and proceeded to fix himself a smoke. He did not say anything until he had exhaled his fifth deep draw, and then it was merely to inform me that reinforcements would be with us before dawn.

We took lodging in the rooms upstairs, one of six vacant rooms the landlord let to transient workers; but, contrary to my expectation, rather than sleep, Holmes arranged the bolsters beneath the blankets to give the illusion of our sleeping bodies and, leaving the door unlocked, retreated to a second unoccupied room to wait out the night. I thought, for a moment, I heard scratching within the walls. Rats. I shivered at the thought, but of course given the hostile climate the rodents would seek refuge just like anyone else. I confess to thinking his precautions were a mite paranoid, but some two hours later, in the darkest part of the night, when two gunshots rang out in quick succession, I changed my mind.

He raised a hand to still me.

I was without my trusty service revolver. Indeed, our only weapon was my cane, though Holmes could easily transform it into a deadly weapon, and I was no slouch in the martial arts myself, but I would always rather things didn't come to that if it could be helped. The mind is the key to set us free, as the great Houdini used to say. I heard footsteps on the landing, and in our room angry shouts of puzzlement and rage. Three voices, so we were outnumbered.

"How did you know they would come for us?" I whispered, barely daring to breathe.

"I did not," Holmes admitted, "but once I placed the call with the master of the hunt, Thurneman, I knew there was no little risk in doing so, and that I would tip our hand should Thurneman be in cahoots with our blackmailers."

"Which he obviously is," said I.

"More than that, I have gravely misjudged the threat. We were to be murdered in our beds, not to be run out of town."

"What now?"

He put a finger to his lips. The plan was obvious: we wait. Outside our second room I heard a brief scuffle as the invaders argued over their subsequent actions. Gunshots cannot go unanswered, even in a small town like this. Those two shots would have been heard, and the police would inevitably respond sooner rather than later. Our best course of action was merely to wait, because their best course of action was to flee the scene of the would-be crime.

I counted silently to thirteen before I heard the first footsteps on the stairs, going down.

Still we waited.

Eventually I heard the outside door slam, and it occurred to me to wonder how our would-be killers had found their way into the public house unhindered in the first place—the door had been left unlocked, pointing the finger at someone, most likely the landlord himself, and turning this into a grand conspiracy indeed.

The police arrived as we emerged from hiding. I was surprised to see the familiar face of Stefan Lindblad, one of Bissmark's special detectives, who had driven up from the capital during the night to lead the investigation and serve as our translator. The man, in his early fifties, wore a grizzled expression of determined confusion, not unlike Gregson or Lestrade back home. He issued instructions to his officers quickly, barking out the orders with a semaphore of movement as he sent them hither and yon, before turning to face us. I don't mind admitting it was good to see a familiar face so far from home.

"Mister Holmes, Doctor Watson," he said, "Would one of you mind telling me what is going on here?"

"Murder," my companion said. "Or at least a very good attempt at it. You will find two very dead pillows in the room upstairs."

"Shot clean through the feathers," said I, much to the policeman's confusion. "A little English humour," I told him.

"Come sunrise I believe we shall find an actual corpse," Holmes said, and now there was no trace of humour.

Lindblad took a small black leather-bound notebook from his pocket and turned over a couple of pages to a blank one. I noticed several doodles on the reverse; the man obviously had a most febrile imagination. He proceeded to jot down notes as Holmes ran him through what we knew, or at least suspected. Rather than wait for morning proper, the detective had us lead him through the empty snow-covered streets to the crooked blue house of the hunt master, and hammered on the gateway door with enough force to wake the dead. Those thunderous blows, however, didn't raise Thurneman.

Lindblad gestured to a couple of his subordinates and stepped away from the door so that they might kick it down. It was no easy task, but eventually the wood yielded, splintering around the lock, and we were inside.

It was obvious that the place had been vacated in a hurry; the remains of a half-consumed supper were still on the table; the chair Thurneman had been sitting at on its back in the middle of the floor where he had cast it aside. The Bakelite telephone was off the hook. Holmes strode across to it, hung up the handset and then lifted it again to get the attention of the operator.

"Who was the last person called from this phone?" he demanded and, when the operator didn't answer in any way he found satisfactory, he thrust the handset towards Lindblad and told him to ask the same question.

The answer was not unexpected, in that the call had been to one Thomas Allwin, the owner of our lodging house. We had our smoking gun. A conspiracy was unfolding around us. Rather than rush back to the pub to arrest Allwin, we took a moment to search the hunt master's home, looking for anything of significance to our investigation. The main house was filled with curiosities that I do not mind admitting made me most uncomfortable, including several examples of amateur taxidermy gone slightly awry. The glassy eyes of the various creatures truly did seem to follow me around the room as I made my search. I discovered his journal stuffed down the side of a battered leather armchair. Lindblad translated the epigram for us: *To take another man's life is no crime; it only means a change in the physical state, since the soul is immortal and lives on in something else, an animal or a human being. To take from another human being only means a change in the state of possession in this life.*

"Cheerful thought," said I.

"It belongs to the teachings of the Raya-Yoga movement from the Far East," said Holmes.

The frontispiece bore a most peculiar symbol, a triangle with a circle within and a circle without. I saw the same image repeated throughout the book, with text beside it I could not read.

Lindblad offered a translation. "The triangle represents the three true members of the church, the circle within symbolises the inner circle of trusted members, and the outer circle represents those who are not truly a part of the church but can be called upon if needs must."

"And there is a roster of names?"

"No, but there appears to be a draft of a contract, which would suggest a paper trail exists to be found."

"Which is something," said I, but Holmes was not so easily appeased. He stalked out of the room. The outer door slammed in his wake. I saw him cross the inner courtyard, but instead of entering the parallel building on the other side, he pulled up storm doors that led down to the cellar and a moment later disappeared from sight.

I followed him out.

By the time I arrived he had lit a gaslight and stood engrossed in the study of what can only be described as a wall of occult madness; each symbol was scratched into the plaster with a knife blade, gouged deep into the surface. I saw again the symbol I would come to associate with the Magic Circle, but there was so much more, too; things recognisable from the work of Madam Blavatsky, Crowley and other charlatans. Holmes was engrossed by them. I found the images more repulsive than fascinating.

He nodded three times in quick succession, digesting everything the wall had to tell him, and then he was off, moving at a loping run, his long legs carrying him up the narrow wooden stairs into the room above, where he snagged a ring of keys off a hook, and then he was out through the door.

By the time I caught up with him, a baying chorus of hounds filled the night.

I hadn't even seen the second gate inside the small courtyard when we had been here earlier in the day. It opened on to kennels where the hunting dogs were kept. Holmes had them gathered around him as he knelt, holding out the tartan scarf the imposter king had worn for the hunt. I didn't need to ask what he was playing at; once the dogs had got the man's scent he released them. It was all we could do to keep up with the half a dozen hounds as they tore through the maze of narrow streets.

"How could they possibly have the scent already?" I asked, as I laboured a few steps behind my friend, but ahead of Lindblad and his fellows, who were slower to react to Holmes's burst of frenetic energy than I was. But then I'd had half a lifetime of getting used to his peculiarities—so much so that they hardly felt peculiar to me at all these days; they were just Holmes being Holmes. He loved the chase. The energy.

I gestured for Lindblad to hurry up before the dogs disappeared out of sight. We rounded the corner on to the main square, only to see the dogs already merging with the night-dark alleys that led away on the other side, past the old church and the stately park. I could hear rather than see the dogs now as we struggled to match their pace. Without torches we were at the mercy of the moon, but strangely the night was not all dark, but rather illuminated by the snow upon the earth. It was a curious trick, but I was grateful for it just the same. The ground was treacherous underfoot, but we made our way through the park, our eyes fixed on the dark skirts of the forest that loomed up ahead of us.

The dogs disappeared into the trees.

We struggled manfully to keep up, drawn on by their ragged barking as it changed in tenor, becoming more aggressively frantic. They'd found whatever it was they were looking for.

We followed a narrow track which ran parallel with the run-off river from the silver mine. The moonlight reflected on the frozen water. Back when the mine was active, they would have had someone out breaking the ice to ensure the boats could progress unhindered. The dogs, I saw, had crossed the frozen water and circled around an empty patch of ground, digging with their paws. I knew what we were going to find before they finished digging it up.

A hand.

"Detective Lindblad, may I ask you to describe what happened next in your own words?" I had called up into the gods.

"*Vist*," the Swede said, then caught himself and corrected the words in his head. "Of course. We approached the area where Mister Holmes was already on his knees, digging at the loose dirt with his bare hands. The dogs had found a shallow grave in the woods."

"And what—or rather *who*—did you find in the grave?"

"The king," the policeman said, to shocked gasps from the assembly. "At least, that is how it first appeared, though as the dogs clawed at his face, their claws tore at some of the prosthetics that had been used to better shape his face and enhance the physical similarities."

"So it wasn't the king?"

"No, and to be honest it did not look much like him. I could not for the life of me imagine how it could fool someone in his inner circle."

"Fascinating," said I, turning my attention to the Royal Box, "is it not, Your Majesty?"

"Most," the king said. "If not a little macabre to think of one's own body in a woodland grave."

"I would imagine so," said I. "Thankfully it is not something the majority of us have to contemplate." I turned my attention back to Lindblad. "So what happened then? Could you talk us through it?"

"It took some time to exhume the body," the grim Swede said.

Thankfully he spared us most of the details. "It was only when it was out of the ground that I noticed something weighing down the right pocket of his top coat. A room key from Allwin's, the public house in the centre of the town."

"And the room in question?"

It was the room we'd taken refuge in when Thurneman's thugs had tried to kill us the night before, and put Thomas Allwin right at the heart of the mystery.

Up until that moment, I'd been content to consider him something of a bumpkin in the play, but he was no innocent, that much was becoming abundantly clear.

Lindblad's men turned the room upside down, ignoring the landlord's protestations. I studied the man as he made a nuisance of himself; he was well dressed, dapper even, in pinstripe trousers and a snug-fitting waistcoat, though his boots were incongruous, heavy miners' steel-toe-capped affairs. They found nothing but, as I studied the man, so too did Holmes, and his eye was far keener than my own. "You," he said to the landlord, "are going to confess your role in this whole sordid affair."

Allwin gave no indication that he understood a word of it, but as my friend moved a step closer, raising a finger as though trying to gauge the wind direction, his eyes darted furtively to the left, towards the dresser in the corner. Lindblad's men had already turned it out so I knew there was nothing to be found in there, yet for all my certainty, the fact that the man's gaze instinctively drifted that way had me puzzled. I took it upon myself to cross the room, then pull open the first drawer, but the man did not so much as flinch. It was the same with the second and third drawers, even as I tipped them out and turned them upside down. Nothing. So it wasn't the dresser that had him anxious, but something in its vicinity.

Outside, the sun was rising.

That was another thing that took some getting used to. We were well into the morning, but the sky outside was still essentially grey and not much lighter than it had been in the middle of the night. The sun was finally beginning to break through the holes in the cloud, offering something approaching daylight. That fact, and that alone, was the only reason I caught the pinprick of light through the flock wallpaper as I turned away from the dresser, defeated.

It took me a moment to register what that tiny pinhole of light *meant*.

I knocked on the wall above the dresser. My fist was greeted by a curious hollow reverberation of plasterboard and space behind it. "It's hollow," I said.

"Of course it is," the landlord objected. "There's a room right on the other side—*your* room," he said. But that didn't match up to my memory of the building.

I rushed out of the room, counting out the paces in the hallway, then unlocked my own room, measuring the distance to the wall. It did not add up. I repeated the pattern of knocking on the wall, moving along the wall as I tried to sound out any differences in the echoes that came back to me. There was definitely some sort of cavity between the rooms. I pushed and probed at the wall, trying to find whatever mechanism would trigger the access, but there was no telltale click to match my endeavours, which could only mean the access panel was in the royal suite. I chuckled at the notion of ascribing so grand a label to the fleapit, and went back through to repeat the search.

Holmes watched my efforts in silence, and only after waiting a good five minutes for me to properly humiliate myself, pointed at the ceiling. It took a moment to register, but of course I should have known he was already one step ahead. Lindblad dispatched two officers to investigate, and a moment later we heard movement in the wall before us.

"Rats in the walls," Holmes said, and I remembered hearing the scratching as we waited for Thurneman's goons to pay their nocturnal visit.

A moment later the wall swung slowly inwards, and we were face to face with Lindblad's two coppers. The space between the walls was actually a narrow room, with a chair, gas lamp, and a few conveniences to make waiting less of a chore.

"What in the world?" I said, more to myself than to the others, but that did not stop Holmes from explaining it.

"We know your secrets. Do you want the world to know them?" said he.

I caught his gist immediately.

This room was the source of the salacious lies Bissmark had been so quick to dismiss. The fact that it was a bedroom was all the explanation I needed. "There is a woman, no doubt?"

"We will have to ask Master Allwin, as I suspect he will have procured her services for the imposter king to make sure that events unfolded the way his paymasters required."

The dapper man shook his head, a look of genuine fear on his face. He obviously understood every word that passed between us.

"I can't tell you," Allwin said.

Not "I don't know". I *can't* tell you, which of course was a matter of choice.

"Now, now, Master Allwin, you quite obviously can tell us, your lips move quite adequately, and there is a tongue in your mouth. The only thing preventing you from telling us is the fact you are labouring under the misapprehension that you have a choice in the matter."

"Please. Please. I can't." He backed up a step, then another, and another, until his back was pressed against the wall. He didn't stop shaking his head the whole time.

"All we need is a name," Holmes said.

"You don't understand; it will be the death of me."

"How very melodramatic," said Holmes. "I understand your co-conspirators will look most unfavourably on such a betrayal, but as their own liberty will last but a few hours longer than your own, I can assure you they will not be in a position to make good on any threats."

"They won't need to," Allwin said. "It's in here." He pressed two fingers against his forehead. "He put something inside me . . . if I betray him I am finished." He was shaking. Clearly he believed what he was saying. "I made a promise. I am bound by it. If I break my vow, I will die. There is no way out. He made sure of that. I am bound to them. Please. You cannot make me tell you. There must be another way." He looked around the room frantically. I was sure in that moment that he was looking for something that might be used to end his own life.

Holmes said something. It took me a heartbeat to register that it was one of the trigger phrases we'd heard the Great Andersen deliver to much amusement, and in response the landlord dropped to his hands and knees and scratched around on the floor like a chicken in search of feed, pecking his forehead at the room's bare boards over and over.

"Mesmerism," I said, in disgust.

"Look at me, man," Holmes said, his voice deep, regular, the rhythms of his words slow and easy.

Allwin had no choice but to do as he was told.

Holmes continued: "You cannot force a man to act against his better nature. I cannot plant some seed in your brain that would make you act against the basic urge of self-preservation. To think otherwise is preposterous." Which was easy to say, but harder to prove. The man looked unconvinced. Holmes said: "I want you to listen to my voice, concentrate on my words. I'm going to put you into a trancelike state and remove the imperatives put in place by Thurneman. To prove that you are free to talk, I will repeat the trigger that had you thinking you were a chicken a moment ago. You will be free of the subconscious imperative, and likewise free to talk. Understood?"

We watched as Holmes focused Allwin's attention, and within just a few moments had him submersed in a deep fugue state, awaiting instruction, neither awake nor asleep. Holmes's voice was gentle, reassuring, but far from removing all of the supposed triggers, he merely told the man he would no longer feel the need to act like a chicken when he heard that word.

"When you wake, you will no longer be afraid of Thurneman; he cannot hurt you or make you hurt yourself, do you understand me?"

"Yes," Allwin said.

"Very good. I am going to count backwards from ten, and when I reach one you are going to tell me the name of the girl who was used by your confederates to falsify evidence against the king. Do you understand me?"

"Yes."

"Very good," said Holmes. "Ten . . . Nine . . ."

There was a woman—there is always a woman. In this case she was the only woman in my audience. I invited her to tell her story. Her name was Maria Nordqvist, and in every way imaginable her life was utterly unremarkable, save for one: she had been a honey-trap for a man she believed to be her king.

She rose awkwardly, smoothing down the bustles of her best dress. Her flaxen hair had been braided and put up in hoops. Her face was striking if not exactly pretty, her nose too sharp, her cheeks too sculpted ever to be called beautiful. She was distinctively Scandinavian in appearance; she had slim, narrow hips accentuated by her skirts. She coughed once, clearing her throat.

"In your own time, my dear," I reassured her.

Unlike Allwin, she didn't speak English, so one of Lindblad's men interpreted for her, repeating her story every couple of lines. "I was told that to betray their cause meant certain death—at my own hand. They proved they could manipulate me into doing what they wanted—simple parlour tricks I could not resist, taking control of my body. All it would take was a word, Thurneman promised, a single trigger word, and I would not stop until I had ended my own life. And I believed him."

"What made you change your mind?"

"Mister Holmes."

"Would you mind explaining how?"

"He put me in a mesmeric state and removed the trigger. You can tell me to bark like a dog, nothing will happen now."

A few of the men in the gallery laughed, but there was an edge to the atmosphere, everyone waiting with baited breath for the truth to finally be laid at their feet.

"Would you care to tell us what happened in that room?"

She nodded. "I was forced to entertain a man while they watched from their hiding place, taking photographs."

"And these photographs were of a lewd nature?"

She nodded, colour rising in her cheeks. I did not wish to push her further or cause unnecessary embarrassment, but I had one last question for her, and needed the woman to spell it out so there could be absolutely no doubt. "Could you identify the man?"

"I should hope so," she said, earning a nervous laugh from somewhere up in the gods.

"Let me rephrase that: would you be so kind as to make the man's name known to everyone here."

"I can do better than that," said she, pointing a finger up in the direction of the Royal Box. "That's him, there."

She'd picked out the king from all the faces in the room, as I'd known she would. I had seen the photographs. The quality was poor, the images blurred from lack of light and the peculiar arrangement they'd been forced to manufacture to better focus on the bed through the pinhole in the wall, going back to the first very basic principles of photography. The images were barely more than blurred suggestions, crude in both senses of the word, but good enough for the purpose of extorting the king. Bissmark had known that from the moment the envelope had landed on his desk. It didn't matter if the man in them was Gustav or some imposter, once they were seen they could never be unseen and people would make up their own minds as to the veracity of the images, meaning he'd be damned before sundown. Holmes was right in his thinking that there was a growing groundswell of opinion in this country that wanted to see the Bernadottes humbled.

"There is only one thing that remains," said I, "and that is to present to you the mastermind behind this whole sorry affair and see that justice is served."

That was a cue, and my man up in the rigging earned his keep, focusing the full beam of one of the theatrical spotlights on a seat right in the middle of the audience.

The man looked up, perturbed. His face was heavily lined, each deep crease well earned, if his bearing was anything to go by, as he slowly eased himself up to his feet. Holmes had been most adamant that this final reveal posed the single greatest risk to the house of cards our case was constructed from but, as this was nothing if not a learning experience for the watchers, failure was not the end.

"I think you will find yourself mistaken, sir," the man said in impeccable English. "I am innocent of any and all of your accusations. Indeed, I am as innocent as your good self, as I have an unbreakable alibi."

"And that would be?"

"Why, you, Watson. And might I congratulate you on a truly fascinating examination of what was a most vexatious investigation." I knew that voice better than I knew my own, and as Holmes slowly peeled the first layer of prosthetic from his jawline, changing the entire shape of his face, I could not help but marvel at how well he had disguised himself in plain sight. "There remains but one thread to pull that we might unravel this entire mystery."

"And that would be?"

"The identity of Mister Thurneman, who, as Inspector Lindblad has highlighted, does not and has never existed. He is a ghost."

"But there is no such thing," I said.

"Indeed," Holmes agreed. "The name puzzled me for a while, until I realised it was nothing more cunning than an anagram, made more complex by being in English as opposed to the man's native tongue. When you have the key it is not difficult to crack; Thurneman is of course a Swedish-sounding rearrangement of the word 'manhunter', a clue to the nature of the man himself, who arrived mysteriously in the town a matter of a month or so before the first sighting of the imposter king. This is the man behind *four* imposter kings, who has practised the art of deception and misdirection. My first thought was that his true identity was actually that of the mesmerist the Great Andersen, a man who in turn appears to have no past. But what would a stage magician stand to gain from blackmailing a king?"

"Power," said someone in the audience to his left.

"Influence," said another, this time from behind Holmes.

"Money."

"The unholy trinity," Holmes agreed. "But it wasn't until I had studied the itinerary for the man's tour that I realised the same man was in the audience at every single performance."

Now he had my attention.

"And who might that be?" I enquired.

"Why, the king, of course. Each show was a gala performance. And at three of the shows, theatre workers reported that the mesmerist had been offered an audience with the king. So I asked myself a question: what could a king want with a man who made a living from parlour tricks? It took some thought, but it was something that Watson said that set me to thinking about the world this king finds himself living in, and how it is a thankless place where his throne is being stripped daily of its power and influence. Then another question occurred to me: *What happens in a game of kings when the monarch truly does not want to be king at all?*"

"Are you saying the king was behind his own blackmail? That makes no sense."

"And yet it is the truth: the grand crime to extort the king himself, a crime that just a few moments ago you dismissed as a stupid story, was never more than half the tale. Misdirection, like the magician's art. The true crime was nothing more than a king looking for a way to leave his throne, is that not the case, Your Majesty?"

The man's brow furrowed, but he offered no answer. No defence. No denial.

"Why not merely abdicate? Cede the throne to one of your sons?" I asked. There were three, each of an age where they could rule with something approaching wisdom.

"Abdication does not solve the problem of a civic uprising and an outdated form of rule, does it? The aim, the end game, is a bloodless revolution, if you like. The king giving his country back to its people. Look at how many lives were lost in the October Revolution and the civil war that broke out in its wake. What man of good conscience would ever want to inflict that kind of suffering upon his people, even if those people appear to have no love left for him? It must be sorely tempting to want to simply disappear. And who better to help with that than a renowned mystic," said Holmes. "A man whose entire life is built around illusion. He helped you plan the whole thing, did he not?"

The king nodded. There was sadness in his eyes. Regret. How must his life have crumbled for it to come to this?

"What about the body in the woods?" I asked. "The first imposter king. Surely you aren't claiming the king was somehow responsible for the murder of a man?"

Holmes shook his head. "Not directly. He most certainly never gave the order. In this case there never was a first imposter, was there, Your Majesty? There were only the two men who bore a striking resemblance to you, and then you yourself, acting out a part. That was you in Sala, was it not? And then again in Uppsala and Stockholm. Who better to play the king than the king himself?"

Gustav nodded, once, solemnly.

I looked from him to the woman as the realisation she had truly bedded her king sank in, my mind wrestling with the reality Holmes was offering up.

"So if it wasn't an imposter king, who was it?"

"Why, Watson, is that not obvious? It was the king's man or, as he styled himself, the *manhunter*. Thurneman had served his purpose. He could not be allowed to walk free, though, as the risk of him telling what he knew was too great."

"Someone still killed him," I protested. "Murder is murder."

"Indeed, but we will never know who. The corridors of power are murky at the best of times. These are not the best of times in this land, my friend. Even so, there isn't a man alive who would willingly betray a king he had gone to such lengths to protect, so we must content ourselves with knowing that we have done what we were brought here to do, assembled as fine a group of minds as could be hoped, and I think in this one lesson given a passing fair introduction to the idea of deductive reasoning and why one should always look beyond the headlines and their sensationalism for the truth that lies at the very heart of the matter."

It was difficult to argue with that, but then it was always difficult to argue with Holmes, as he had the frustrating habit of being right all the time.

The Adventure of the Orkney Shark
Simon Bestwick

——

I

RNAS Cladach Duillich, Orkney, 15 November 1927

We'd waited two days for the storm to end – and, in my case, with mingled excitement and dread, for the long-delayed moment of truth. Now three hundred men, hanging on to mooring ropes, walked the airship from her shed in the windless dawn.

A voice-pipe shrilled. "Clear of the shed, sir," said Church, the duty rigger.

My stomach grew tight as all eyes in the control car turned to me. Church, the navigator, the coxes at their wheels – and the neatly suited men at my side.

It was hard to tell which of these had drawn more attention from the crew. One stood out because of his race – he was an Australian Aborigine – and the silent, cold contempt with which he eyed all present. To my shame I'd never succeeded in pronouncing his true name, and he – not a patient man – had given up the attempt. I knew him only as Mr Blacksmith.

The other man drew attention for his fame. Although in his seventies and leaning on a stick, his hair remained jet black, his long, aquiline face surprisingly smooth and his eyes as sharp and undimmed as his intellect. Every man there knew him: the famed detective, Sherlock Holmes.

"At your leisure, Commander," he said.

The moment had come. "Up ship, Mr Church."

"Up ship," he said into the tube. A moment later Flight Sergeant Hunt, at the observation hatch on top of the ship, repeated the order through his megaphone.

There was an odd feeling of weightlessness – unique to airship travel – as two million cubic feet of hydrogen cancelled gravity's pull, and the ship rose. It was at once familiar and new: I'd experienced it often during my war service but, until last week, not since the Armistice of '18.

Holmes swayed slightly; Blacksmith remained unmoving and impassive. Below us the field, the airship sheds, the gasworks, the station and the island itself all shrank away, to reveal the cold grey North Sea around them.

The ship's ascent slowed and stopped; she hung in the air, shifting in the wind. "Start engines," I ordered.

Church relayed the command; the ship's three Sunbeam Maoris and twinned German Maybachs coughed and growled into life. "Set course and speed," I told Flight Lieutenant Bowman, the navigator, who chalked the bearing on a board in front of the steering coxswain, then went to the telegraph board to ring down the order for "full speed".

The ship rocked slightly as we crossed the hills near the coast, steadying once we were out over the open sea. "Hold altitude at sixteen hundred feet," I told the height coxswain.

"Aye, sir."

I went to gaze out of the control car window, and His Majesty's Airship R.36 sailed out across the North Sea, in search of the Orkney Shark.

II.
1 Russell Square, London, two weeks earlier

I'd read of Mr Holmes as a boy, but had never expected to meet him. I'd thought both him and his elder brother Mycroft long-since retired, if not dead – yet here they both were, hale and hearty despite their years, in a room as out of its time as they were.

Stuffed animal heads, Zulu assegais and Indian *tulwars* were mounted on the walls, alongside paintings depicting Waterloo,

Ondurman and Rorke's Drift. Perhaps they thought that, as a former officer, raised in the Empire's glory days, I'd find comfort in memories of the past. They were wrong.

"In an area of the North Sea east of the Orkneys and Shetlands," said Mycroft, "twenty ships have vanished without trace in the past three months."

I nodded. "I take it this exceeds the normal rate of loss?"

"The North Sea is a dangerous place to ply any sort of trade," said Holmes. "Nonetheless, one might expect to lose no more than two ships a month in the usual course of things. Also, these have mostly disappeared in excellent weather, and—"

"And while most of the losses were trawlers or cargo ships," said Mycroft, "the last two were military vessels. HMS *Achilles*, a prototype of the newest destroyer class, and HMS *Ostia* – likewise, one of our latest mark of submarine – searching for wreckage or survivors from the *Achilles*."

"Certain fishermen of the Orkney Islands," Mr Holmes put in, "apparently believe the sinkings to be the work of a sea monster – the so-called Orkney Shark, said to be several hundred feet in length."

"Allegedly it has been seen," growled Mycroft, "but we have been unable to determine by whom."

"Besides which," said Holmes, "it's improbable any shark could grow to such size – or chew through steel plating. So it is the second least likely of four possibilities."

"And the least likely?" I asked, sipping the whisky and soda they had provided.

"Coincidence, which I distrust as an explanation at the best of times. Discounting this, or sea monsters, we are left with two possibilities: a newly arisen natural phenomenon, such as an underwater volcano or magnetic anomaly – which, like the others, lies outside my area of expertise, or – most probable of all—"

"Foul play," I said. "More exactly, a submarine."

Holmes looked briefly put out by the interruption, but nodded. "No other vessel could operate so near the British coast undetected, or despatch one of our own submersibles so effectively."

"Some suspect Russia," said Mycroft, "with whom our relations are anything but cordial. Others, unwilling to forget past enmities, suspect the Germans. In either case, the peace of Europe is at risk – therefore I, and my colleagues in the Diogenes Club, have persuaded the prime minister to keep the affair secret."

I knew of the Diogenes, of course – outwardly a gentleman's club, but in reality dedicated to the nation's defence.

"Under the terms of the Versailles Treaty, the German Navy has no submarines, surely?" I said.

Mycroft nodded. "A secret programme is possible, but unlikely. The Soviets have no submarine that could outclass the *Ostia*. Indeed, neither country has designers with the skill to build one." He smiled. "The Germans did once, but the Great War—"

"In short," Holmes cut in, "we need data."

"And," said Mycroft, "a rapid, *discreet* solution."

"To find and destroy this 'Orkney Shark'," I said, "the search must be from the air, or the searchers would risk the same fate. And it could only be made by a craft that can remain aloft for hours, even days. In short, an airship."

"Precisely!" Mycroft beamed.

"Never having travelled by dirigible," said Holmes, "I look forward to it."

"You, Mr Holmes?"

"For the most part, my activities are now confined to teaching duties here. But I am, on occasion, persuaded to take on a case – usually by Mycroft, as now."

"The defence of the realm requires it," said Mycroft. "And, of course, it also requires an experienced airship commander."

I lit a cigarette. "My experience, gentlemen, is a decade old. I've only just been recalled from Australia for the new Imperial Airship Scheme. Why not use Bird or Mouldy?"

"Who?" said Holmes.

"The men of the Royal Air Force," said Mycroft, "delight strangely in peculiar nicknames. Flight Lieutenant Irwin and Squadron Leader Booth are 'Bird' and 'Mouldy' respectively; Lieutenant Commander Atherstone here – *Grabowsky* Atherstone, to give him his full name – is 'Grabby', I'm told."

"Fascinating."

"Irwin and Booth are the designated commanders of the new airships, *R.100* and *R.101*," Mycroft told me. "They are too much in the public eye, whilst you have only recently returned to Britain. Your absence will go unnoticed."

As would my death. "I'm still badly out of practice," I said. "Moreover, Mr Holmes, *R.100* and *R.101* are still under construction. The only remaining British airship, *R.36*, was deleted last year and broken up."

"Officially, yes," said Mycroft. "However, I and others thought it ill-advised to leave Britain without an operational airship. *R.36* was in fact repaired and flown – in conditions of utmost secrecy – from RAF Pulham to a former RNAS station on the Scottish island of Cladach Duillich – a secret base used during the Great War for very *special* operations. Cladach Duillich has its own gasworks, two airship sheds – and two Submarine Scout blimps, preserved from the Great War. You can reacquaint yourself with lighter-than-air flight with these before taking command of *R.36*. But I'm sure it'll come back quickly."

"I admire your optimism," I said.

"Well, you *do* have one other important qualification for this mission. As First Officer of HMA *R.29*, you stalked and sank the German U-boat *UB-115*."

"Assisted by several armed trawlers and two destroyers," I pointed out.

"Even so, it was the *only* success of its kind achieved by a British airship during the War," said Mycroft. "You'll help?"

A thought occurred to me. "Might I make a telephone call before answering?"

"A telephone call? Commander—"

"I'll say nothing of this," I assured them. "But it *is* necessary, gentlemen."

Mycroft sighed. "Very well."

A servant ushered me to a side-room, from which I telephoned Eve. "Noel?" she said. "What is it?"

"Nothing to worry about, old girl," I told her. "Is Mr Blacksmith there?"

"Where else?"

I heard the strain in her voice. Eve was loving, steadfast and unwavering – but it remains hard to share a home with a non-paying guest who despises you. "I think I may have found how to discharge the debt," I said.

"Really?"

"Depends on him. Can you get him?"

"Of course."

Blacksmith came on the phone. "Yes, Mr Atherstone?"

"I have a proposition for you, Mr Blacksmith," I said.

A couple of minutes later, I replaced the phone; the servant conducted me back to the two brothers.

They looked at me, these guardians of Empire – thinking I was, like them, a champion of that faded, dying dream. They were mistaken, of course – but innocent men were dying in the North Sea, and another war would harm only more innocents still. Besides which, the life of an airshipman was the only one in which I truly belonged – and, finally, I had a chance to repay the debt I owed.

"I will help," I said, "on one condition."

"Condition?" Mycroft spluttered.

"I have an acquaintance," I said, looking at Sherlock Holmes, "alone in the world, whose particular skills and background leave him unqualified for most occupations – with one possible exception."

"The science of deduction?" smiled Holmes. "And your condition, of course, is that he be inducted into my School for Detection?"

"Yes."

"A counter-proposal, Commander," said Holmes. "I must approve all entrants to my school. Let your protégé accompany us on this mission; if he acquits himself satisfactorily, I shall take him on. Is this acceptable to you?"

"Yes."

"Then it's settled," said Mycroft. "You'll need to ask your wife to send along a case, Commander: you leave for Cladach Duillich at once."

III.

Over the North Sea, 15 November 1927

The riggers' distant singing echoed in the hull. Armed with needle and thread, rubber patches and pots of glue, they climbed among the cage of girders, looking for holes in the envelope of doped fabric that formed *R.36*'s outer cover, and leaks in the great drum-shaped gas-bags of goldbeater's skin, chained at intervals within the hull.

They sang because it was the simplest way to find a hydrogen leak; when inhaled, the gas affects the vocal cords, turning the voice high-pitched and squeaky. It could also make you light-headed, and if you lost your footing on the higher girders you might fall straight down, through the outer cover and into empty space. It was a job that required a steady nerve, and nimbleness of both body and mind.

I watched the rolling grey water through binoculars as we flew, as did Blacksmith. Other eyes kept watch from *R.36*'s gondola, or from hatches dotted along the hull. During the War, Britain's airships had patrolled its coastal waters, seeking the telltale signs of German U-boats: oil slicks, gulls wheeling over open water, the ripples where a periscope broke the surface.

After several hours, I turned, rubbing my eyes, and saw Blacksmith leaving the control car. Holmes stared after him, frowning, then followed.

"Maintain course and speed," I told Bowman. "Alert me if anything is sighted."

"Yes, sir," he said as I followed Holmes and Blacksmith into the gondola.

Half built when the Great War ended, *R.36* had been redesigned as a civilian vessel, with a twenty-five-cabin passenger compartment attached behind the control car. Several of those cabins had been removed to accommodate bombs, depth charges and small arms; one of the remainder served as accommodation for Holmes and Blacksmith, and another as an office in which the detective could assess his beloved 'data'.

It was here we found Blacksmith, studying a chart on the wall. It showed the waters east of Orkney and Shetland, the missing ships' last known positions marked by red drawing pins. He leant forward, hands on his knees. I'd seen that pose before.

"Something interests you, Mr Blacksmith?" said Holmes.

Blacksmith nodded. "There must be a lair," he said. His English was excellent: very precise, and only slightly accented.

"Lair?"

"All creatures have them."

"The so-called Orkney Shark is—"

"The Orkney Shark is not a beast," he said. "Nonetheless, the principle applies. All things eat, Mr Holmes." He nodded upwards. "This eats petrol. So does a submarine."

"Diesel, to be exact," I said.

Blacksmith ignored me. "Airship, aeroplane, submarine, boat – all require a home. They must return to it. Replenish."

"Your point?" said Holmes.

"Where is the lair of the Orkney Shark?"

"If we knew that, Mr Blacksmith, our troubles would be at an end."

"Look." Blacksmith pointed at the red pins; his finger made a slow circle. "The missing ships all surround one area of open sea. You observe?"

"I observe, Mr Blacksmith."

"Fish or machine, the Orkney Shark is a hunting beast. Such beasts venture from their lairs to hunt." Blacksmith's pointing finger moved from the space at the centre of the map, out to the dots, then in once more, over and over. "All this points to its lair being here – and yet there is nothing. I suggest, Mr Holmes, that this area of sea may repay investigation."

Holmes half smiled, and opened his mouth to comment, but before he could answer there was a sound of running feet and the curtain at the entrance to the cabin was pulled back. "Commander – Mr Holmes . . ."

It was the duty rigger, Church, tasked with carrying messages to and from the control car: a tall young man with a long, intelligent face and a brush of brown hair. "What is it, Mr Church?"

"We've sighted something."

"A submarine?"

"No, sir." Church swallowed. "A ship of some sort, but she's drifting and isn't responding to hails. She's dead in the water."

I looked at Holmes; he raised an eyebrow. "Further data may be at hand," he said. "Come!"

He strode past myself and Church towards the control car. I nodded to Church, and the tall young man followed him.

Blacksmith straightened his tie. "We should join them," he said, and went too.

IV.

The ship was a cargo steamer, wallowing in the grey water. She was listing, and from the control car I could see bodies on her deck. In faded lettering at the bow, I made out the name *Ourang Medan*.

"This, I think," said Holmes, "bears closer investigation. You would agree, Mr Blacksmith?"

"I would, Mr Holmes."

Holmes looked expectantly at me. I nodded. "Sergeant Greene, break out small arms and prepare to disembark."

"Aye, sir." Greene, a wiry, dark-haired man, was in command of a squad of Royal Marines attached to *R.36*.

"Mr Church," I said, "ready mooring ropes and the basket." As he nodded and dashed off, I turned to the coxes. "Take us in, Mr Potter. Mr Hunt, can you bring us to six hundred?"

Hunt, a stocky, grey-haired man with bright blue eyes in a square, leathery face, nodded. "No problem, sir." I knew him – and Potter – well; both were veterans of the Airship Section. Potter had been one of only five survivors when *R.38* had broken up over the Humber in '21, and Hunt had been aboard *R.33* when a storm had torn her loose from the Pulham mooring mast and blown her out to sea. Under "Mouldy" Booth's command, he had organised emergency in-flight repairs and helped bring the ship back in under its own power. He was less in the public eye than the new airship commanders, so Mycroft had arranged for him and Potter to serve on *R.36*. An astute move, ensuring the potentially rusty commander was bolstered by solid NCOs. As *R.36* cruised towards the stricken boat, he adjusted the height wheel.

A nautical ship has one steering wheel, a rigid airship two: one for the rudder, one for the elevators that control its altitude. It's the second that requires true artistry – and "Sky" Hunt was a true artist.

We could lose height by "valving off" some of our hydrogen, but that would reduce the ship's useful lift and the engines would have to consume more fuel to shift the added weight. The longer we conserved such resources, the longer we put off returning to Cladach with our mission unfulfilled.

A large wicker basket was lowered on mooring ropes, containing five marines. When they were down, they secured other ropes to the steamer, enabling us to maintain position above it, while on the airship, riggers stood ready with knives to cut the ropes should the ship be endangered.

The deck of the *Ourang Medan* was clear, occupied only by her crew's bodies. The basket was winched back up, then lowered again, now holding two marines armed with rifles, plus Holmes, Blacksmith and myself, each armed with a revolver.

Holmes knelt by one of the dead crewmen. "Blue lips," he said, "and petechiae in the eyes. Do you see, Mr Blacksmith?"

"As if he had been strangled," said the Aborigine. He tilted the dead man's head back. "But there are no marks on his throat."

"Indeed." Holmes inspected several other bodies. "The same with these. Smothered, perhaps? But how?"

"Sir?" Greene called; he and his fellows were standing beside the open hatch that led to the hold. "Permission to proceed?"

"Carry on, Sergeant."

Greene nodded and descended the steps below decks, but a moment later there was a choking sound and the thud of a falling body. One marine shouted and went after him, rifle raised.

I ran for the hatch, Holmes and Blacksmith at my heels, reaching it in time to see the other marine, midway through his descent to the hold, turn and try to climb back up. Choking, he collapsed on the steps; below him, Greene lay unmoving on the floor of the hold.

A red-haired marine corporal made to run down, but Blacksmith seized his arm. "No!" he said.

"Let go of me, you bloody savage—"

"A boathook," said Blacksmith. "Fetch one, quickly, if you want them to live. If you go down there, the same will happen to you."

"Do as he says," I barked.

A boathook was found and fetched. Blacksmith grabbed it and started down the steps, extending it in one arm. "Hold on to my other arm," he told the corporal, "in case I fall."

The man scowled, but obeyed. Blacksmith took a deep breath and held it, then reached out with the hook. He succeeded in snagging the fallen marine's uniform, pulling him up until he was in arm's reach of the hatch. "Quickly!" snapped Blacksmith, and the man was hauled to safety. His lips were already blue.

"The kiss of life," ordered Holmes, "and quickly."

"What about the sarge, sir?" said the corporal.

"It is too late," said Blacksmith.

"I'm afraid," said Holmes, "Mr Blacksmith is right, Corporal . . .?"

"O'Hara, sir."

"Corporal O'Hara, that man is dead." Holmes studied Greene and the dead men on the deck. "Carbonic acid gas, unless I miss my guess. That is what killed these men – and doubtless those below decks."

He crouched and picked something up – it resembled a piece of porcelain. "Do you observe this, Mr Blacksmith?"

Blacksmith crouched beside him. "The gas was in here?"

"I believe that if we search we will find more such fragments, if they were not swept overboard in the storm. These containers shattered on the deck, stifling those up top, while the rest—"

"Mr Holmes, sir!" O'Hara called. Three other marines had tied a rope around his waist and lowered him through the hatch, enabling him to shine a torch around the hold. "You should see this."

The beam of the torch picked out what appeared to be a long sharp tube, jutting into the hull through a buckled plate. Water had seeped in around the breach, partly flooding the hold – and, presumably, accounting for the list.

"That came in below the waterline," said Holmes. "A torpedo, I would imagine, albeit of rather novel design – injecting gas into the ship's interior, thus eliminating everyone below decks. The canisters shattering on the top deck completed the work." He stood and looked about, then pointed. "There! Mr Blacksmith, with me!"

Blacksmith followed Holmes aft; the rest of us quickly joined him, and we saw what Holmes had seen. Near the stern, a section of the *Ourang Medan*'s metal hull had been partly peeled back: I observed a long, deep cut, as if made by a welder's torch.

"The butchering of the kill," said Blacksmith.

Holmes looked at him. "Do I understand you correctly, Mr Blacksmith?"

The Aborigine knelt. "The missing ships," he said, and rapped lightly on the steel plating. "All were made of metal?"

"Indeed they were!" Holmes sprang to his feet, then winced. "Ah. Sometimes I forget my years. I think I begin to understand."

He turned to face me. "Trawlers, cargo vessels, a destroyer, a submarine – all had one thing in common. Metal. This ship, too, would have vanished, but the recent storm tore it from the grasp of the 'Orkney Shark'. Our enemy doesn't sink his prey, Commander – he captures the vessels undamaged, then dismantles them."

"But to what end?" I said.

Holmes went still. "We must return to the ship," he said. "And contact Cladach Duillich immediately."

As he strode up the deck, Corporal O'Hara approached Mr Blacksmith. "Mate," he said, offering his hand, "I'm sorry for what I said."

Blacksmith looked at the offered hand, but didn't take it. "Good," he said, then went after Holmes.

O'Hara stared after him, then looked at me.

"I'm afraid Mr Blacksmith is not a forgiving man, Corporal," I said.

As well I knew.

V.

Back in the control car, Holmes made straight for Atkins, the wireless operator. "Instruct Cladach Duillich to get me Mycroft," he said, then turned to Bowman. "I require detailed charts of the area within the following latitude and longitude."

Bowman hurried to his charts; Atkins began sending. Holmes strode off to his "office". Blacksmith and I both followed; we found him studying the chart. "You were quite right, Mr Blacksmith. I must thank you for commending this gentleman to my attention, Commander. He has the makings of a fine detective."

Blacksmith merely raised an eyebrow.

Holmes paced, leaning on his stick. "A submarine that preys only on metal ships – no other common denominator links the missing vessels. An advanced design, with hostile intent – yet it strikes neither at our Navy nor our coast. All it apparently seeks is steel – but both Germany and Russia have that in plentiful supply.

"Furthermore, as Mr Blacksmith observed, there is this." Holmes pointed to the area of the chart Blacksmith had indicated. "A submarine's base of operations should be in its native land – unless it is not controlled by any government at all."

"A criminal conspiracy?" I said.

"Not criminal, political. Our enemy, Commander, is driven not by avarice, but fanatical devotion to a cause. Do you recall Mycroft saying no German or Russian could build a submarine capable of outclassing the *Ostia*?"

"Yes – but then he said that Germany *had* had such an expert . . ."

Holmes rubbed his hands together. "Mycroft has hinted as much in the past, but is sworn to secrecy regarding his war service. Now, however . . ."

Church pulled the curtain back. "Mr Holmes – your brother."

"Excellent!" Holmes clapped his hands. "If nothing else, I will have the satisfaction of hearing Mycroft break silence on a topic that has long intrigued me."

VI.

"The man you allude to," Mycroft said over the speakers, "was Count Melchior von Eisenholm. Do you recall, Sherlock, the affair of the Bruce-Partington plans?"

"I do indeed. A submarine design," Holmes told me. "We were led a pretty dance some years ago, keeping it out of the hands of the Nachrichten-Abteilung."

"And all, as it proved, for nought," said Mycroft. "Less than a year later, the Kaiserliche Marine deployed a new class of U-boat which rendered it obsolete. Thereafter, we raced frantically to outmatch the Germans in submarine warfare – up to the outbreak of war, and beyond.

"And all throughout, one name came up again and again: von Eisenholm. Prussian aristocrat, scientist and inventor, he was somewhat like your Professor Moriarty, Sherlock: a man of formidable intellect, wedded to monstrous intent. But while Moriarty was a criminal, von Eisenholm was a fanatical militarist, utterly convinced of Germany's destiny to rule the world itself."

I suppressed a smile, given how we British had hardly been innocent of such designs – although both Holmes brothers would doubtless have considered the comparison heretical.

"Von Eisenholm's hero was Count Zeppelin," said Mycroft. "Zeppelin did not *invent* the dirigible, but *perfected* it; he revolutionised its development and set the pattern for all future airships. Von Eisenholm believed this was yet to be done for the submarine – but would be, by him."

His voice ringing through the wireless speaker, Mycroft explained that von Eisenholm had established laboratories and workshops at Schloss Kalterstein, on the shores of the Kaltenzee, three miles from the Baltic coast. The wide, deep lake had been an ideal testing-ground for submarines; a deep inlet, at the foot of the *schloss* itself, a perfect U-boat pen.

Working in absolute secrecy, von Eisenholm and a handful of trusted assistants had presented a succession of brilliant new designs to the Kaiserliche Marine. Time and again, he'd almost turned the War in the Central Powers' favour; only Mycroft, tireless in gleaning his machines' secrets and devising counter-measures, had stopped him.

Von Eisenholm's string of successes ended when he unveiled new, more grandiose plans. He spoke of a new breed of submarine: self-sufficient, self-repairing, able to leave dry land behind for ever, if required – even able to manufacture more of its kind. It was too radical a vision for the conservative German High Command. Von Eisenholm fell from favour, but continued his work unaided at Schloss Kalterstein, recruiting a private army to crew his experimental submarines and guard his estate.

"Some thought von Eisenholm a spent force." Every word Mycroft spoke came with absolute clarity from the radio speaker. "But I never doubted he remained a menace. I strove to penetrate Kalterstein's security, but without success – until the very end."

In November 1918, when Admiral von Hipper abandoned his plans for a last-ditch naval assault on Britain, Mycroft learned that the count, believing his prototype submarines ready for action, intended to sail them down the river that flowed from the Kaltenzee to the Baltic, deploying them first against the British naval blockade. Once loose, they could roam at will permanently, while constantly increasing their numbers – a submarine guerrilla army to bring about an ultimate German victory.

"In reality, of course, the War was lost," said Mycroft over the soft crackle of radio static, "but von Eisenholm could have prolonged it another two, even three years, at the cost of millions of lives."

"What action did you take?" asked Holmes.

Mycroft sighed. "I passed what I had learned, through an agent, to those of the German High Command who had accepted the inevitable. They, as I, knew there would be no dissuading him, and that Germany's greatest asset was now a deadly threat to her. That night, the Kaltenzee was surrounded, the river mined; Germany's own bombers blew Schloss Kalterstein, the U-boats and all therein to fragments."

"So, Brother Mycroft," said Holmes, "you deduced that Melchior von Eisenholm was dead and his submarines destroyed. I offer the following scenario: anticipating his compatriots' treachery, von Eisenholm escaped in one of his submarines via the river before it was mined, and has, ever since, roamed the seas like some underwater Flying Dutchman – until now."

"But *why* until now?" pondered Mycroft.

"If the *Ourang Medan* is any indication," said Holmes, "the crews of the vanished ships were gassed, and the ships cannibalised."

"To build new submarines?" said Mycroft.

"That would have been his intent when he left Schloss Kalterstein," said Holmes. "He doubtless planned to bide his time, let Germany's enemies think their victory secure, before emerging as her champion and rallying all true Germans to his side. But even genius can only bend reality so far to its will. He may manufacture ships, but not men to crew them."

"True," said Mycroft. "So why act now?"

"For the same reason, I think, that although von Eisenholm's submarines needed no permanent base, he appears to have one now – a lair, to use Mr Blacksmith's term. His ship has been in continuous service for almost a decade, and the salt sea is notoriously punishing. Self-sufficient or not, time and decay claim their due of man and machine."

I understood what he was driving at. "A replacement ship."

"Not merely a replacement." Mycroft's voice rumbled from the speaker. "He has taken enough steel to build a fleet. But a fleet without a crew?"

"The realisation that time is marching relentlessly on," said Holmes, "may have spurred him to action. As for his fleet – I have my suspicions, but they must await further proof." Holmes motioned to Bowman. "Bring those charts. Mycroft, we may require additional help to bring this business to its end."

"What do you have in mind?"

"Torpedo bombers – as many as you can move to Cladach Duillich. Fuelled, armed and ready to take off at a moment's notice."

"Within the hour," Mycroft assured.

"Good. Stand by for further announcements, brother of mine. Mr Blacksmith?"

Blacksmith moved to Holmes's side as Bowman spread out the requested charts. "Here," said Holmes, "is the still centre of the raging storm. Do you see?"

"There," said Blacksmith, stabbing a finger at a point just left of centre, dotted with a spray of black specks.

"What are these, Mr Bowman?" enquired Holmes.

"The Skule Skerries, sir," said the navigator. "That's what the Scots call them."

"A shoal of rocks," said Holmes. "The topmost points of an undersea mountain range – meaning shallower waters nearby. Von Eisenholm may no longer trust his ship to endure the pressures found at extreme depth. But here, in the middle of the North Sea, he has a resting-place close to the surface, where his strength can be conserved." He chuckled. "One cannot help but admire the man's sheer deranged ingenuity."

"Mr Bowman," I said, "plot us a course to the Skule Skerries."

Blacksmith nodded. "Now, we hunt the hunter."

VII.

"Full speed," I said. "Take her up to fifteen hundred, Mr Hunt, and hold her steady."

Bowman chalked the new bearing on the board in front of the steering wheel; Potter turned *R.36* on to her new course, while Hunt adjusted the height wheel.

"If neither of you have need of me," said Blacksmith, "I believe I shall sleep."

"Sleep?" said Holmes.

Blacksmith shrugged. "It will take us some small time to reach our destination. In the meantime, there is little to be done. Our enemy is known, his lair detected; we know what we must do. It would be wise to face him rested and alert."

"By all means," said Holmes, "if you can. I doubt I could sleep at any price."

Blacksmith nodded and left the control car. Once we were under way, I went to a window, looking out across the sea.

Nothing compares to flight in an airship. Aeroplanes are fast and noisy, fighting always to stay aloft: dirigibles have stateliness and grace.

The day I first flew in one – a Submarine Scout identical to the one I'd retrained on at Cladach Duillich – I'd known it was where I belonged. It had been too long, and till now there had been no opportunity to savour the experience.

I lost myself in silent contemplation for some time, before Holmes joined me at the window.

"Most remarkable," he said at last. "I wonder, Commander, if I might ask a question of a somewhat personal nature."

"You're free to ask, Mr Holmes."

"The nature of your relationship with Mr Blacksmith puzzles me. You do not conduct yourselves as master and servant."

"That's because we're neither," I said.

"Nor quite as friends, I think."

"No," I said, "nor that."

"If anything," said Holmes, "I could believe he disliked you profoundly."

"He detests all white men."

"Then why entertain his company?"

"You'll remember," I said, "that I and my family lived in Australia for some years before I was recalled for the Imperial Airship Scheme."

"Of course."

"For a period," I said, "I was a farmer. Those years were a strange time – some people were beginning to change their view of the Aborigines."

"In what way?"

"They questioned whether the Aborigines were indeed 'lower types', to treat or mistreat as we pleased; whether they should not be recognised as fellow human beings and accorded the same rights and privileges any white man would think himself entitled to. Others, of course, continued to regard them as little more than animals – and, as such, either useful – or vermin to be exterminated."

"To which school of thought did you incline?"

"At first – to my shame – the second. Until one day – some of our cattle were stolen, and I set out in search of the thieves. I never found them, or the cattle. Instead I heard a baby crying, and went to investigate."

For a moment I was back in the dry gully on that baking-hot day: the heat and the dust, the stink of blood and ordure and decay, the buzzing of flies.

"There were between thirty and fifty of them, all told," I said. "Men, women and children. Almost all had been beaten and tortured – cuts, burns. Virtually all the women – even some of the children – had been violated in the most brutal, disgusting manner. The only sounds were the flies, and the wailing of the child. I found it trapped under her mother's body."

Holmes was silent.

"She was a tiny thing," I remembered. "More or less newborn. I'm not sure if she'd been injured in the fall, or simply left there in that stifling heat for too long. She was howling, crying – I gave her water, but it was too late. The baby died in my arms. Have you ever experienced such a thing, Mr Holmes? To hold a new life in your hands, and to feel it end?"

"I have not," he said.

"Nor had I, till then. You might say this was a Damascene moment, Mr Holmes. One man's blood is as red as another's, one child's death the same. There was nothing I could do in that gully. That child had been the only living soul left there – almost the last, I later learned, of an entire tribe." I nodded aft-ward. "Blacksmith's tribe. Friends, family – wife, child – all died in that gully. And it was plain they had been killed by white men. I am no detective, but found enough evidence to make *that* deduction. And I knew, as well, that they would pay no price for what they had done."

I looked down at the smooth grey sea that passed below us. "I don't know how long I stayed in that gully. But eventually I moved out – and found tracks leading away. I had my rifle, so I forgot my cattle and set off in pursuit of the killers."

"To mete out personal justice?"

"To mete out the only kind those men would receive."

"And where was Mr Blacksmith at this time?"

"Tracking the killers himself, along with two other surviving tribesmen. They found them, and they fought well. But they were outnumbered and outgunned. When I arrived, Blacksmith's companions had been killed, and he himself wounded and disarmed. I am a reasonable rifle shot, and killed enough of the gang for him to get free and settle accounts."

"He does not seem particularly grateful," said Holmes.

"In his eyes, he has no cause to be. What I did – even though it led to our being ostracised by our neighbours, and the failure of our farm – was as nothing weighed against what had been done to him and his by other whites. We are no more friends than we are master and servant, but I owe Mr Blacksmith a debt. Until it is repaid – insofar as it can be – he is my companion."

Holmes said nothing. In silence, we watched the grey sea pass.

VIII.

Ahead, the sea was punctured with bursts of black and white. The skerries jutted up out of the water in little nubs and spines and flat tables of black rock, like so much discarded furniture, and the water around them frothed white.

"Mr Atherstone." Blacksmith had joined Holmes and me at the window, straightening his tie and smoothing his hair and not looking remotely like a man just roused from sleep. "This is the place?"

"This is the place, Mr Blacksmith," said Holmes. "So now we watch."

Lookouts were already in position, searching the shallows for any sign of our quarry – assuming it was there; that any of the story Holmes had spun from a handful of clues was other than fancy. Passing over the shoals of wet black rocks, the idea of the vengeful Melchior von Eisenholm and his submarine seemed ridiculous.

We had, at least, the clear weather to assist us. To any surface ship the rocks would have been a lethal and treacherous hazard, unseen until it was too late; to us, they were easy to see. But there was no sign of any submarine: only rock, occasional traces of sand . . .

"There," said Blacksmith, pointing from an open starboard window.

"Where?" Holmes and I ran to his side, peering out – but we had already passed over the spot.

"Reduce speed," I told Church. "Mr Potter, bring us around. Mr Hunt, maintain altitude."

Slowly the airship turned. It wasn't a quick process; *R.36* was 675 feet long from nose to tail, and almost eighty wide. But in the end, she cruised back the way she had come, at a more sedate pace.

"What did you see, and where?" demanded Holmes.

Blacksmith pointed to an area of swirling water between two flat, tabular skerries.

"There," he said. "It does not move."

"I see nothing," said Holmes.

"Nor I," I said. "Just rock, weed, barnacles . . ."

"Barnacles, yes. There are none elsewhere on these shoals."

He was right, now I considered: for whatever reason, the tiny shell-fish didn't appear on any visible part of the rocks and skerries. They lay only in this one area, in a long, wide cluster. As we drew closer, I saw its outline was distorted by the water's churning, but there was something about the shape – a regularity, a symmetry.

The barnacles had not grown here; they had grown somewhere – or on something – else. Something that had spent a great deal of time in other parts of the sea, more conducive to their survival.

Blacksmith was right: I saw it now. A great mass, encrusted in barnacles and weed, in the shape of a huge fish – a long, teardrop body, but with fins, almost like wings, jutting out from its sides, and another, a thin sharp triangle, rising from its back. But it was larger than any fish – four hundred feet, if it was an inch. A little over half *R.36*'s length, but for a submarine, it was a titan – and where *R.36*'s hull was a cage of light duraluminium girders, the Orkney Shark's would be solid steel.

"The Orkney Shark, indeed!" said Holmes, pointing. "Von Eisenholm departed from traditional submarine design, taking the fish as his model: and what better model than the shark could there be?"

"Mr Atkins," I said, "consult Mr Bowman and transmit our *precise* location to Cladach Duillich – tell them to get the bombers in flight *at once*. Corporal O'Hara, ready the depth charges and stand by. Mr Hunt – maintain altitude. Mr Potter, bring us around for another pass."

I clasped my hands behind my back; they shook slightly.

"We're in your hands, Commander," said Holmes. "What now?"

"We'll force her to surface with depth charges," I said. "That should make her vulnerable to the torpedo bombers. If she isn't aware of us yet, she soon will be: I'd be astonished if von Eisenholm doesn't have look-outs, and they couldn't miss something our size."

"Will they attack?" said Holmes.

"More likely run," said I.

"I think they will fight," said Blacksmith. "The beast is tired and sick, and has nowhere else to go. Even a beast without hope will fight, if cornered."

I reached for a voice-pipe. "O'Hara?"

"Sir?"

"Target is ahead, between the two flat rocks." I gave him a brief explanation of what to look for. "Depth charges at the ready. It mustn't escape."

"Aye, sir."

I peered out of the window. The barnacled hulk of the Orkney Shark – it seemed impossible now that I could ever have missed it – rested on the rocks below.

"Drop charges at will, Corporal."

Bubbles flurried up to the surface; the great submerged shape shifted. Slowly the Shark rose, and began moving away from the rocks.

"She's running, O'Hara," I began to shout, but already the first depth charge was falling, then another; a moment later the water exploded into great hissing spouts and R.36 rocked in the blast. As the water settled I looked for any sign of the submarine. Perhaps she was already gone; perhaps the blast had crippled her and she'd fallen clear of the plateau she'd rested on, tumbling into the depths where the pressure would crush her weakened hull like paper. But no: she was intact, and she was rising. Her shark-like fin broke water; a moment later, the rest of her followed.

"There," said Blacksmith. "We have her. We must keep her in the – Mr Atherstone!"

He pointed, but I had already seen it: the back of the submarine suddenly bristled, hedgehog-like, as two dozen thin sharp spines shot out. But they were not spines; they were the barrels of guns, and as I watched they all swivelled to point at R.36. And a moment later, they fired.

IX.

Blacksmith caught both Holmes and I and flung us to the deck as the control car windows shattered. There were shouts, cries, and the guns thundered again and again; the airship shuddered as they flailed it.

"Take us up!" I shouted. "Engines to full power!"

Hunt was already spinning the elevator wheel; the deck tilted as we climbed. Rigger Church scrambled to the telegraph board, wrenching the handles to "full speed"; bells rang and the engines' growl became a roar.

"Let go a quarter-ton of ballast aft," I shouted, and R.36's deck levelled off again.

Blacksmith helped Holmes to his feet. Below, the Orkney Shark wallowed; her guns still fired, but we were now out of range. Two bodies lay on the control car floor: an assistant wireless operator and Bowman, who'd been almost cut in half. "Get those out of here," I ordered, reaching for a voice-pipe. "O'Hara?"

"Sir."

"What's your status?"

"Two men dead. We still have the charges, but we won't be able to aim with accuracy above eight hundred feet."

Which, I guessed, would be well within the range of the submarine's guns. I looked at the control panel – the manometer, which monitored the gas pressure, was falling. "Church!" I said. "Get the other riggers – check every gas-bag immediately."

"Sir."

"Mr Atkins, what's your status?"

"Shortwave's still functional, sir, but the telegraph's gone."

"See if you can raise Cladach. We need an ETA for those bombers."

The Orkney Shark remained afloat and motionless in the water, so I surmised that our attack had immobilised her, at least for now. Without special anti-airship ammunition, her guns might damage R.36's gas-bags often enough to cause a critical loss of hydrogen, but that would be a long, slow process; however, the control car and passenger gondola were essentially boxes of thin sheet metal – easy targets with no protection against bullets.

So, on the face of things, a stalemate. But, given time, they might repair the submarine and escape: and if they did, there was no guessing when or where von Eisenholm might reappear.

"Altitude, Mr Hunt?"

"Twelve hundred, sir."

"Hold her steady at that. Mr Potter, bring her round. Circle her. If she tries to get away we'll attack, but for now, let's try and keep her for the bombers."

"Trying to raise Cladach, sir," said Atkins, "but there's too much interference. Another transmission—"

"*Achtung!*" A voice came from the speakers. "This is the SMS *VEUB-1*, calling enemy airship. To whom am I speaking?"

I exchanged glances with Holmes and Blacksmith, and took Atkins's microphone. "Lieutenant Commander Atherstone of His Majesty's Airship *R.36*," I said. "Count Melchior von Eisenholm, I presume?"

A pause. "I congratulate you, Commander."

"I can't take the credit, Count. We also have Mr Sherlock Holmes on board – I'm sure you've heard of him."

"Indeed." The English was precise and unemotional, but the voice had a harsh, almost jagged quality: a murderous rage, barely contained. Years of lonely exile had taken their toll. "I crossed sabres with his brother during the War. A worthy opponent, but ultimately I evaded him."

"But not me." Holmes took the microphone. "You are run to ground, Count."

"You forget, Herr Holmes, my vessel is self-repairing. I need only time."

"Which you do not have," said Holmes. "And your ship is inevitably succumbing to its ravages."

"But not yet, Herr Holmes. It will last long enough for me to set my plans in motion."

"You have had ten years to do so, Count," Holmes said. "You can build ships, but not men."

"True," agreed the Count, "but a ship is a machine, and any machine can be automated. You would be astonished, truly, Herr Holmes, how easily one man can operate a machine of this size – if the necessary devices are included. I did not begin this voyage alone, but necessity forced me to ensure that I could so continue."

I wondered if von Eisenholm's men had jumped ship, perished through illness or accident, or if he'd disposed of them for insufficient dedication to his maniac dreams.

"My agents," he continued, "sought to find crews for my new ships, but without avail. Therefore I have worked to build a new generation of submarines that *require* no crews – they are automata, and once activated will be under my absolute control. You believe I am alone, Herr Holmes? That all the vanished ships were to build one new vessel? *Nein*. If I so desire, I alone can unleash terror on the seven seas and bring devastation upon you all."

"Even so," said Holmes, "you yourself are trapped aboard a damaged and decrepit ship – immobile, unable to submerge, and at our mercy."

"You have dropped no further charges, Herr Holmes," Von Eisenholm's voice purred coldly from the speakers, "since you cannot do so without once more coming within range of my guns. We are at an impasse – but this is unnecessary. Your brother was a worthy opponent, and so both yourself and Commander Atherstone have also proven—"

"And also Mr Blacksmith," said Holmes. "A colleague whose insights brought us to this location."

"Good day, Count von Eisenholm," said Blacksmith politely.

"Maintain your distance," said the voice. "I will leave, and you may live long enough to see Germany restored to her rightful destiny."

"You must know," said Holmes, "that as Englishmen we cannot allow that."

Blacksmith raised an eyebrow; I was tempted to do the same. If anything, my family were Scots by way of Poland (the source of the "Grabowsky" part of my name), but my duty as a human being was to forestall von Eisenholm's schemes. I met Holmes's gaze and nodded agreement. After a moment, so did Blacksmith.

"I confess," said von Eisenholm, "that I would have been disappointed in you had you chosen otherwise. One judges a man by the quality of his enemies. Very well! Make your attempt. You will not survive it. *Auf Wiedersehen!*"

The radio went dead.

"Mr Potter, bring us round for another pass," I said. "Mr Hunt, take us down to eight hundred. And Mr Church," I told the young rigger as he returned, breathless, to the control car, "instruct Corporal O'Hara to stand by."

X.

I moved again to the front of the control car as the ship turned, descending towards the sea before levelling out.

"Should we clear the bridge, Commander?" said Holmes.

I shook my head. "There's no safe place on board, Mr Holmes. I expect they'll rake the gondola from end to end."

"I see." Holmes sighed. "You know, Commander, this may be the longest I have ever gone without a cigarette."

"You get used to it," I assured him.

"I hope to live long enough to do so."

Tiny flashes of orange fire prickled across *VEUB-1*'s back as *R.36* approached; the gondola shuddered as the first rounds hit it. The bullets that punched through the envelope and gas-bags would encounter so little resistance that no one would feel their impact. The riggers would now be racing against time to find and patch all holes.

"Maintain course and speed," I said.

VEUB-1 passed under the control car. Hunt cursed as a shot tore the sleeve of his jersey; a ragged line of bullet holes wove along the floor.

O'Hara released a depth charge; it exploded a hundred feet from the Orkney Shark. But the submarine's guns crashed again in answer, and the deck was jerked from under me like a pulled rug, as a single volley, precisely and lethally aimed, smashed into the centre of the gondola.

There were screams from aft, shouts and cries of panic and alarm, running footsteps. The guns chattered again, but already we were climbing: "Sky" Hunt had known from the force of the impact – as I had – that this volley had done real damage, and if more of the same kind followed, the danger to the ship would be mortal. And so we rose – but slowly, too slowly.

"Let go ballast!" I shouted. *R.36* shuddered, then lurched upwards. From the window I saw depth charges falling – along with several bodies, and then the whole mass of racks and aiming equipment that held the remaining charges, trailing smoke. The last volley must have damaged them, leaving no choice but to jettison them before—

The charges blew as they hit the water in a huge concussive blast of foaming spume, some of which sprayed in through the windows.

"Dear God," I said, my ears ringing from the explosion. I looked to see Church stumbling on to the bridge. "O'Hara – the marines . . .?"

"All dead, sir." Church was pale. "That last salvo. And the charges . . ."

"That was your doing?"

Church swallowed, nodded.

"You did well." I squinted out of the window into the vast white haze of smoke and steam, hoping the action that had saved us had doomed von Eisenholm – but *VEUB-1* remained undamaged, her guns still firing. A few shells fell back and shattered on the surface, white vapour billowing outward.

"Carbonic acid gas," said Holmes. "Those will be the weapons that finished the torpedoes' work on the *Ourang Medan*."

I'd come close to pitying von Eisenholm, alone with his ailing ship and doomed dreams – but pity fled, now that I recalled the bodies on the cargo ship. Not to mention the men on the *Ostia*, the *Achilles* and the rest – or *R.36's* own dead.

"Maintain altitude, Mr Hunt," I said.

"Do my best, sir," he said. "But we're still losing gas."

"I'll get the bags seen to, sir," said Church.

"Carry on," I said. "Mr Potter, keep us circling."

"We no longer have any means of harming the submarine," said Holmes.

"I know," I said. "Mr Atkins, raise Cladach now. Find out where the Hell those bombers have got to."

"No need, Mr Atherstone," said Blacksmith, pointing out of the window. I looked: in the distance, two dozen black spots were approaching from the northwest. A moment later, I made out the droning of their engines.

XI.

The bombers were Blackburn Dart biplanes, and flew in rows of three. The first trio pulled ahead of the group, then swept down, flying in a straight line at surface level towards the target, preparing to release their torpedoes.

The bristling spines of *VEUB-1*'s guns swivelled and aimed to meet them. Fire-points flashed; one of the Darts spewed black smoke and veered off, losing height and ploughing into the water. A moment later, a white geyser erupted as its torpedo blew.

Another salvo tore the wings off the second bomber. The third climbed, fighting to gain altitude as the second aircraft came down, but *VEUB-1*'s guns followed it; a moment later the Dart exploded in mid-air.

The next group of bombers was now diving; three more dropped in behind them and they spread out. *VEUB-1*'s guns chattered. Two bombers exploded; a third spun off-course and collided with a fourth, both of them dropping into the water in a tangle of torn fabric and splintered steel.

The guns swivelled, all volleying together at one of the surviving aircraft again and again. As it fell in pieces into the sea, the last of the six loosed its torpedo.

VEUB-1's guns locked on to it and fired till it burst into flames, but the torpedo's wake was already streaking across the water like an arrow. For a moment I thought von Eisenholm's reckoning had come at last, but the torpedo went wide, exploding harmlessly against one of the skerries. The remaining bombers spread out, but the Orkney Shark's guns bristled and shifted, ready to meet them.

"Mr Potter?" I said.

"Sir?"

"Bring us around once more. Set a direct bearing for that thing."

The cox'n swallowed, but nodded. "Sir."

"When you've done that, lock the wheel into position. Mr Hunt, I'll take the height wheel. Mr Church, ring all engines to full speed."

"What are you doing, Commander?" asked Holmes.

"If von Eisenholm can hold off the bombers long enough, he'll escape," I said. "That cannot be allowed."

"Commander—"

"There are inflatable rafts stored aft. Mr Blacksmith, can you see to Mr Holmes?"

"Of course, Mr Atherstone." He hesitated for a moment. "Good luck."

"Thank you," I said, and gave my last command as captain of HMA R.36. "All hands, abandon ship."

The bells rang; the engines growled and R.36 surged forward, the sea coming up to meet us.

XII.

Blacksmith hurried Holmes aft-ward; Church, Potter and Hunt hesitated at the control car's door. "Off you go, lads," I told them.

Alone at last, I looked ahead, grappling with the elevators to keep the ship steady. For all the carnage on the sea, the weather remained clear and calm, but despite the riggers' best efforts, R.36 was losing gas and listing to port. But her bearing remained constant: all I needed to do was control and direct her final descent.

Pinpricks of fire danced across the submarine's hull as she fired at the oncoming bombers. Another Dart dropped into the sea, towing a banner of smoke. Von Eisenholm's only concern now, he doubtless thought, was the bombers; without depth charges, we had only a pair of Maxim guns, which would scarcely dent VEUB-1's hull. R.36 had no other armament, save one: the ship itself.

VEUB-1's guns swung upward, then swept round towards R.36. I locked the height wheel into position and sprinted aft, towards the hatch through which the rafts had ditched. By now we were flying almost level with the surface; the grey sea skimmed by. I took a deep breath, and jumped.

I struck the water, plunging under the surface into shocking cold. I surfaced, floundering, and one of the aft engine cars rushed towards me. With the ship listing as it was, the whirling propeller blades almost touched the sea, flurrying the surface into foam.

A hand seized my arm, dragging me clear – Blacksmith, leaning over the side of the raft. He dragged me on board, then ducked low as R.36's empennage swept by, the massive fins missing us by inches.

The Orkney Shark's guns fired, launching furious volleys at the airship in an effort to shred her gas-bags. But her engines drove her on and, even if she struck the sea, her momentum would not be denied: von Eisenholm had seen her too late.

The long sleek silver shape crumpled and split into twisted metal and torn aluminium-painted fabric; there was a flicker of orange, a blinding flash, then a great rush of heat and a deafening boom. The blast almost capsized us. Two more explosions tore through the ship, reducing R.36 to a cage of red-hot girders, crumpling in the heat of burning hydrogen and fuel – and caught in that cage was the Orkney Shark.

For a moment I thought it might break free of its half-molten cage. But the remaining bombers spread out in an arc, flew in for the kill, loosing their torpedoes one by one. Two streaked wide and ran out to sea; a third detonated against a skerry, but the others struck home in great gouts of thundering spray.

Spume, smoke and steam hid everything for a few seconds; when it cleared, we saw the airship's wreckage collapse into a seething roil of boiling water, steam and smoke. And R.36, carrying with her the Orkney Shark and its creator, sank to rest forever in the depths of the North Sea.

XIII.

The surviving torpedo bombers, with no means of making a sea landing, were unable to come to our aid. However, Mr Atkins had managed to alert Cladach Duillich before abandoning the ship, and four seaplanes were despatched to the Skule Skerries.

Along with the marines, Bowman and the luckless radio man cut down at his side, one engineer had been killed at his post by a stray bullet, and four riggers had died inside *R.36*'s hull. But those of her crew who had made good their escape were pulled from the water within an hour of the airship's end, wrapped in warm blankets and plied with flasks of cocoa laced with good Navy rum.

Most of us suffered from the cold, and were ordered to several days' bed rest in a fine Edinburgh hospital. Blacksmith was not among them; seemingly none the worse for wear, by the time of my final meeting with Sherlock Holmes, he'd already departed for new lodgings provided by the School for Detection.

"A satisfactory conclusion," said Holmes. He sat, well wrapped, in one of the day rooms, chain-smoking to make up for the cigarettes he'd been deprived of during our flight. "I only regret that there was no opportunity to confront von Eisenholm face to face."

"What about the other von Eisenholm submarines?" I asked. "They must still be out there somewhere, waiting to be used."

"Only von Eisenholm knew where," said Holmes, "or could activate them. They can be safely left to rust."

"There's no chance," I said, "that the count himself might have survived?"

"The probability of his death is so great as to constitute a certainty," said Holmes. "The only mystery remaining has nothing to do with him."

"Oh?"

"It concerns yourself, and Mr Blacksmith. You spoke of a debt to him."

"Yes."

"But *you* saved *his* life. Surely, then, the debt is his?"

"No," I said. "My personal guilt or innocence is of no account; we all profit, by birth, from an Empire that has left Mr Blacksmith, and countless others, alone in a way you or I can barely comprehend – or, God willing, ever will. Do you wonder he holds us in contempt? The wonder would be if he did not."

He did not understand, I could see.

"What I owed him, Mr Holmes, was a place in the world. Now he has one."

XIV.

Today is the fourth of October 1930. This evening *R.101* takes flight for India, with me as her first officer, and the future of airships largely depends on what sort of show we put up. There are many unknown factors and I suspect that the thing we call "luck" will figure rather conspicuously in our flight. Let's hope for good luck and do our best.

We have a decent crew, at least, including several men who served on *R.36*'s final flight: Hunt, Potter, Atkins the radio man, and young Rigger Church.

I have not seen Mr Blacksmith since that day; I trust that he flourishes in his new career. Mr Holmes, no doubt, continues as before. For a brief time I worried I had been too candid with him, but to my knowledge he never repeated what I have revealed.

We were, of course, all sworn to secrecy, but nonetheless I have decided to set down the events of that November. Facing the unknown, a man takes comfort in his achievements, and two of mine remain unknown to the world at large. That I have married a good woman, raised two fine sons, and am the only British airshipman to sink a German U-boat is common knowledge. But I am also the only airshipman to have used his ship to ram a submarine . . . and perhaps the only man or woman, of any land, to present Sherlock Holmes with a mystery not even he could solve.

Noel Grabowsky Atherstone, Lt Cmdr, RN (Retd).

The author's historical notes:

Lieutenant Commander Noel Edward Alexander Carl Eugene Grabowsky Atherstone was born Noel Grabowsky in 1894 and joined the Royal Navy in 1912. Transferring to the Airship Section in 1917, he served as first officer on R.29, in which capacity he stalked and sank a German U-boat – the only such success by a British airship. After the War, he retired, took the name Atherstone (his wife's mother's maiden name) by deed poll, and emigrated to Australia with his family. (The Australian composer Paul Grabowsky is his nephew; his granddaughter, Rebecca Atherstone, is a well-known news presenter.) After a stint as a farmer, he worked in a cannery before being recalled for the Imperial Airship Scheme. As first officer of R.101, he was killed, along with forty-seven others, when R.101 crashed into a hillside near Beauvais, France, in the early hours of 5 October 1930. Both Mr Blacksmith, and the Australian experiences Atherstone describes in this story, are fictional.

Flight Sergeant George "Sky" Hunt was born in 1888 and joined the Royal Naval Air Service in 1913. Perhaps the most experienced airship NCO in Britain, he was awarded the Air Force Medal for his part in helping to bring R.33 safely home, after a heavy storm blew her out to sea. Serving as chief coxswain on R.101's India flight, despite having retired a week before, he died at Beauvais on 5 October 1930.

Flight Sergeant Walter Potter joined the RNAS in 1915, serving on numerous airships. One of only five survivors of the R38 airship crash in 1921, which claimed forty-four lives, he continued in service and was an assistant cox on R.101. He and Hunt were close friends; according to one account, Hunt escaped R.101 after she crashed, but went back into the wreck to try and find Potter. Like Hunt, he died at Beauvais.

George Kimberley Atkins was born in London in 1900 and joined the RNAS in 1917. He was part of R.100's crew on her flight to Canada, and also served on R.101 as a wireless operator. He died at Beauvais.

Sam Church was born in Cardington in 1904. Selected for training as a rigger – a demanding twenty-six-week course – he joined R.101's crew in 1929. (Historically, I have taken a small liberty by making him an airshipman in 1927.) When the ship went into her final dive, he attempted to release water ballast from the bows, which might have prevented the crash. He suffered severe burns; his father and fiancée made a frantic sea crossing to Le Havre and car journey to Beauvais in order to be at his side, but he died only hours before their arrival, on 8 October 1930. He was twenty-five.

The Spy and the Towers
Nick Oldham

———

As if he possessed a sixth sense, which on many occasions I thought entirely feasible (although I am certain he would have denied the accusation), Sherlock Holmes looked up from his copy of that morning's *Times* newspaper, folded it, unfolded his long, stick-like legs, and stood up.

We were in his rooms and I was sitting opposite him on the other side of the unlit fire in the hearth, for it was a warm enough day as we were almost a fortnight into the month of May, the year 1894. I glanced up from my reading pleasure of the moment, once more revisiting my dog-eared copy of Charles Darwin's *On the Origin of Species,* which was, as ever, holding my complete fascination.

Holmes scowled at my choice of reading material. We have had many an intense argument over Darwin's theory, not least because Holmes simply considered it an inconsequence, of no interest or value to his occupation as a consulting detective. I, as a medical man, however, was astounded by the findings and deductions, which were still controversial, even so many years since publication.

"Do you still believe we come from the ape?" Holmes asked sourly, even though I knew he was impressed by Darwin's investigative philosophy.

"Yes I do," I began, raring for a verbal joust, "and I'm very surprised by your stance on this . . . how can it be inconsequential to your thought process?"

"Inasmuch as it makes little difference to me if the Sun revolves around the Earth or vice versa," he said, echoing a conversation we'd had previously.

Tilting his finely pointed chin in a highly superior manner, he gave a dismissive "tut" and strode over to the window overlooking Baker Street below. It was only then I realised why he was at the window, although at that moment I could not say how he knew before me, hence my passing thought about his sixth sense.

Holmes slid his fingers under the transom and raised the window a few more inches, allowing more sounds of the street below to invade the room.

However, even though I knew I was a few moments behind him, I could not keep an expression of smugness from my countenance as Holmes turned slowly from the window and arched his thick eyebrows in an encouraging gesture: I could tell from the way his body spoke he wanted me to guess why he had crossed the room.

I placed down my book and announced with a voice as conceited as my expression, "Lestrade has arrived."

The look that then crossed Holmes's face was one of hard-won victory.

"My dear Watson," he beamed, "I may make a detective out of you yet . . . but why do you say Inspector Lestrade has arrived? Can we dissect that pronouncement, rather like Darwin dissects his monkeys?"

Ignoring the jibe, I said, "Simple, Holmes, I have two ears and a modicum of a brain between them."

I tried to keep Holmes waiting, but then I relented.

"Several things. Firstly the transom window was open half an inch before you opened it further."

"Good," Holmes nodded.

"Which means the sounds of the street below, though more muted than now, were audible. I have heard the fishmonger walk along the street, peddling his wares, and also the voice of Noreen, our local lady of the night; also I heard the distinct, familiar metallic click of the heel protectors of Constable Johnson's boots, our local bobby, on the pavement; also someone whistling as they, presumably, strolled with a dog."

"Good, good."

"I could also hear, quite clearly, the sound of horses' hooves and the turn of carriage wheels upon the cobbles – which leads me to Lestrade," I said. "His usual hansom, in which he has just arrived," I said confidently, "has a nail or piece of iron wedged into the tread of the nearside wheel, making it sound quite distinctive as it turns, and I have no idea why he does not get it repaired. It would infuriate me."

"And . . .?" Holmes urged me on.

I gave him another of my slightly arrogant smiles. "And his usual horse, Old Jackie, has a marginally unusual gait to the trot which is a tad out of time, but it is something which does not seem to affect his speed or balance."

"And?" Holmes continued to push me.

I was becoming slightly weary of the game by now, but I added, "The cab door squeaks like a mouse and requires lubrication."

Holmes nodded. "All in all, a mess."

"But am I right?" I demanded with an irritation that made me begin to twirl my moustache.

Holmes merely shrugged and said, "I don't know, Watson. You have completely astounded me by your observational and listening skills."

"What?" My mouth drooped open, flabbergasted.

"Now I too will know when Lestrade's hansom carriage approaches."

"But . . . but . . . you knew even before I did . . . how . . .?"

He tapped his nose like a conspirator, turned to the window and closed it, instantly cutting out the sound from the street.

There was a loud rapping on the front door – Lestrade using the tip of his cane on the beautifully polished wood instead of the brass knocker, a habit that exasperated Mrs Hudson, Holmes's housekeeper, to distraction.

I heard her scurrying from her living accommodation downstairs, along the hallway, shouting shrilly, "I'm coming, I can hear you," and then the sound of the door being unbolted, followed by a curt exchange of words, mainly from Mrs Hudson, followed by the sound of footsteps quickly climbing the stairs, whilst from the bottom of the flight, Mrs Hudson shouted sarcastically, "I know you know your way, Inspector, but this is not done. I show visitors in, they do not barge past me."

There was a loud knock on Holmes's door, this time from Lestrade's knuckles as opposed to his gold-tipped cane.

"Holmes!" he called through the closed door.

Holmes exchanged a mischievous look with me and said quietly, "One, two, three, four, who's that knocking on the door?"

I was quite astonished by this ploy of making Lestrade wait, but when I made to rise, Holmes gestured for me to stay sitting. Clearly the only person allowed to annoy Mrs Hudson was Holmes himself, and this was a little payback for Lestrade's rudeness to her.

Lestrade knocked again and called, "Holmes? I know you're in there."

Smiling wickedly at me, Holmes said, "Five, six, seven, eight, maybe I should make him wait."

As he said this he was walking across the room and Lestrade was knocking even louder. Holmes unlocked the door and opened it just as the inspector was about to bang again. Lestrade almost fell through the door.

"I . . . er . . . I . . ." He flushed.

"He barged in past me, Mr Holmes," Mrs Hudson said apologetically. She had mounted the stairs and now stood behind Lestrade with her hands on her hips, affronted. "He had no right."

"In which case you should apologise to the dear lady," Holmes told Lestrade.

"Holmes!" he barked seriously. "I do not have time for trivialities, sir. I need to see you and speak urgently." He glanced over his shoulder at Mrs Hudson. "Apologies," he said brusquely.

Holmes stepped aside and allowed the detective into his rooms, then smiled his best smile at Mrs Hudson and said, "Tea?" before closing the door on Mrs Hudson's clearly audible "Tch!"

Lestrade strutted across to the hearth, turned and surveyed both of us, then said gravely, "I think we may be dealing with a matter of national safety and security, gentlemen."

"And how do you surmise that?" Holmes asked.

"He's missing," Lestrade said, losing his composure, placing his right hand across his chest, splaying his fingers wide across his heart. "Ace is missing and he was on a mission of national importance."

Holmes and I looked at each other quickly.

"Sit," Holmes instructed Lestrade. "Tell."

He was known as "Ace" simply because it was decided by the shadowy provost of the School for Detection that his identity – like that of the provost – should remain unknown for our safety and for Ace's safety. His future role was also kept from Holmes and myself, but it seemed clear to us he was destined for hush-hush work within the intelligence community, and the less we knew about him, the better. No one, not even Ace himself, told us that for certain and, if I was honest, I am not even sure Ace knew what his future would be, but he had a great deal of natural talent, and he and Holmes had quickly formed some kind of bond between themselves as, in task after task set by Holmes, Ace proved himself almost beyond teaching.

As an aside, Holmes once confessed to me, "All I need do with this lad is tweak a little."

He was a natural when it came to foot surveillance, not least because he had the ability, like a chameleon, to blend into the background or pass himself off as someone else. In short he was phenomenal, and astounded both Holmes and myself, although at first I had some doubts.

In one of our early training exercises from the School for Detection's headquarters at 1 Russell Square, I was simply tasked by Holmes to go for a stroll around central London for an hour or so to see if I could spot Ace following me at any stage. Just a simple foot surveillance test.

I laughed derisively at the notion, knowing it would be easy for me, simply because I knew what Ace looked like and what he was wearing that particular morning – a grey suit, gaiters, brown brogues and a flat cap. Holmes even briefed Ace and myself together, so I knew this would be ludicrously easy.

Nodding confidently, I set off.

I walked diagonally across Russell Square to Montague Place, then left on to Bloomsbury Street, deciding I would make this a pleasant constitutional. It was at this juncture I checked surreptitiously over my shoulder and stifled a grin as I realised how very simple my task would be. The young man simply did not have any idea how to follow someone discreetly.

However, my initial thoughts began to waver slightly when, half an hour later, not having seen Ace once in any of those thirty minutes, I was sitting in a teashop on the corner of Duncannon Street looking towards Trafalgar Square. I truly thought he had given up the pursuit.

My reveries on the matter were interrupted by a heavy-set, swarthy-faced gentleman, with thinning hair and a sandy moustache, who was dressed in tweeds. He asked if it was possible for him to sit opposite me while he drank his cup of tea. The teashop was quite congested and I of course agreed to his request, although I found myself unable to engage in the conversation he was trying to force, and was somewhat irritated when he asked if I would "Keep an eye" on his cup of tea whilst he visited the "gents".

When he returned he was accompanied by another fellow – tall, thin, round-shouldered, bearded; they both sat across from me at the table and engaged in a conversation between themselves to which I paid no heed.

I was still desperately trying to spot Ace skulking out on the street.

Eventually I took my leave and returned to the house on Russell Square, where I was shown into one of the drawing rooms, and waited to report my findings to Holmes. My conclusion about the surveillance skills of Ace was that he was either very good or had given up trying to follow me and had returned to headquarters. My inclination was towards the latter.

I played with my walking stick until a man I did not initially recognise knocked and entered. He was thin, bearded. I frowned at him for a few moments then said, 'Sir, may I help you?'

Without replying, and to my astonishment, his posture changed, his shoulders straightening slightly, and he slowly peeled off his beard and moustache to reveal my good friend Sherlock Holmes behind the disguise.

"Holmes!"

"Ah, Watson, do you remember me?"

Again, my brow furrowed.

"And, possibly, my good friend?" Holmes turned slightly and made a sweeping gesture with his arm as the door opened and in walked the man whose cup of tea I had guarded whilst he visited the toilet in the tearooms on Duncannon Street. I recognised the man but, beyond recalling the encounter, he meant nothing to me . . . until he removed his tweed jacket, then his waistcoat, unbuttoned his shirt, and proceeded to remove several layers of padding over his vest which he dropped on to the floor. He then took hold of his hair at the crown of his head, pinching it between his finger and thumb, and removed what was a sandy-coloured wig, and followed this by peeling off his moustache and beard. After that, he drew a damp handkerchief across his face to wipe away foundation makeup to reveal the young features of Ace underneath the disguise.

He smiled modestly at me.

"Well I never!" I cried, my eyes leaping from one man to the other – both grinning, incidentally – in front of me.

Holmes had done it again. He was a master of disguise and had deceived me as to his identity on many occasions. But I had to say that Ace was certainly his equal. His disguise was simple, but tremendous.

"I thought you had given up following me," I said, visualising the man who had sat down at my table with his cup of tea. "But . . . but I saw you duck out of sight on Montague Place, at which point you were in the clothes I had seen you in at the briefing. You must be a quick-change artist."

"He is," Holmes said, "and, begrudgingly, I must concede he is my equal."

"But you also had me fooled, Holmes," I admitted.

"Surveillance is deception," Holmes said mysteriously.

"You must have assisted him," I accused.

Holmes shook his head. "Not at all . . . I kept back a respectful distance and watched the situation develop. It was only in the teashop I revealed myself to him, by which time I also wanted a cup of tea, and from there we both followed you back here."

I exhaled a long sigh and smiled at Ace. I was very happy to have been duped in this way. I extended my hand and we shook. "You are very good," I congratulated him.

Holmes cleared his throat.

"As are you, Holmes, as are you."

Ace's skills went far beyond mere surveillance, extending to interrogation techniques, spy craft, crime investigation, martial arts, weapon handling and sharpshooting.

As I said, he was very, very good.

My attention returned to Lestrade, who had now taken a seat and was rubbing his narrow, ferret-like chin with worry.

Holmes and I waited silently as Mrs Hudson brought in a tea tray and laid out the cups, saucers, milk and teapot, slamming them down on the occasional table to show her disapproval of Lestrade, who seemed immune to her scathing glances or the noise. Eventually, after pouring the tea, she withdrew.

"We wanted to give him a simple, yet important assignment for his first deployment," Lestrade said.

Holmes, who seemed to have gone quite cold on the man, said with a suspicious chill in his tone, "Which was?"

"To follow someone, keep them under surveillance and report back."

"Who was this someone?" Holmes asked.

"A man by the name of Thomas O'Hara." Lestrade averted his eyes but Holmes and I looked sharply at each other.

"An Irishman?" I said.

Lestrade nodded, but seemed reticent about expanding on the subject.

"Tell us, man!" Holmes exploded, making both myself and Lestrade jump in our skins.

The inspector looked worriedly at Holmes. "Scotland Yard's Special Branch received information that a man called Thomas O'Hara would be arriving in London from Ireland, and that is all. Except O'Hara is suspected to have links with Irish rebels bent on Home Rule, and he was thought to be planning something to take place on English soil." Lestrade then produced a photograph of the man O'Hara and gave it to us.

Holmes looked furious. "So instead of walking a puppy on his first assignment, he has been asked to ride a tiger!"

I concentrated on Lestrade and said, "The 'something', I suppose, refers to an attack or atrocity of some description?"

Lestrade licked his lips. "Yes."

Holmes emitted a hiss of contempt.

"But," Lestrade continued defensively, "we did not know what sort of attack it was supposed to be, or even if the threat was genuine . . . all this was based on whispers and rumours picked up by Special Branch . . . you know how they operate . . ." His voice tailed meekly away.

"So, just to confirm," I said, "you put Ace on the trail of a suspected terrorist?"

"But with firm instructions merely to report back anything he believed to be of value and on no account to become involved, but if anything were to happen, to call in the police immediately."

Holmes regarded Lestrade with an expression of such disdain that I thought, for one moment, he might be on the verge of violence.

"And what, if anything, did Ace report back to you?" Holmes asked icily.

"Well, O'Hara arrived seven days ago on the train," Lestrade began. "He came into Euston Station from Holyhead and Ace began to follow him from that location. Unsurprisingly he tailed him to Kilburn, and then to a public house called The Old Toad." Here I glanced at Holmes, for we both knew the Toad, a less than salubrious hovel supposedly frequented by an Irish-based clientele with a reputation for plotting against the Empire; Holmes did not look at me, but held his steel gaze firmly on Lestrade, who was beginning to quake under the force of the glare. He continued, "It seemed Ace managed to pass himself off as an Irishman and ingratiate himself with some of the people in that area. He overheard O'Hara in discussion with other suspected rebels . . . at least, that is the conclusion to which I have arrived."

"What did he hear?" Holmes asked.

Lestrade fumbled in his jacket pockets, mumbling something about a "dead letter drop" and found a folded piece of paper in his waistcoat. He handed this to Holmes, who unfolded it carefully, read it, then handed it to me.

Scribbled on it in handwriting I knew well – Ace's – were the words, *No time for detail . . . plotting to bomb the tower, pm, all I know.* It was signed, "A."

My mouth popped open. "Seemed like he was in a rush," I commented.

"What have you done since retrieving this?" Holmes asked.

"Why . . . I came straight here."

"Do you know when this was deposited in the dead letter drop?"

Interrupting, I asked, "I'm afraid I may show my ignorance here, gentlemen, but what is this 'dead letter drop' to which you refer?"

"Simple tradecraft. A means, my dear Watson, of passing information between an agent and his or her handler so neither have to meet, thereby retaining security," Holmes explained to me, then looked back at Lestrade and said, "My question, please."

"Um, sometime between the time of O'Hara's arrival at the Old Toad and about one hour ago."

"That is a rather wide timescale," Holmes said with massive

understatement. "The point of a dead letter drop, I would have thought, is to check it regularly, not on a whim."

Lestrade hung his head in shame.

"It seems our boy could well be into something deep and dangerous, and might perhaps be out of his depth," I said.

"He was briefed simply to follow and not engage," Lestrade protested.

"Inspector, things are not always so clear cut," Holmes told him, "and knowing Ace, those instructions would be rather like telling a cat just to play nicely with a mouse, not kill it."

"What do we do?" Lestrade asked weakly. "We don't even know what it means. The 'Tower', what does it mean by the 'Tower'?"

I scratched my head. Holmes stood up abruptly and crossed to where he had been sitting by the hearth a few minutes earlier. Both Lestrade and I watched him, expecting some dramatic pronouncement, as so often is the case. Instead he picked up the folded copy of *The Times* newspaper he had been reading and began to flick quickly through the pages.

He spoke as he did this. "What you have to do, Lestrade, is to muster your police force."

"And do what, exactly?"

"Two things: round up the usual suspects and then throw a ring of steel around the tower because I fear that Ace is, as they say, up to his neck in this thing and in grave danger."

Lestrade shook his head, completely confused. "How . . .? What . . .? Which tower? The Tower of London? That hardly needs a ring of steel."

Holmes gazed levelly at him. "Have your officers pick up all known ringleaders in Kilburn and then protect this . . ."

Holmes opened the newspaper and showed Lestrade the article he had been searching for. The inspector grabbed it from his fingers, his eyes running quickly through the words and taking in the photograph.

I found I was holding my breath, desperate to read it, and when

Lestrade looked up, his face ashen, I snatched it from him and read through the article as quickly as he had done.

"My God," I gasped, "they're going to bomb Tower Bridge – and the Prince of Wales . . . and this afternoon."

As it happened, Tower Bridge – a combined bascule and suspension bridge spanning the River Thames – had not yet been officially opened to the public; though after eight years of construction, the bridge was almost complete. I knew the Prince of Wales, our future king, would be presiding over the opening ceremony at the end of June. I also knew, for it was quite common knowledge, that the prince had maintained a keen interest in the bridge since building had begun in 1886. He often paid, sometimes unannounced, sometimes announced, visits to see how construction was progressing. Today's proposed visit, together with his good lady wife, the Princess of Wales, had been announced in the royal court pages of *The Times*. This would be his last visit before the official opening in a few weeks' time.

"There is no time to lose," Holmes said, pulling on his overcoat and hat.

I grabbed my outer coat also, and a minute later the three of us hared down the stairs, rushing past a wide-eyed Mrs Hudson with no time for explanations.

"We'll need to use your hansom," Holmes told Lestrade.

"Yes, yes, yes," the detective said as we emerged through the front door on to Baker Street.

Holmes opened the carriage door to allow Lestrade and me to climb in. I expected him to jump in after us, but he paused a moment as a young street ruffian approached him. I recognised the lad as one of Holmes's army of helpers known affectionately by him as The Baker Street Irregulars. They were a ragtag bunch of street urchins who had occasionally proved useful to our investigations, but only if silver coins crossed their grubby palms.

And Holmes did indeed thumb a coin into this lad's hand, said a few words to him, and jumped into the hansom as the lad – whose name I knew to be Jimmy – strolled smugly away, tossing the coin up with his thumb, catching it with a downward flap of his fingers – and whistling.

I recognised the tune instantly – "Down at the Old Bull and Bush" – the same one I'd heard not many minutes earlier coming up through the window from the street below. Then it dawned on me how Holmes had known that Lestrade was on his way before I had even heard the sound of the hansom: Jimmy had warned him by whistling the tune.

I rolled my eyes to myself at the revelation. It should not have surprised me that Holmes had his little band of watchers keeping their eyes out for him. They were everywhere, doing his bidding.

He sat in, crushing myself and Lestrade against the side of the hansom, which was only designed to seat two individuals, and grinned across at me, no doubt realising I had "rumbled" him, as they say.

"Where to?" Lestrade asked.

"Tower Bridge, without delay," Holmes said, and Lestrade shouted up to his driver, who cracked his whip; his misbalanced horse and creaky hansom pitched forwards and away.

Not long later, having raced along the Thames Embankment, we drew up on Iron Gate on the north bank of the river, from where the new bridge spanned the waterway over towards Horselydown Lane on the south. It was a magnificent construction, having cost in excess of one million pounds, but well worth it in my estimation. It would allow road traffic to pass over and river traffic to pass under, as the bridge was effectively split by two equal bascules which could be raised to allow large ships and yachts to travel through.

We disembarked from the hansom and Lestrade said to Holmes, "What now?" He was very much in a tizzy, unable to marshal his thoughts.

"Now, my dear Lestrade, you must show what a practical policeman you are. I would suggest firstly you return to Scotland Yard, then round up and deploy as many officers as possible to this location to seal it and search it for possible explosive devices; then you must hurry to Buckingham Palace and plead with the Prince of Wales to seriously consider cancelling his visit this afternoon." Lestrade did not move. Holmes said, "Now go, shoo!"

Lestrade's hansom bore him away, leaving Holmes and myself by the river, which was lined with numerous ships and boats of all shapes and sizes. Tower Bridge, despite the pleasant enough day, was almost consumed by the smoke from their funnels.

Holmes surveyed the scene. I could almost see his mind working as he lit his pipe, applying that formidable intelligence to the problem at hand, so I was slightly taken aback when he turned to me, "papping" his pipe as it came to life, and said mockingly, "Could you see a troop of monkeys building this?"

Before I could answer, he stalked away towards a fenced-off area, behind which was a huge construction yard for the bridge on this side of the river. With me at his heels, he went to the site manager's office and interrupted a meeting of about a dozen men that was taking place there.

At first, each one scowled at our intrusion, but when Holmes introduced himself, the atmosphere changed: Holmes's reputation clearly preceded him.

A small man bustled forwards, holding out his hand to shake that of Holmes, and introduced himself as E. W. Crutwell, the resident engineer. Holmes and he stepped to one side and began an earnest discussion out of my hearing. I waited, smiling at the assembly of gentlemen whose meeting we had invaded.

Holmes and Crutwell finished their conversation and Holmes came towards me.

"As I thought," he ruminated. "Many of the construction workers on the site are of Irish origin, continuing on from the Navvies who built the canals and railways a few years ago. There may be some republican sympathisers amongst them."

"Surely we could root them out?"

"First of all, there are over four hundred workers on site and we have, perhaps – " he consulted his fob watch – "two hours in which to firstly identify them, then weed them out, then interrogate them, by which time, even if we moved quickly, it would be at least six-thirty p.m." Holmes's sarcasm at my expense, I thought, was sometimes uncalled for. "No," he declared, "the only way in which we can achieve this is to firstly stop the visit taking place, and then flood the place with constables . . . neither option being likely. Come," he beckoned me, "at the very least we can poke our noses into other people's business."

Many of the construction workers were out on the bridge itself, putting the final touches to the granite and stonework cladding the steel structure underneath. The area in which most of them lived, a squalid sort of shantytown in my opinion, was devoid of all workers, but populated by their wives and children. Many had lived there since construction had begun eight years before. In about a month the whole place would be dismantled and demolished and the workforce would move on.

We gained little from the exercise, other than to draw deeply suspicious looks from the womenfolk, who clearly regarded our presence as meddling. Holmes and I sensed palpable resentment directed at us.

Lestrade was back within the hour, having mustered about two dozen men, who arrived in coaches and were immediately deployed on searching duties. Although, to me, it looked a thankless task, bearing in mind the size of the bridge and the multitude of places in which explosives could be secreted.

The inspector came up to us, breathless and worried. "I have been unable to make contact with the prince or princess. I am informed they have been on private business this morning and will come to the bridge directly from wherever that is. They will be in a private carriage . . . so the visit in on," he said forlornly.

"In that case, Inspector," Holmes said, "we must protect the future king."

"My dear Sherlock," the Prince of Wales beamed brightly as he stepped down from his carriage and instantly spotted Holmes's tall, lean figure amongst the small crowd who had gathered in Iron Gate. This was a fairly discreet visit, and although some brief detail of it had appeared in *The Times*, it had not been widely publicised. The prince beckoned Holmes to approach him, much to the consternation of the two body-guards flanking the royal – and also to my shock.

The Prince of Wales knew Sherlock Holmes!

Holmes threaded his way through the onlookers, who were being held back by a very thin, dotted, blue line of constables who, to a man, looked terrified by the whole situation.

"What brings you to these parts?" the prince asked him.

"Sir, may I – we – " Holmes glanced at myself and at Lestrade, who was similarly stunned by this new relationship – "talk urgently to you?"

"But of course, my man." The prince frowned. He looked at Crutwell, the engineer, who was expecting to greet him and who obviously knew him from previous visits. "Crutwell, could you give us a few moments?"

"Sir, yes sir."

"Perhaps we could retire to my carriage?" the prince suggested. He waved regally at the onlookers and promised to be back shortly, and we three, plus the prince, stepped into the most opulent carriage I had ever seen.

We sat across from the Prince of Wales who smiled and said, "Now then, Holmes, what new mystery are you about to unravel before my very eyes?"

"Sir, we have good reason to believe a bomb might be planted some-where on or around Tower Bridge and timed to coincide with your visit," Holmes explained quite bluntly.

"With me as a target? Well, by Jove!"

"Yes sir, you and your wife, who I see is not present.'

"No, she was feeling faint and returned to Lambeth ahead of me. I am alone . . . but what is this nonsense?"

"It is not nonsense, sir," Lestrade cut in excitedly, then checked himself when he remembered who he was talking to. "With respect, sir, we have a highly placed spy within the Irish republican movement," he boasted, stretching the facts almost to breaking point and drawing looks of horror from both myself and Holmes. "Our information is that a bomb is set to go off this very afternoon."

Holmes shot Lestrade another look – but with an accompanying frown that puzzled me – which seemed to do the trick of shutting the man up.

When the prince said to Lestrade, "And may I ask exactly who you are?" it merely added to his unease.

"Lestrade, sir, Inspector Lestrade, Scotland Yard.'

The prince turned to me, knocking the smirk off my face when he said, "And you, sir?"

"Doctor John Watson."

"Ahh . . . I know of you . . . you are Sherlock's assistant and diarist, am I correct?"

"In a way, sir."

"I have read many of his exploits written by you . . . very charming," he said, and glanced at Lestrade once more. "And you are the less than efficient detective referred to, now I recall."

Lestrade coloured up, but Holmes stepped in. "Sir, if I may? Would you consider postponing your visit?"

The prince leaned back and gave the impression of consideration, but then shrugged and said, "No, the visit goes ahead."

"Three-fifteen p.m.," I informed Holmes.

Each one of the last ninety minutes had been filled with high tension. That is, everyone who knew of the threat, with the exception of Holmes and the prince, were wound as tightly as any screw I had ever seen, as the prince stubbornly made his tour of Tower Bridge, inspecting every nook and cranny, chatting amiably with workers and management alike, none of whom displayed any malice towards him in the slightest.

Ahead of him, in effect clearing a path, a squad of police searchers looked for a possible bomb and found nothing untoward.

As the prince finally drew away in his carriage, my relief was so great I almost stumbled weakly to my knees, while I saw Lestrade duck behind a wooden shed and heard the sound of him retching.

Only Holmes seemed unaffected, but distracted, as though his mind was churning again. He had lit his pipe and was staring thought-fully across the river.

After his bout of nausea, Lestrade and I went to stand with Holmes.

"How have the arrests gone?" Holmes enquired.

"We are still searching for suspects. They seem to have gone to ground."

"And Ace? Any news of his whereabouts?"

"Nothing."

"And that *nothing*, therefore, means something significant," Holmes said. "He is in danger still, of that I have no doubt and, also, we – I – have missed something very simple yet crucial to all this.'

"His information was clearly wrong," Lestrade insisted.

Holmes turned his head slowly and glared like the devil at the policeman. "That young man does not give false information."

Lestrade shrugged. He was simply relieved the day had gone with-out incident: no bomb had been found, or detonated, and the Prince of Wales was still breathing. The fate of Ace was now not so important.

Holmes looked at me. "Baker Street," he said.

"You know the Prince of Wales?" I asked Holmes.

We were back in his rooms at Baker Street. It was early evening and, despite everything else happening, curiosity chewed at me over this issue.

"Only a little."

"How would that be?" I enquired. "I certainly did not know you knew him."

He sighed. "I dealt with a small, confidential matter, a trifle." Holmes shrugged it off, then leaned forward on his chair conspiratorially. "One day, in the very distant future, I shall regale you with the strange case of the prince and the Maltese prostitute – although you may wish to retitle that when you come to write it, and change some names to protect the guilty."

"The prince and the—?" I blurted, but Holmes raised a hand to stop further probing.

"We have more pressing matters," he reminded me.

"Of course, of course," I agreed, although my curiosity was hugely stirred.

The transom window overlooking Baker Street was again slightly open, and from below I heard a shrill whistle.

Holmes leapt up from his chair and hurried downstairs.

I crossed to the window and saw him emerge from the front door and walk towards a couple of street ruffians, one of whom I recognised as being Jimmy, the young lad Holmes had earlier given a coin for having warned him of Lestrade's arrival. The other lad I knew to be called Potter.

The three had an earnest discussion. Clearly they had information for Holmes.

Coins once again changed hands and the youngsters disappeared quickly into the evening traffic, whilst Holmes ran back upstairs into the room, unfolding a piece of paper he had taken from his pocket.

I recognised it as the note Lestrade had received from Ace via the dead letter drop. And I did not know how it had come into Holmes's possession. As far as I knew, the last time I saw it, it was going into Lestrade's jacket pocket.

Holmes must have dipped for it, I guessed, but did not ask. Amongst his many fields of expertise he was a great pickpocket.

He slumped back into his favourite armchair and reread the crumpled note, his lips moving silently to the words thereon. Then he looked up beyond my shoulder at the wall behind me (in which bullet holes were still visible and unfilled after his target practice months before). His eyes were glazed in concentration, then suddenly became focused again and he looked at me a moment before snatching up that morning's *Times* and furiously going through the newspaper, discarding page after page until he was surrounded by a mass of paper, before finally finding what he was searching for.

He sat back and read the article, then raised his piercing eyes at me.

"I am a fool," he declared. "I have misled myself and everyone else. I have made the schoolboy error of jumping to a conclusion."

"Holmes, what on earth do you mean?"

"There is more than one tower in this world and the letters 'PM' do not necessarily stand for post meridiem." His eyes danced. "Add to that what I have just learned from the Baker Street division of the detective police force, and I find myself about two hundred and fifty miles and at least a good day's travel from the intended target."

He handed me the newspaper article and stood up.

"We have no time to waste.' He ran to the door and bellowed down, "Mrs Hudson, hail a cab, please – quickly."

I read the article quickly and exclaimed, "By goodness, you could be right."

"Could be? *I am*, Watson. *I am*."

The article was quite brief and, ironically, on the same page as the royal court reports in which we had found details of the prince's visit to Tower Bridge. But this was about the visit of another man to another tower, another construction that, like Tower Bridge, would over time become one of England's most iconic landmarks but, as Holmes rightly pointed out, was about two hundred and fifty miles away.

I said, reading and paraphrasing slightly, "The prime minister is to visit Blackpool tomorrow to officiate at the opening of the Blackpool Tower to the general public. Inspired by the Eiffel Tower in Paris,

Blackpool Tower, at five hundred and eighteen feet, is constructed from five million Accrington bricks, two and a half thousand tons of iron and ninety-three tons of cast steel. The prime minister, William Melville, will open the tower to the public at one p.m. tomorrow, the fourteenth of May, in a ceremony to take place on the platform at the top of the tower."

I looked questioningly at Holmes, who was thrusting his arms into his heavy overcoat. "That is the tower referred to in Ace's note. The PM referred to is not the afternoon, but the prime minister."

"But how have you made this connection?"

He donned his ear-flapped travelling cap, then exhaled to steady himself. "Because since his graduation from the school, Ace has been under surveillance by my Irregulars . . . not constantly . . . but I had an inkling that, due to his skills and abilities, Lestrade would thoughtlessly assign to him a dangerous mission immediately, and I was correct."

"No one could have foreseen that," I argued.

"Not as such." Holmes gazed coldly at me. "But I was right, wasn't I? Following Thomas O'Hara, a vociferous supporter of Irish Home Rule and suspected planter of bombs, a man who despises the prime minister, is not the same as following Jack Jones the pickpocket down Chancery Lane. Only an idiot like Lestrade would fail to foresee grave danger and would take the chance of putting someone of Ace's undoubted skills up against such a man, knowing that he would try and infiltrate O'Hara's people. Ace may be skilled and may relish the challenge, but he is still young and inexperienced and, therefore, vulnerable – hence the Irregulars keeping an eye on him from time to time."

I waited for more.

"They lost his trail for several days – not unusual and not worrying – but they found him early this morning boarding a train at Euston for Manchester, with an onward ticket to Blackpool. He was with a man fitting O'Hara's description, given to us by Lestrade earlier. The Irregulars could not get this information to me sooner because they were being chased by the police – some misunderstanding, it seems, about a quantity of stolen beer – and had to lie low this morning, which is why I tasked Jimmy to find out if anyone knew anything and get back to me."

"My God, Holmes!"

"Indeed . . . now get into a warm hat and coat. We are making our way north, so expect it to be cold. Blackpool is in Lancashire, after all."

We had a choice of the express train from Euston to Manchester or the slow overnighter. The express would have meant a very long cold wait in Piccadilly Station for an onward connection to Blackpool, so we opted for the late, slow train, even if it would be frustrating, and even though we could not secure bunks for the night. At least we were able to get a first-class carriage in which we could stretch and doze. Holmes settled himself in, pulled down the peak of his hat and folded his arms across his chest, dropped his chin low and instantly fell asleep.

My mind was awash with questions which I longed to put to Holmes, but they would have to wait, so I tried to settle, but my sleep was poor and frequently interrupted.

We pulled into Manchester at eight a.m. and waited for the Blackpool connection at ten a.m., filling the time by eating a hearty breakfast at a large hotel close to the station.

Refuelled and revitalised by the food, we boarded the train that took us west across Lancashire, calling at such stations as Bolton and Leyland, travelling through a lush green landscape unfamiliar to myself and Holmes. We stopped at Preston for a short while, then were off across the flat and very fertile Fylde plain and our first tantalising glimpse of the Blackpool Tower itself, sitting on the edge of the Irish Sea.

It grew from the size of a pin to a sewing needle in the distance, to become a knitting needle; as we drew closer, it widened, and we could see its metallic structure and eventually even the flagpole at its summit on which the Union flag fluttered.

Both Holmes and I were transfixed by a magnificent piece of

engineering and construction combined – I half expected him to mention monkeys, but he did not.

The train pulled into the terminus at North Station, Blackpool. We disembarked with many others, mainly day tourists visiting with the expectation of ascending the tower.

"Do you have a plan?" I asked Holmes.

Holmes thought about that for a moment and then responded, much to my surprise, "No."

Within five minutes of leaving the station, we were on the street behind the tower in a huge crowd, a section of which was a snaking queue up to the entrance. I could see a board displaying the cost of admission – 6d; a further 6d was the cost of a lift to the top and another 6d for the tower circus.

By my quick calculation, at least two thousand people were on the street, including street performers, fortune-tellers, magicians and beggars – plus pickpockets, I supposed.

"This is impossible," I said.

Holmes was his own tower amongst these people, his height making him stand out, giving him a view over their heads. He caught sight of two uniformed constables from the local borough and made a beeline towards them, splitting the crowd as he pushed through.

I followed, literally in his wake.

"Officers," he called.

They were two ruddy-faced fellows. "Yes, sir?" one replied.

"The prime minister, where is he?"

One of the coppers pointed towards the sky and the top of the tower. "Up there, sir."

"My name is Sherlock Holmes. The prime minister could be in grave danger . . . how well is he protected?"

The other constable rolled his eyes with a "We have a lunatic here" expression, whilst the other looked merely uninterested.

"Sherlock Holmes, you say?"

"Yes."

The constable regarded me. "And you'll be Doctor Watson, I presume?" he said, making light of our claims and not believing a word.

"Actually, I—" I began, but was cut short by a collective eruption of noise from the crowd behind me; a rushing thing, mass intakes of breath, screams of fear, shuffling of feet, some cursing from both men and women. I spun quickly to see what the hubbub was about and, like some minor miracle, the crowd suddenly parted and there was a pathway open as people stepped and stumbled backwards, revealing a lone figure at the end of this path.

The figure staggered towards us, battered, dragging one foot, clearly in severe pain, his head, face and upper chest soaked in blood.

It was Ace – our errant School for Detection graduate.

And he had a revolver in his right hand.

He dropped to one knee and held out his left hand pleadingly.

Holmes and I rushed to him. I managed to lower him gently to the ground; his eyes looked imploringly at me and then changed as he recognised me.

"Watson," he gasped hoarsely, then saw Sherlock Holmes and said, "Holmes, thank God . . . he's on his way up now . . . to . . . to . . . kill the PM . . . the whole thing, primed to explode . . . he just needs to connect the wires as the PM cuts the ribbon . . . you must stop him. . . he is a martyr and will die for the cause." His head lolled to one side as everything overcame the poor young man: pain, effort, weakness, blood loss.

I looked urgently at Holmes.

"Come, Watson," Holmes said brutally. "You must leave him – these fellows will care for him." He jerked his thumb at the constables standing by, virtually useless. Holmes yelled at them, "Now do you believe us? See to this man, get him medical attention."

"Yes, sir," the eye-roller said, coming out of his trance.

"Watson – with me."

I laid Ace's head carefully on the ground, torn because as a medical man I was loath to leave anyone suffering, but I knew at that moment other matters were more important.

Holmes deftly scooped up the revolver that had dropped from Ace's fingers and we both ran towards the tower entrance. Holmes led the way, forcing his lithe, slim, but strong frame through the crowd. He vaulted the cashier's desk, as did I, but less nimbly.

Then we were in the ground floor of the tower, rushing quickly through its corridors. I drew my revolver from my waistband whilst Holmes quickly checked if the gun he had just purloined was loaded; after that, he sniffed the muzzle.

"This gun has been fired recently," he said, then released the cylinder and tipped the bullets out on to the palm of his free hand, discarded two and replaced the other four back into the gun. "Two fired," he said.

We burst through a double door and found ourselves in a large ballroom. We ran down the steps past the stage, across the dance floor on which several couples were dancing, although not to any music as there was no orchestra playing.

The silent music dancers split in horror at the sight of two gun-toting men dashing determinedly across the mahogany floor. Ladies screamed and a couple of gallant gentlemen stepped in front of them to offer protection.

We hurried through and out of the doors at the opposite end, coming on to a mezzanine floor where the lift entrances were located. Many people were waiting here and, at the moment we appeared, a lift door opened and people began to file in.

Holmes raised his gun and fired a shot into the ceiling. He shouted, "Everyone, get out of the lift!"

More people screamed, but they instantly deserted the lift as instructed. Holmes and I entered the lift car, which was being operated by a uniformed staff member, an old man cowering in the corner.

"To the top, my man," Holmes demanded. The lift man did not move.

Holmes shut the lift doors, turned a brass wheel on the control panel, and the contraption started to rise slowly.

"Is the prime minister still up there?" Holmes asked the poor man.

"Y-yes . . . he was waiting for this lift to arrive and then he would perform the opening ceremony. Are you going to kill him?"

"Not this time," Holmes said, and put his face to a tiny window that looked out across the resort as the lift rose up through the central structure of the tower.

It seemed to take a very long time, creaking noisily all the way.

Then we arrived. The doors opened on to the platform, which ran all the way around the top of the tower, providing a truly magnificent 360-degree view across the Irish Sea and back over Lancashire, though we had no time to appreciate it.

As we stepped out, there were probably fifty people around the platform, all looking away from us. I assumed the prime minister was on the opposite side of the platform, about to perform the opening ceremony.

People seemed to be pushing and looking over other people's shoulders, with the exception of one man to our right. He was kneeling in one corner of the platform, concentrating on something neither Holmes nor I could see, but he turned to us and immediately saw our guns. At the same moment, we saw he had the ends of wires in each hand, between his finger and thumbs.

It was Thomas O'Hara. We both recognised him from the photograph Lestrade had given to us.

Realisation that the game was up struck him, but then I saw the decision in his eyes and he shouted, "For a free . . ." and tried to bring the ends of the wires together.

He never uttered those last words, for both Holmes and I made our decision instantly. Our guns came up. We had to shoot – each of us going for the head, the only way to ensure O'Hara would be unable to make the connection with the wires. He died instantly.

They had beaten Ace badly. It took several weeks for him to recover at a private hospital in Blackpool. We stayed by his side until he was very much on the mend, whilst at the same time putting together the pieces of the attempt on the prime minister's life.

It seemed that Ace had managed to ingratiate himself into the section of the Irish community in Kilburn who were plotters in favour of Irish Home Rule, but in all the time he spent there, he was watched carefully by them, which accounted for the hastily written note that Lestrade recovered from the dead letter drop. It had been the only chance he had to warn Lestrade of the impending plot. Still posing as a supporter, Ace learned that some of the construction workers responsible for building the Blackpool Tower had Fenian sympathies and had hidden a bomb at the top of the structure. The bomb simply required two wires connecting to detonate it and, if someone was willing to die for the cause, the prime minister could be assassinated at the top of Blackpool Tower in a spectacular blow against the oppressors.

O'Hara was that man, willing to die for the cause.

But when he arrived in London for his final briefings from his masters, he became a little reckless, drank too much, said too much, trusted too many, knowing he was living his final week. This was how Ace had learned of the fiendish plot.

When O'Hara left for Blackpool, Ace had gone with him, along with two other sympathisers who were not taken in by Ace: they thought he was a traitor in the making. When O'Hara had gone to complete the final task of his life, Ace had tried to slip away and warn the authorities, but the two men prevented him. A terrible fight to the death ensued and Ace killed them both with his pistol, but not before they had almost beaten the life out of him.

Holmes and I stayed for the inquests, at which our actions were exonerated and commended by the coroner, and during which Ace's actions were also deemed to be self-defence. His real name, by an order from the government, was never revealed.

Holmes and I paid one last visit to the Blackpool Tower, merely as day-trippers, before our return to London, where a new case awaited us.

At the top of the tower, Holmes took in the view, which was truly awe-inspiring. He lit his pipe, pulled his ear-flaps down and walked around the platform several times. I simply stood and gazed out across the sea until I became aware of Holmes standing next to me.

"An ape," Holmes said, "could never build anything like this . . . but neither would an ape plot to kill a fellow ape."

I nodded.

"You know, that young man, Sidney, will go far. He has an aptitude for espionage far beyond anything I possess," Holmes said.

"Sidney?" I said. "You know Ace's real name?"

"Yes, of course. Always have. Don't you? You surprise me."

"No, never have . . . so what is he called?"

"His name is Sidney . . . Sidney Reilly, and I feel that one day he may, possibly, become the best spy the world has ever known."

The Monster of the Age
Paul Finch

------

1 March 1922

Dear Mr Holmes and Dr Watson,

Letty Feltencraft here. With any luck, you will remember me. I don't think I have been a particularly noteworthy student, but several times, Mr Holmes, you have complimented me on the questions I have asked in class, and on at least one or two of the essays I have handed in for your inspection.

I apologise for this very impersonal way of contacting you gentlemen, but out of necessity I am not able to make this presentation to you in person. As you are both well aware, we have now reached the part of the course where we fledgling detectives must submit proposals for dissertation so that you may consider them and then discuss them with us during seminar. However, I am afraid that I must circumnavigate the normal protocols of the School for Detection and inform you that I have already settled on a topic, and in fact have now embarked in pursuit of it. As I say, this was out of necessity, as there simply was no time for debate. I found myself in a position of having to act, and having to act fast.

In short, gentlemen, for my dissertation, I propose to uncover the true identity of the infamous Whitechapel Murderer . . .

"That's ridiculous!" I said, putting the letter down. "Is the girl out of her mind? The dissertation accounts for a whole third of the marks. She'll fail the course . . . and she was doing so well."

Miss Leticia Feltencraft might have held herself in such low estimation that she thought neither Holmes nor I would remember her, but I doubted it. She'd been a more than capable student up until now, and I suspected she knew this without needing to be told.

Holmes remained in the armchair opposite, wearing his blue dressing gown and sucking on his old black pipe. Somewhat to my surprise, he made no comment.

"Holmes!" I remonstrated with him. "Surely you agree? Miss Feltencraft will throw it away!"

"Is there much more?" he asked.

"Several pages or so."

"Then perhaps, Watson, we should read on and try to fathom her reasoning from whatever facts she has accumulated."

Somewhat abashed, I did as he asked.

Dr Watson, I can imagine that you in particular will advise against this. No doubt you will consider it far too ambitious a scheme.

I felt the heat rise on my neck, but I persevered with reading aloud.

You would never say it, at least not in so many words, but I suspect you will feel that a murder case, the solution to which eluded even the great Sherlock Holmes, would be too much of a challenge for an up-and-coming detective like myself. However, Mr Holmes, it strikes me that even a genius such as you would struggle to make something out of nothing, and in terms of factual evidence, that was all the investigators back in 1888 had at their disposal – nothing. Looking back on the case, it is no surprise to me that the Whitechapel Murderer was never apprehended. We did not even have fingerprint technology back in those long-ago days.

I myself have several new techniques to my advantage, though more about this in a moment. I know it has long been Scotland Yard's contention that the mysterious Whitechapel Murderer was most likely dead by the end of the nineteenth century, or at least incarcerated. But personally, I have never been convinced of that. It always sounded like guesswork to me. And now, at long last, I am on the trail of evidence that I hope will disprove it once and for all.

It all began for me when I was nursing. You may recall that I was part of the auxiliary TFNS from 1914 to 1918. In '17, I was based at St Michael's Cottage Hospital in Folkestone, where I was attached to a unit specialising in treating soldiers who were shattered both in body and mind. What I am about to disclose to you, gentlemen, is a breach of patient confidentiality, but I trust it will go no further, and I would not be imparting this information did I not think a much greater good would come from it.

One of our patients at that time was a certain captain in the Lancashire Fusiliers. His name was Arthur Bishopbourne. I remember thinking him somewhat old for that rank. He was almost fifty, as I recall, but the circumstances of his wounding were quite terrible. Apparently, he had been somewhere called the Scarpe, which was an action fought during the Battle of Arras. He had been caught in a shell-burst there, which left him and the corpses of his men buried under earth and rubble for at least a couple of days. When he was dug out again, he was semi-deranged. He had also suffered multiple physical wounds, though the worst was his left arm, which had been all but torn from its socket. When he finally came to us, the arm had been successfully re-attached, but was paralysed from the shoulder down, so there was no possibility of him returning to active service. He was thus due to be invalided out; only the resulting mental problems were delaying this. Of course, Captain Bishopbourne was only one among many such severe cases. He was certainly not the only patient at St Michael's who exhibited strange behaviour. Yet, in his case there were oddities that stood out even in that company.

I did not have much contact with Captain Bishopbourne personally, but I heard the following from other staff members who did. Read into it what you will.

For much of the time he was affable and polite, but there were occasions when he would become withdrawn and even menacing, particularly in his attitude to female nurses. Once or twice, while a couple of the girls were trying to tend to him, he would address them foully and even outrage them with his remaining good hand. You must not get me wrong. We dealt with countless wounded soldiers, most of whom had been under constant fire and now existed in a kind of happy-go-lucky Limbo. We were not unused to cheeky behaviour, but there was something about Captain Bishopbourne's which took it further than mere sauce. At times, his attitude was so predatory that some girls did not even wish to be on the same ward as him.

We had a Doctor Bertrand at St Michael's who specialised in the new psycho-therapeutic methods. Several times, Doctor Bertrand put Captain Bishopbourne into a trance to try to get to the root of the problem, and on these occasions some very strange phrases came from the patient's mouth. He talked about the streets of London running with blood – he was not a Londoner, by the way, but came from somewhere in the north. He talked about ladies of the night; those were his exact words, gentlemen: "Ladies of the night, with their welcoming thighs and generous bosom . . ." I am sorry to be crude, gents, but these are those facts that you, Mr Holmes, are so fond of. He raved at length about how he needed these women, how he wanted them. But he also talked about seeing their flesh torn and bodies in pieces – or something to that effect, and, I am led to believe, he became wet-mouthed and wild-eyed during these sessions.

Captain Bishopbourne's nerves were evidently damaged, but even Doctor Bertrand admitted it was somewhat disconcerting that the patient's thoughts were awash – and again, that was Doctor Bertrand's exact term, "awash" – with this combination of eroticism and horror.

In due course, he put it all down to the patient's shell-shocked state, deciding that he had once been a frontline soldier who, when rotated back to the rear, might have sought comfort among the tavern girls (he might have sought this to an inordinate degree if he was unmarried, which apparently he was, despite his age), and who had brooded deliriously on this while buried alive in that charnel pit, surrounded as he was by dismembered corpses – and as such it all became mixed up in his mind and froze into a torturous mess.

But if that was the case, it was not plain to me why Captain Bishopbourne talked about the streets of London running with blood, as opposed to the streets of Poperinge or even Paris, where so many of our combat troops were sent for their rest and recovery.

Of course no one cared what I thought, and eventually Captain Bishopbourne was deemed cured and discharged, both from hospital and the armed forces. Whatever he had been before, he was now a shadow of it. His left arm was useless and he walked with a pronounced limp. To be blunt, he was a right old mess. But mentally, while I would not say he had recovered – he was still very withdrawn, and he still had a feverishly wandering eye – there was no real reason for him not to be released from care.

I joined the Metropolitan Police the following year, and soon had other, more immediate matters to occupy my mind. However, I always wondered if Captain Bishopbourne was someone we ought to have looked into a little more carefully. Finally, when I left the police force last year and enlisted on your course at Russell Square, I found I had the time to do a little research to that end. And all I can say is that what I uncovered, in the library section of the British Museum of all places, set me on the path I am reporting from today.

I must be brief now, gentlemen, for at noon I am due to catch a train from Euston Station, which will take me to the far north of England. I have learned that Captain Bishopbourne is back at his family home, Trawden House, which is in the parish of Trawden Forest in the Pendle district of Lancashire. That may seem a considerable distance from London; you may rightly wonder how I could ever have considered this gentleman a suspect in the Whitechapel Murders. But I have also learned that the Bishopbournes are copper and gold merchants of long-standing and wide interest. They have – or at least did have until recently – a business presence in many major cities, and our capital was no exception. It is a coincidence *verging on the incredible, I am sure you will agree, that the Bishopbournes owned a factory shop and trading office in Whitechapel itself during the very year in question – 1888. More so, maybe, that one Arthur Bishopbourne, while still a young business-man, was stationed there. And even more so, perhaps, that this office closed less than one month after the death of the Whitechapel Murderer's supposed final victim, Mary Jane Kelly.*

I say "supposed final victim", gentlemen, because another terrible unsolved murder has also come to my attention. Only last year, on Christmas Eve no less, sometime between nine o'clock and eleven, a poor street-woman named Valerie Blye was found stabbed thirty-nine times in a dismal backstreet of Colne, which is a factory town in northeast Lancashire – only five or so miles from Trawden House.

With this additional information now in hand, Mr Holmes and Dr Watson, I might as well be honest with you and admit that only last night the emphasis of my proposed dissertation completely changed. It is no longer my intent simply to name a name, but to take into actual custody the disturbed personality known during his terrible heyday as Jack the Ripper.

Your good friend,
Letty Feltencraft

By the time I had finished reading the letter, Holmes was standing at the window, pipe in hand. He said nothing as he peered down on Baker Street's mid-morning rush.

"Miss Feltencraft is nothing if not spirited," I finally said. "But I rather fear, as she seemingly expected I would, that she is letting her imagination run away with her."

Holmes pursed his lips. "You consider this a nonsense, Watson?"

"So much so that I feel we should summon the girl to Russell Square and give her a talking-to."

"On the basis of what . . . theorising? Sometimes, in the pursuit of unknown criminals, one must theorise."

I was surprised by the apparent seriousness of his tone. "Never without evidence though, Holmes. Isn't that what you always used to say?"

He puffed on his pipe. "The girl *has* evidence. It is entirely circumstantial, but there is plenty of it. Plenty."

"Holmes, surely these links between Arthur Bishopbourne and the Whitechapel Murders are completely coincidental? One could probably cast similar aspersions on a hundred others who were in Whitechapel at the same time."

He turned his limpid, grey-eyed gaze upon me. "All of whom, while under the mesmeric influence, would reveal sexually sadistic tendencies?"

"Well . . . maybe," I blustered.

"Ah . . . *maybe*."

"But Holmes, she's approached this thing the incorrect way. She has a single suspect. No solid evidence. And now she seeks anything she can that will put this suspect further into the frame. She is bending the facts to fit the thesis."

Holmes nodded. "Yes, she only has one suspect, which ordinarily I would consider a weakness in her case. However, it happens – not often, but occasionally – that the suspect leads the investigator to the crime rather than the other way around."

"But Holmes!" I protested. "Surely Jack the Ripper is dead? Even if he didn't die in 1888, as many suspect, thirty-four years have passed. What are the chances he could still be active?"

Fleetingly, Holmes almost looked amused. "*You* were alive in 1888, Watson. So was I. We both still live, breathe, walk upon the Earth."

"You're seriously saying you think there may be some truth in this?"

"I have no factual evidence on which to base an assessment. However, the murder of Valerie Blye may bear further consideration." Again, he looked thoughtful, even pensive.

"Holmes . . . thirty-four years! What has the fiend been doing in the meantime?"

"A great deal has happened since 1888, Watson. Not least the War. We have all found ourselves with different preoccupations."

"He had twenty-six years before the War even started. At the rate he was murdering, it was almost one victim a month, surely we'd have received many more corpses?"

"That is true. And I fear Miss Feltencraft will need to explain this aberration."

I tried not to sound as dismissive as I felt. "I fear Miss Feltencraft is letting her pointless ambition lead her into a completely blind alley."

He glanced at me again. "Pointless ambition, Watson?"

"Don't you think?" I said. "She applied several times during her service with the Metropolitan Police for a transfer to the Criminal Investigation Department, and on each occasion was passed over, which never sat easily with her."

"Yes, well . . ." Holmes nodded. "I never thought the senior officers in the Metropolitan Police ever really held the cause of Suffrage close to their hearts."

"By the deuce, Holmes . . . it's hardly work for a woman! Miss Feltencraft and all those other girls were only appointed back in '18 because there weren't enough men to fill the vacancies."

I will admit to feeling a little disloyal having uttered these words. I did not intend to disparage the hundred or so women police constables who were appointed at the close of the War. In truth, they could not have had a more difficult task. There wasn't just the rank-and-file criminality to deal with; there were many damaged men wandering the streets in those days: men who were unfit for work, men who'd taken to drink, men who couldn't shake the violence from their souls. And yet the police force was down in numbers, so those brave young women were often forced to confront these unstable characters alone, without the consolation that male colleagues would come rushing to their assistance if they called.

Miss Leticia Feltencraft was the only one I'd known personally, but I'd instinctively liked her. She was not especially tall – perhaps five feet and five inches – but with a strong, stocky frame and fine, even features; soft, red-gold hair, a dusting of freckles and the most piercing cat-green eyes. She went about her daily work in a keen, alert fashion, and when she spoke, she did so quickly and sharply, like a schoolmistress issuing rebukes. For a young woman of no more than twenty-six or -seven, I'd say, she carried remarkable natural authority. In so many ways, she was the stuff that police constables are supposed to be made of. And yet – what can I say? – she was a woman. To my mind at least, this reduced her effectiveness and trebled the danger she faced, because so many felons would be less respectful of her, less intimidated, less inclined to come quietly when she boxed their ears and felt their collars.

"As I recall, she resigned from the police force in sheer frustration," Holmes said.

He also had liked Miss Feltencraft. He'd been especially approving of her written work, which he'd once described as "so thoroughly considered and presented that a copy should be set on the wall in every British police station as an example to all grammar assassins and thick-fingered scribblers".

"That's correct," I said. "That's why she had time to join the detection course. But if I'm allowed an opinion, Holmes . . . I think *frustration* is too light a word. More likely *obsession* is Miss Feltencraft's true motivation."

"What makes you say that, Watson?"

"Surely you remember the girl's history? Her father had been decorated after the Sudanese campaign, and during the War her two brothers were both in France. She joined the TFNS first, if I remember, but ultimately nursing wasn't enough for her. She feared she was missing out on the real action. So, as soon as the call was made for women police constables, she was among the first in the queue."

"She was an avid reader of yours, was she not?" he said.

"So she told us on first arriving at Russell Square. She followed your investigations closely, Holmes, and is very eager to emulate you. On completion of the course, she intends to reapply. And if the Metropolitan Police won't have her back, she will offer her services to a different force. She is quite determined to be a police detective."

"And the only way to make that happen is to catch the most infamous murderer of them all?"

"There you have it."

I expected this would be sufficient to convince Holmes that Miss Feltencraft needed to be brought back to the school for a reprimand. I could not imagine he'd think personal ambition an admirable enough cause for raking up again all the blood and darkness of the Whitechapel Murders. But instead he contented himself with re-filling his pipe and lighting it. And this concerned me a little.

Holmes was now in his late sixties, but though he had never mentioned it once, I strongly suspected that Jack the Ripper's original evasion of him still rankled. My friend measured himself by his ability to solve complex puzzles. Words like "insoluble" or phrases like "give up" did not exist in his vocabulary. If he failed to break a case quickly, it remained on hold; it was never closed. But that did not mean it wasn't a sore point. Lack of evidence during the Whitechapel Murders had defeated him at the time, as it had so many Scotland Yard detectives, and that was something he could not abide.

Miss Feltencraft was correct about one thing: back then there had been nothing to go on but supposition. But, likewise, the theory that Jack the Ripper must now be dead was also supposition. In Holmes's eyes at least, there was always a possibility the killer might one day return. Not that I considered this anticipatory attitude healthy. It didn't preoccupy his thoughts as such – Holmes hadn't mentioned the case at all for at least ten years, and then only in passing. But it was a blot on his landscape. It niggled at him from time to time.

Reflecting on all that, perhaps it should not have surprised me that he didn't instantly dismiss this foolhardy errand the Feltencraft woman had embarked upon.

"So you don't intend to call her back?" I said, somewhat lamely. "To admonish her, I mean?"

"Miss Feltencraft needs far more data before she can reach any firm conclusions," he replied. "But, even as we speak, she is out there looking for it. Can we ask more of a detective than that?"

3 March 1922
Dear Mr Holmes and Dr Watson,

Fortune favours the brave, they say, and thus far that old proverb appears to be holding good for me. I like to think of myself as brave, though I know others, perhaps your good selves included, would more likely describe me as headstrong, maybe reckless. For which reason I am writing to you again, as I think it only fair after maybe alarming you the other day with my first letter, to keep you regularly updated on my progress.

I am now in the Lancashire village of Beardshaw, in the heart of Trawden Forest, which is a wild part of the world to be sure: great sweeps of rugged hills and moorland broken here and there by belts of wildwood. Most of the people hereabouts are farmers and farm labourers. Everyone I have spoken to seems bemused to hear my London accent, while to my own southern ears the Lancashire dialect is somewhat guttural. But they are a friendly enough bunch, and I have managed to find a room upstairs in a village pub called The Roundhead's Rest.

As I recall, Mr Holmes, you advised that if ever we were to go "incognito", as you call it, we needed a good, solid cover story. Well, mine is a simple one but it appears to be doing the trick. I am still Letty Feltencraft, but I am here because I have travelled as far as my money will allow in order to get away from a troublesome ex-husband, and I am now looking for work in a completely different environment. As luck would have it, the local postmistress, who was the first person I spoke with to this effect, directed me to a vacancy card in her own front window. You will not believe this, but the post being advertised is for a chambermaid up at Trawden House itself, which is no more than two miles' walk from Beardshaw.

I consider this an amazing stroke of luck, and intend to take the card up to the house tomorrow, and apply. I was given a word of warning by the postmistress, who advised me that Trawden House is not all it once was. Apparently, the Bishopbourne family have let it go to rack and ruin in recent times. Again, those are her words, not mine: "rack and ruin". It seems that old Sir Randolph Bishopbourne, who was the founder of the family's wealth and rather a domineering personality, died on 3 January 1916, at the ripe old age of eighty-four. His wife, Lady Clara Bishopbourne, having had some long-standing nervous problem, followed him to the grave on 14 June 1919.

I mention these dates specifically because I took note of them on the headstones erected in the local churchyard, and I know how keen you are, Mr Holmes, on collating actual facts rather than relying on mere gossip. Anyway, this left only the son, young Arthur Bishopbourne, who had lived all his life in the shadow of his father and, as such, never amounted to much. This might explain why he joined the Colours in 1914, at forty-four years old – only one year before reaching the end of permissible enlistment – because he was desperate to make something of himself in the world. We all know what happened to him while he was over there, of course. My understanding is that he now leads a solitary, dissipated lifestyle, doing very little apart from drinking and indulging himself in curious substances, which initially he took for the pain of his wounds, but now takes for recreation. I'm told that everything of consequence – the estate, the household, the family's business affairs, such as they are – is run by the Bishopbournes' housekeeper, a lady called Miss Abigail Simm, who is very efficient but has the temper of the Devil.

You may wonder how I came by all this additional information. Well, it was not from those gravestones or from the postmistress, but from one Dora Page, a barmaid at The Roundhead's Rest, who, as you can tell from all this, is a right old chatterbox. Mind you, she is another who does not think it a good idea my looking for employment up at Trawden House. She says the place is near enough a ruin and its grounds all overgrown; in short, that she finds it rather eerie. Again, I use the exact parlance: "rather eerie". She also says the place is haunted, but I suppose tales like that are par for the course, this being such an old structure. Eighteenth century, according to Mr Peabody, the local vicar. Of course, like Mr Holmes, I do not believe in such guff and, even if I did, none of that will put me off. I won't even be dissuaded by the most scandalous bit of gossip I have now heard, which Dora Page imparted to me in a very confidential manner. It seems that Captain Bishopbourne, though he has never married, is much like his father in that he has an eye for the ladies – and not a good one. Well, we already had an inkling about that, though it is interesting that he seemingly had this reputation before he went off to war and not just as a result of his mental injuries. Anyway this, it seems, is why maidservants are in short supply up at Trawden House. The card in the Post Office window had been there almost eight months without a single applicant enquiring about it.

For this reason, I am confident I will get the job, and no ... before you even ask, I am not concerned about Captain Bishopbourne. I can look after myself, as I proved many times during my service as a WPC. And anyway, this is detective work. If I was looking for a non-hazardous occupation, I would sign on somewhere as a nanny.

Your good friend,
Letty Feltencraft

"I wonder if there is such a thing as having too much pluck," I said, pocketing the letter as we strolled in Regent's Park.

It was a bright day, the first sunshine we'd seen since the previous September. The flowerbeds were a riot of daffodils, but the air was cold. Everyone out and about was thickly wrapped.

Holmes took a pinch of snuff. "You consider that Miss Feltencraft runs the risk of becoming the next victim of the Whitechapel Murderer?"

I didn't rise to that bait. "It just strikes me that she may be taking this whole thing too far."

"It strikes *me*, Watson, that she has the courage of her convictions. The lady is far from home, completely alone and, where she herself is concerned, on the trail of a dangerous madman."

"Don't get me wrong, Holmes . . . I admire her single-mindedness, but there must be limits. For instance, we received another letter today." I produced a second envelope. "It was written by the provost at Russell Square in response to your recent enquiry."

Holmes indicated that I should read it. I opened the envelope and took out the note.

"It seems that Miss Feltencraft hails by origin from Spitalfields."

He nodded. "It was plain from her accent that she was born within the sound of Bow Bells."

"But this is exactly the point, Holmes. That district of London was terrorised by Jack the Ripper. Even respectable women didn't feel safe. Perhaps Miss Feltencraft feels there is a score to settle?"

"Perhaps so."

"And is that not another reason to call her back?"

Holmes gave this more consideration that I felt was necessary. Again, I wondered about his curious indifference to Miss Feltencraft's unorthodox approach. In some ways, it was almost like tacit approval, though of course he would never say as much, and if I pressed him on the subject he would rightly reply that it was his function to lecture, not produce the students' coursework for them. But again I couldn't help wondering if the real reason was his long-standing desire to see the Whitechapel mystery resolved.

"She *does* have the air of a young woman on a personal mission," he finally remarked.

"A mission that might now have led her to make trouble for a Lancashire family who could be entirely innocent."

"A Lancashire family whose home base is very close to the scene of Valerie Blye's murder."

I was not able to deny that, nor that it had been a horribly familiar type of crime. Since Miss Feltencraft's first letter, we had read up on the Valerie Blye case in the archive basement at *The Times*. The attack on that poor woman, a forty-four-year-old streetwalker in the factory town of Colne, had been ghastly. Almost identical, Holmes had pointed out – even down to the number of knife-wounds – to the stabbing of Martha Tabram in Whitechapel back in 1888, though Scotland Yard investigators had never been certain that Tabram was a victim of Jack the Ripper.

"More important, however, is the new development," Holmes said. "This revelation that Arthur Bishopbourne's unpleasant attitude to the fairer sex was not caused by the brain damage he suffered on the Western Front . . . but was something he had already manifested before."

I must admit, that had also given me pause for thought.

"Then there is the small matter of the Bishopbourne office in Whitechapel," Holmes added, "which mysteriously closed less than one month after Mary Kelly's murder."

"There may be an entirely non-mysterious reason for that, Holmes."

"Indeed there may, Watson. And I feel we should make it our next priority to discover exactly what that reason was."

We continued to stroll, but I was startled by this.

"Holmes . . . you don't intend to involve us in Miss Feltencraft's enquiry?"

"I merely seek to satisfy my curiosity, Watson."

"But is that proper? This is part of the girl's dissertation."

"I asked you earlier if you feared that Miss Feltencraft might fall victim to the Whitechapel Murderer. You declined to answer."

"I suppose that's because I don't know."

"I don't know either, Watson," he replied. "And I rather wish I did."

4 March 1922

Dear Mr Holmes and Dr Watson,

I have got the job. But, I must say, it was not as easy as I expected. Considering no one will apparently work at Trawden House, I was only appointed under strange circumstances which have not left me comfortable. But more about that shortly.

First of all, the house itself. I was led to believe the Bishopbournes were once a successful merchant family; if this is all that remains of their empire, then something went badly wrong. It was clearly once part of a great estate. The main house is a big red-brick structure, Georgian in style, with a west wing and an east wing, and a pillared portico at the front. But it is in a near-dilapidated state. There is a gauntness about it, and a coldness. A couple of the windows are cracked, I noticed, and no one has bothered to repair them. Much of the guttering is loose or crammed with birds' nests. In terms of its position, it is tucked into a fold in the land, its eastern end fast against a great, rocky, tree-covered rise, down which a hillside torrent called the Mill Race pours in a small but copious waterfall. It gathers in a noisy plunge-pool, which is only fenced off by flimsy wrought-iron railings standing right next to the house's east wing, before disappearing in a fast stream down a gully and into an underground cave system. Everything down that side is damp and covered in spongy yellow moss – it is not a very healthy place.

As for the rest of the surroundings: the driveway, which is beaten earth, is largely overgrown with weeds, which shows how little traffic arrives here these days, while the grounds themselves – officially known as Trawden Plantations – are more a jungle than a manicured park. Various walks lead away from the main building, but they soon vanish amid profusions of thorns, bracken and deeply tangled thickets.

Inside, Trawden House is equally dismal. Those tall, airy chambers which Georgian palaces used to be famous for are noticeably lacking. The passages are dim and narrow, the rooms poky, with most of their windows covered by heavy, dusty drapes, which accounts for the general gloom I suppose. The furniture is very rustic, made from heavy, dark wood, and is not comfortable. There is a constant smell in the air. More damp, I suspect, though it might also come from the carpets, which are old and worn, or the wainscoting, which is mildewed in many places and rotted along its skirting boards. I have only been here a short time, but I have already seen mice scampering about. The whole building is fitted with electric lighting, but none of it works. Faulty wiring, apparently.

On this basis, it is plain why they were looking for an extra servant. Something must be done to spruce this place up a little, but I fancy it will take more than a willing girl like myself. Not that the folk who live here seem hugely motivated to do anything about it themselves; at least not all of them.

There are three members of staff, if you can call them that. Henry Smallwood-Smythe is the official estate manager, but he does not do very much. I have not met him yet, but apparently he is at retirement age and lives in a gatehouse at the south end of Trawden Plantations. It seems he was a former business associate and close friend of old Sir Randolph, and his appointment here was little more than honorary; a replacement home for him after he lost his own through some bad investments. There is also a groundsman/ gardener/gamekeeper named Norbert Growther. He is pretty typical of his sort. He wears work-clothes all day, a big heavy coat and scarf, and a slouch-brimmed hat. But at seventy-five, he is far too elderly to hold any one of these posts, in my view, let alone all three. This might explain why I hardly see him doing any work, though I have observed him pushing a barrow from time to time, and carrying hoes, forks and the like.

Conversely, Miss Abigail Simm does work. In fact, I have never seen her take a moment's rest. But it is not surprising that she too makes little impact, given that she is alone and the house so big and sprawling. But she is a strange woman. She too is somewhere in her early seventies, but far from frail. She is tall, straight and thin, with a very severe aspect. She has the whitest skin I have ever seen and the darkest eyes. It seems she once was attractive; apparently she began her association with the Bishopbournes many, many years ago when she was appointed as Captain Bishopbourne's governess – I have seen a photograph of her posing with Baby Arthur on her knee, and she was very beautiful back in those days. Even now, her hair is pure ash-grey and would hang down to the small of her back if she didn't keep it furled in a tight bun. It does not help that in her old age she favours dark dresses, dark stockings and heavy clumping shoes made of dark leather. There is a funereal air about her these days but, as I say, she is forever on the go, trying to do what she can about keeping this old place shipshape, though ultimately failing.

Which made her attitude on my first arrival all the more strange.

I intimated at the start of this letter that I had some difficulty acquiring the post. Well, that was mainly down to Miss Simm. From the outset, she did not seem to want me. She was suspicious that I was even interested in the job. Maybe I could understand that – we are in the back of beyond out here – but to say that some of her questions were verging on the personal would be the understatement of all time.

For instance . . .

Why would a young girl like myself seek work in a remote part of the world like this? Would I not be more comfortable in the town or the city where I could socialise with others of my own age group?

Is there a young man in my life? (I ask you, Mr Holmes and Dr Watson – imagine posing a question like that to a girl you have only just met.)

If there is a young man in my life, where is he now and what are his intentions? (You see . . . it got even more intrusive).

If there is not a young man in my life, why not? (Again, I ask you . . .)

I obviously did not give her my cover story about being an abused wife on the run. I felt sure that was all she would need to show me the door. Instead, I told her I was an orphan, that my mother had died in penury and that I had left London as it held nothing for me but unhappy memories. She did not seem convinced by that and asked for references. Can you credit that – references? To work in a place like this? It threw me a little, and then she asked what experience I had. I told her a pack of lies, of course – about working in various sizeable houses down south. She asked me for names and addresses. I could not really give her any for fear she would check up on them. By now I had a strong suspicion I was about to be thrown out. When suddenly Captain Bishopbourne intervened on my behalf.

This was a frightening thing in its own right. I had long considered the possibility that the captain might recognise me from St Michael's Cottage Hospital. I did not expect that he would – I had so few dealings with him face-to-face back then and, as you can imagine, he did not notice very much happening around him – but the mere thought was ugly. As it turned out, he did not recognise me, but his intervention was unnerving all the same.

Captain Bishopbourne is fifty-two now, and he looks every year of it. His left arm is stiff, pale and twisted like a dead tree branch, and he still walks with a noticeable limp. He is a thickset bloke, but not overly heavy. That said, he has dark rings under his eyes, wizened, pockmarked cheeks and saggy jowls. His hair was once fair, I understand, but now is thin, wispy and colourless. From what I have seen thus far, he is inclined to be well turned-out. He wears a morning suit before noon, a lounge suit in the afternoon and of course he always dresses for dinner. And it is all quality stuff. I know a good bit of material when I see it, Mr Holmes. But he still strikes me as a gentleman who has gone to seed. His jackets are crumpled, his collars and cuffs grimy. But I digress . . . Captain Bishopbourne strayed into the kitchen where I was being interviewed. Quite by accident, I feel. But as soon as he set his eyes on me, he smiled like a cat. A big, broad grin, it was, the corners of his mouth stretching up to his ears. He has these pale, watery-blue eyes, which fixed on me intently.

"And who is this, Miss Simm?" he asked.

In response, Miss Simm stiffened. She was coldly furious, I could tell, as if she knew that she was about to be overruled. Once informed about me, his response was immediate.

"If she desires to work for us, Miss Simm, you must appoint her."

I felt very queasy just to be near him. For a brief time, I was actually thankful for the presence of Miss Simm. She clearly did not want me, but now that her master had spoken she had no option. I was offered the job, given a round of the house and advised what my duties will consist of – and they are many (it is not so much a chambermaid they want, as a general dogsbody).

I know that one must never judge a book by its cover, and that murderers do not walk around looking the part. But Captain Bishopbourne has a predatory air. My undercover investigation continues, gentlemen, but I now feel strongly that I must watch my host very carefully.

> Your good friend,
> Letty Feltencraft

"This is far from satisfactory, Holmes," I said, closing up the latest letter.

Holmes gazed from the omnibus window as we rode across London. "How so?"

"The girl is certainly making headway of sorts . . . but towards what? The case does not add up. Arthur Bishopbourne may well be a strange and frightening chap. But if he's fifty-two now, he would only have been eighteen when Jack the Ripper was at large."

Holmes removed his pipe and tapped out the ashes in the armrest tray. "You remember George Newton, I take it? Charles Ashton? Jack Field?"

"I remember them all, of course I do!" I replied, somewhat grouchily.

Even now, after so many years, whenever I proposed a hypothesis at variance with Holmes's own views, he had the tendency to put flies in my ointment almost as a matter of course. Jack Field, for instance, had been hanged only the previous year at Wandsworth for murdering a young girl in Eastbourne. George Newton had committed the same heinous crime in Stratford in 1911, and paid the price at Chelmsford, while Charles Ashton died at Hull in 1903 for the same offence again. All were either eighteen or nineteen years old at the time.

"Very young men are frighteningly capable of atrocious crimes," Holmes said.

"But isn't there a notable difference between these offences?" I said. "The original Whitechapel Murders turned steadily more gruesome, the mutilations and disembowelments increasingly wild and horrible – as if the murderer was building up an uncontrollable head of steam. In contrast, Valerie Blye was merely stabbed."

"Those are the dissimilarities, I agree," Holmes said, tamping fresh tobacco into his pipe. "However, similarities can also be seen. None of the original Whitechapel victims had been indecently assaulted before being slain. Neither was Valerie Blye. In all these cases, the pure object of the exercise was to brutally, bloodily kill. In addition, all the victims, both in 1888 and in 1921, died in a most frenzied attack. You forget, because it suits your argument to forget, my dear Watson, that Valerie Blye was not 'only stabbed' – she was stabbed thirty-nine times. This implies that the new perpetrator – if indeed he is a new perpetrator – is of a similarly unsound mind to the old one. And now I put something else to you . . ." He lit the tobacco and puffed out several fragrant clouds. "Take a disturbed fellow who has impulses he cannot fight. He gives in to them again and again when he is young. But as he grows older, he gains greater control, especially as it becomes plain to him that the price he will pay if caught is a date with the hangman. And then suppose this fellow was to embark on a military career. Later in life than most, but he still undergoes intense training – as such, he learns even greater self-control."

"And then he goes to the front line?' I added, attempting to follow the logic. "And on a daily basis he watches fellow soldiers blown to bits or machine-gunned. He sees bayonet work and men hanging on the wire . . . his lust for blood is further sated? Is that what you're saying?"

Holmes pondered as he smoked. "I rather fancy that would have the opposite effect. In my experience, Watson, homicidal tendencies may be stimulated by the sight of blood rather than sated. And just supposing Arthur Bishopbourne *is* our man . . . if his instinct is to derive pleasure from such horror, would a re-engulfment in it not drive him to greater acts of foulness?"

"So this is why he took up his knife again on returning home from the War?"

"When he was fit enough, perhaps. A couple of years later. Maybe so, yes."

"This is still supposition, Holmes," I said.

"Not entirely. Slowly but surely, we are acquiring facts."

By this, Holmes referred to that morning's research. We were now en route back to Baker Street from the records office of the London Metal Exchange, where it had been confirmed to us that, in 1888, Bishopbourne Copper & Gold Ltd, as it was known, whose official London trading address was 10 Commercial Street – only a stone's throw from two of the original Whitechapel murder sites – had been officially represented by young Arthur Bishopbourne and his clerk, a certain Solomon Ezer. This proved beyond doubt that Bishopbourne had been present in Whitechapel at the time of the murders. But it also provided us with another potential witness: Solomon Ezer, who apparently was not just still alive, but still in the precious metals business.

6 March 1922

Dear Mr Holmes and Dr Watson,
I have now been three days settled in Trawden House. My room is at the end of the east wing on the first floor. And a small cubbyhole of a place it is, with a basic iron bed, a feather mattress, a table, a stool, a water jug, and not a single picture on any one of its blank walls. It is very cold in here. In fact, the whole house is cold. It is not just that awful waterfall so close by. The wind wails across the encircling moors, droning in the rafters, penetrating every part of the interior. This is proving a difficult investigation, but again, Mr Holmes, as you said during one of your lectures, good detective work is all about taking pains.

I am certainly being kept busy here, scrubbing floors, dusting shelves, washing pots, fluffing the ceilings and corners for cobwebs, of which there is no shortage. But I can scarcely complain, as Miss Simm sets the example. For an older lady, and one who is somewhat imperious in manner, she is very industrious, cooking and cleaning as though there is no end to it. As yet, I have seen no sign of that fearsome temper, but that may be because I have proved a willing worker.

But my, she is a chilly soul. She does not indulge in pleasantries or exchange banter. I perhaps should not expect that from her, as I am so new. But she is brusque and clipped with everyone, particularly old Growther, with whom she only has occasional dealings. He seems to keep to his world out in the grounds, and Miss Simm to hers, which is indoors – though I have sometimes known her take food and drink down to the shed on the edge of the orchard, where he lives. She has an even odder relationship with Captain Bishopbourne, whom she mostly ignores. They interact so little that, quite often, it is almost as if neither master nor servant are even aware of each other.

Before you ask, Captain Bishopbourne has had surprisingly little time for me. Yes, I originally expected trouble from him. But since then he has largely kept to himself. His private bedroom is on the upper floor in the west wing of the house, and when he comes downstairs, which is never any earlier than mid-morning, he tends to keep to his solar, which is apparently a kind of gentleman's day-room next to the conservatory at the back.

This solar is one of two rooms that Miss Simm has advised me I have no business in. This has made me curious. I have occasionally glanced in there when the door was partly open, but all I have managed to see thus far is what looks like an old drawing room gone to waste. The walls and ceiling are stained brown, and there is ash on the table-tops – presumably all this is down to Captain Bishopbourne's smoking habits, which are excessive. There are books on the shelves, and though many of these look like fine volumes, being old and bound with leather, they are in a frayed and disorderly state. I also see bottles in there: some along the sideboard; some lying on the floor amid scattered papers and other such detritus. And these are not just drinking bottles. Don't get me wrong, gentlemen. Captain Bishopbourne does drink – there are decanters in there aplenty. Oftentimes, when I am taking out the rubbish, I find empty bottles for brandy, whisky and port. But there are medicinal bottles too, for tablets, elixirs and the like, and yet as far as I am aware, he is under no doctor. If I am honest, gentleman, I think that Captain Bishopbourne, whether he be a murderer or not, is a very debased man . . .

I glanced purposely at Holmes as I read this part of the letter aloud, but he studiously refrained from returning my gaze.

Everything I have heard about the captain's lifestyle appears to be confirmed – except, as I say, that so far there has been no threat from him to my person.

Until . . . maybe, last night.

This is why, despite my heavy workload, I was inclined to write to you today.

Not wanting to be here for ever, I reached a decision yesterday that I needed to investigate Trawden House without the beady eye of Miss Simm constantly fixed on me. She is always the last in the household to retire – usually at around midnight. Her own apartment – which is large and well furnished for a servant's, I must say – occupies the top floor in the west wing. As my own room is on the first floor, I felt it would be relatively safe, once she was in bed, to venture downstairs in my nightgown and have a poke around. Initially, it seemed like an enormous task. What was I looking for? What solid evidence could I find that might connect Captain Bishopbourne with those ghastly murders of so long ago? Where could I even start?

However, if nothing else, I knew I ought to try to examine those rooms to which I am forbidden entry. The first one, as I mentioned, is Captain Bishopbourne's solar. That one, I suspect, will be out of bounds to me permanently, as it is always kept locked when the captain is not present, and he keeps the key on his person. But the second one is a room leading off the stairway connecting the kitchen to the cellar. The cellar itself is a complex of bare stone chambers and corridors, all damp and cluttered with thrown-away furniture and boxes of household bric-a-brac. But this locked room, which is only accessible from the small landing at the turn on the cellar stair, has a more lived-in look about it. I am not sure if that makes sense, Mr Holmes, but using your own deductive methods, I have noted how worn the carpet is in front of this door, and how shiny the brass door-handle is, whereas so many others connecting to little-used rooms in Trawden House are tarnished and green with age . . .

At this point of my reading, Holmes nodded and muttered his approval.

This room is also kept locked, but there are bunches of keys hanging throughout the house, particularly in the kitchen itself. It ought only to be a matter of trial and error.

So it was late last night, gentlemen, when I finally opted to make my move.

I said that Trawden House is supposedly haunted, but that I hold only contempt for such stories. It occurs to me that maybe these tales first spread because the house is so dreary and desolate. However, it was about one o'clock in the morning and I had not been down on the ground floor more than a couple of minutes before I sensed a presence.

It was pitch-dark. I hadn't dared risk a lamp or candle, and had expected that I would have to blunder about until my eyes attuned to the thin moonbeams penetrating those heavy downstairs curtains. But I had no sooner crossed the main sitting room, when I heard what I took to be slippered feet coming through the open door behind me. I am ashamed to admit I was, briefly, overcome by fear – I ran through into the morning room, and cut left into the central hall. Again, I heard those feet in pursuit, but now there was a dim silvery glow from the stained-glass fanlight over the front door, and when I looked back, I glimpsed an alarming shape, a figure all muffled in dark cloth, emerging from the room behind me. I fled to the foot of the main staircase and hastened up it. When I reached the top, the figure had arrived at the bottom, where it stopped. It had no discernible head or face – it was simply a shape covered completely in material, yet I sensed that it was staring up after me.

In appearance, this thing was your archetypical ghost, though I knew that in truth it was a flesh-and-blood man, and in my mind there was only one person it could be. I dashed back to my room and rammed home the bolt on the door. I then sat up for several hours, listening for the sound of feet in the passage beyond, or maybe for the sly knock of someone requesting admission. My head was filled with thoughts of poor Mary Kelly. She answered her door to a late-night knock, did she not? And what followed was the most gruesome death any person could suffer. Like the unfortunate Miss Kelly, I too have a small grate in my bedroom and, owing to the threadbare clothing I have brought with me, I feared the malefactor would find no shortage of rags to burn there, thus creating sufficient light for him to work on my poor suffering form for as long as he felt like it.

In all my time in the Metropolitan Police, even when walking the night-time beat in the thickest pea-soup of a river fog, I have never been as nervous and alarmed. But as you will gauge, that knock on my bedroom door did not come. At present, I am still very much alive, but whether or not this house is the house of Jack the Ripper, let no one tell me that nothing is amiss here. What else would you call it, sirs, when a figure – cloaked and hooded to complete anonymity – silently roams its passages in the depths of the night?

Your good friend,
Letty Feltencraft

"Well that isn't very encouraging," I muttered, slipping the letter back into my pocket.

"It certainly is not," Holmes agreed.

"But eccentric behaviour does not equate with murder, nor even a desire to commit murder."

"That also is true, Watson."

"And as Miss Feltencraft said, the night-time knock never came."

Despite this, I was unnerved by the latest missive, and perhaps Holmes was too. He didn't respond as our cab deposited us at the lower end of High Holborn and, while I paid the cabbie, he walked swiftly away along a narrow, low-roofed arcade lined on either side by jewellers' shops.

"Holmes?" I said, hurrying to catch up. "What do you think we should do?"

"Continue our own enquiries," he replied. "We have *some* facts, but not nearly enough."

I think both of us hoped this lack of hard evidence would in some way be resolved by the interview due to follow – which was with none other than Solomon Ezer, Esq., Arthur Bishopbourne's right-hand man back in the days when Bishopbourne Copper & Gold had had a presence in London's East End.

We found him at the far end of the arcade, in the rear office of a small silversmith's.

Ezer was eighty now, at least, but still a hale and hearty fellow of corpulent girth, shaggy white hair, and equally shaggy white whiskers. He currently sat stripped to his waistcoat and sleeves, poring over a mass of ledgers and accounts, a foul-smelling cheroot clamped between his broken, yellowing teeth. When the workshop boy introduced us, he sat ponderously back, pushed his bottle-thick spectacles up his nose and regarded us through wreaths of cigar smoke.

"Solomon Ezer, I trust?" Holmes said.

"That's correct." Ezer's voice was chesty, crusty, his face inscrutable, though his small dark eyes gleamed as he surveyed us.

"Good of you to make this time available," Holmes said.

"Who would not find time to meet with the legendary Sherlock Holmes?" Ezer replied. "Forgive me, though . . . I thought you would have retired by now, Mr Holmes?"

"Not so long as there are criminals at large, Mr Ezer."

"A laudable sentiment."

"I'd like to speak to you about Bishopbourne Copper & Gold."

Ezer's expression remained blank. "You are aware I left that company several years ago?"

"We are," Holmes said. "On the death of its chairman, Sir Randolph Bishopbourne. But during the year we are interested in, Mr Ezer, you were very much a part of it. How clearly do you recall the events of 1888?"

Ezer's bristle-filled nostrils flared as he expelled great plumes of cigar smoke through them. But his expression remained unreadable. "You ask an enormous thing, gentlemen. That was thirty years ago."

"But I'm sure you remember?" Holmes said. "Few who were present in Whitechapel at the time do not."

"I take the point." Ezer stubbed out his cheroot in a black-stained dish on his desk. "But all I really recollect of that dark time is the noise in the streets when the hue and cry arose. It was particularly bad at night. The mob would carry firebrands. Increasingly, you see, they were looking for Jews."

This was true of course. Almost from the commencement of the 1888 murder spree, there'd been rumours the madman was a Jewish barber or bootmaker called 'Leather Apron'. At first this was attributed to a general anti-Semitic feeling in Whitechapel, an area increasingly colonised by immigrants. But in the event of the fourth murder, that of Catherine Eddowes, a piece of bizarre graffiti was discovered close to the scene, which read: *The Juwes are the men that will not be blamed for nothing*. Though the message made almost no literal sense, the possibly misspelt word 'Juwes' served to convince the local populace, and a great many of the local constabulary, that Jack the Ripper was indeed Jewish.

On reflection now, it must have been quite a difficult time for Ezer and his family.

"We had to keep a low profile," he said, as though he'd been reading my thoughts.

"Did you attract attention from the police?" Holmes asked. "The company, I mean."

"They visited us on Commercial Street," Ezer confirmed. "But only inasmuch as they visited everyone. I believe it was Inspector Lestrade himself who came to our door. We were a respectable firm, after all. I imagine he felt it only proper that a senior man should deal with us."

"Whom did Lestrade speak with?" Holmes asked. "Specifically."

"Master Arthur, of course. He was our managing director."

"At eighteen, wasn't he a trifle young to hold such a post?" I asked.

Ezer eyed me, for the first time with interest, perhaps wondering what on Earth it might be that had already led us to establish the age of his former manager. "Personally, I thought so, yes. But it was his father's whim that he be brought into the company at an early age and assigned a role that would challenge him. Of course, he had help. I myself was not inexperienced. I'd been working at the Whitechapel office twenty years by then, as foreman and clerk. On Master Arthur's arrival at the end of that summer, I was reassigned as his adviser and senior assistant."

"Why?" Holmes asked.

Ezer frowned. "Excuse me?"

"Bishopbourne Copper & Gold had company offices in Manchester, Newcastle . . . all closer to young Master Arthur's home than London. Why was he sent so far away?"

Ezer shrugged. "As I say, it was part of a learning process that Sir Randolph was forcing his son to undergo." His eyes fleetingly twinkled.

"Something amuses you?" Holmes asked.

"Well . . . to a young gent from the country, a new life in Whitechapel should have been a shock. A sharp learning process, indeed. But Master Arthur was in many ways cosseted. The apartment allocated to him above the company offices was more than comfortable, and of course he'd brought a servant, a domestic to look after his every need. So perhaps in the event he learned very little."

"It seems odd," I remarked, "that a gentleman of Arthur Bishopbourne's status never attended a university."

Again, Ezer regarded me with interest. "May I ask what this is about, gentlemen? These events are many years past, and I feel the least you can do is—'

"The usual thing," Holmes interrupted him. "Murder."

"Murder?"

"Several murders, in fact," Holmes explained. "Murders that happened in the past. And murders that may happen in the future."

"Indeed? And do you have a crystal ball, Mr Holmes? Is that your secret?"

"I said murders that *may* happen, Ezer, not *will*. Surely you've no inclination not to prevent such a terrible possibility turning real."

Ezer blew out a long, low breath as he pondered his position. Clearly, even though he was no longer part of Bishopbourne Copper & Gold, he retained some loyalty to his former employers. Breaching close confidences did not come easily to him, but the affair of the Whitechapel Murders always had the power to shake a man's convictions.

"Master Arthur was destined for Cambridge," he finally said. "But then some scandal broke at his school . . . close to the end of his final year. Involving one of the housemaids."

"A maid?" I said.

Ezer raised a hand. "That was the rumour on the shop floor at Whitechapel. But no one knew for certain. Obviously it was never openly discussed."

"Was there police interest in that case?" I enquired.

"Not as I understand it," Ezer replied. "But a decision was taken inside the family that young Master Arthur was not to go away to university."

"And, instead, his father forced him into the harder world of business," Holmes said. "Perhaps not just to make him grow up, but maybe as a punishment?"

"I imagine there was an element of that, yes."

"What was he like, Master Arthur?"

Ezer shrugged again. "Affable enough, though I never thought him bright. He groped his way through business matters. A slow learner, if you follow. And . . . well, he had *other* interests."

"Such as?"

Again that warning hand. "It was most likely his age. He went out nightly. Enjoyed the pleasures of the district."

"We're all grown men here, Ezer," Holmes said, "so let us be frank. When you say 'enjoyed the pleasures of the district', do you mean that Master Arthur courted prostitutes?"

"I mean that he enjoyed pubs and clubs, Mr Holmes, and yes . . . the favours of women of easy virtue. As I say, he was a young fellow. Lazy in the flesh, but maybe wild at heart."

Another man might have coloured in the cheek at this admission; after all, Ezer was supposed to have advised and guarded his one-time protégé. But he clearly had never regarded such immoral behaviour as anything more serious than a rite of passage and, if he hadn't been ashamed of it then, how likely was it he'd feel shame all these decades later?

"There was no suggestion," I asked bluntly, "that he might have been Jack the Ripper?"

"Jack . . .?" Ezer's bushy eyebrows knitted together. For the first time since we'd arrived, he looked genuinely shocked. "That idea is preposterous!"

"In what way?" Holmes said.

"For one thing . . . as I say, Master Arthur was slow."

"Do you mean slow-witted?" I asked.

"Not that, no . . . but he rarely became animated." Distractedly, Ezer struck a match and relit what remained of his cheroot. "He was uninterested in work. Became bored easily – in short, gentlemen, he was a sot, a bumblehead. He lounged in his office, even slept. He had no real motivation to do anything."

"Except to go out at night and see these women of low virtue," I said.

"He went to them for pleasure, not violence," Ezer retorted.

"You seem very sure of that," Holmes said.

"We had many male workers in those days. Some were of a rough breed, others refined but single men nevertheless. *They* enjoyed the pubs and bawdy houses too. In truth, they're most likely the ones who introduced Master Arthur in the first place."

"They drank and whored alongside him, did they?" Holmes said.

"With him, in the next room to him . . . either way, they always reported back to me."

"You kept a close watch on him?"

Ezer glanced away – evasively, I thought. "I had no such role . . . but I was officially his assistant. It helped to know what he was doing. Either way, if you'd seen him in those days, Mr Holmes, you could never picture him as Jack the Ripper."

"From what I know of him, I can't picture him leading a troop into battle either," I said. "But apparently it happened."

Ezer now glowered at me, as though these remarks were verging on insolence. "Doctor Watson . . . there was no suggestion from the police that Master Arthur was the Whitechapel Murderer."

"So let us get this straight," Holmes said. "When Lestrade visited, he never asked Master Arthur to account for his whereabouts on the nights of the thirty-first of August, eighth of September, thirtieth of September and/or eighth of November?"

Ezer looked at him askance. "November the eighth?"

"Forgive me." Holmes raised a hand of apology. "Mary Kelly was murdered on November the ninth."

"On all those nights, Mr Holmes, Master Arthur was accounted for. I can vouch for it."

"In which case, why did the Whitechapel office close before the end of that month?"

Ezer made a breezy but frustrated gesture. "The company was in good health overall. But there were fluctuations at that time in the value of certain metals. It was an exercise in cost-cutting more than anything else."

"What happened to the workforce?"

"We were offered employment elsewhere in the company. I continued, but in the shipping office at Southampton, only returning to London many years later."

"And what happened to Master Arthur?"

"When the Whitechapel office closed, he went back to the family estate in Lancashire."

"And he never returned to London?"

"As far as I am aware, Mr Holmes. The rest, as you know, is history. As Sir Randolph aged and his health failed, so, gradually, over a period of years, failed the company – a process that Master Arthur never had the knowledge, skill or interest to arrest. Now, if you'll pardon the impertinence, my own company – small and humble enterprise though it is – will fail too if I continue to dedicate valuable time to such frivolous pastimes as this. If there is nothing else, gentlemen, I'd like to bid you good day."

Almost from force of habit, I was tempted to get heated with him, to say that this was not a frivolous pastime and that we were seeking to bring a criminal to justice. But for once that would not strictly have been true. As such, we made our apologies and withdrew, and about half an hour later found ourselves in Whitechapel, on Commercial Street itself.

There was a dank March chill, but it was late afternoon, and the bustle of the East End was all around us, traffic clamouring, hordes of working folk thronging the pavements. In the midst of this mayhem, one building remained silent. On the other side of the thoroughfare, directly opposite, the brown brick edifice that had once housed Bishopbourne Copper & Gold stood boarded and grimy.

"I know what you're thinking, Holmes," I said. "Young Bishopbourne left London and the Whitechapel murders ceased. But why did similar crimes not occur elsewhere?"

Holmes stroked his chin. "Perhaps Sir Randolph took him home for that purpose. Because out in the wilds of North Lancashire there would be fewer such temptations."

I could scarcely believe what I was hearing. "So, not only do you suspect that Arthur Bishopbourne was Jack the Ripper, you suspect that old Sir Randolph knew about it?"

"Sir Randolph had a reputation himself, Watson."

"For philandering, not for murdering women."

"Nevertheless, it reveals a certain, shall we say . . . *disrespect*."

"It hardly means he'd approve of murder."

"I'm not suggesting he approved of it, Watson. But I can't help wondering if maybe Sir Randolph had suspicions about his son from the start. Suspicions stemming from whatever scandal it was that ended the boy's education prematurely. It was interesting, was it not, that Solomon Ezer, though he initially claimed only vague memories of those days, was familiar enough with them to correct me when I stated that Mary Kelly had died on November the eighth?"

"That was a deliberate mistake on your part?"

"Of course it was. Evidently, Ezer has a very clear recollection of those days. Better than most, I'd say, despite denying this when we initially spoke to him. Even though it was thirty-four years ago, he remembered that time well enough to assert that Master Arthur was safely accounted for on all the relevant occasions."

I had to admit that Ezer had seemed inordinately certain about this.

"A strange thing to be sure of if there was never any suspicion about his young master," Holmes said. "An even stranger thing that Ezer insists he had no remit to keep a close watch on that young man, when it is plainly evident that this is exactly what he was doing. I put it to you, Watson, that once the Whitechapel Murders commenced – not long after Arthur Bishopbourne first arrived there, you'll have noticed – Sir Randolph knew his son well enough to feel concern. And who in London would he trust adequately to communicate these fears to, if not the same man he'd appointed to be his son's senior adviser?"

I grunted in acknowledgement of this.

"That is why, even three decades later, Solomon Ezer is so sure of his facts," Holmes added. "Because he checked up assiduously at the time, at Sir Randolph's behest."

"But if that is the case," I said, "and Arthur Bishopbourne was innocently engaged on the nights of the murders, why would Sir Randolph still close the Whitechapel office a month later?"

Holmes considered this as he surveyed the empty building.

"Maybe, as Ezer said, the fluctuating value of precious metals was costing the firm money. More likely, though, Sir Randolph was still unconvinced about his boy."

"So why not contact Scotland Yard? They would establish it one way or the other."

Holmes began to walk. I followed.

"Put yourself in the shoes of the industrial gentry of the nineteenth century, Watson. Like the landed gentry before them, their dirty laundry was not to be washed in public. Almost certainly, this would be a matter dealt with at home."

"Holmes, I . . ." Still, I shook my head. "We have nothing solid to support this conjecture. It's too much of a leap."

"I agree, Watson. We are still painfully short of data." He increased his pace. "We shall return to Baker Street forthwith, in the hope that our correspondent on the ground may finally have supplied some for us."

7 *March* 1922

Dear Mr Holmes and Dr Watson,

I have made another nocturnal ramble and, this time, at last, I have something factual to report. I would even go so far as to say that I now feel vindicated in all my suspicions.

I will come to the detail soon.

First, despite my previous fright, I ventured straight out again the following night. You may wonder why I took such a risk, but quite simply I could see no other way to investigate this mysterious household. By the same token, I knew that if I gave in to fear and cowered in my bedroom like a mouse, it would only weaken my resolve. On this occasion, I ensured to take a stout walking stick, which I had found in an under-stair cupboard. If that hooded horror approached me in the darkness again, I would give the rascal a good what-for. I took one other precaution too: this time I did not wait until it was late, but left my room almost immediately after I heard

Miss Simm ascend the stair. It struck me that Captain Bishopbourne might not go wandering straight away if his housekeeper was only just in bed, as his room was in the same region of the house as hers, and she would likely hear him moving around.

Of course, this meant that I too had to go quietly. I even went barefoot this time. It was agony on the brick floor in the kitchen, which was ice cold. However, for all this, it was the kitchen that was to prove most rewarding.

As I mentioned previously, several bunches of keys hang in there. The first I took from a hook near the water pump. I went down the cellar stairs, feeling my way as my eyes just would not adjust to such deep gloom and, one by one, I inserted each key into the locked door at the stairway's turn. None was a fit, but I was determined to be patient and methodical – that is another lesson I learned from you, Mr Holmes – and as I knew the next bunch of keys was hanging under the stone hood over the top of the kitchen stove, I did not get frustrated.

I went back up to reclaim this second bunch – at which point I thought I heard movement somewhere overhead, a footfall on a creaking floorboard possibly.

I waited for several minutes, barely breathing, but there was nothing further – by which time, my eyes were finally adjusting. The moonlight filtering through the grimy, gauze-covered kitchen window was very poor, but it enabled me to distinguish the main fixtures. In fact, it gave me quite a start. For half a second I fancied a figure was standing right next to me, but then I realised that it was merely a coat-stand with some old oilskins on its pegs.

Relieved, I reached for the second bunch of keys above the stove, but accidentally dislodged them, and they fell down behind the appliance. They clattered on the floor, but it was muffled. When I dropped to my knees and reached underneath, I learned why. There were heaps of unswept ashes down there, and many fragments of half-burned paper. As I clawed the keys out, one such came with them. It looked like a charred railway ticket. I was about to push it back out of sight, when, despite the poor light, I noticed some important details printed on it. I stood up to try and examine it more closely, only to receive a very sobering shock.

That same cloth-covered form was standing right there.

Before I could move, it grabbed hold of me. I saw a gleaming white face under a hood, and a long white arm with a white talon on the end of it. And the grip of that talon on my elbow was vicelike. I almost shrieked in horror – only for the thing to speak to me.

"Leticia! What in Heaven is this?" I recognised the voice of Miss Simm. "Why do you wander the house at night, child?"

"Why do you, Miss?" I replied.

I considered it a fair question; I could have asked another – why did she also wear dark, heavy garb that reached to the floor, if not to deliberately camouflage herself? But as it was, she flew into a rage, calling me an "impudent baggage" and demanding an answer to her question.

"Miss Simm, I apologise for that rudeness," I said, "but you scared me so!"

"I asked why you wander the house, Leticia!"

"I don't sleep well, Miss Simm," I said. "This mansion is so cold and lonely, and I'd rather walk about than lie in bed listening to that terrible wind. It's just to tire me out, so's I can sleep."

"And crawling around the kitchen floor will serve this purpose?"

"If you please, Miss . . . I dropped my stick and could not find it in the darkness."

"Why do you arm yourself?"

"Please Miss, I was followed by someone the previous time I did this. I thought . . . well, the stories about this old place . . ."

"And that stick will protect you against ghosts?"

"Please Miss, I couldn't think of nothing else to do."

"You're an impudent baggage!" she told me again. "But I suppose you have a right to know. There are no ghosts here. That is idiot *village gossip. The person you saw last night was me. I don't sleep easily either, Leticia. Or should I say I sleep lightly . . . and if I hear someone up to no good, I am duty-bound to investigate."*

"I don't mean nothing wrong with my night-time wandering, Miss."

"That remains to be seen, Leticia. If anything is missing, I swear there'll be a reckoning."

"I'm no thief, Miss. Search me now, if you need proof."

I said this bold as brass, though I obviously hoped she would not as I still had that half-burned ticket in the sleeve of my nightgown.

"I may search you," she said. "And your room. But that will be on another occasion, when you least expect me . . . so that you won't have sufficient time to conceal any ill-gotten gains."

"I swear, Miss, you'll find nothing bad there."

"We shall see about that, Leticia. In the meantime, go back to your bed. A girl who has the energy to walk abroad at night clearly has inadequate chores to perform during the day. We must remedy that tomorrow. Besides, this house is no safe place to wander in the dark." She saw my questioning look and – hastily, I thought – added: "It has loose stair-treads and slippery floorboards. A chambermaid is no use to me laid up with injuries."

Which, if you don't mind my saying, Mr Holmes and Dr Watson, is purest bunkum.

I know for a fact there are no dangerous floorboards in this house, as I spend most of each day on my hands and knees cleaning them. One thing she said to me I did give credence to – "if I hear someone up to no good, I am duty-bound to investigate". That much I believe, because she must have heard my movements downstairs – she clearly does have sharp ears – but I suspect the person she expected to find was Captain Bishopbourne, and the "no good" was most likely me.

Did she think the captain was en route to my bedroom? Is that why she reacted so quickly?

Could she know about his terrible inclinations? Is this why she did not want to hire me in the first place?

Forgive me, Mr Holmes . . . I know that all I am doing here is asking yet more questions rather than providing answers, and theorising without any solid evidence . . . all things you deplore. But this story at least has an intriguing outcome. It is that ticket I mentioned. I later examined it in the firelight of my bedroom, and what I suspected I had glimpsed in the kitchen was confirmed. It was a return ticket from Beardshaw Halt to Colne. More important than this, it had been punched, which indicated to me that it had been used.

More important still was the date of it: 24 December 1921.

As you may recall, that was the very evening on which Valerie Blye was murdered.

Your good friend,
Letty Feltencraft

Lestrade, formerly Inspector Lestrade of Scotland Yard, now happily retired, lowered his newspaper. The cigarette visibly sagged between his lips. To his credit, he didn't seem completely displeased to see us, but up until our arrival in the smoky corner of the public house where he was taking his luncheon, he had looked much cosier than he did now.

"Holmes," he said. "Watson. To what do I owe this pleasure?"

Holmes sat at the table without asking permission. "We are merely here to pick your brains, Lestrade. We shan't keep you long."

Lestrade removed his cigarette. "*You* . . . wish to pick *my* brains?"

"How are you on the events of thirty years ago, old chap?" I asked, also sitting.

Lestrade looked perplexed. "No better than you'd expect me to be, I'm sure. If it's a case you're interested in, you're better off going to the Yard and checking the files."

"It's your personal impression I'm interested in, Lestrade," Holmes said. "Of a suspect. A fellow who, in the event, was never even charged."

Lestrade shook his head. "My memories are somewhat muddled these days, Holmes. Especially if it's a suspect who never finished up in court."

"I have an inkling you'll remember this one, Lestrade . . . considering that he might have turned out to be Jack the Ripper."

There was a long silence, during which Lestrade placed his cigarette in the ashtray and casually sipped his beer. Superficially he feigned disinterest, but I could already tell that he was intrigued. "You any idea how many suspects I interviewed during that enquiry, Holmes?"

"You were heavily involved. I know that."

"I was central to it. I reported direct to Chief Inspector Abberline. But just out of interest, which suspect are we talking about? Druitt, Kosminski, Ostrog . . .?"

"As none of those characters are alive now, they can hardly be of interest to me," Holmes replied. "The fellow I wish to know about is a certain Arthur Bishopbourne."

Lestrade frowned. "That name doesn't ring a bell."

"You interviewed him personally, Lestrade. He was a young fellow, yet he managed a factory shop and trading office, Bishopbourne Copper & Gold, at 10 Commercial Street."

Briefly, Lestrade's eyes glazed over. He placed his beer on the table. "I think . . . now you mention it, I *do* recall that young chap. Not that he was a real suspect." He glanced round at us. "*Is* he a suspect?"

It was the same reaction I'd seen from Holmes himself, though somewhat less guarded: a hunter long ago denied his ultimate prize and then suddenly, in his twilight years, gaining a sniff of it again. How could he not be interested?

"We are seeking to establish this very fact," Holmes replied. "But first, tell me if you would, why you didn't consider him a viable suspect at the time?"

Lestrade shrugged. "He was young. Very young, in fact, while we had the Ripper down as an older bloke . . . someone who was experienced and cunning. Someone who could prowl that neighbourhood without being noticed, who could talk to the street-women without standing out."

"But Bishopbourne *did* talk to the street-women," Holmes said. "He regularly enjoyed their company."

"Well, that's what drew our attention to him. We interviewed him under the pretence we were just canvassing the neighbourhood. But in truth, it wasn't unusual for someone like him to visit the pubs and brothels. Whitechapel was a den of vice in those days. Plenty of toffs came down to join in the fun. Didn't make them murderers."

"Nothing else about Arthur Bishopbourne aroused your suspicions?" Holmes persisted.

Lestrade mused. Clearly, his memory of those events was restoring itself rapidly. "I wouldn't say *nothing*, Holmes."

"Go on . . .?"

"Bishopbourne was baby-faced, all right. But we've had baby-faced killers before. As you know, they're often the worst because you don't see them coming. Plus, there was something slightly *off* about him."

"Something *off*?"

"He was ill-at-ease to be spoken to. I told him it was merely because he had premises in the area. Had he seen or heard anything suspicious? But even then, he seemed jumpy."

"Why wasn't this followed up?" I wondered.

Lestrade shrugged again. "I considered it, but ultimately he matched none of the descriptions we had. No one who claimed to have seen the murderer in action talked about it being a top-hatted gentleman. On top of that . . . well, what I just said about baby-faces notwithstanding, I was never convinced he had what it took to be an actual murderer. It was plain that he was only nominally in charge of that company. Even in his private life he was coddled."

"Coddled?" I said.

"He'd come down from the North Country, as I recall. They're supposed to be tough as old boots up there, but he'd even brought a servant to look after him. Stern-looking woman, she was. Seems she'd been his governess when he was a child."

Neither Holmes nor I, well versed as we were in the stone-faced interview technique, were able to conceal our surprise at this revelation. Lestrade chuckled.

"That's correct, gentlemen. This bloke came to London to make his way in the world . . . and he still had his nursemaid with him. She cooked for him, shopped for him, cleaned . . . even tried to stop him going out at night, as I recall. No success there, though . . . if he went on the town with his workmates, what could she do? That bloke who ran the factory for him, Solomon . . .?"

"Solomon Ezer," Holmes said.

"That's right, Solomon Ezer. He didn't care for her. Had to ban her from the shop because she was even keeping Bishopbourne company during work hours. Strange arrangement. But, as I say, the bloke was so pampered. Couldn't picture him as Jack the Ripper then. Still can't now."

That was not Lestrade's final word on the matter, but it was his final word of value.

He rambled for another minute or so, but I quickly gauged from Holmes's increasingly brusque demeanour that nothing else useful was forthcoming. It was some time into our cab ride back to Baker Street before either of us spoke again.

"Lestrade couldn't be more wrong, could he?" I said. "We've both of us known maniacs who were excessively useless in normal life but became predators in the darkness."

"It's a familiar form of insanity, I agree," Holmes replied. "But the implications are even more alarming. I doubt Miss Abigail Simm would have referred to herself as a governess when Bishopbourne was eighteen years old, but her role would have been more or less the same."

"To keep an eye on him, you mean?"

"Again, almost certainly at the request of his father."

"That obviously vexed Solomon Ezer," I said.

Holmes pondered. "It may be that Miss Simm overstepped her mark. Clearly, Ezer considered himself to be in charge in Whitechapel, even if, overall, he was somewhat lax in that duty."

"But if all this is true . . . and both of them had a watching brief where Bishopbourne was concerned, that implies that this was one young man considered *highly* likely to go off the rails."

"Indeed."

"And yet, Holmes . . . that still doesn't prove he was, or could ever be, a murderer."

Holmes said nothing. I could tell that he was at least as undecided on the matter as I was. I could tell something else too – whereas before he'd merely been interested in the case, now he looked troubled by it as well. Deeply troubled. We returned to 221b within half an hour, to find that the second post of the day had delivered another letter from Lancashire.

"Open it, Watson," Holmes instructed. "Forthwith, if you please. Time may not be on our side."

8 March 1922

Dear Mr Holmes and Dr Watson,

So sorry about this. I had genuinely hoped that while all these clues I have so far gathered amount to no more than circumstantial evidence, we would shortly be uncovering something of real significance . . . a "smoking gun" as Dr Watson referred to it in the case of "The Gloria Scott".

But ultimately I have again been disappointed.

I did discover something interesting today, though it has done little more, in truth, than muddy the waters. As you know, I have long been convinced that answers to this puzzle may lie in one of those two locked rooms here at Trawden House. Today, an unexpected chance arose to investigate at least one of them, Miss Simm announcing that she would be out for some time this afternoon, as she was going down to Beardshaw to buy supplies. Ordinarily, that would be my task – usually, when there is heavy shopping or baggage to carry, it is down to me and me only – but today it seems she is making an exception. I asked no further questions because of the good opportunity this presented. It also meant, of course, that I would be alone in the house with Captain Bishopbourne. I wasn't totally happy with that. Whenever I meet him, he regards me with that same lascivious glint in his jaundiced eye. This unnerves me, but I'll be honest, it is rare I encounter the captain during the course of my working day, and as such, when the time came and Miss Simm departed for Beardshaw in the pony and trap, I was eager to get going.

Captain Bishopbourne's solar was obviously out of bounds – no sense in pushing my luck on that front. But the room off the cellar stairway was now mine to examine.

I returned immediately to the kitchen, only to find that all the keys had disappeared. Did Miss Simm suspect me? She must have hidden those keys for some reason. However, at this late stage I was not to be put off. Even the gloomiest and dingiest of the cellar rooms have high, grated windows, usually visible from the outside at the bottom of deep, leaf-filled recesses. But this room would not be as low down as they are, and if that too has a window, it should be much more easily accessible.

Thus, I began looking around the exterior of the house, mainly on its west side. As I have already described, the gardens here – particularly at this opposite end from the Mill Race – are very over-grown. It beggars belief that old Growther is kept on as gardener because he seems to make no difference. Quite a comfy old age he has for himself, if I'm honest – full lodgings, full pay and very little work. Makes me wonder if he knows something he shouldn't.

Anyway, the underbrush at that west side of the house is particu-larly dense and tangled. I battered my way through a mesh of twigs and thickets using the walking stick, but it still plucked at my clothing and scratched my face. I hadn't seen Captain Bishopbourne all day, but as I fought my way on, I glanced continually over my shoulder just to ensure I was still alone. At first, I neither heard nor saw anything to alarm me. But only a short while later, I thought I detected movement in the corner of my eye. When I looked harder, I saw nothing out there amid the twisted branches. But it was another grey day, and the whole coppice was dappled with deep shadow – so I held my ground, squinting to try and see better.

That was when I did spy something: a half-concealed figure about forty yards to my right.

Or did I?

Was it somebody keeping very still, or a simple illusion created by a mix of light and shadow?

Gentlemen, my heart almost skipped a beat. I kept a tight grip on that stick, but for a moment didn't know whether to go forward or back. The house was somewhere on my left, but I hadn't reached it yet. I hastened on, looking again over my shoulder, but now – where I'd thought there'd been a man, I saw nothing. Had the illusion vanished because I had changed position? I didn't waste time wondering, but traversed what remained of the undergrowth, now covered with moss and bark and bits of ragged leaf – only to suddenly hear what could have been the sound of pursuit after all: a rattle and crackling of boughs, a snapping of twigs under heavy feet. I peered back again, still seeing no one.

At last, I came up against the west wall of the house, and was able to move more freely. I kept it on my left side as I hurried forward, desperate to come to a window, but taken a little by surprise when I suddenly did. It was composed of three individual panes, but it was horizontal and lay at ground level, the upper part of its frame only reaching knee height.

Instinctively, I knew this was the window I'd been looking for, but again I held my ground, listening for further sounds of pursuit.

As before, it had gone quiet, and though I scanned the foliage, it was very still. For the first time now, it occurred to me that I might have put myself in dire peril. If Captain Bishopbourne had been waiting for Miss Simm to depart so that he might attack me, how much easier had I made it for him by ensconcing myself in the most remote and hidden corner of the grounds? Even the window to the locked cellar room would be little use in this regard. There'd be no further avenue of escape should someone chase me inside there. All that said, now that I had discovered the object of my interest, it would be sheer folly not to at least investigate further.

Regardless of whatever might be happening in the brush behind me – though I kept my ear cocked, I can tell you that – I dropped to my knees and felt my way around the edges of the panes. They were thick with grime and other forest muck, but also very old and rickety. I managed to fit my fingers into a few gaps, and prised them apart further. At last, the middle pane of the three creaked open. It wasn't particularly ladylike of me, but I got down on all fours to waddle my way backwards through the gap. There was a drop on the other side, but only about six feet or so. I had done it, gentlemen; I had entered the locked room that had eluded me all this time.

And what a spectacle met my eyes.

Clearly it had once been a lady's boudoir. There was plush furniture, there were wall hangings and a fireplace. But much of this was in a poor state, covered in dust and mildew, the fireplace cluttered with soot and feathers. Cobwebs so thick and dirty they were more like rotted drapery extended from wall to wall. But the strangest thing were the photographs.

That is correct, gentlemen. Framed photographs adorned every flat surface: the shelves, the mantel, the bureau. And, stranger still, they were all of the same person: Captain Bishopbourne in various stages of his life – from being a baby in his nursery cot and then a boy at school, until his days as a dapper young business-gentleman, and then as a not-quite-so-young commissioned officer in the army.

I've never seen as many pictures of a single person in one place.

At which point I had the shock of my life.

"Lord bless me, girl!" a gruff voice broke in. "What're you doing in here?"

I spun around, and there was old Growther in the open window. Not only that, he was pointing a shotgun through it at me.

"Lord bless me!" he said again.

"Are you going to shoot me, Mr Growther?" I demanded to know.

"I'm sorry, girl, I fancied I heard someone mooching around the house. We do occasionally get vagabonds in this neighbourhood."

"Was that you . . . who followed me through the woods?"

"I thought you might be a burglar," he said. "But what are you doing in here?"

I tried to sound as innocent as I could. "This is the one room I can't get inside to clean."

"You aren't supposed to be in here. So just get yourself out right now." He wasn't angry. If anything, he seemed concerned. "Thank your lucky stars it's me who found you, and not Captain Bishopbourne. He wouldn't want anyone intruding in his mother's old parlour."

That was one mystery solved then. This subterranean room was once the private quarters of the late Lady Bishopbourne. No wonder there were pictures of her boy everywhere. If I'd been a little more keen-eyed, I'd have realised that before Growther found me, because just before I climbed out again, I spotted a calendar on the wall, on which all the dates had been crossed off right up until that tragic day, 20 June 1919.

Still looking to try and gain something from my ill-fated expedition, I tried to engage Growther in conversation as we made our way back around to the front of the house.

"Does Captain Bishopbourne have a wicked temper too?" I asked.

Growther didn't look at me, just grunted: "Best keep away from him is all I'd say."

"He seems pleasant enough," I persisted.

"Don't they always."

That comment certainly set me wondering. "Mr Growther, what—?"

"Miss Letty, you're a young girl!" he interrupted. "And very naïve, no doubt. So just you keep away from him."

And that is all he would say on the matter.

Anyway, that is my latest epistle, gentlemen. I am sorry we are none the wiser, but Miss Simm will be back shortly and I have chores to perform. Tonight, we have a guest. Every Friday evening, the old business partner and sometime estate manager, Henry Smallwood-Smythe, attends the house, where he joins Captain Bishopbourne for dinner, brandy and cigars and a game of cards. Apparently it is a custom neither of the gentlemen ever misses. I will be sure to write to you again in due course if anything more interesting crops up, but at present I have few other lines of enquiry.

Your good friend,
Letty Feltencraft

By the time I put the letter down, Holmes was standing by the window. Even now, at our age, he was a tall, lean figure, an impression enhanced by his tight grey suit and close-fitting cloth cap. On this occasion, his posture was distinctly rigid.

"Watson . . . how quickly can you put a bag together?"

"Are we going somewhere?" I asked.

"Indeed we are. We're going north."

"When?"

"This very night."

We travelled north via the London-to-Scotland sleeper service, but neither of us really slept. For much of the journey, I ploughed through the various notes and writings we'd now accrued in reference to the original Whitechapel investigation. There seemed no end to the theories and counter-theories, so it was a torturous exercise. Holmes remained deep in thought, barely responding when I passed comment. Only once did he pick up any kind of book to read, and this, to my bewilderment, was a copy of last year's diary. He didn't ponder it for long; merely flipped a few pages, checked a single detail inside, and reinserted it into his travelling cape, his pensive frown fixed in place. When I finally attempted to engage him in a proper conversation, he only replied distractedly.

"We have a problem here, Holmes." I tapped a finger on one of the original police surgeon's statements. "According to this, because of the direction of knife-strokes across the victims' throats and because of the manner in which the poor women were manually strangled before the blade came into play, there is a strong suspicion that Jack the Ripper was left-handed."

"I have heard that, yes."

"Don't you see? Arthur Bishopbourne cannot be a suspect. His left hand is useless."

"His left hand was rendered useless during the War, Watson. The Whitechapel Murders occurred before the War."

"I'm talking about the murder of Valerie Blye . . . last Christmas Eve."

Holmes remained distant. "Do the police reports in that case also express a belief the killer was left-handed? If so, I must have missed it. No . . . the unfortunate Valerie Blye was simply stabbed until she died. Over and over again. There was no technique, Watson. No finesse."

"Even so, could any man carry out such a crime – thirty-nine puncture wounds to the poor woman's body! – when he only has one hand available?"

"I fear so, if the victim is taken by surprise and the first blow is deep enough to penetrate the vital organs."

"The victim drops to the ground immediately, you mean?"

"At which point he is able to stab her again and again . . . at his leisure."

It evoked a horrible image in my mind. If there was any mercy to be found in the original Whitechapel slayings, it was that, for matters of expediency, the assailant either killed or knocked his victims unconscious before slicing them open. One could only pray that, somehow or other, the same swift death had come to Valerie Blye.

"Good Lord, Holmes . . ." It was strange how only now the full and dreadful import of this case was dawning on me. "If all this is real, we are tracking a genuine monster here . . ."

"The monster of the age, Watson. The monster of the age."

These were dramatic terms for Holmes to speak in, and though he delivered them without emotion, I could tell that he was agitated. From this point on, he glanced repeatedly at his watch. By mid-morning, when we arrived at Preston in central Lancashire, and waited on the platform for our connection to the east of the county, he strode about as if in a state of growing anxiety. This was not his normal manner, and so it affected me too. But it was mid-afternoon before we finally arrived at Beardshaw Halt, by which time I was deeply fatigued. As I say, we'd barely slept overnight, and at my age that often translates into stiff joints and aching limbs.

Needless to say, Holmes was in no such condition. He led the way out of the small country railway station at speed. We found the tiny village all but deserted. It was much as Miss Feltencraft had described it, comprising a small green encircled by stone cottages, with The Roundhead's Rest at one end, and at the other just two shops: a greengrocer and a pharmacist.

Holmes assessed the shops, chewed his lip concernedly, and went back inside the railway station. The counter clerk endeavoured to help, but was only able to tell us that there was no cab service here and no omnibus. He added that we might be able to persuade a local man to take us to Trawden House in his cart, but that at present the majority would be out lambing. Holmes decided that we had no time to knock on doors and hope to get lucky. Once the clerk had pointed us in the right direction, a narrow lane heading north from the village, we set off walking.

Holmes strode ahead and, as we'd been instructed, after about a mile veered off the road.

Everything Miss Feltencraft had written about the region was true. It was much colder up here than in London, bare hills ranged along the grey March sky, in several cases capped with snow. We trudged over meadow and pasture, most of it boggy and covered with bracken. We had also to cross ditches, which invariably were flooded, and dry-stone walls, which proved no less problematic. Only after a couple of hours did we enter the so-called Plantations. From here, we quite literally had to hack and chop our way through a jungle of naked, interwoven thickets.

"Is this really the shortest route to Trawden House?" I panted.

"Only in terms of mileage, I'd imagine," Holmes replied.

But not long after that we emerged into open space on the edge of a small, neatly furrowed vegetable garden. This was attached to a building that looked as if it had once been a fortified house. It possessed two storeys and covered no more than forty yards square, but it was built from grey granite and battlemented around its eaves. Alongside it ran a roadway of beaten earth, presumably the driveway leading up to the main property.

As we stood gasping for breath and brushing off scraps of vegetation, the latch on the house's side door lifted, and an elderly man came out wearing a weathered coat, fingerless gloves and a long, ragged scarf. He was middle-aged but heavily built, balding on top, with podgy cheeks and an immense walrus moustache. Somehow, it all combined to render him puffed-up and ludicrous. Had I not been so out of breath, I'd have chuckled at the sight.

"I hope you have good reason to be here, gentlemen," the man said sternly.

Despite his current status, his voice betrayed upper- or middle-class origins.

"I hope so too," Holmes replied, approaching around the edge of the vegetable patch. "Whom do I have the honour of addressing?"

Our host straightened up a little. "My name is Smallwood-Smythe. I am—"

"The estate manager here," Holmes said. "At least nominally. You, in return, are addressing Sherlock Holmes and Dr John Watson."

Smallwood-Smythe's plump cheeks visibly paled. Briefly, his mouth sagged open. "Gentlemen . . . you had only to—"

"We just *have* said," Holmes interrupted him.

"Erm, yes . . . of course. Would you care to come inside? Perhaps take a hot mint tea?"

As well as the chill in the air, my clothing was damp with sweat, so my extremities were turning numb. As such, I was minded to say "yes", but as usual Holmes answered for us both.

"We have no time, alas. But Mr Smallwood-Smythe . . . I have a question for you."

Smallwood-Smythe looked distinctly nervous. "You have a question . . . for *me*?"

"By answering truthfully you will not implicate yourself in any criminal enterprise, I assure you. Lying to us, on the other hand, could have a very serious outcome. I need to know about these Friday evening dinner engagements of yours with Arthur Bishopbourne."

The estate manager's eyes bulged and his cheeks coloured, as though he couldn't quite fathom how he'd simply stepped from his front door, only to be confronted by the legendary Sherlock Holmes in a none-too-conciliatory mood. He gazed searchingly at Holmes and then at me, though I was unable to help him. The question had taken me by surprise as well.

"It's an old arrangement that began with Sir Randolph," he finally explained. "Friday was always the evening when dinner was held at Trawden House. Guests came from far and wide, though, gradually, as circumstances changed, there were fewer of these. Eventually there was just me. Sir Randolph having now passed on, his son maintains the tradition."

"This is every Friday, is it?" Holmes enquired.

"It is, Mr Holmes. Without fail."

"And if for any reason you must miss the engagement . . .?"

Smallwood-Smythe stiffened again, as though this was a matter of pride for him. "I never have. Not once."

"Not even on Friday 24 December last year?" Holmes asked. "Christmas Eve?"

Immediately, I realised why he'd been reading his old diary on the train.

Smallwood-Smythe looked affronted by the mere suggestion. "I have never rejected an invitation to dine at Trawden House, not even last Christmas Eve."

"And Captain Bishopbourne was present on this occasion?" I asked. "He didn't at any stage that evening leave you alone?"

Smallwood-Smythe looked bewildered.

"Answer truthfully," Holmes urged him. "Only the truth will serve you well here."

"He was . . ." Smallwood-Smythe lifted his shoulders, as if this whole thing was too ridiculous. "Arthur was in my company all evening, gentlemen . . . all evening."

"How long did the evening last?" Holmes's expression remained inscrutable, despite the disappointment I imagined he must have felt at this response.

"From seven until close to midnight," Smallwood-Smythe said. "You look doubtful, Mr Holmes. I assure you this is correct. I recall that evening *particularly* well . . . Arthur made rather a mess."

"Explain that, if you would," Holmes said.

"Well, his arm is withered due to a wound he received at Arras. This gave him great difficulty serving the soup."

Holmes's reaction to this was astounding; even I was taken by complete surprise.

Without another word, he lurched away from us to the drive and walked quickly in the direction that I presumed led up to the house. I hastily apologised to the startled estate manager, and scrambled in pursuit.

"Holmes, wait!" I said, breathless. "Aren't we wrong about this . . . terribly wrong?"

"I *was* wrong, I admit," Holmes replied, walking fast. "At first. But only yesterday Miss Feltencraft provided us with vital new information, and now Smallwood-Smythe has confirmed it."

I hurried alongside him. "But Arthur Bishopbourne cannot have murdered Valerie Blye!"

"You conclude that because Bishopbourne hosted dinner, this means our prime suspect was present here for the whole duration of that fateful Christmas Eve?"

"We've just been told that he was. Seven until midnight, whereas Valerie Blye died between nine and eleven. And it's not as if Bishopbourne could simply have slipped away when his guest was not looking. The town of Colne is five miles distant. In any case, Smallwood-Smythe said that Bishopbourne had difficulty serving the soup . . . which indicates that he is not just hampered by his crippled arm, but *very* incapacitated."

"You miss the most important thing it indicates, Watson," Holmes replied. "Not so much about who *was* here last Christmas Eve, but who *wasn't*."

"I don't follow."

"Why would Bishopbourne be serving his guest at all? He is the master of this house."

"And? Miss Simm is the housekeeper, so she . . . Good Lord!"

"Exactly, Watson. And yet that railway ticket had been punched, had it not? So *someone* from these premises took a journey to Colne that night."

"You can't . . . you can't mean *Miss Simm*?" The mere thought of this staggered me.

"The same Miss Simm who was present in Whitechapel during Jack the Ripper's depredations," he added.

"But Holmes . . . *Miss Simm!*"

"On this basis, Watson, so much falls tragically into place. There were more police officers on duty in Whitechapel during that long autumn of 1888 than anywhere else in London. They stood on every corner, skulked in every alley. It's a miracle they did not catch Jack the Ripper by accident, let alone design. Each man they saw they stopped and questioned. Each *man*, Watson . . . does that not explain a great deal?"

"But Miss Simm is respectable. A governess, a housekeeper . . ."

"It would not be unheard-of for a demented person, no matter how respectable on the outside, male or female, to resent with homicidal rage the affections a loved one shows to others."

"You're saying Miss Simm was jealous of Bishopbourne's relations with ladies of the night?"

"Did she not watch him constantly when he lived in Whitechapel? Did she not try to cosset him? So much so that his own clerk had to ban her from the office?"

"We've already seen that Ezer was lax in his care," I argued. "He believed men should be men, and as such he and she had an altercation. That is all."

"That altercation itself may have had consequences." Holmes glanced sidelong at me. "A Jewish man defies her, and the next thing we know, a message has appeared near a fresh corpse, directing the police to the Jews."

As I pondered this, it made an outrageous kind of sense, but still I tried to shake it from my mind. "Miss Simm, as a former governess, would be well educated, Holmes, and that message was misspelled and well-nigh incomprehensible."

"It would not be the first time a clever felon has employed misdirection, Watson."

"No . . . no!" I stammered. "It just won't do. We are talking mass murder!"

"Correct, Watson. Mass murder of a most foul and comprehensive type . . . the victims' very gender was removed, their femininity annihilated. Did that not send out a clear message?"

"But Holmes, it's preposterous! Miss Simm is merely a servant. Why would she feel so insanely jealous . . .?"

"Is she *merely* a servant, Watson? Are you sure? Consider the curious room in the cellar."

"Lady Bishopbourne had mental health problems. It's hardly curious that she decked her old parlour with photographs of her son."

"What is curious, Watson, is that Lady Bishopbourne, the mistress of the house, had her parlour on the subterranean level at all."

I could not deny this, though it was something I had not previously considered.

"Did we not also learn that Miss Simm's top-floor apartment was unusually grand for that of a serving woman?" Holmes said.

"You're saying the top-floor rooms originally belonged to Lady Bishopbourne, and the subterranean parlour was Miss Simm's?"

"Doesn't it stand to reason? Proof positive came in the form of the subterranean calendar Miss Feltencraft referenced in her final letter. Its days had been marked off up until June the twentieth 1919. Yet Lady Clara Bishopbourne died on the fourteenth of June. The eagle-eyed Miss Feltencraft noted this herself the first time around, though she overlooked it the second time."

"So Miss Simm waited a few days before—"

"Before moving upstairs and taking charge of the household, yes."

"But old Growther said that underground room belonged to Arthur Bishopbourne's mother . . . *great heavens!*"

Holmes looked disappointed in me. "Did the photographs not tell you that already, Watson? Arthur Bishopbourne is Miss Simm's son."

I was stunned, and yet again it made sense in a terrible, twisted kind of way. "Holmes, how is all this possible?"

"Sir Randolph was a man of gross appetite. Why wouldn't it extend to the servant girls, especially the beautiful young governess?"

"But how could Lady Bishopbourne have tolerated having her

husband's mistress on the premises, not to mention spending every hour with her husband's illegitimate child?"

"You've already pointed out Lady Bishopbourne's mental weakness, Watson. Was she even aware of these sad events?"

"If this is true, it would certainly explain Miss Simm's overprotective attitude . . ."

"Perhaps, as one who had suffered at the hands of the older Bishopbourne, she was determined their son would not follow in the same path. Obsessively so – to the point where, if she could not prevent these sinful dalliances, she would punish them afterwards."

"The deuce!"

"An approach I now fear she will apply to our brave Miss Feltencraft."

I tried to tell myself there was no danger of this. "Miss Feltencraft is a chambermaid, Holmes, hardly a woman of the night."

"Do the disturbed make such distinctions?"

"But Miss Simm kept watch on the girl's behalf. When she feared Bishopbourne was prowling, she came out to defend her."

"Or to defend Bishopbourne, Watson . . . from the evil temptress who will lead him to sin. She adores her son to the point where she sees no wrong in him. She *must*. Allowing him to wallow in a world of indolence and waste, her only reprimand a wall of feigned indifference – which he is quite happy to return."

A small structure emerged on the side of the drive: a wooden shed with a tarpaper roof. It nestled amid a clutch of leafless apple trees, but a wavering, red glow filtered from its grime-encrusted window.

"Growther lives on the edge of the orchard, does he not?" Holmes said, diverting over there.

We banged on the shed's door. When there was no response, we opened it. A musty, cramped interior, reeking of soil, grass cuttings and human sweat, greeted us. Norbert Growther – it could only be Growther, given his heavy boots, rugged, mud-spattered apparel, and the hanks of scruffy whiskers on either side of his wizened face

– slumped lifelessly amongst a clutter of outdoor oddments: rakes, hoes, sacks of seed and the like. Set on the small table in front of him was a half-eaten meal, a fragment of pie and a crust of bread. But several empty beer bottles lay at his feet, and his head rested on a shelf next to a flickering oil lamp.

Holmes shook him violently. The gardener stirred and murmured, but he did not wake.

"Drunk to the world at this hour," I observed. "Little wonder the Bishopbourne empire has crumbled if they keep employees of this quality."

"He knows about Arthur Bishopbourne's habits," Holmes replied, scanning the squalid little room. "They have no option but to keep him."

"What are you looking for?"

"Growther owns a shotgun, does he not?"

"I don't see it here."

"Nor I."

"I have my revolver."

"For the time being that must suffice." Holmes darted out and thrust his way onward through the trees. "Hurry, Watson. Pray that the murderer this time went about her scheme in slow and methodical fashion, and that we are not already too late."

I stumbled after him, tripping on roots. "Won't it be quicker to go via the driveway?"

"The driveway will take us to the front door," he replied. "And I rather fancy no one will answer the front door. Not this evening."

A few moments later, the main house emerged in front of us. A great rambling structure it was, scowling down through the gloom. It was built mainly from Georgian-era brick, but with minimal artifice or decoration. Much of it stood in darkness, but we hurried westward along the side path, finally closing in on a tiny light. It brought us to a purpose-built annexe, a Victorian conservatory – a cast-iron structure fitted with miniature panes of glass, several of which had cracked

– jutting out into the thorny chaos of the rear garden. The light emanated from a window alongside it, in the wall of the main building.

I recalled Miss Feltencraft writing that Bishopbourne's solar was located in this area.

When we glanced through the window, the room was exactly as she had described it: a once-elegant chamber now gone to seed. There was dust a-plenty – on the casements, the shelves, and on the mantel over the fireplace, where a few meagre flames guttered. Arthur Bishopbourne was also present, and he too matched his description. He wore evening dress, but it was crumpled and dishevelled. In addition, he was slumped in a wingback armchair, his head tilted on one side, a mop of lank, greasy hair hanging to his shoulder. As with Growther, a tray of food sat in front of him, with an empty wine bottle alongside it. When Holmes rapped on the glass, there was no response.

"Bishopbourne!" he shouted. "Wake up, man!"

The motionless figure did not even stir.

"Another one lying in a drunken stupor . . . and at this early hour," I said, disgusted.

"I doubt it, Watson," Holmes replied. "One of them maybe. But not two."

"Either way . . . we're at the rear of the property. There should be a tradesman's entrance."

"No time for that, I'm afraid. Stand back, if you please."

Holmes crossed the path, searching quickly through the bracken and hefting a heavy stone.

"Holmes!" I protested.

He ignored me, heaving it at the solar window, which exploded inward, its diamond panes collapsing in a heap of jangling shards. Still there was no movement from the armchair.

"Bustle, Watson!" Holmes shouted as he clambered through.

I followed him inside, only to stop briefly in my tracks at the sight of a colossal oil painting above the fireplace. It depicted a towering male figure: square-jawed, heavy-browed, thickly moustached, wearing a fur-collared overcoat and a bowler hat, with a King Edward cigar between his leather-gloved fingers, and what looked to be a turbulent night sky behind him, lit red, orange and purple by a sprawl of foundries and factory chimneys.

Randolph Bishopbourne, no doubt: merchant, businessman, self-made millionaire and inveterate womaniser; perhaps the agent of all this misfortune.

Holmes, now alongside the chair, urgently beckoned to me. I scrambled over there and checked the younger Bishopbourne's pulse. He was alive but unconscious. I leaned down to smell his breath, immediately detecting a familiar bitter scent.

"Laudanum," I said. "He's an addict, of course . . . or so we're told."

"Was Growther an addict too?" Holmes wondered. "Perhaps we should check the food?"

I lifted the plate and sniffed at the fragments of sandwiches and cold beef. Again, it was unmistakable – laudanum.

"Drugged deliberately," I said.

"Of course." Holmes edged towards the inner door. "As was Growther. Because tonight there must be no interruptions. I suspected something like this when Miss Feltencraft advised us that very soon after their encounter in the kitchen – in other words, when Miss Simm's worst fears about her new employee were seemingly confirmed, namely that she was a night-time hussy – she elected to travel to Beardshaw herself. As she always sent her junior to collect the groceries, it stood to reason that this mission was to acquire something else." He glanced around at me. "And the only other shop in the village is a pharmacy."

In response to this, I drew my revolver and cocked it – only for a distant, muffled cry to echo down from the upper reaches of the house. Hurriedly, Holmes yanked the door open. Only darkness lay beyond. We listened intently.

"If Miss Simm is the killer," I whispered, "why did she not take similar precautions with her previous victims?"

"Because even if Miss Simm is insane," Holmes whispered back, "she is no fool. Her predatory instinct almost overtook her in Colne – Valerie Blye's corpse was not mutilated, but the murderess came very close. Even so, when the blood had cooled afterwards, she must have realised that it might conceivably be linked to the Whitechapel Murders of so long ago – as indeed it was – and that if she made the same mistake here, in this very house, it would take considerably less than a sharp-eyed pre-graduate from the School for Detection to become suspicious. No, on this occasion, I fear the victim must simply disappear, along with her baggage – just another of these flighty chambermaids who come and go as they please."

Another muffled cry sounded, though now it was more of a shriek.

"That does not mean to say – " Holmes lurched into the darkness – "that the method of her dispatch would not be the same as the others. *Quickly, Watson!*"

We progressed through various rooms and passages, now so dark that our eyes attuned with painful slowness. I detected rotting boards and threadbare carpets, decayed wainscoting on the walls. Here and there, a lamp fitting dangled cobwebs. It was such a complex path that we took to the bottom of the main staircase that I doubt I could have found my way back easily. From here, the treads rose steeply into blackness, a rickety banister positioned on the left.

Overhead, all had gone quiet again.

We ascended with as much stealth and caution as we could manage – but were no more than halfway up when a female figure ghosted into view above.

Despite the oil lantern she carried, almost the entirety of her tall, thin body was blotted out by her jet-black garb, which seemed to consist of a hooded gown with a huge shawl over the top. Such attire had served her well when prowling this house in pursuit of Miss Feltencraft, of course; perhaps even when stalking her other victims – it would have hidden her nicely in the Whitechapel fog.

We gazed up as, slowly and purposely, she placed the lantern at her feet. Her face was framed between straggling tresses of ash-grey hair, though in the under-glow of the lamp it was wizened and hatchet-like, and white as alabaster, which was in sharp contrast to the blood-red gleam of her lips, the glassy green glint of her eyes. Her long, pale forearms slid into view as she raised a double-barrelled shotgun and aimed it down the stairwell at us.

"Miss Simm, I presume?" Holmes said, talking very quickly. "Allow me to introduce ourselves. My name is Sherlock Holmes. This is my friend, Dr Watson. Another friend of mine is Miss Leticia Feltencraft. We are here to reclaim her from you."

Miss Simm's face registered no emotion at all – until it abruptly split into a demonic, V-shaped grin. As she lifted the shotgun to her shoulder, I pointed my revolver.

"Too late for that, Watson!" Holmes clutched my collar and drove both our bodies sideways at the banister, which collapsed beneath our combined weight.

It was a six-foot drop into the passage below, but it was worth it to evade the barrel-load of shot that Miss Simm now blasted at us, tearing away the remaining spindles like matchwood.

Swiftly and silently, she descended. Once in sight, she took aim again.

"Madam, I too am armed!" I shouted up at her, though I was badly winded from the fall and had struggled to regain my feet.

"There'll be no sauciness here!" she said in a voice of strict reprimand – as though we were children. To this day, I feel certain that Miss Simm did not really see us for who we actually were, or was even vaguely concerned about that. We were a threat. This was all that mattered.

Holmes dragged me aside and we burst through a doorway – as another hail of shot struck the corridor, splinters flying every which way. We found ourselves in a half-curtained room filled with shafting moonlight. Outside, meanwhile, light feet descended the rest of the stairway. With a *clunk*, the firearm was broken open.

With eyes fixed on the open door in front of us, we retreated side by side – until we bumped into a dining table, which rattled as though loaded with crockery. Urgently, we tried to circumnavigate around it, but as we did the shadowy shape of Miss Simm appeared in the doorway. Again she fired, wildly, blindly. Fleetingly, the detonation lit the room: panels on the walls, dusty paintings, a table laden with dinnerware, which flew into fragments.

Thankfully, Holmes had seen something else: another door, directly behind us.

He opened it and hauled me through into a dim corridor. Some twenty yards on our right, we spied a wedge of red firelight. Holmes strode swiftly in that direction.

"This is a God-fearing house," came Miss Simm's flinty voice from the room behind.

"Yes, madam, you set a fine example," Holmes called over his shoulder. "Following Master Arthur everywhere he goes, putting his wrongs right in the cruellest way possible."

"He is his father's son! There is only so much one can do!"

Holmes pushed open the next door, and bundled me back into the familiar fire-lit environs of Bishopbourne's solar. I hadn't expected this. I was completely lost in the darkened geography of this awful house. Holmes meanwhile, shoved me violently to one side and hurled himself the other way – just as the shotgun roared a fourth time. Shot rained through the open door, smashing a low table and the crystal decanter on top of it to smithereens.

Bishopbourne still lay senseless in his wingback chair, but Holmes now darted over there, positioned himself behind it and indicated I should do the same.

"A human shield?" I said, appalled.

"All this is for the good of her son," he replied. "She won't risk a single shot."

It was a well-judged decision. I did as Holmes said, and when our tormentor emerged through the smoke-filled doorframe, she tottered to a halt, eyes slitted. I levelled my revolver at her.

"I have you dead-on, madam. Don't force me to shoot."

For several long seconds she regarded us, her thin features pale as ice, her crimson mouth crooked, as though half in frown and half in smile. And then, in a swirl of skirts, she withdrew.

Holmes dashed across the room after her.

"Holmes, wait!" I shouted. "Ambush."

"I think not, Watson. The woman knows she is finished. She seeks now to complete her devilish work before it's too late!"

We blundered again through the maze of passages. At any time I expected to round a corner and find the madwoman waiting. Even when we located the stair and hastened up it, slipping and stumbling on shattered woodwork, it struck me that if she were to reappear now we'd be easy targets. But renewed shrieks from overhead, which I suddenly felt sure came from Miss Simm herself, seemed to emanate from a more distant reach of the house.

At the top of the stair, Holmes turned sharp left. I tottered after him down a long, straight corridor, which dwindled to what looked like a stained-glass window at the far end of the house. More shrieks sounded from directly in front of us.

As the tall window neared, I saw that it ran more or less from floor to ceiling. Glacial moonlight shimmered through it, illuminating its imagery: in the background green Lancashire hills but also factory chimneys with smoke furling; in the foreground Randolph Bishopbourne again, this time flat-capped and wearing tweeds – at which point two silhouetted shapes flitted past the window from right to left, one evidently in the grasp of the other.

"Miss Simm . . . *desist!*" Holmes shouted, his voice a whip-crack. "*This folly must end!*"

Rather to my surprise, the two shapes came to a standstill. Despite one of them clearly being a hostage, there was no obvious struggle. I was puzzled by this. Miss Feltencraft, as a sturdy young woman, ought to have been able to overpower a septuagenarian like Abigail Simm. But they now backed into the moonlight near the window, and I saw the truth of it. Miss Feltencraft, who was wearing a nightgown, had her hands bound in front of her and was gagged, a great mass of cloth stuffed into her mouth and held there by a strip of material, while Miss Simm, who had discarded the shotgun so that it lay near a skirting board, had drawn a short, thin blade and held it point-first at her captive's throat. The deranged woman's features were fixed in icy stone, her chin tilted upright. She was a haughty one. Even as we advanced, my revolver trained squarely on her breast, she stood clearly in view – which in itself was disconcerting. Miss Feltencraft moaned something through her gag, but it was inaudible. We halted ten yards short; at such close range I felt sure a bullet would be faster than Miss Simm's hand. But now Holmes wanted to talk.

"I understand your pain, Miss Simm," he said in a low, even tone. "You bring a child into the world with all the agony that involves, and suddenly he is taken from you. You are permitted to raise that child, of course, but not in the role of mother."

"It was the perfect solution," she replied in a voice of casual disdain, as though it was no surprise to her that we completely misunderstood this situation. "Everything Sir Randolph decided was to the good."

"I imagine you told yourself that many times as you loyally sat in your corner," Holmes replied. "Darning socks, reading a book maybe . . . but covertly watching while your son cavorted at your mistress's knee."

I saw a tremor in Miss Simm's lip, but her knife-hand remained steady.

"A mistress so hare-brained that most of the time she scarcely knew where she was," Holmes added. "I expect the care you provided – as Arthur's wet nurse, nanny, governess, skivvy – was little consolation when the boy knew you only in that role. When he neither felt nor showed a hint of love or affection towards you."

"What hope did he have of understanding the real world?" she blurted. "His father always gallivanting. His so-called mother twittering away to herself . . ."

"And so you sought to exert a positive influence . . ."

"With limited success." Her mouth quivered again, her eyes now shining with tears. "He was always a strange one. Distant, idle . . . with an unhealthy interest in the serving girls. You heard about his school?"

"We did, alas."

"I tried to discipline that coarseness out of him. But discipline ends when boys become men."

"So instead you disciplined those others."

"Before the War, he visited Colne," she said. "Regularly. A dirty, dissolute place. It pained me to permit it, but what else could I do . . . so close to home. Too close to take any real action. But then the War came, and though Arthur had no intention to serve, I cajoled him, thinking it would mature him. His father was old by this time, dying, riddled with diseases of the flesh, unable to manage his affairs – but his greatest horror was that his son would come to nothing. So he too persuaded Arthur to serve, certain that as an older enlistee he would never see battle. But after 1916, with so many officers dead, even the senior men were called to the front. And yet, against all expectations, Arthur excelled himself." The tears ran freely down her cheeks. "He became the man I always knew he could be . . ."

"He gave much for his country," Holmes said. "We understand that. But then he came back broken, did he not? In mind *and* body. And as such he returned too readily to his old degenerate ways. In fact, it was worse this time than before. That wasn't the future you'd envisaged for him, was it, Miss Simm? – when last Christmas Eve, while your son was more innocently engaged in entertaining Henry Smallwood-Smythe, you travelled to Colne yourself."

"I could avoid it no longer!" she snapped. "My Arthur should have been a hero, Mr Holmes! The lauded man who would restore the Trawden estate and the Bishopbourne name. Instead, what was he . . . a brute, a beast of the field!"

"And a regular client of Valerie Blye's?" I asked her. "Or was it a case that anyone would do as long as the warning was sent?"

She turned her icy stare at me. "What does it matter, Dr Watson?"

"It matters, madam, because it might be the difference between a hospital and the gallows."

"Miss Simm . . . surely you can see this has ended?" Holmes said. "Not in the way you wished it to, but in truth it could never have ended that way, could it?"

"I only wanted the best for Arthur. I'd have done anything to prevent him becoming a replica of his terrible father."

"Everyone will sympathise with that. Now please put the knife down."

Though her gaze remained riveted on Holmes's face, she slowly lowered the blade. And when he advanced a few steps, offering his palm, she delicately laid it on the flat of his glove.

Relieved, I uncocked my revolver.

Miss Feltencraft promptly struggled free, roaring beneath her gag. She continued in this vein as Holmes led her aside and used the small knife to saw at the bonds on her wrists – only to stop, fleetingly puzzled. He inspected the blade more closely.

"This is nothing. I doubt this could butcher a mouse . . ."

Miss Feltencraft was now able to wrench her hands free, and so yanked the gag from her lips. *"That's because she has another!"*

I spun back to face the suspect, but it was too late. She had drawn a second knife from under her gown, and this was a monstrous thing: ten inches in length, made from thick steel, yet curved like a dagger and honed to glittering sharpness. Even as I turned, she swept it down at my gun-arm, slicing the sleeves of my coat, jacket and shirt, and the flesh underneath. I shouted hoarsely as the pistol dropped from my hand. Miss Simm thrust me aside and rounded on Holmes, raising the steel on high. He backed off, attempting to push Miss Feltencraft to safety, only to see her fall to the floor. But the murderess had lost interest in her former victim. She closed in on Holmes, grinning dementedly, eyes like green embers.

He backed to the wall. But there was nowhere else to go from there. When those blows fell, they would skewer him like a pig, then hack, cut, slash . . . And with a cataclysmic *BOOM!*, the shotgun was discharged from the floor, where the prone Miss Feltencraft had retrieved it.

Miss Simm was blown backwards into the stained-glass window, which exploded outward.

All of this happened in front of me, but briefly I was so concerned by the blood throbbing from my wound that it barely registered. Frantic, I shrugged my overcoat off and wrapped it around my arm as tightly as I was able. Holmes lurched forward to assist, stripping off his tie to bind the dressing in place. Only after several rather desperate moments did we turn to the casement. The ornate pane was completely gone, the hill-country wind streaming in on us.

Miss Feltencraft leaned to one side of it, the shotgun still in her grasp but tilted to the floor, smoke seeping from its muzzle. She shook her head weakly as she regarded us.

"I . . . I had to . . ." she stammered.

"Of course you did," Holmes replied.

We reached the casement and peered down at the plunge-pool far below. The moonlight illuminated a vague, dark form, very ragged and tattered, driven this way and that by the crazed current, but finally sliding sideways over a lip of rock and dropping out of sight down the gully to the caves.

"Mr Holmes, I . . ." Miss Feltencraft tried to speak again. Only now did I note how ashen she was.

"Are you injured, Miss Feltencraft?" I asked her.

"No, I . . ." She made an effort to straighten up. "Miss Simm drugged my food. I'd eaten half of it before I detected the scent. She was still able to overpower me—"

"Where does this thing come out again?" Holmes interrupted.

"Anyone's guess, Mr Holmes," Miss Feltencraft replied. "I've heard there's a whole labyrinth of tunnels and underground rivers."

I sighed as I imagined the difficult conversation we were due to have with the local constabulary. "And I thought that once we became teachers we were done with complex matters like this?"

"There's never been any case as complex as the Whitechapel Murders," Holmes responded.

"Well . . ." I tried to sound stoic, though my arm was hurting terribly and I was feeling weak from blood-loss. "At least that's *one* famous mystery laid to rest."

"You think so, Watson?" He turned to look at me in that determinedly detached way he always affected when matters weren't quite as he wished them. "Even in the unlikely event we manage to retrieve Miss Simm's body, or even just her knife . . . how will we prove it?"

"With our testimonies," I replied. "All three of us heard the woman admit to murder."

"That was the murder of Valerie Blye, in Colne, Lancashire," Holmes said. "Miss Simm made no reference to the deaths of the Whitechapel prostitutes."

"*Mr Holmes!*" Miss Feltencraft protested.

"Miss Feltencraft, your work has been exemplary," he told her. "You will in due course become a very fine detective. But at no stage did your chief suspect admit or imply that she was responsible for Jack the Ripper's crimes."

"Bishopbourne," I said. "When he recovers, we'll make *him* talk!"

"An indolent fool?" Holmes wondered. "A sot? A bumblehead? Wasn't that what Solomon Ezer called him? Would Bishopbourne even have known these things were going on?"

"He clearly knew something," I argued. "He raved about it in the military hospital."

Holmes scanned the plunge-pool again, intensely, longingly almost – as if the answer to this one problem that had dogged him all his career, horribly mangled though it now doubtless was, would magically re-emerge from the boiling foam.

"Bishopbourne raved about the long, lurid autumn of 1888, Watson," he finally said. "Because he was there at the time and it left its indelible mark on him, which it no doubt did on countless others. Besides . . . he will be told by the first lawyer he consults that even to hint that he knew the perpetrator of these crimes would make him an accomplice. Dullard though he is, Bishopbourne won't wish to spend the rest of his days in prison. No, I rather think that, though Miss Abigail Simm is a very likely candidate to be Jack the Ripper, that is all she will ever be." A frown of frustration etched deeply into Holmes's face. "In which capacity, I'm afraid ... she joins a long, long list of others."

The Contributors

Simon Bestwick once roamed the Lancashire wilderness, wild and free, until a cunning lass from Liverpool charmed and trapped him before carting him off to Merseyside and marrying him. He is now adjusting to life on the Wirral whilst writing feverishly. Already responsible for the novels *Tide of Souls*, *The Faceless* and *Hell's Ditch*, the story collections *A Hazy Shade of Winter*, *Pictures of the Dark*, *The Condemned* and *Let's Drink to the Dead*, the ebook serial *Black Mountain* and the novella *Angels of the Silences*, he is about to unleash two new novels, *The Devil's Highway* and *The Feast of All Souls*, and a new collection, *And Cannot Come Again*, in his ongoing bid for world domination. In the meantime, he's doing his best to avoid getting a proper job again.

Website: www.simonbestwick.com

Simon Clark has written many short stories and novels, including *Darkness Demands*, *The Fall*, *Secrets of the Dead* and *The Night of the Triffids*, which continues John Wyndham's classic, *The Day of the Triffids*. *The Night of the Triffids* has also been adapted as a full-cast audio drama by Big Finish.

The year 2014 saw the publication of *Inspector Abberline and the Gods of Rome*, a crime mystery, featuring the real-life Inspector Abberline, who led the hunt for the notorious serial killer Jack the Ripper, and who went on to become head of Pinkerton National Detective Agency in Europe.

Simon lives in Yorkshire, England. His website is www.nailedbythe-heart.com

Paul Finch is a former cop and journalist, and, having read History at Goldsmiths College, London, a qualified historian, though he currently earns his living as a full-time writer.

He cut his literary teeth penning episodes of the British TV crime drama, *The Bill*, and has written extensively in the field of children's animation. However, he is probably best known for his work in thrillers, dark fantasy and horror, in which capacity he is a two-time winner of the British Fantasy Award and a one-time winner of the International Horror Guild Award.

He is responsible for numerous short stories and novellas, but also for two horror movies (a third of his, *War Wolf*, is in pre-production), for several full-cast *Dr Who* audio dramas, and for a series of bestselling crime novels from Avon Books at HarperCollins, featuring the British police detective, Mark 'Heck' Heckenburg.

Paul lives in Lancashire, UK, with his wife Cathy and his children, Eleanor and Harry. His website can be found at paulfinch-writer.blogspot.co.uk, and he can be followed on Twitter as @paulfinchauthor.

Liverpool-born **Cate Gardner** lives on the windy shores of the Wirral with the horror and crime writer Simon Bestwick and a ghost called Kneecap. Her short stories have appeared in many weird and wonderful places including *Postscripts*, *Black Static*, *Shimmer*, *Shock Totem* and *Best British Fantasy*, and in her story collection, *Strange Men in Pinstripe Suits* (Strange Publications). She's had five novellas published: *Theatre of Curious Acts* (Hadley Rille Books), *Barbed Wire Hearts* (Delirium Books), *This Foolish & Harmful Delight* (Egaeus Press), *In the Broken Birdcage of Kathleen Fair* (Alchemy Press) and *The Bureau of Them* (Spectral Press). Perched on the bones of previously attempted novels, she is currently working on two novels while avoiding being sucked into the wormhole of Facebook where good intentions die. You can find her on the web at www.categardner.net

A writer of science fiction and fantasy, **Guy Haley** is the author of *Crash*, *Champion of Mars*, and the *Richards & Klein* and *Dreaming Cities* series, among others. He is also a prolific contributor to Games Workshop's Black Library imprint.

Previously a journalist and magazine editor, Guy finds making up his own strange worlds even more fun than writing about those created by other people. 'The Bell Rock Light' is his first Sherlock Holmes story.

British Fantasy Award winner **Carole Johnstone** is a Scottish writer living in north Essex. Her short fiction has been published widely, and has been reprinted in Ellen Datlow's *Best Horror of the Year* and Salt Publishing's *Best British Fantasy* series.

Her debut short story collection, *The Bright Day Is Done*, is available from Gray Friar Press, and her novella, *Cold Turkey*, is part of TTA Press's novella series. Both works were shortlisted for a 2015 British Fantasy Award.

She is presently at work on her second novel, while seeking fame and fortune with the first – but just can't seem to kick the short story habit.

More information on the author can be found at carolejohnstone. com

Alison Littlewood is the author of *A Cold Season*, published by Jo Fletcher Books. The novel was selected for the Richard and Judy Book Club, where it was described as "perfect reading for a dark winter's night". The sequel, *A Cold Silence*, has recently been published, along with a *Zombie Apocalypse!* novel, *Acapulcalypse Now*.

Alison's short stories have been picked for *Best British Horror 2015*, *The Best Horror of the Year* and *The Mammoth Book of Best New Horror* anthologies, as well as *The Best British Fantasy 2013* and *The Mammoth Book of Best British Crime 10*. She won the 2014 Shirley Jackson Award for Short Fiction with her story 'The Dog's Home', published in *The Spectral Book of Horror Stories*. She also contributed to *The Mammoth Book of Sherlock Holmes Abroad*.

Alison lives with her partner Fergus in Yorkshire, England, in a house of creaking doors and crooked walls. You can talk to her on Twitter @Ali__L, see her on Facebook and visit her at www.alisonlittlewood.co.uk

William Meikle is a Scottish writer, now living in Canada, with twenty novels published in the genre press and over three hundred short story credits in thirteen countries. He has books available from a variety of publishers including Dark Regions Press and DarkFuse and has two Sherlock Holmes and a Professor Challenger collection available from Dark Renaissance along with a handful of Holmes stories in anthologies. Willie lives in Newfoundland with whales, bald eagles and icebergs for company. When he's not writing he drinks beer, plays guitar, and dreams of fortune and glory. He can mostly be found lurking on Facebook. Mostly.

Nick Oldham was born in April 1956 in a house in the tiny village of Belthorn – mums were very hardy in those days – up on the moors high above Blackburn, Lancashire. After leaving college then spending a depressing year in a bank, he joined Lancashire Constabulary at the age of nineteen in 1975 and served in many operational postings around the county. Most of his service was spent in uniform, but the final ten years were spent as a trainer and a manager in police training. He retired in 2005 at the rank of inspector.

He lives with his wife, Belinda, on the outskirts of Preston.

Nick is the author of the popular series of crime thrillers featuring DCI Henry Christie, now numbering twenty-three titles, including *A Time for Justice, Nightmare City* and *Unforgiving*. These are set mainly in the northwest of England. He has also written two thrillers in the Steve Flynn series, *Onslaught* and *Ambush*, as well as the novelisations for two independent British crime films, *Vendetta* and *We Still Kill the Old Way*.

He can be followed on Twitter as @NickOldhamBooks and on Facebook as, strangely, NickOldhamBooks

Saviour Pirotta has always loved and read detective stories, from Enid Blyton to Agatha Christie and Conan Doyle. As a child he set up a detective agency called the Friendly Five, which had its headquarters inside a hollow mulberry tree. The society could never find any mysteries to solve, so the young Pirotta filled in the time with writing detective stories of his own, a hobby which turned into a profession in adulthood.

Originally from the small island of Malta, he emigrated to the UK in the early 1980s. He has written many books for children, winning an Aesop Accolade in the US for his version of *Firebird* and an English Association award for a picture book called *A Seed in Need*. 'The Pressed Carnation' is his first work of fiction for adults.

Saviour has a passion for Victoriana, Art Deco, Ancient Greece and Italian Renaissance art. He loves travelling and a lot of his work is inspired by places he visits. He lived in London and Brighton for many years before moving to Yorkshire ten years ago. His home is a nineteenth-century cottage in the world heritage site of Saltaire on the outskirts of Bradford.

For more about Saviour please visit www.spirotta.com

Steven Savile has written for *Doctor Who*, *Torchwood*, *Primeval*, *Stargate*, *Warhammer*, *Slaine*, *Fireborn*, *Pathfinder*, *Arkham Horror*, *Rogue Angel*, and other popular game and comic worlds. He won the International Media Association of Tie-In Writers award for his novel, *Shadow of the Jaguar*, and the inaugural Lifeboat to the Stars award for *Tau Ceti* (co-authored with International bestselling novelist Kevin J. Anderson). Writing as Matt Langley, his young adult novel *Black Flag* was a finalist for the People's Book Prize 2015. His latest books include *Sherlock Holmes and the Murder at Sorrow's Crown*, published by Titan in September 2016, *Parallel Lines*, a brand-new crime novel coming from Titan in January 2017, and *Glass Town*, a mythic fantasy novel to be published in hardcover by St Martin's Press in April 2017.